RED PHOENIX BURNING

RED PHOENIX BURNING

LARRY BOND AND CHRIS CARLSON

RED PHOENIX BURNING

Published by Larry Bond and Chris Carlson
Map by Erik Carlson

ISBN-13: 9781519635389

DEDICATION

This book is dedicated to the people of the Koreas and their long struggle for a free and united homeland.

CONTENTS

ACKNOWLEDGMENTS

Our deepest thanks go to Dr. Andrew Erickson and Ms. Jean Hyun for taking the time out of their busy schedules to review the manuscript. We greatly appreciated Dr. Erickson sharing his Chinese political-military expertise, and Ms. Hyun for helping us get the cultural aspects correct. This novel is better because of your efforts.

Authors' Note

This book is a sequel to the novel *Red Phoenix*, written by Larry Bond and Patrick Larkin, and published by Warner books in 1989. It described a hypothetical invasion of South Korea by the North, an oft-discussed scenario on that troubled peninsula.

The world has changed in many ways since *Red Phoenix* was published, but the two Koreas remain, a fossilized relic of the Cold War and the East-West polarization that touched many parts of our lives before the fall of the Soviet Union.

At the end of *Red Phoenix*, the invaders were defeated by UN forces and retreated back across the 38th parallel, with the cooperation of the Chinese, who supervised a caretaker government. Kim Jong-il, the "Dear Leader" who had ordered the invasion was assassinated, and his young son Kim Jong-un was installed by the Chinese as the new leader of the country under the tutelage of his aunt and uncle who acted as regents.

Thus, the North Korea described in the world of *Red Phoenix* does not differ too much from our real world, except that there was no invasion of South Korea in late 1989.

With this bit of fictional background, you can read this story without having to have read *Red Phoenix* first. If you have read it, you will find familiar names, both of original characters and the next generation.

We hope you will enjoy their story.

This time, I worked with my long-time partner, Chris Carlson, to describe a different but equally dangerous scenario. Chris' knowledge and storytelling ability were vital in making this the best story we could, and the only reason my name comes first is that "B" precedes "C" in the alphabet. I will refuse to claim any passage as mine, or point to one and say Chris wrote it. We could have each written a story based on the same scenario, but together, we've created one much better than either of us could have done alone.

Dramatis Personae

American Characters

Carter, Randall	Lieutenant General, commanding officer, US Seventh Air Force
Christopher, Tony	Brigadier General, vice commander, US Seventh Air Force
Dougherty, Jeff	Team leader, North Korea section, Central Intelligence Agency (CIA)
Fascione, Thomas	General, commanding officer, Combined Forces Command and US Forces Korea
Fowler, Kary	Aid worker, Christian Friends of Korea
Graves, Andrew	Colonel, commanding officer, Eighth Fighter Wing, US Seventh Air Force
Jenkins, Rick	Commanding officer, USS *Hawaii* (SSN 776)
Yeom, George	CIA-NIS liaison, CIA
Little, Kevin	Colonel, commanding officer, Headquarters and Headquarters Battalion, US Eighth Army
Miller, Mike	Lieutenant Colonel, commanding officer, Joint Security Area battalion
Mitchell, Ralph	Commanding officer, USS *Gabrielle Giffords* (LCS 10)

O'Rourke, Dan	Major General, chief of staff, US Forces Korea
Olsen, George	Brigadier General, intelligence officer, US Forces Korea
Sawyer, Chris	North Korea senior analyst, CIA
Tracy, Robert	Lieutenant General, commanding officer, US Eighth Army
Waleski, Gabriel	Rear Admiral, commanding officer, US Navy in South Korea
Wallace, Joshua	Lieutenant Commander, executive officer, USS *Hawaii* (SSN 776)
Wyman, James	President, United States of America

South Korean Characters

An Kye-nam	President, Republic of Korea (ROK)
Guk Yong-soo	Lieutenant, Ninth Special Forces "Ghost" Brigade, ROK
Gung Ji-han	Lieutenant, Ninth Special Forces "Ghost" Brigade, ROK
Ji Sang-hoon	General, commanding officer, ROK Air Force
Kwon	Major General, commanding officer, Special Warfare Command, ROK
Lee Joon-ho	Major, operations officer, UN Command Security Battalion
Ma	Corporal, Ninth Special Forces "Ghost" Brigade, ROK
Moon Su-bin	Volunteer nurse, Christian Friends of Korea
Oh	Master Sergeant, Ninth Special Forces "Ghost" Brigade, ROK

Park Joon-ho	General, deputy commander, ROK-US Combined Forces Command
Rhee Han-gil	Colonel, commanding officer, Ninth Special Forces "Ghost" Brigade, ROK
Sobong	Lieutenant Colonel, Mike Miller's second-in-command
Sohn	General, commanding officer, Third Army, ROK
Yeon Min-soo	General, chief of staff, ROK Army

North Korean Characters

Cheon Ji-hyo	North Korean refugee, mother of two children
Cho Ho-jin	North Korean citizen, Russian intelligence asset
Choi Sung-min	Sergeant, neighborhood supervisor, Ministry of Public Security
Gong Kyeong-pyo	Vice Admiral, KPA Navy
Kim Jong-un	Supreme Leader, DPRK
Koh Chong-su	Vice Marshal, Chief of the General Staff, Korean People's Army (KPA)
Lee Ji-young	North Korean defector, daughter of Lee Ye-jun
Lee Ye-jun	Senior Politburo member, DPRK
Maeng	Sergeant, special forces, KPA
Ri Il-chun	Deputy Chairman, Second Economic Committee
Ro Ji-hun	Captain, special forces, KPA
Ryeon Jae-gon	Captain, aide to General Tae, KPA
Sik Chol-jun	Colonel, bodyguard to Kim Jong-un

| Tae Seok-won | General, Sixth Bureau, General Staff Department; then commanding officer, Thirty-Third Infantry Division, KPA |
| Yang | Major General, deputy commander, Thirty-Third Infantry Division, KPA |

People's Republic of China Characters

Long	General, deputy commander, Southeast Security Force
Shu	General, chief of staff, People's Liberation Army
Wen Kun	President, People's Republic of China
Yu	General, defense minister, People's Republic of China

Russian Characters

| Malikov, Alexei Fedorovich | Deputy Director, Directorate S, Russian Foreign Intelligence Service |
| Telitsyn, Pavel Ramonovich | Asian Department chief, Directorate S, Russian Foreign Intelligence Service |

Map

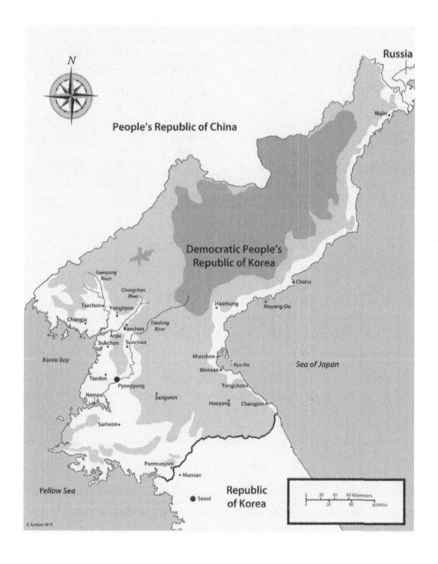

PROLOGUE

20 July 2015
Heungnam Union Fertilizer Plant
Hamhung, North Korea

A gust of wet wind blowing off the Sea of Japan sent acrid vapors from the plant's tall stacks swirling through the maze of rusting sheds, massive steel piping, and storage tanks. For a brief moment, the scarred, treeless slopes rising beyond the tangle of industrial buildings were visible. But then the wind shifted back, and the desolate hills were blotted out again.

General Tae Seok-won coughed, hacked, and then spat to his right, narrowly missing the highly polished shoes of the dapper, middle-aged man at his side. Even a brief exposure to the Heungnam plant's caustic fumes made his eyes water. Some of the substances manufactured here—precursors and stabilizers for Sarin nerve gas—were used for the chemical weapons he controlled as chief of the Sixth Bureau of the General Staff Department.

The others, heroin and crystal methamphetamine, were essential to him and to many others in the hierarchy of the Democratic People's Republic of Korea. Money from the sale of these drugs in China, Japan, and other countries around the world helped pay for the luxuries enjoyed by

Pyongyang's military and political elites—Mercedes sedans, gourmet food, and elegant furnishings for their spacious apartments and country homes. Making sure this plant ran smoothly was a vital task.

Vital or not, Tae felt uncomfortably exposed. This facility was dangerous in its own right, as the annual toll of fatalities from industrial accidents and exposure to toxic chemicals attested. And if one of his rivals decided to strike at him here, this labyrinth of pipes and tanks could easily be turned into a deathtrap.

He scowled. In ordinary times, he could have deployed a full battalion of security troops to guard against sabotage.

But these were not ordinary times.

"You seem uncomfortable, Comrade General," a smooth voice said quietly, barely audible over the background noise of clanking machinery, pumps, and the blare of patriotic music from the loudspeakers.

Tae forced a smile as he glanced at the dark-suited man beside him. Ri Il-chun was the deputy chairman of the Second Economic Committee—the group in charge of coordinating North Korea's military production and procurement. Ri was not a friend. On the other hand, he was not an open enemy, either. Their political and economic interests often coincided. Amid the ever shifting, complicated, and covert war waged between Pyongyang's competing factions, this made him almost an ally.

Many in the West looked at North Korea and saw a monolithic tyranny dominated by the "Supreme Leader," Kim Jong-un, and his cadre of close supporters. That was a façade, as Tae and his peers knew all too well. The political turmoil and economic stagnation of the past three decades had fractured the monolith.

Cold-eyed Kim Jong-un and his ruthless cronies presided over a precarious balance as the many factions within the Korean Workers' Party and the armed forces struggled for wealth and influence. Whenever any one group seemed on the edge of amassing enough power to be truly dangerous, Kim could rely on jealous rivals to pull it down and tear it apart.

The system worked, however imperfectly and inefficiently, but it depended entirely on the maintenance of a rough balance of terror among those contending for power.

And now Tae knew that balance was threatened. This was why he and Ri were "inspecting" this foul-smelling labyrinth of poisons, so far from the convenience, and the constant surveillance, of their respective offices in Pyongyang.

He turned to face the other man squarely. "Comfort is not a concern of those who serve the Supreme Leader . . . and the state."

Ri smiled slyly back at him. "Aptly expressed, Comrade General." He shrugged. "That is good, because the news I bring is not especially comforting."

Tae frowned. "The rumors were accurate, then?"

"Completely accurate," Ri confirmed, his lopsided smile fading. "General Chu will be appointed as the head of the Department of the Economy."

"When?"

"A few weeks, at most."

For an instant, Tae stood frozen in place as he contemplated a future filled only with catastrophe. It was as though he were trapped on a sheer cliff, condemned to helplessly watch the avalanche of ice and rock roaring down the mountain toward him.

Ri's report confirmed what his own sources had conveyed earlier. Chu and those in his circle were among the bitterest enemies of the factions to which Tae and Ri belonged. Chu's old post as the head of the State Security Department, the secret police force enforcing the Kim family's preeminence, had made him dangerous enough. His spies and agents were seeded throughout the military and the government, a constant threat to those with whom his interests clashed.

But control over the Department of the Economy would magnify Chu's power exponentially. This new bureaucracy was a recent creation of Kim Jong-un. Tasked with tightening the party's control over every aspect of the North's economic life—including the shadowy trading companies that ran drugs and exported weapons—its chief could pry into the secret finances of any enemy, any rival, exposing all the illegal payoffs, bribes, and kickbacks that were the common currency of every transaction in the DPRK.

With that kind of information at his disposal, Chu could break anyone he desired, consigning them, their wives, and their children to torture, firing squad, or exile to a death camp almost on a whim. And he would not show mercy to anyone he deemed a competitor.

Tae felt his hands tighten into fists. Previous directors of the Department of the Economy had been relative nonentities, easily swayed and easily frightened into ineffectiveness. What madness had possessed Kim Jong-un to hand so much power to someone like Chu? And this wasn't the first unwise decision by the young Kim. He seemed even less stable than his father.

Tae forced himself to speak calmly. "Can anything be done?"

"Officially?" Ri shook his head. "No. The Supreme Leader's decision is final."

"And unofficially?"

Ri hesitated for a long moment. He glanced over his shoulder, making sure that no one else was in earshot. "Others are . . . concerned," he admitted softly.

"Who?" Tae demanded.

He listened intently as the other man quietly ran through a list of names. Tae knew them all. Some he could tolerate. Others he despised. Some he feared. All held high positions in rival factions within the party and the military, with many commanding the allegiance of units in the Pyongyang Defense Command, the Guard Command, the III Corps, and the State Security Department—the interlocking security apparatus of the regime and the Kim dynasty.

The general felt cold. Even hearing this list of names could mark him for a lingering and infinitely painful death. Were Ri and these others serious? Or was this a trap, designed to ensnare him and others like him? A way for Ri to curry favor with Chu and his allies?

He looked up to find Ri watching him closely.

"You are wary," the other man said. "That is wise. This is no time for rashness." Then his voice hardened. "But neither is it a time for hesitation or cowardice. Like the rest of us, you must decide. And soon."

Tae nodded stiffly. "I understand."

Ri handed him a small sheet of rice paper. "There are two futures, Comrade General. The choice is yours."

Tae glanced down at the paper. On one side, it bore the words 큰 위 험, "Great Danger." On the other, it carried the message 기회, "Opportunity," and a telephone number. He looked up again.

Ri nodded slowly. "That number is secure...for now. But do not delay too long, Tae." With that, he turned on his heel and walked toward the black limousine waiting to take him back to Pyongyang.

General Tae Seok-won stood silently, watching the bureaucrat as he got into his car, unconsciously flipping that single small scrap of paper from one side to the other.

CHAPTER ONE
WARNING FLARES

15 August 2015
The Demilitarized Zone
Korea

The dead were everywhere, huddled at the bottom of the trench. Some had been shot. Others had been bayoneted. Some of the soldiers lay curled up, frozen in the agony of death. The rest stared up at the gray, cloud-covered sky with unblinking eyes and white, bloodless faces. Smoke from burning bunkers drifted slowly in the still air.

Kevin Little stumbled down the corpse-strewn communications trench. His combat boots skidded through a mixture of frozen blood, mud, and blackened snow. He locked his jaw tight to keep his teeth from chattering. He was cold—colder than he could ever remember being. Every movement sent pain surging through his body, as though jagged shards of ice were being driven deep through his flesh.

He knew these dead men. They were his soldiers. They were the men he had led. Sergeants Pierce and Caldwell. Corporals Ramos and Jones. Privates Smith, Donnelly, and Jackson. They were the men he had failed.

He blinked back tears.

WHUMMP!

Kevin swung around in horror. Twenty yards behind him, dirt and bits of shattered rock fountained skyward.

WHUMMP!

Another explosion, closer this time, knocked him to his knees. Shrapnel hissed past, ripping at the compacted earth walls on either side.

God, he thought, fighting for breath. The North Koreans were walking a mortar barrage right down the trench. He staggered to his feet, trying to run . . . and knowing that it already was too late—

"Colonel Little? Sir?"

Colonel Kevin Little opened his eyes. The green, glowing numerals of the digital clock on the table beside his cot blinked from 2352 to 2353. He wiped away the rivulets of sweat running down his face. Summer nights in South Korea were hot and humid. *My God, not again*, he thought wearily. It was the old dream—the nightmare that had haunted him off and on through twenty-plus years and three wars.

He focused on the here and now. He wasn't trapped in the ruins of Malibu West, the tiny DMZ outpost he'd commanded, and lost, as a young second lieutenant so long ago. Instead, he was in the small, plainly furnished quarters set aside for any senior officer staying overnight at Camp Bonifas, right at the edge of the Demilitarized Zone on the road to Panmunjom.

There was another knock on his door. "Colonel?"

"Come!" Kevin sat up and swung his legs off the cot. He bent down, already pulling on his socks and boots. Then he looked up at the short, wiry South Korean officer who'd entered the tiny room. Major Lee Joon-ho was the S3, the operations officer, for the UN Command Security

Battalion that kept watch over the Panmunjom Truce Village and its surroundings—otherwise known as the Joint Security Area.

"What's up, Major?" he asked quietly, hoping that the other man wasn't here to check on him because he'd been screaming in his sleep.

"Lieutenant Colonel Miller would like to see you in the CP, sir. We have a situation."

Kevin nodded. "I'll be with you in a second."

The Joint Security Area battalion, whose motto was "In Front of Them All," was the only combined Korean-American unit in existence. Since the US was handing off more and more front-line DMZ duties to South Korea, most of its soldiers were Koreans like Lee. But the battalion commander, Mike Miller, the command sergeant major, and about forty others were Americans.

While the other man waited outside his door, Kevin quickly finished lacing up his boots and shrugged into his battle dress uniform jacket.

He had just taken over command of the US Eighth Army's Headquarters and Headquarters Battalion, and the HHB provided logistics and administrative support for Miller and his troops. That provided the official reason for Little's visit to Camp Bonifas on an inspection tour.

The Joint Security Area was the one place where Allied and North Korean soldiers routinely came face-to-face. And over the decades since the first, and then the second armistice, it was a place where some of those daily confrontations turned violent, even deadly. Despite that, or perhaps because of it, Panmunjom was also a magnet for tourists, politicians, and presidents who wanted to peer into the armed hellhole that was North Korea.

Kevin snorted. It was the same morbid fascination that drew people to stare at the man-eating tigers in a zoo. But in a zoo, there were iron bars or wide moats between you and the tigers. At Panmunjom, there were only a few signposts and a line of concrete blocks ten centimeters high between the five small buildings that straddled the demarcation line.

Then he smiled to himself. So how exactly was he any different from the rest of those thrill-seeking tourists? Sure, he could rattle off a list of official-sounding justifications for watching the UN Command Security Battalion handle the conflicting duties of playing VIP tour guide while staying ready for war, but mostly he was here to see how things had changed in the long years since he was last up on the DMZ.

And now, Kevin thought, clipping the drop-leg holster for his Beretta to his trouser leg, he would go see what the tigers were doing that had Miller worried enough to wake a visiting colonel. He grabbed his body armor off the bare floor and followed the South Korean major at a fast walk toward the camp command post.

Lieutenant Colonel Miller was on a secure phone when they came into the command post. Other officers and non-coms were busy at computers scattered around the room, scanning through feeds from the remote cameras liberally emplaced around the Joint Security Area. Major Lee went into a huddle with a couple of young-looking South Korean lieutenants typing frantically at laptops in one corner.

"Understood, Terry," Miller said calmly in a soft West Texas drawl. "Stay on it. Keep me posted."

He hung up and turned toward Kevin with a tight smile. "Looks like we'll be putting on a bigger show for you than I'd hoped, Colonel."

"Don't go to any trouble on my account, Mike," Kevin said, matching his expression. "I'm really just here for the golf."

Camp Bonifas boasted that it possessed "the world's most dangerous golf course," a single par-3 hole surrounded by razor wire, machine gun bunkers, trenches, and minefields.

"Yeah, right," Miller said, grinning a little bit wider. But the grin vanished as he nodded toward the phone. "That was one of my platoon leaders up at OP Oullette. They're hearing a lot of small arms and machine gun fire from the north. They can't see any of it, but it's echoing off the surrounding hills."

"Could it be some unscheduled KPA battle drill?" Kevin suggested. Under various standing agreements, each side was supposed to notify the other of any planned military exercises close to the DMZ. But the Korean People's Army was notorious for ignoring such agreements.

Miller shrugged. "Maybe. But they don't usually pull that kind of shit after dark."

Kevin nodded. North Korea's regular armed forces didn't have a lot of the night vision gear that was widely used by the US and its allies. Without such equipment, live-fire exercises after sunset were pointless.

"Sir!" Major Lee broke in suddenly.

The two American soldiers turned toward him.

"Voice of Korea has gone off the air," Lee reported.

Kevin felt a shiver run down his spine. Voice of Korea, the new name for Radio Pyongyang, was North Korea's main channel for propaganda and news to both the world and to its own citizens. It never went silent. Never.

"When?" Miller asked.

"Twenty minutes ago," Lee said. His voice was flat, unemotional, but there were beads of sweat on his forehead.

"Without any warning. There is only static on all its broadcast frequencies."

"Crap." Miller looked at Kevin. "I don't like this at all, Colonel. Not one damned bit."

"Nor I," Kevin agreed. He fought down the urge to take command and start issuing orders. He outranked the other man, but he was here as a visitor, and this was Miller's patch. The battalion commander knew the turf, his unit's capabilities, and his responsibilities.

Miller looked at Major Lee. "Tell Lieutenant Colonel Sobong that I'm activating ROUNDUP immediately. He's in charge. But let's do this by ground only. I don't want any helos in the air right now. There's no point in spooking those bastards across the wire if we don't have to."

"Yes, sir."

Kevin nodded to himself. Miller's move made sense. One of the security battalion's chief duties was guarding Daesong-dong, the only village inside the DMZ. In exchange for the risks they ran just by living so close to the border with North Korea, the two hundred or so civilian farmers were well paid— but they had to accept a number of restrictions like nighttime curfews and obedience to military orders. ROUNDUP was the code word for an emergency evacuation of Daesong-dong. Sobong, Miller's South Korean second-in-command, and the unit's civil affairs company knew the drill. It was an operation they rehearsed with the villagers every three months.

"Now that is weird. Just wild-ass weird," one of the young officers manning a computer console said abruptly. He swiveled around to face Miller. "Sir! None of the guys at our checkpoints or watching the remote cameras have eyes on any KPA guards inside the JSA."

"What?"

"They're gone, Colonel," the lieutenant said. "Or they could be sheltering real deep. But we've got no visual contact or thermal trace on anyone on their side of the line."

"How long have they been gone?" Miller demanded.

The lieutenant swallowed hard. "Maybe ten minutes. Maybe more. Maybe less." He gestured at the screen in front of him. "We were focused on spotting any infiltrators trying to sneak across the line . . ."

And not paying enough attention to the normal goons who stood guard, Kevin realized. It was a form of target fixation; the less technical term was tunnel vision.

He saw Miller's jaw tighten. The officers and men at those checkpoints and those monitoring the remote cameras were going to catch hell during the morning debriefing on this incident.

If any of them are still alive when the sun comes up, Little thought grimly.

There were a number of scenarios that might explain why North Korea's radio station would go off the air around the same time its soldiers at Panmunjom vanished. Unfortunately, none of them seemed likely to do much for the life expectancy of anyone at Camp Bonifas.

Kevin shook his head, half-amused and half-disgusted by his own sudden fit of pessimism. Maybe, just maybe, he should have pulled his twenty and gone back home to run the family ranch in eastern Washington like his parents had always wanted. Hell, he'd seen a lot of combat over multiple tours in Korea, Afghanistan, and Iraq. His luck had to be running mighty thin by now.

Then he shrugged. He'd make a lousy rancher. You had to like cows and horses to be a good rancher. And he hated cows. And horses. Especially horses.

7

Miller's voice broke in on his thoughts. "Captain Shin! Call the MAC Joint Duty Officer and tell him to report here, pronto. I don't want him caught outside the wire if this situation turns sour."

The UN's Military Armistice Commission kept specially trained officers on duty twenty-four hours a day to monitor a telephone hotline linking the two sides at Panmunjom. Their office was just thirty feet away from a North Korean guard post and right in the line of any fire.

"Checkpoint Three reports lights moving on the Reunification Highway, near Kaesong!" Major Lee said suddenly, listening to one of the CP's secure phones. "Many lights."

Christ, Kevin thought, not really believing it. Here they come. Again. The Reunification Highway was bound to be a major axis for any new North Korean armored offensive into the south.

"Get me a count," Miller snapped. "And ID those vehicles."

"Yes, sir!" Lee said. He spoke urgently into the phone, dropping into Korean while he demanded more information from the soldiers manning Checkpoint Three, a blue-painted building perched on a hill overlooking the western perimeter of the JSA. Anyone stationed there had North Korean territory on three sides.

Kevin watched the South Korean major's face closely. For a moment, Lee stayed calmly professional, listening to the reply. Then he blinked once. His eyebrows rose in astonishment. At any other time, his expression would have been funny as hell.

"The lights are from automobiles," Lee said slowly, as though he couldn't really believe what he was saying. "A group of at least six civilian cars driving out of Kaesong on the highway. They are coming toward the DMZ at fifty or sixty kilometers an hour. With their headlights on."

"You have got to be fricking kidding me, Major," Miller said.

"No, sir," Lee said stubbornly. "I am not kidding you."

Miller shook his head in disbelief. He glanced at Kevin. "This is getting stranger and stranger, Colonel Little. What in the name of God's little green earth is going on? Could this be some kind of hush-hush diplomatic thing that Seoul and DC forgot to tell us about?"

Kevin shrugged helplessly and shook his head. He hadn't heard a thing, and he doubted there was anything to hear. The striped-pants folks in the US and South Korean state departments could be slow to tell their respective armed forces what they were up to, but even they had to know that running an unannounced diplomatic mission up to the DMZ in the dead of night was asking for major-league trouble. That kind of trouble could get people killed and wreck a lot of promising bureaucratic careers.

"Well, whatever the hell this is, I'm going up to Checkpoint Three to see for myself," Miller decided. He turned toward another of the South Korean officers. "Captain Shin, I want the ready platoon mounted and on the way to Checkpoint Three in five minutes. And tell my driver I'm on the way."

Miller looked at Kevin with the hint of a sardonic smile. "You want to ride along, Colonel? Things could get . . . interesting."

Are you willing to stick your head out of the cozy, relative safety of Camp Bonifas and play headquarters tourist at the most exposed site on the whole DMZ . . . right as the proverbial shit is flying toward the fan, Kevin silently translated. He snorted. The smart move would be to head back to Seoul right now. Going with Miller was just an excuse to stare again at the tigers prowling around right across the line. Then again, he decided, sometimes that was the safest thing to do. It was usually the predator you didn't see who pulled you down.

He grinned back at the other man. "I wouldn't miss it, Lieutenant Colonel Miller."

Checkpoint Three, Joint Security Area
The entire Panmunjom Truce Village was brightly lit by floodlights mounted on buildings and tall metal lampposts. Once past the entrance to the UN side of the compound, the convoy of trucks and Humvees carrying the security battalion's ready platoon swung left onto a two-lane road heading west, and then turned sharply onto an even narrower one-lane road heading uphill toward Checkpoint Three. Trees and underbrush lined both sides.

"Stop here, Harmon," Miller told his driver. They were near the top of the hill and within a hundred meters of the demarcation line, but still just out of sight of the closest North Korean guard post.

Kevin swung himself out of Miller's Humvee, stifling a grunt as his knees and feet briefly took on the full weight of his body armor, ammo, and other gear. Counting the M4A1 rifle one of the security battalion's sergeants had issued him before they drove out of Camp Bonifas, he was probably carrying around forty-five to fifty pounds of extra weight. That wasn't the full load carried by an infantryman on an extended foot patrol, but it was more than enough—especially for someone who was closer to fifty years old than to forty.

"Better leave that in the Humvee, sir," Miller said quietly, nodding at the assault rifle. "This close to the line, we only carry sidearms. Our KPA pals get nervous if they see heavier firepower."

"And if we see some of those 'pals' are toting something a bit bigger?" Kevin asked.

"Then the rules have changed."

"Swell." Kevin slid the rifle back into the Humvee but left the door slightly ajar. If the rules had suddenly "changed," he didn't want to have to fumble with the latch.

The two 6×6 trucks carrying the ready platoon pulled in behind them and parked. South Korean soldiers dropped off the back of the trucks, quickly forming up in the shadow of the trees. Their camouflage gear had more pixelated greens and browns than the US Army pattern did, and they blended well with the tangled woods on either side of the road.

"Keep your men below the crest for now, Lieutenant Kim," Miller told the officer commanding the platoon. "Colonel Little and I will go up to Checkpoint Three first. I don't want to escalate this situation unless I need to. Clear?"

"Yes, sir." The South Korean lieutenant turned and began issuing low-voiced orders to his NCOs.

Satisfied, Miller took his helmet off, clipped it to his tactical vest, and donned a soft, camo-patterned patrol cap. He watched as Kevin did the same. "No point in putting on our war paint if we don't have to," he said, his drawl deepening.

Together, the two officers walked up the road. It struck Kevin as surreal to step out into the fully illuminated patch of short-cropped grass and gravel in front of Checkpoint Three. During his time on the DMZ, light discipline was strictly enforced. Back then, if you were lit up, you were a target. *Old habits die hard,* he thought grimly, especially if those habits kept you alive. Just seeing their elongated shadows rippling across the grass ahead of them made his skin crawl.

He moved out toward the western edge of the hill, in front of the lights, and peered through his night vision binoculars. About two kilometers to the southwest, he could make out the huge, 160-meter-high flagpole the North Koreans had erected at the fake village they had built for propaganda purposes opposite South Korea's Daesong-dong. He swung right, scanning across the landscape of low hills and fields beyond the woods and brush that marked the DMZ. The night vision binoculars showed everything in an eerie green. The highway came into focus, running straight through the fields outside Kaesong toward Panmunjom.

Miller joined him. "That damned caravan is about five klicks out and still coming this way."

Kevin raised his binoculars higher and saw them. Six, no, seven cars were driving east with their headlights on. This far away it was hard to tell for sure, but they looked like a mix of luxury models—big Russian-made ZiL limousines and Mercedes sedans. His jaw tightened. In North Korea, vehicles like that were restricted to high-ranking party officials and top army brass.

"They're heading for the Bridge of 72 Hours," Miller said. "Which means we're going to have these guys, whoever they are, right in our laps in about five minutes."

Kevin nodded. Back in 1976, after axe-wielding North Koreans had murdered two Americans, Captain Bonifas and Lieutenant Barrett, the UN Command had closed off the only road access to the North Korean side of Panmunjom. Working feverishly over three days, the KPA had built the aptly named Bridge of 72 Hours as a replacement.

Movement beyond the oncoming cars caught Kevin's eye. He focused his binoculars farther west along the highway, closer to Kaesong. There. He could make out a low-slung, eight-wheeled armored vehicle with a small, round turret up top. *Hell,* he realized, *that was a BTR-60, a North Korean APC.* It was driving flat-out and it was only a few hundred meters behind the caravan of limousines.

Suddenly a series of bright flashes, blindingly green in the night vision glasses, erupted from the BTR's turret.

Almost simultaneously, the last car in the caravan swerved wildly and slammed head-on into one of the tall poplar trees lining the highway. Its doors popped open, but no one got out as a second burst of heavy machine gun fire ripped through the car—tearing it open from end to end.

Ten seconds later, the sound of a rapid-fire burst—a crackling staccato—arrived, rippling uphill at the speed of sound.

Everything fell into place in that instant. In the DPRK, modern luxury cars could only belong to high-ranking North Korean officials. Unexplained small-arms fire in the hills beyond the DMZ erupting almost at the same time as communications from Pyongyang goes off the air; and then the guards around Panmunjom pulling a sudden disappearing act could only mean something real bad was going down. Kevin lowered his binoculars and swung toward Miller. "That's not a diplomatic mission, Mike. They're trying to defect."

"Agreed," the other man said slowly. Then he nodded toward the highway. "But someone blew the whistle on those poor bastards."

Kevin took another look, just in time to see a second car, this one a ZiL, spin across the highway with pieces of metal and rubber flying away in all directions. It crashed into a Mercedes and sent the sedan pinwheeling into the trees. Three figures scrambled out of the smashed cars onto the pavement and then crumpled as machine gun fire from the oncoming BTR caught them.

"Shit!" Miller growled. "They're getting murdered. And there's not a damned thing we can do about it."

Another limousine skidded off the highway into a field. More men tumbled out of this wreck. They carried assault rifles and submachine guns, but another burst from the BTR tore them apart before they could shoot back.

There were just three cars left.

A dazzling speck of fire streaked westward down the highway from a squat building near the Bridge of 72 Hours and hit the lead vehicle. The ZiL exploded. Loyal KPA troops equipped with antitank guided missiles were manning the bridge defenses, Kevin realized.

The two surviving cars turned sharply, veering off the highway and onto a narrower road that ran southeast toward the western edge of the DMZ.

"They're trying for the Bridge of No Return," Miller said.

Kevin nodded. The old, crumbling bridge, used for prisoner of war exchanges after the First Korean War armistice but now closed to traffic, was the only other place where anyone could cross the Sachon River and enter the Joint Security Area. "You'd better get some of your guys down there, Mike."

"Yeah—"

"We've got movement in KPA Four!" their radios squawked.

That was the two-story North Korean guard post with a direct line of sight on Checkpoint Three.

Kevin swung around and then felt himself hurled backward as the whole world around him flashed white. He hit the ground, bounced hard, and then found himself lying flat on his back. Everything seemed to be happening in slow motion. Trailing streamers of flame, shards of wood, and jagged pieces of concrete arced across the sky overhead, tumbling away in all directions.

Time abruptly accelerated back to normal.

Acting on reflex, he rolled over and fumbled for the helmet clipped to his tactical vest. Once it was on, he cautiously lifted his head, trying to see what the hell had just happened.

The rules had changed.

Checkpoint Three was a blazing mound of rubble. A few years back, the UN Command had rebuilt the post, installing blast-resistant glass and thicker walls. But no one had planned for it to withstand a direct hit from an antitank missile.

Kevin caught a flurry of movement off to his left. It was Miller, dazed and bloody, rocking back and forth on his hands and knees and obviously trying to get to his feet. *Oh, God*, he thought, opening his mouth to shout a warning—

Crack.

Miller went down, hit in the head. His patrol cap went flying off into the darkness.

Kevin swallowed hard. The North Koreans had a sniper zeroed in on this hilltop. Without thinking, he rolled away to his right, angling downhill.

Crack.

Dirt and torn grass spurted from the spot he'd just abandoned.

He kept moving, scrabbling down the hill, seeking cover in the taller grass and clumps of brush. Twenty meters down, he stopped and risked a quick check of his surroundings.

Above him, the hilltop glowed red and orange in the light from the burning building. To his right, he could make out Miller's Humvee and the two trucks parked beneath the trees. Shadowy, camouflaged figures flickered into motion, darting across the road in ones and twos and spreading out across the slope. Good, he thought. Lieutenant Kim was on the ball. He was already deploying his platoon for action.

Kevin glanced to his left, eyeing the thick forest that marked the winding trace of the Sachon River. There, on the slightly higher ground rising beyond the trees, he could just make out two pairs of headlights bucketing up and down along the rutted, potholed road that led to the Bridge of No Return. Some of the would-be defectors who had triggered this murderous attack were still alive, and still trying to escape to the South.

His resolve hardened. If Pyongyang wanted those people dead badly enough to risk reigniting the war, then it was his duty to try his damnedest to bring them across the line alive. But he wasn't going to be able to do that on his own. It was time to get back in the fight.

He groped for his radio. It was gone, probably ripped away by the blast or torn off during his scramble down the hill. Swell. He really hoped that Lieutenant Kim's men weren't trigger-happy.

Slowly, carefully, Kevin got to his feet, making sure that his empty hands were clearly visible. He saw a South Korean soldier swing toward him, sighting down his rifle. He froze.

"Colonel Little?" a voice hissed.

"That's me."

Lieutenant Kim materialized out of the darkness. "Where is Colonel Miller?"

"He's dead, Lieutenant," Kevin said flatly. "Hit by a KPA sniper after they blew Checkpoint Three to hell."

The young South Korean officer stiffened. For a moment, he was silent. Then he asked, "What are your orders, sir?"

"First, radio Major Lee and report the situation here," Kevin said, thinking fast. With Miller's second-in-command, Lieutenant Colonel Sobong, busy managing the evacuation of the civilians from Daesong-dong, Lee would have to assume operational control over the rest of the battalion. "Then you defend this position with two of your squads and your machine gun teams. Watch your flanks. Under no circumstances will you cross the demarcation line."

"And if we see the enemy?" the young officer asked carefully.

"Then you shoot them, Lieutenant."

"Yes, sir," Kim nodded tightly. "And what about my third squad, Colonel?"

"I'm taking it," Kevin told him. He nodded downhill toward the darkened blur that was the Bridge of No Return. "We've got company coming, and I plan to meet them personally."

"I understand, sir."

"There's just one more thing, Lieutenant," Kevin said as the other man turned away to begin relaying orders to his men.

"Colonel?" the Korean asked, puzzled.

"I need a rifle."

The Bridge of No Return
Swearing under his breath, Kevin slid downhill, bulling his way through the overgrown tangle of underbrush and low-hanging tree branches by brute force. He could hear

Sergeant Jeong and his eight men crashing through the woods behind him.

This kind of stunt was just plain nuts, and he knew it.

Running full-tilt through these patches of forest at night was just begging to be ambushed by the KPA. And he would have fried any junior officer who pulled this kind of dumb-ass maneuver in a peacetime exercise. But there wasn't time for anything clever, or slow, or even safe. They had to get to the bridge before those defectors reached it.

Kevin broke out into the open at the bottom of the hill and dropped to one knee, breathing hard. Jeong and the others went to ground behind him, rifles pointed to the west.

They were at the edge of the road leading to the bridge. About sixty meters ahead, he could make out the rectangular shape of the old UN checkpoint. Sited at the east end of the span, it had been abandoned years ago as too dangerous a post.

KPA Post Seven was at the west end of the bridge. It was a bigger, more solidly built structure than the deserted UN checkpoint. If those people trying to escape the North were lucky, the bribes or fake orders they were relying on would have cleared Post Seven. Somehow, though, Kevin wasn't willing to bet that they were that lucky.

He could hear engine noises now. Those last two cars must be getting pretty close. He glanced back at Jeong. The South Korean noncom looked young for his rank, but he seemed perfectly calm. "Follow me, Sergeant. You take the south side. I'll take the north."

Jeong nodded.

Suddenly, the staccato chatter of a heavy machine gun drowned out the sound of the approaching cars.

Whummp.

Beyond the river, to the north of their current position, a wavering orange glow marked the wreck of another fleeing car. That damned North Korean BTR-60 was still on the hunt.

They were out of time.

"Let's go!" Kevin pushed himself to his feet and out onto the empty road. Boots pounded on the pavement behind him as the South Korean soldiers followed at a fast trot. The eight riflemen split up smoothly, with four tucking in behind him and four behind Sergeant Jeong to his left.

Forty meters. Twenty meters. Ten. Kevin's pulse was speeding up, accelerating steadily with every footfall. The bridge loomed up out of the darkness, hemmed in on either side by tall trees.

They passed the empty UN checkpoint and threaded through the rusting, blue-painted bollards placed to close off the bridge to vehicles. Off at the other end, a flat-roofed building, KPA Post Seven, came into view, visible only because it was lighter-colored than the surrounding trees.

God help us now, Kevin thought, as they crossed onto the span, moving toward the almost undetectable border between South and North Korea. Toward what might be the line between relative peace and all-out war. The air was still, without even a breath of wind, and almost unbearably humid. Despite that, and despite the weight of his armor, rifle, and other gear, he felt cold, chilled to the bone.

Lights flickered at the other end of the bridge. That last car was almost here. It sped up. They were close. Very close.

Shit! No! There were shapes moving in that KPA guard post. It *was* manned. A sudden blaze of light flared as one of the North Korean soldiers inside tripped the searchlights—revealing a black Mercedes sedan slewing to a stop about fifty meters away.

And then its windshield shattered, smashed by shots from the building. More rounds lashed the sedan's right side, puncturing metal, fiberglass, and plastic. Screams echoed above the rattle of automatic weapons fire.

A door flew open on the other side of the Mercedes and a dark-haired Korean man in a business suit scrambled out. He turned, reaching back inside the car, and then spun away in a spray of blood and shattered bone—hit by several bullets at the same time.

"Damn it!" Kevin snarled. He raised his voice. "Sergeant Jeong. Kill those bastards."

Kevin dropped to one knee, raised his own M4, and peered through the sight. He aimed at a North Korean soldier firing an assault rifle and squeezed the trigger, holding the rifle steady as it kicked back against his shoulder. And again. And again.

Hit at least twice, the enemy soldier slumped forward, dead or dying.

One of the South Koreans from just off to his left fired a grenade launcher with a muffled *thump*.

The grenade went off inside the KPA guard post in a blinding burst of white light. A North Korean staggered outside, bleeding from a dozen places where shrapnel must have caught him. But he still clutched his rifle.

Half a dozen rifles cracked simultaneously. The KPA guard fell and lay still. Blood flowed black across the dirt.

Another grenade went off inside the building. Smoke and dust curled away through the blown-out doors and windows.

"Cease fire! Cease fire!" Kevin yelled. He made rapid chopping motions with one hand.

One by one, the South Korean soldiers lying prone or kneeling around him stopped shooting.

As the sound of firing faded, Kevin could hear another engine, this one deeper and throatier, roaring closer. It must be that BTR-60, he thought wildly. The wheeled North Korean armored vehicle was still out of sight and several hundred meters up that road to Kaesong, but it would be here in just a minute or two.

"Not good," he whispered. Rifles and grenade launchers weren't going to be of much use against that armored beast. They'd have to bug out and fast.

But not before he took a closer look at those poor, dead fools who had sparked all this carnage.

"Sergeant Jeong!" he called out. "Come with me! Send everybody else back across the bridge. Move!"

Without looking to see if his orders were being obeyed, Kevin ran toward the bullet-riddled Mercedes. He could see the driver splayed up against the dashboard. He came around to the open door, stepped over the body of the man who'd been killed while getting out, and peered inside.

It was a slaughterhouse. Four people, two of them women, lay sprawled in a heap in the back. One of the dead men clutched a briefcase. It had broken open, spilling stacks of hundred euro notes onto his lap.

Kevin swallowed hard and looked away. *My God*, he thought. What a waste. Mike Miller and the men in Checkpoint Three were dead; and for nothing.

"*Dowa juseyo!*" a soft, pain-filled voice moaned from inside the Mercedes. Kevin knew enough Korean to understand: "Please help me!"

He stared back into the darkened interior. One of the women, the younger one, maybe in her late twenties or early thirties, was still alive. Her long black hair had fallen over her face, but he could see her trying to move slender fingers.

He whirled around. Sergeant Jeong stood there, his mouth open in shock as he heard the young woman's tearful pleading. "Get her out!" Kevin snapped. "We'll carry her across the bridge!"

Moving her without treating those wounds might kill her, he knew. But staying here was certain death.

With the young woman slung between them, they sprinted back across the Bridge of No Return. Halfway across, Kevin felt her clutch his arm. He looked down at her.

"It has begun," she said quietly, tears falling onto the cracked concrete along with the blood from her wounds. "The burning has begun."

CHAPTER TWO

FOG OF WAR

16 August 2015
USS *Hawaii* (SSN 776)
North Korean East Coast, Sea of Japan

Commander Rick Jenkins was a troubled man. "Any change, Chief?" he asked as he poked his head into the ESM bay.

The intelligence specialist shook his head and pointed at the nearly empty screen in front of him. He was just as bewildered as his captain. "No, sir. The airwaves are damn near empty. No radio. No TV. No long-haul communications. I'm not even seeing the harbor coastal surveillance radar. It's like everyone at the Wonsan naval complex decided to take the day off."

"What about the air base?" pressed Jenkins.

"Nada, sir. But it still could be a little early for them. They mostly have MiG-19 and MiG-21 fighters stationed there, and those old birds don't usually fly at night."

"I've never seen it this quiet, Chief, ever," Jenkins said, remembering previous surveillance missions. "Even during national holidays, the North Koreans always have their coastal surveillance radars up, and they keep their patrols out and about. We haven't seen a single patrol boat sortie in the last eighteen hours. That's just not right."

"Beats me, Skipper. I've never seen anything like this either. It's possible the naval base could be using landlines, but that only lets them communicate with the head shed at Toejo Dong. It won't help with any of their local tactical units. And that doesn't explain the radars, or the lack of them."

"Total EMCON?" Jenkins suggested out loud. The only reason he could see for such a drastic move would be as a possible precursor to hostilities. The very thought sent shivers down his spine.

"It's a possibility, sir. But I'll let you know the moment I see anything."

Jenkins walked slowly back to the command workstation, mumbling under his breath. His executive officer, Lieutenant Commander Joshua Wallace, was watching the feed from the raised BVS-1 photonics mast on the port vertical large-screen display when he heard his captain grunt.

"Excuse me, sir?"

"Nothing, Josh. Just thinking how damn peculiar this whole situation is, that's all."

"Well, things are getting stranger with each passing minute, Skipper. We're about an hour from sunrise and none of the fishing vessels have left port yet. For a country that routinely teeters on the edge of famine, not sending your fishing boats to sea means something very not good is happening."

Jenkins ran his fingers through his hair and sighed. What the hell was going on? He knew the North Koreans were a strange people, but the complete absence of activity from one of their larger ports was weird even for them. Pulling up the geoplot display on the command workstation, he noted over a dozen contacts that his sonar techs had identified as fishing trawlers—all of them were far behind them.

"Everything else seems more or less normal," remarked Wallace pointing toward the screen on his left, where the upper half of the Wonsan skyline was cast in the greenish hue of the infrared display. All looked quiet and serene. "We could try and get a little closer if you'd like, Skipper. The main naval facility is tucked away in the back of the bay. And we don't have the best vantage point from out here."

Both men turned and looked down at the digital chart on the navigation display. Since the BVS-1 mast also had the ability to receive GPS signals, their submarine's exact position was constantly being updated. Wallace ran his finger along the fifty-meter line. "We could run right up along here without crossing over into North Korean territorial waters and still have some decent water beneath us."

Jenkins nodded his approval. Their mission was to keep an eye on the DPRK's East Sea Fleet, and he had the authority to walk right up to the Conventional Twelve-Mile Limit if he believed he needed to do so. "Very well, XO. Bring her around to course three three zero. We'll close on the coast up to, but not across, the CTML."

"Come about to course three three zero and close the coast to the CTML, but not across, aye, sir," replied Wallace.

As *Hawaii* turned to the northwest, she began to inch closer to the coastline. Jenkins also brought his boat shallower, putting another few feet of mast out of the water. He wasn't too concerned about being detected. There were no active radars nearby and the soon-to-be rising sun would be behind him. The early morning glare would be more than adequate to hide the exposed masts from any snooping eyes.

As the submarine drew nearer to the coast, the large flat-panel display began to show more and more of the city. An eerie greenish pulsating glow suddenly appeared on the screen. Its center was close to where the naval base was located. Both Jenkins and Wallace leaned forward as they tried to make out what they were looking at. It was bright green on the low-light display.

"Is that a fire?" Jenkins wondered.

"Possibly," Wallace said slowly. "But if it is, it's a damn big one."

Their concentration was abruptly broken by the squawk of the ship's intercom. "CAPTAIN TO ESM BAY."

Jenkins pivoted and skirted around the fire control consoles and jumped to the ESM bay. "What do you have, Chief?"

"Once we got a clear line of sight, we started to pick up some short-range tactical radios, Skipper, probably army shortwave sets. Petty Officer Johnson has been trying to make out what they're saying."

A deep frown of confusion popped on Jenkins' face. "The transmissions aren't encrypted?"

"No, sir. They're in the clear."

The captain shifted his gaze to the young cryptologic technician; he seemed lost in concentration, listening intently to the Korean-language chatter a dozen miles away. "What are they saying, Petty Officer Johnson?" Jenkins asked quietly.

"It's very jumbled, sir," Johnson responded. "The voices are rather excited, and very intense—shouting actually. It's tough to be sure, but I think this major just ordered his men to fire on the naval base headquarters building."

The sailor's report stunned Jenkins. He paused briefly, struggling to maintain his composure, then looked the petty officer square in the face. "Let me get this straight. You're telling me that a North Korean army officer ordered his men to fire at the base headquarters? That he's ordering his troops to shoot at their own countrymen?"

Johnson swallowed hard, but answered firmly. "Yes, sir. I'm pretty sure that's what he said."

Before Jenkins could press the young CT further, he heard his XO behind him shout out, "My God! Skipper, you better get out here and see this!"

Jenkins bolted back to the command workstation just in time to see several bright flashes on the large-screen display. Moments later, another set of flashes flared up— they were explosions, possibly RPG or even mortar fire. Johnson had been right. The North Koreans were fighting each other.

"Holy shit," whispered Jenkins in disbelief.

"What the devil is going on, Skipper?"

"I have absolutely no idea, XO," Jenkins replied more firmly. "But that doesn't matter right now. I want you to prepare an OPREP-3 Pinnacle message ASAP. The whole chain of command needs to know that North Korea is flushing itself down the toilet."

16 August 2015
Sixth Intelligence Squadron
Osan Air Base, South Korea

The sudden deep yawn caught Brigadier General Tony Christopher by surprise. *Oh Lord*, he thought, it was much too early in the morning to be staring at so many flat-panel displays.

Awakened by the US Forces Korea senior watch officer immediately after Eighth Army raised the alert, he had rushed over to the Seventh Air Force's Air Operations Center while his boss jumped into a waiting staff car and headed for Seoul.

Tony frowned. He hadn't even been back in country a month before the North Koreans started playing their usual games again. He should have expected it though; the Korean peninsula just didn't seem to like him very much.

The first time he'd been stationed here, he'd found himself dragged into a full-scale war. Of course, he could have said the same thing about Iraq. Then again, he hadn't been shot down during the two conflicts he flew in the Middle East. Now it looked like the North Koreans were getting feisty again, and Tony wondered just how bad things would get this time. He was glad Ann was still back in the States.

"Looks like you could use some coffee, General," announced a staff sergeant as he placed a steaming mug on the table next to Tony.

"Absolutely! Thanks," replied Tony gratefully, grabbing the mug and taking a cautious sip. "Ah, and a fine brew it is."

"Glad you like it, sir," the noncom said, smiling. "We go through a lot of the elixir of consciousness around here. It's not exactly exciting watching a UAV video feed for hours on end."

"I can imagine," grunted Tony as he took another drink. As a fighter pilot, he shared the dislike of unmanned aerial vehicles held by all true aviators. He couldn't argue that they weren't effective and useful, but the idea of "flying" from a ground-based station was anathema. Where was the exhilaration, the joy, the sheer fun you experienced when you climbed into a high-performance aircraft and roared skyward? By comparison, a slow, klutzy, unfeeling UAV, with a limited field of view, was a very poor substitute.

"The remaining Reapers should be in position soon, General," said the staff sergeant as he handed Tony a remote control. "You can use this remote to walk through the video feeds. The UAV's position and altitude will be in the upper right-hand corner of the display, the heading scale will be top center, the target's location . . ."

"I think I got it, Staff Sergeant, thank you," Tony interrupted curtly. He'd spent ample time becoming familiar with the MQ-9 Block 5 Reaper. He even had some stick time, if one could call it that, so he was well-versed in the unmanned aerial vehicle's capabilities.

The airman nodded and beat a hasty retreat. It was never a good thing to get caught patronizing a general officer.

Tony smiled slightly. That minor incident should make his life a little easier in the future. As the brand-new vice commander of the Seventh Air Force, he fully expected to be put to the test by its officers and enlisted personnel, if only to see if the rumors they'd all heard about him were true. Being the air force's only living triple ace with seventeen combat kills had definite disadvantages, the chief of which being that everyone would want to see if he really *was* that good. Politely nixing the good staff sergeant should help a little in that regard.

As Tony continued slurping his coffee, he began thumbing through the live video stream from the six Reaper UAVs spread out along the DMZ. Fitted with a multispectral optical and infrared sensor package and a high-resolution multimode radar, the Reaper was truly an eye in the sky. Flying at thirty thousand feet, it could peer far beyond the North Korean border. Although the MQ-9s could be armed with an assortment of precision-guided munitions, for this mission all of them were unarmed. Without the extra weight of the ordnance, each Reaper could stay on station for twelve hours. Right now, information was far more valuable than bombs.

The initial sweeps were along the DMZ and just inside the border. Everything looked quiet—*a little too quiet*, Tony thought. The North Korean garrison buildings were visible, but there weren't very many people moving about. And there were few, if any, guards and no patrols. *This is just bizarre*, Tony said to himself.

"Sir! You'll definitely want to take a look at the video from Merlin Two Seven. It's the MQ-9 covering the east coast corridor," called out one of the sensor operators.

"Understood," Tony replied. He switched over to the proper channel. But as soon as the image came up on the screen, his curiosity became confusion.

"What the hell?" he muttered, half to himself.

"Yes, sir," spoke up the sensor operator. "That column of vehicles is heading north along Asian Highway 6, *away* from the DMZ. At their current speed, they'll be in Wonsan a couple of hours after dawn. I . . . I can't explain it, General."

"General Christopher," interrupted the senior watch officer, "we're getting similar data from the other Reapers. Merlin Three Two has an armored column heading north on Reunification Highway. It looks like they're moving toward Pyongyang."

Tony launched out of his chair, a sudden surge of adrenaline relieving his weariness. "Major, I want a full accounting of DPRK units withdrawing from the DMZ. Get extra bodies in here if you need to, but I need to know which units are bugging out and where they're going. Move!"

"Yes, sir!" The major began issuing a rapid series of orders to his Reaper teams while reaching for the phone.

Marching through the video feeds, Tony saw that four of the six UAVs showed similar scenes with North Korean army units heading north along major highways. Even around Panmunjom, the site of the earlier incident, troops were moving away from the DMZ. The hair on the back of his neck stood on end, even though he couldn't begin to explain what was happening. All he knew was the KPA was conducting a large-scale withdrawal from the DMZ. It was unprecedented, and unexplainable, and therefore unnerving.

Fifteen minutes later, the watch team provided a very rough sketch of what was going on along the DMZ. It wasn't precise, but the data was good enough for Tony to order an alert sent out to all Combined Forces Command units.

He moved over to a video teleconference–capable computer, inserted his common access card, and logged into the secure computer network. Pulling up his address menu, he located the chief of staff, US Forces Korea, and hit the "Video Call" button. Tony waited impatiently while the connecting icon spun on the screen and the sound of a ringing phone filled the cubicle. After what seemed like an inordinate amount of time, the ringing suddenly stopped. A text box popped up on the monitor.

CONNECTION FAILED. PLEASE TRY AGAIN LATER.

"Oh, for the love of . . ." Tony growled. He reached over, grabbed the handset for the secure line, and aggressively started punching buttons. The phone rang twice before a female voice answered.

"US Forces Korea Headquarters. Chief of Staff's office. How may I help you, sir or ma'am?"

"This is Brigadier General Christopher at Seventh Air Force. I need to speak with Major General O'Rourke immediately."

"Yes, sir!" exclaimed the woman. "Stand by while I put you through."

Seconds later, a tired voice came on the line. "Hey Tony, what can I do for you?"

"Dan, we have a major situation developing on the DMZ. Multiple UAVs are showing elements of the KPA First, Second, and Fifth Corps withdrawing from the DMZ and heading north. I've issued an alert based on this information to all CFC units."

The initial response to Tony's report was dead silence. When O'Rourke finally spoke again, his voice was tense. "Please repeat your last message."

Tony grinned. He couldn't blame the other man for wanting to hear it again. If he hadn't seen the UAV video with his own eyes, he wouldn't have believed it either.

"We have multiple Mike Quebec Niner eyes on target," Tony said patiently, emphasizing every word. "They're showing elements of the First, Second, and Fifth Forward Army Corps on the move. These units are heading north, I repeat, heading north, away from the DMZ. I've ordered an alert sent to all CFC units."

"The NKs are pulling back from the DMZ? That doesn't make any sense," O'Rourke said flatly.

Tony shrugged. "I hear you, Dan, but that doesn't change the facts. The North Koreans are abandoning their positions along the DMZ in droves."

"Okay, okay, can you send me some video clips? I need to get this to General Fascione ASAP!"

"I've already got the Sixth Intel Squadron watch team putting together a representative collection," replied Tony. "I was going to walk you through a couple of shots on the video link but I couldn't get through to your account."

An exasperated sigh came from the other end of the phone line. "Yeah, my computer's been disconnected. The headquarters element is moving from Yongsan Garrison to Camp Humphreys this week and this whole place is completely FUBAR. Have the Sixth IS send the clips to the USFK watch officer and he'll get them uploaded for the bigwigs. They should be convening here in about an hour."

"Will do." Tony hesitated for just a second. "But, look, please do me a favor and tell my boss *before* he sees the videos in the conference room, okay? Blindsiding a superior isn't my normal operating procedure, and I really don't want to do that to General Carter with less than a month on the job—it could make for a strained relationship."

"No problem," O'Rourke assured him.

"Thanks, Dan," Tony replied. Out of the corner of his eye, he noticed a set of waving arms trying to get his attention. At the other end of the room, the Sixth IS major pointed to his watch and then held up five fingers. Tony nodded and gave the man the "okay" sign. "You'll have the video clips in about five minutes."

"Great. That'll do just fine, thanks," O'Rourke said. Then, in a lower voice, he asked, "Look, do you have any wild ass theories as to why they're moving away from the DMZ?"

Tony sighed and shook his head. "This withdrawal goes against everything I thought I knew about North Korea. It just doesn't make any sense. But if you want wild speculation, I can come up with two possible scenarios. Either we are seeing one of the best fake-out maneuvers in history, or something has gone seriously wrong inside the DPRK. Neither of those bode well for our long-term health and well-being."

16 August 2015
US Forces Korea Headquarters, Yongsan Garrison
Seoul, South Korea

The USFK conference room was filled to capacity and then some. The twelve leather chairs surrounding the main table were occupied by either an American or a Republic of Korea general officer. The more junior staff officers were bunched together in four rows of seats at the back of the room or lined up against the walls. All watched with rapt attention as Brigadier General George Olsen, the USFK intelligence officer, or J2, narrated the video clips sent up from Osan.

"In this clip, you can see elements of the Fifth Corps heading north toward Wonsan along Asian Highway 6. Based on rough estimates of column length, we're looking at brigade-size units. Those vehicles are also packed in pretty close to each other, and they're moving damned fast, considering it was still dark when this video was shot. Whatever the North Koreans are up to, they are in one hell of a hurry."

"What types of vehicles were seen heading north?" General Ji Sang-hoon, chief of the ROK Air Force, asked.

"In this clip, sir, all the vehicles appear to be two-and-a-half-ton utility trucks, basically troop carriers. The majority of the other videos show the same thing," Olsen told him. "But we've seen tanks, Chinese Type 69s, Russian T-62s or the North Korean Chonma-ho variants, in battalion strength, in two other clips. That's on the order of sixty tanks on the road, and they're heading toward Pyongyang."

"That would suggest division-level redeployment, wouldn't it, George?" observed Lieutenant General Robert Tracy, commander of the US Eighth Army.

Olsen nodded. "That's our current assessment. Based on some very rough OOB accounting, we're estimating that between five and seven regular infantry divisions are currently on the move. This represents about one-third to one-half the regular strength of the three Forward Army corps along the DMZ. And I must remind you that this only takes into account what we're able to see. The true extent of the North Korean redeployment could be even larger."

A low murmur broke out as the men and women crowding the room began talking with their neighbors. The J2 waited until the noise had settled down before wrapping up his presentation. "Are there any other questions?"

"Just the most important one, George," chimed in General Thomas Fascione, commander of the Combined Forces Command, and Commander, US Forces Korea. "Why?"

Olsen shrugged. "To be honest, sir, we don't know. The best theory we can come up with, based largely on the UAV footage, the incident at the Joint Security Area late last night, and the complete shutdown of North Korean radio and TV, is that there may have been a coup."

Speaking through a translator, the ROK Army Chief of Staff, General Yeon Min-soo, strongly disagreed. "Are you suggesting, General Olsen, that the North would dramatically reduce its combat strength on the DMZ to deal with a coup attempt? Surely the Pyongyang Defense Command and the KPA Third Corps are more than capable of dealing with such a situation!"

The American intelligence officer nodded. "That's true, sir. Those units should have been quite capable of dealing with a coup attempt." He paused briefly. "But what we are suggesting is that the coup was successful."

For a brief moment, there was dead silence. But then the room erupted as officers reacted to Olsen's statement. Voices rose as individuals either agreed with him, or flatly dismissed the possibility as absurd. Many of the South Koreans were visibly shocked by the notion of a sudden regime change in Pyongyang. Only General Park Joon-ho, the Deputy Commander of the ROK-US Combined Forces Command, remained calm.

"Gentlemen, ladies!" a deep voice roared. "Quiet!"

Broad-shouldered and bull-necked, Fascione still looked more like the West Point linebacker he had been than the clear-eyed strategist who had pacified two die-hard provinces in Iraq. He was taller than anyone else in the room. He also outranked them all.

The noise subsided almost immediately. Fascione turned back toward his intel chief and said, "That's one hell of a hypothesis, George. If that's true, we may be facing a possible civil war in North Korea."

Olsen looked very uncomfortable. He knew he had gone way out on a limb. "Yes, sir, I realize that is the logical conclusion of our analysis."

"General Olsen," interrupted Ji. "By your own admission, your order of battle analysis on these withdrawing units is very rough. And you also said the redeployment could be even greater, correct?"

"Yes, sir, that's an accurate summation," the J2 agreed slowly.

The ROK Air Force commander smiled thinly. "Then is it not just as possible that we are only looking on the dark side of things, and that the situation is not as grave as your worst-case scenario suggests? Is there any other information that bolsters this . . . theory . . . of yours?"

Before Olsen could reply, Rear Admiral Gabriel Waleski, commander of the US Navy units stationed in South Korea, raised his hand. "General Fascione, if I may?"

"Go ahead, Gabe."

Waleski nodded his thanks and looked around the crowded conference room. "When I arrived at Yongsan Garrison this morning, I was handed an urgent message from one of our submarines patrolling off the North Korean coast, near Wonsan. The commanding officer reports intercepting verbal orders given by a North Korean army officer for his troops to attack their own naval base headquarters. The submarine also observed multiple explosions near the base. It would appear that North Korean military units *are*, in fact, fighting each other—at least at Wonsan."

Ji was momentarily surprised by Waleski's report, but he regained his composure quickly and bowed slightly. "Admiral, I would very much like to read this report. Would it be possible for your government to release it to us?"

Waleski nodded. "Absolutely. I've already been given permission by my CNO to share this report with our ROK counterparts. Admiral Ban will have a copy before he leaves."

Pleased by Waleski's gracious response, Ji bowed again, silently expressing his thanks.

"Anyone else have any last questions before I give you your running orders?" Fascione asked.

"Yes, sir, I do," Tracy replied. The Eighth Army commander turned to face the South Korean general who was Fascione's deputy. "General Park, is there any new information from the defector that our people rescued at Panmunjom?"

Park's expression remained stoic as most of the assembled officers looked at him with amazement. This was the first they'd heard that someone had actually survived the slaughtered convoy as it attempted to flee the DPRK.

"Unfortunately, General Tracy," the South Korean said slowly, "the young woman was very badly injured. She had suffered multiple gunshot wounds. Our National Intelligence Service agents only had a few moments with her before she went in for surgery. To my understanding, she is still in the operating room."

"Did the NIS agents get anything, sir?" Tracy's voice had a bit of an edge to it.

Park shrugged. "They were only able to obtain her identity, along with the identities of those traveling with her. Her name is Lee Ji-young. She is the daughter of senior politburo member Lee Ye-jun."

It was the Americans' turn to be astonished. Fascione and Olsen, however, looked more annoyed.

"That's not an insignificant detail, General," Fascione responded tightly. "And one that should have been made known earlier."

Park shrugged again, apologetically this time. "Forgive me, but at the time the significance wasn't obvious." He looked at the Americans. "It is not exactly a rare event when a high-ranking Communist Party official defects."

"I grant your point, sir," Tracy countered. "But my chief of the headquarters battalion was the guy who pulled this Lee Ji-young out of that car. And it was only one of *seven* cars that attempted to run the checkpoint, which *is* unusual. Colonel Little also specifically reported that woman was lucid when he carried her across the Bridge of No Return.

And he stated that she said something like 'the burning has begun' before passing out."

Park's face hardened. Clearly, he did not appreciate where this conversation was going. "I was unaware of her reported statement, General Tracy. But now that I know of it, I would agree that it supports our J2's theory."

"Particularly since Lee Ye-jun was a staunch supporter of the Kim family," Olsen said flatly.

Fascione abruptly intervened. From the look on his face, the USFK commander was not inclined to see the disagreement descend into bickering.

"Let's get beyond this, people," he snapped. "Our two governments are going to be breathing down our necks in the very near future. General Park and I need your best assessments, pronto. Is that clear?"

Heads nodded all around the room.

"Good." Fascione ticked off what he wanted. "First, is Kim Jong-un still alive? Second, if he's dead, who the hell is running things in Pyongyang? Or are various contenders for the throne still duking it out? Third, who controls the DPRK's nuclear, chemical, and biological weapons?"

He turned to Olsen. "George, get with your ROK counterparts and put together a point paper that fleshes out your theory. Don't give us the *Encyclopedia Britannica* version. Make it short and sweet, but highlight why you believe it's likely that a North Korean civil war has started. Then answer those other questions I just rattled off."

The J2 nodded somberly.

"And I want a draft on my desk in three hours," Fascione ordered.

There were soft whistles from around the room. In the usual run of things at headquarters, just deciding who should be on the distribution list for a report like this often took longer.

"As of this moment, people, we are on a war footing," said Fascione bluntly. He eyed them coldly. "And if you think I'm overreacting, I suggest you talk to Lieutenant Colonel Miller's widow."

That shut them up.

"The rest of you begin your planning on the working assumption that North Korea is imploding," Fascione continued. "If so, what options do we have to deal with this mess?"

He looked around the room. "Don't forget that we may have to worry about a lot more than the pure military side of this. If the DPRK falls apart, we'll be facing a flood of refugees across the DMZ; in the tens or hundreds of thousands, possibly even in the millions. Where the hell will we put them? And how in God's name will we feed and care for them?"

Fascione's jaw tightened. For a moment, he looked his age. "We may be facing the most dangerous situation on the Korean Peninsula since the last war." He stood up. "Only this time, those sons of bitches in Pyongyang have nukes. So we have to get this right."

16 August 2015
Foreign Intelligence Service Headquarters
Moscow, Russia

Pavel Ramonovich Telitsyn read the morning worldwide intelligence summary with great interest and concern. Initial reports indicated that something very wrong had occurred in North Korea, but they contained almost nothing beyond vague references to fighting on the outskirts of the capital, and the complete lack of national level broadcasting. He sighed. It was useless. As the Asian Department chief for Directorate S of the Foreign Intelligence Service, he knew his superiors were going to be demanding more. And soon.

He was right.

Deputy Director Alexei Fedorovich Malikov arrived in Telitsyn's office fifteen minutes later. He looked agitated and worried.

"Good morning, sir," greeted Telitsyn. "Please, sit down. May I offer you a cup of fresh tea?"

"You may," Malikov nodded, glowering. "I could use something fit to drink. That lukewarm bilge water they serve in the main conference room is hardly satisfying."

Telitsyn fought down a laugh. His superior's naval past tended to slip out whenever he was annoyed. "I take it the morning staff meeting was more arduous than normal," Telitsyn observed.

"That, my dear Pavel, would be a gross understatement."

"North Korea?"

"Of course!" Malikov snapped. "What else could it be?" The deputy director took the tea offered him by the younger man. He sighed. "I'm sure you saw that pathetic report from our embassy in Pyongyang?"

"Yes, sir," Telitsyn replied. Shrugging, he added, "It was lacking in depth and specifics."

"Polite, Pavel. Very polite. It was a worthless piece of shit!" Malikov said bluntly. "We need reliable information on exactly what the devil is happening there. The president and the premier are deeply concerned. Which means the director is seriously disturbed, and that means I'm greatly troubled. Which means you should be practically pissing in your pants."

Telitsyn waited patiently. The deputy director might be bad-tempered, especially after a night spent reliving old memories with former shipmates and a bottle of vodka apiece, but he was no fool.

"Very well," Malikov said finally. He eyed his subordinate. "Do you still have that pet North Korean on a leash?"

"Cho Ho-jin? Yes, he is still operational," Telitsyn answered hesitantly. He was not sure he liked where this was going. Cho was one of his best deep-cover agents—an agent Telitysn had groomed ever since the renegade North Korean stumbled into Vladivostok as a starving teenager more than twenty years before. Ruthless, cunning, and highly intelligent, Cho was too useful to risk lightly.

"Well?"

"He's done very good work for us recently," Telitsyn said. "His reports on those new North Korean missile silos near the frontier were most informative—"

"And you don't want me or some other damned bureaucratic fool interfering with him, eh?"

There was no way to answer that question honestly, Telitsyn knew. Not and keep his post.

Malikov nodded, as though he'd read his subordinate's mind. "Unfortunately, your wishes do not count in this matter, Pavel Ramonovich. Nor do mine, frankly. Our masters want accurate answers from inside North Korea. Our task is to supply those answers. Understand?"

Slowly, reluctantly, Telitsyn nodded.

"Good! Then contact this agent of yours. Tell him to get his skinny yellow ass to Pyongyang and find out what the hell is going on."

CHAPTER THREE

PLUNGE

16 August 2015
Office of Asian Pacific, Latin American, and African Analysis
Directorate of Analysis, Central Intelligence Agency
Langley, Virginia

Chris Sawyer kept the CNN news channel on while he worked, although he'd muted the sound as soon as he was sure the anchors weren't saying anything new. The satellite photo the networks were all showing didn't need much in the way of explanation.

What had once been a building the size of a city block was now a huge mound of broken concrete and twisted steel. Any disaster on that scale would have made the news. But what had all the news anchors and talking heads in a lather was that this building had been identified as part of the massive Korean Workers' Party office complex in Pyongyang, North Korea.

With all of the DPRK's official media off the air, speculation that had first focused on sinkholes or shoddy construction was now shifting quickly to more ominous and sinister causes for the apparent implosion. Before he'd hit the mute button, they were also zeroing in on the possible significance of this catastrophe, as it occurred on August 15.

As the CIA's senior analyst for North Korea, Sawyer knew the talking heads were right. That pile of rubble had been the Party Banquet Hall, used for formal dinners and celebrations by the North's ruling political and military elite. And August 15, Liberation Day, was a national day of celebration set aside for parades, pomp, and parties to commemorate the end of Japan's decades-long occupation of Korea.

He also knew a few other things he fervently hoped would *not* appear on CNN or the other channels. Leak investigations were always hell. And the last thing he needed right now was to have his team wired up to polygraph machines and cross-examined.

He stared again at the image of the ruined building plastered across the screen.

A network of tunnels ran under Pyongyang, connecting Kim Jong-un's offices and residence with other official buildings. Extending for dozens of miles, it included escape routes out of the city and a lavishly appointed underground bunker, a refuge against air attack. Many of the tunnels had been bored through solid rock to a depth of three hundred meters, and they were wide enough for cars and other vehicles to use. In peacetime, they provided passage for Kim and other members of the regime to move about in secrecy and safety.

The fact that these tunnels existed was public knowledge, but Sawyer and his people, by piecing together overhead imagery, defector reports, and other information, believed they had about two-thirds of the network mapped. If the US ever went to war with North Korea, the air force would suddenly find a few dozen new targets added to its bombing list: innocuous-looking buildings or subway stations that were the entrances and exits to Kim's secret labyrinth.

And one of those tunnels ran right under the Korean Workers' Party office complex. From defector reports, Sawyer and his team knew that the banquet hall itself ran deep underground, with multiple basements filled with kitchens, storage areas, and air raid shelters. Analysts also believed that a set of internal high-speed elevators connected the building with the deeper tunnel system. It was an obvious destination for Kim's private transportation system.

So what had caused a massive steel-and-concrete structure to collapse in a matter of seconds?

Sawyer was convinced that it had to be a bomb—a very big one. He'd had weapon effects experts from the agency examine all the available images, both the commercial ones shown by the networks and the more detailed photos taken by US spy satellites. Their reports showed that the lowest point in the rubble matched the estimated location of those elevators. They also argued that only an explosion that completely destroyed some of the hidden underground basements could account for so much damage to the banquet hall itself.

A demolitions expert attached to the CIA's Special Activities Division had gone further. Over his many years in the military and then in the agency, Scott Voss had blown up enough stuff to take out a whole city. "No way was that an accidental gas explosion, Chris," the big man had told him. "Not enough explosive power from natural gas, for one thing. Plus, there's not enough fire damage. Ninety-plus percent of the time that you have a natural gas explosion, you're going to get one hell of a fire."

Instead, Voss believed it would have taken at least a thousand kilograms—a metric ton—of military-grade high explosives to destroy the assembly hall from within. A ton of explosives planted in one of those deep elevator shafts. "Nothing kills like overkill," he'd said.

There were other clues.

All the satellite photos showed large numbers of emergency vehicles and military trucks surrounding the ruined building, with hundreds of civilians and soldiers swarming over the floodlit rubble pile. Rows of bodies were set aside, left waiting while ambulances took survivors to nearby hospitals. Sawyer winced, imagining the carnage. If the banquet hall was being used that night for a celebration, more than a thousand people could have been inside when it imploded.

Signals intelligence satellites had captured some of the radio transmissions made by emergency crews combing the wreckage. Most were the kinds of communications one would expect in any disaster—urgent requests for information on the scope of the emergency, reports on the numbers of potential victims, and finally, reports about the efforts being made to rescue survivors trapped in the rubble. But in this case, there had been a second thread, a series of frantic transmissions detailing a separate, panicked search for "higher priority" victims.

Since many of those buried in the ruins were likely to be among the North's most powerful politicians and generals, who could possibly be "higher priority"?

Sawyer listened again to the audio files of those transmissions. The teams involved in this second search did not use any names of those they were seeking, just code words.

There. He stopped the playback.

One of the voices suddenly called out, "We've reached the dais! He is alive, but gravely wounded. The wife is dead. Four of the others are critically injured, the remaining six are dead." That was the last snippet the satellites had picked up.

And the voice repeated it. "He is alive."

Sawyer was sure they were talking about Kim Jong-un. It all fit, he thought. That bomb-shattered building, the near-simultaneous blackout of state media, and the failed mass defection attempt up at the DMZ. Someone had tried to kill—and he might die yet—the absolute ruler of North Korea. The "wife" they were talking about must've been Ri Sol-ju. The "others" were quite likely secretariat heads who helped Kim Jong-un rule as Supreme Leader. *Sweet Jesus*, he thought. Kim Jong-un, his wife, and the ten highest-ranking people in the DPRK government. The same number he'd just heard reported as dead or critically wounded on the dais.

He spun back to his keyboard, working through the possibilities again. Inside the paranoid police state of North Korea, it would take unparalleled access, information, and resources to pull something like this off. That meant a conspiracy set firmly in the regime's inner circle.

Everything suggested a coup, and even a successful coup would be bloody. A failed coup might be even worse.

He pulled up the most recent report on that North Korean woman the military had rescued from the DMZ. The ROK National Intelligence Service had reported her name was Lee Ji-young, which placed her as a member of one of the ruling families; her father had been a senior politburo member. There was no way to know for certain which side her family had been on, but he had been a strong supporter of the Kim family in the past.

Were they Kim loyalists getting out ahead of a purge? Or were they conspirators fleeing a failed assassination attempt? According to the US Army colonel who'd carried her across the line, she'd kept talking about "the burning."

The CIA analyst was willing to bet that the violence that would necessarily accompany any coup—whether it succeeded or failed—was well underway.

Sawyer took another pull on his cold coffee, his second cup since a hurried lunch at his desk, and began typing. The White House and his own superiors were screaming for his best guesses about exactly what was going on in Pyongyang. It always made him itchy to make sweeping assessments with so little hard evidence, but that was inevitable for anyone trying to analyze the DPRK. Paranoid and ultra-secretive, what the West knew about North Korea might fill a thin volume. What they didn't know was incalculable, but undoubtedly immense.

Despite that, it was Sawyer's assessment, with high confidence, that an attempt had been made on Kim Jong-un's life. But that bald statement raised more questions than it answered. Where was the North's all-important Supreme Leader now? Was he alive or dead? Who were the plotters? Would North Korea's armed forces hold together or splinter into different factions?

He added a number of indicators that would help produce answers to some of those questions. The rest would require additional collection. Some could be handled by the CIA, with its own resources, but most would require combined efforts by a host of organizations—the other US intelligence agencies, the military, the South Koreans, the Japanese, and many others.

Wrapping up the final paragraph in the report's conclusions, he wrote, "The power struggle now apparently taking place could involve numerous factions armed with nuclear, chemical, and possibly biological weapons. Given the DPRK's strategic location between two important US allies and two powerful US adversaries, and with US forces present in the Republic of Korea, there is a grave risk of violence spreading to any or all of these countries—threatening American interests and lives."

Chris Sawyer sat back and read that passage over carefully several times. Its dry, analytic language was the type required in any official agency report, but it didn't convey even half the anxiety he felt. At the moment, he could see only one possible future where the violence could be contained inside the boundaries of North Korea. There were at least a dozen more where death and chaos spread across the whole region . . . and maybe the whole world.

16 August 2015
Headquarters, 33rd Infantry Division, IV Corps
South of Pyongyang, North Korea
General Tae Seok-won had set up his battle headquarters in a courtyard just east of the mammoth Arch of Reunification. The Reunification Highway swept under the arch, heading straight north toward the center of Pyongyang.

He scowled. The arch, a project of Kim Jong-un's father, showed two women in traditional Korean dress leaning forward to hold a sphere showing a united Korea. Given the circumstances, with the DPRK teetering on the edge of civil war, it was a painfully ironic piece of propaganda.

From the arch, Pyongyang's skyline would be visible through the thick haze, with its spectacular, Stalinist-style hotels, universities, and government ministries dotting the horizon. He and his troops were just seven kilometers from the heart of the nation's capital.

Tae had hoped to get farther faster, but both his luck and the willingness of troops from the Pyongyang Defense

Command to accept his orders had run out at a checkpoint about a kilometer north of the arch. That was where loyalist soldiers had stopped the lead elements of the 33rd Infantry Division, demanding confirmation from the National Defense Commission itself before allowing his units into the city proper. They had refused to be bluffed, and, when Tae's men tried intimidation, pushing and shoving had quickly escalated into shooting.

After a brutal, close-quarters melee that left bodies and burning trucks strewn across the highway, both sides had sought cover among the apartment buildings, shops, warehouses, and small factories on Pyongyang's outskirts. A wide avenue, Tongil Street, intersected the highway at the checkpoint, offering any defending force a ready-made kill zone.

Now Tae could hear sporadic gunfire. They were sniping at each other while scouts from the 33rd's lead regiment, the 162nd, probed for loyalist strongpoints. His men were not well-trained for urban combat, and they were making slow progress. But they were still moving. The closest bridge across the Taedong River was just a few hundred meters beyond Tongil Street. *Take that bridge*, he thought, *and we'll have a clear road to the inner city.*

Meanwhile, Tae was trying to contact Vice Marshal Koh Chong-su, chief of the General Staff, and the first among equals in their coup against the Kim family and the other factions. Tae's troops were fighting their way into position, and he was supposed to have received further instructions by now. The problem was that Koh wasn't answering. Not by radio. Not by cell phone. Not even by dispatch rider.

And the clock was ticking.

Aware of the nervous glances being exchanged by the staff officers clustered around map tables and radios, Tae tried to buy time to think by pretending to study the most recent situation reports.

Time, he thought bitterly. A few of his fellow conspirators had advocated waiting for confirmation of Kim Jong-un's death before acting, but Tae and the others knew that time was too precious. It was all about control. Three generations of North Koreans had been raised to look to the party and the armed forces, and they, in turn, looked upward to their own leaders, rising higher and higher through the hierarchy until all eyes rested on Kim Jong-un. For a few brief hours, if they were lucky, there would be no one to give orders—no one to stop them.

But as soon as it was confirmed that Kim Jong-un was dead, others would vie to take his place. So it was essential that Tae and his fellow plotters were organized and in charge before their rivals from the other factions sorted themselves out.

The plan had worked so well at the beginning, he remembered. Perhaps that should have worried him. Every separate piece had run smoothly, like a well-oiled killing machine—starting right from last night's nerve-wracking helicopter flight to the 33rd Division's headquarters just outside Kaseong . . .

The Soviet-made Mi-8 helicopter shuddered and rattled as it banked, heading for the lighted landing pad starkly visible against the darkened countryside.

"We are two minutes out, Comrade General," the pilot told Tae.

Tae nodded tightly, teeth clenched against the vibration. He glanced at his aide, Captain Ryeon, who sat belted in beside him.

Ryeon leaned closer. "Twenty minutes, sir."

Tae checked his watch. By now, the waiters in the banquet hall would have finished serving dinner. The older soldiers and party bosses would be knocking back round after round of soju, a cheap grain liquor. Kim Jong-un and the younger members of the elite favored expensive, imported single malt Scotch and looked down on the "peasants" who swilled rather than sipped. *Well,* he thought coldly, *it was a divide that soon would not matter.*

He turned his head, peering back into the darkened cabin. Twelve soldiers in crisp, camouflaged uniforms looked back at him with expressionless faces. They were special operations troops, a handpicked squad from one of the Reconnaissance Bureau brigades. Each man carried a Type 68 assault rifle, the North's version of the Soviet-made AKM.

When the helicopter landed, Tae was the first one out.

Just beyond the slowing rotors, he saw a cluster of officers waiting. One of them hesitantly moved forward to greet him. Tae recognized the man from his briefing photos. Major General Yang was the deputy commander of the 33rd Infantry Division. He had a reputation for blind obedience, not initiative. And he was a born staff officer, not a combat soldier. He was perfect for Tae's purposes.

They exchanged salutes.

"I regret that Lieutenant General Seon is not here," Yang said nervously, eyeing the special forces troops lining up on the tarmac. "He is out on an overnight inspection of the Third Battalion of the 162nd Regiment."

"I see," Tae said flatly. Inwardly, he rejoiced. Seon, the 33rd Division's commander, made a habit of spending as much time as possible visiting and inspecting the battalions under his command. It was a habit they had counted on.

Seon was one of the good ones. The IV Corps, stationed near the DMZ, was a breakthrough formation, and the 33rd had the highest readiness scores in the corps, in fact, in the entire western sector. His political credentials were impeccable, of course, but he was also intelligent and energetic. That would make him a dangerous enemy. And that, in turn, required direct action.

Tae checked his watch. Ten minutes left. He looked up at Yang, narrowing his eyes. "Are Major Paeng and Captain Han with you?"

Yang was visibly surprised. Paeng and Han were junior staff officers in the division headquarters, ordinarily well below the notice of a senior commander from the KPA's General Staff. He looked back over his shoulder at the others waiting just out of earshot. "Yes, Comrade General," he said quickly.

Of course they are, Tae thought. Paeng and Han were covert agents planted inside the division by the General Political Department and the Military Security Command respectively. Equipped with separate channels of communication to their superiors, they were tasked with ferreting out treason and subversion. Any unusual activity, like this unexplained visit, could be expected to draw them like moths to an open flame.

"Excellent," Tae said. He lowered his voice. "A critical situation is developing, Yang. We have received credible reports of a plot against the Supreme Leader."

Yang's mouth fell open for a moment. Sweating, he visibly struggled to master his expression. "But—"

Tae cut him off. "Your commander is one of the conspirators."

The other man's knees started to buckle. He looked horrified.

"We know, however, that you are loyal," Tae continued, planting the hook.

Yang couldn't nod his head fast enough. "Yes, Comrade General!"

Tae fought down his disgust. He could practically smell the other man's fear. Then he shrugged. Yang might be a cowardly worm, but he was a worm they needed. For now.

"Good," he snapped. "Then you will continue to serve as deputy commander of this division. If this plot is not crushed in time, the state will need your steady hand and loyal service in the days ahead."

Yang moistened his lips. "And Lieutenant General Seon?"

Tae nodded toward the hard-faced special forces soldiers waiting beside his helicopter. "Seon and the other traitors in this command will be eliminated. At once."

The other man swallowed hard and then forced himself to stand up straight. "I understand. This is no time for weakness or hesitation."

Tae allowed the hint of a smile to cross his face. "Your eagerness does you credit, Yang."

"Sir!" A shout came from behind him.

Tae whirled toward his helicopter. Captain Ryeon came hurrying toward him. "What is it?"

"Pyongyang Defense Command reports a major explosion in the city!" Ryeon said, sounding horrified.

"Where?"

"I do not know, Comrade General," his aide lied. "All of our secure communications channels went down immediately after that first report."

Tae nodded crisply. "So the traitors are in motion." He spun back to Yang. "Put your headquarters on full alert!

Nobody leaves or enters until we have dealt with Seon and the other conspirators in this division. Understand?"

Yang nodded, sweating harder now.

Tae looked carefully at his aide. "Captain Ryeon, take your troops to the Third Battalion immediately. You know what to do?"

"Yes, sir," Ryeon said calmly, as though receiving orders to execute a division commander and his closest aides was a routine duty.

"And take Major Paeng and Captain Han with you," Tae continued, with a slight edge in his voice. "You can brief them on recent events on the road. Clear?"

Again, his aide nodded. Somewhere between the helipad and the Third Battalion's cantonment, the two Kim loyalist agents would each receive the reward their covert services to the regime had earned—a pistol shot to the back of the skull.

Ryeon moved away, already signaling the Special Forces soldiers toward a pair of trucks parked beyond the pad.

Satisfied, Tae turned his attention back to Yang. "Until we can reestablish communications with the capital, I am taking command of the Thirty-Third."

Yang looked relieved. He must have been dreading the prospect of issuing orders, rather than following them.

"I want this division on the road as soon as possible," Tae said firmly.

"Comrade General?"

"We are moving north, Yang," Tae explained patiently. "If this is the coup we feared, it is vital that we help secure the capital and its approaches against any further action by traitors or those they have misled."

He took a thin sheaf of papers out of his uniform jacket. "These are orders from Vice Marshal Koh, prepared for just such a contingency. Our mission will be to guard the southern edge of Pyongyang and to take control of certain key points inside the city. We will coordinate with the Third Corps as the situation requires."

"Yes, sir!"

"And shut down all communications, Yang, unless I give specific permission," Tae said. "No radio or telephones, and search the entire division for contraband cell phones. We can't risk traitors or sympathizers sending information or receiving instructions. Now, I suggest you and your staff get moving!"

Tae stood on the tarmac, watching Yang bustle away toward the waiting officers.

The plan formulated by Koh and the other plotters called for units loyal to the General Staff—and others taken over by deceit and force, like this division—to encircle Pyongyang. Once that was accomplished, they would use this show of strength to negotiate a stand-down of the Pyongyang Defense Command. With the capital firmly in their grip, the rest of North Korea would follow. *As long as III Corps comes over, this will work,* Tae thought coolly, weighing the odds. *Otherwise it will be a bloody mess . . .*

The sound of gunfire from up ahead intensified, breaking Tae's momentary contemplation. He looked up from the reports he'd been pretending to read and listened closely. That wasn't just sporadic small-arms fire now. He could hear the chatter of machine guns, the sharp *crack* of rocket-propelled grenades going off, and even what sounded like mortar fire.

That was bad.

It meant his troops were running into resistance from organized units from the Pyongyang Defense Command, not just a few scattered and stubborn checkpoint guards.

Tae swore under his breath. Where the hell was Vice Marshal Koh? And why hadn't he heard anything from the III Corps over his secure radio channels? Motorized rifle and tank units from that corps were supposed to be moving into the city from the southeast, off on his right flank.

Whummp. Whummp. Whummp.

Tae stiffened.

That was artillery. Heavy guns, at least 122mm, were in action somewhere to the east.

"Sir!" Yang hurried over. The deputy division commander looked pale. "The 161st Regiment reports that it is under artillery fire."

This is going from bad to worse, Tae thought coldly. He had deployed the 161st out along the Pyongyang-Wonsan Highway. It was there to guard his right flank against any loyalist troops pushing west to take him by surprise. If they were being shelled, that meant that at least some units belonging to III Corps hadn't joined the coup as expected.

Ryeon joined them. He had been monitoring higher-level radio transmissions. Despite everything, the younger officer still seemed calm, almost unnaturally so.

"Yes, Captain?" Tae asked, forcing himself to match his aide's wooden expression.

"Terrible news, sir," Ryeon replied. "The Supreme Leader is dead."

Tae stood motionless for a moment. They had done it. Even though this was what they had hoped for, the reality was almost overwhelming. That callow young fool, Kim Jong-un, and his vicious followers were dead—wiped off the board with one violent move.

But Ryeon was not finished. "Ohk Yeong-sik has announced that he is taking command."

That was bad news indeed. As chairman of the Supreme People's Assembly, Okh was one of Kim's most loyal supporters. And he was a logical candidate to fill Kim's shoes, at least as an interim leader. But Okh was not the General Staff's man.

Yang stared at Tae and his aide. "The Supreme Leader is dead? This is confirmed?"

Ryeon nodded.

"Then what shall we do?" the deputy division commander asked brokenly. To Tae's astonishment, tears were running down the other man's cheeks. Still reeling from the execution of his former commander, and then the outbreak of serious fighting, it was clear that the death of Kim Jong-un, by declaration and law the source of everything good in North Korea, had shaken Yang to his core.

"Do?" Tae snapped. He stepped closer to Yang. "We fight, Comrade Major General!"

He turned away, facing the other officers of the divisional staff. "Ohk Yeong-sik was on Vice Marshal Koh's list of conspirators. He and those who support him are enemies of the state. Is that clear?"

Slowly, they nodded. Blood had already been spilled. And whether or not they believed that Tae was telling them the truth, it was too late to go back. Besides, they were all too aware that their new commander's special forces bodyguards were stationed at key points around the headquarters.

Tae looked back at Yang, who was still standing there glassy-eyed and blank-faced. "Snap out of it!" he growled. "Pyongyang is in the hands of those who murdered the Supreme Leader! It is our duty to reclaim the capital and exterminate the traitors!"

He raised his voice. "Put artillery fire on every enemy position blocking our advance to the bridge. Hammer those bastards for five minutes. I want the 162nd Regiment to attack as soon as the barrage lifts! This is a general assault. I do not want anything held back. Not a man. Not a gun. Not a shell!"

Galvanized by his stream of orders, the 33rd Division's staff swung into action.

From here on, this was going to be a straight fight, Tae realized, and a hard one. True, they were disorganized. But so was the enemy. There was no turning back. So be it, he decided grimly. When opponents are evenly matched, it is the strength of their minds that guarantees victory. Then he smiled thinly. That was a quote from the late and unlamented Kim Jong-un's grandfather, Kim Il-sung.

17 August 2015
CIA Headquarters
Langley, Virginia
Chris Sawyer loved hunting for scattered bits of information and fitting them into a recognizable pattern. The intellectual challenge had drawn him to intelligence work. He was providing real answers to people who made very important decisions.

But every job had its downside. The decision-makers needed their eight a.m. briefing, which meant the briefers needed input from the different intelligence agencies by six, which was why the CIA Joint Crisis Team was meeting at five o'clock in the morning. Even with the long summer days, sunrise was a ways off.

The news of Kim's death and fighting in the capital, and of multiple "pretenders to the throne," had put Washington's national security organizations on a near-war footing. In addition to Sawyer and the rest of the North Korean section, the crisis team, run by Chris's boss, had pulled in people from all over CIA, including the proliferation shop and the China and Russian desks. There was even an economist.

Jeff Dougherty, the team leader and head of the North Korean section, started the meeting the instant he walked in the room. He spoke loudly enough to cut through the buzz of conversation. "George, what can you tell us?"

George Yeom had Korean parents who'd immigrated to the US. He was fluent in Korean and kept in close touch with his extended family back in the "old country." It was his job to also keep in close touch with the National Intelligence Service. The NIS was the South Korean equivalent of the CIA, and Yeom managed the exchange of information between the two agencies.

Seoul was thirteen hours ahead of Washington, which meant George was more accustomed to the odd hour than his colleagues. Short and square-faced, Yeom avoided the podium and stood near a map of the Korean Peninsula. "The South Korean agencies live and breathe HUMINT, of course. They don't have our satellites or ELINT aircraft, but then again, satellites won't tell them who's loyal to whom.

"Most of that HUMINT used to come from defectors and their spy network in the North. That network is now in a shambles. Their assets are either unable to communicate, gone to ground, or possibly arrested. NIS just can't tell. The channels the agents used to pass information are unavailable. Phone exchanges, dedicated tie lines, and the private networks used by some of the foreign organizations that operated in the North are all down, either by design or disrupted by the fighting in Pyongyang.

"On the other hand, the number of defectors, or more properly, refugees, is through the roof. They give a consistent picture of fighting around the capital, along with witch-hunts and random arrests throughout the country-side, but few useful details.

"My opposite number says they are 'taking measures to get more information,' but wouldn't provide specifics."

Dougherty asked, "What about their take on the communications we've intercepted?" The US and ROK operated joint listening stations along the DMZ, and the US shared the information it gathered by ferret aircraft.

Yeom shrugged. "Civilian traffic is way down, and what's left is disjointed and contradictory government pronouncements. If you're talking about cultural or linguistic insights, they can't see any pattern or purpose, because they think there isn't any purpose.

"They agree with our assessment that there are three major factions: Kim loyalists, a group of party bigwigs, and the General Staff. They have absolutely no idea who's going to come out on top."

Yeom saw Dougherty looking at the clock and wrapped it up quickly. "At a higher level, my contacts tell me there's a huge fight within the ROK cabinet. A lot of people in the South want to send the army across the DMZ, right now, while the Kim regime is tied up in knots."

Many around the room looked either amused or worried. "President An is not one of them," Yeom announced firmly, "and has pointed out to the hotheads the danger of presenting the different factions with an external enemy."

"Sounds like what's been going on in Congress," Dougherty remarked.

"And the ROK armed forces are remaining at something called 'Invasion Alert,' and the reserves are being mobilized," Yeom finished, then returned to his chair.

Dougherty nodded and started working his way down the table. "Ben, what about China? Anything to add?"

"They're keeping the embassy in Pyongyang and consulate in Chongjin open, but the last bus carrying noncombatants left Pyongyang for the border yesterday morning. The Chinese are beefing up their border security, but it's all border troops. The three group armies in the Shenyang Military Region are still in their barracks or engaged in routine training. There's been a major clampdown on the Korean refugee community. We're all agreed that China's worried, but is keeping clear."

Dougherty nodded and turned to a thin woman with short white hair. "Russia?"

"No changes since they closed their embassy. There's been some increased activity near the border, but nothing like China. Our assessment is that the Russians have enough on their plate. They'll keep out. Of course, they love anything that gives us and China problems."

After Dougherty had consulted all the subject experts, he called on Sawyer. "Chris, does this all agree with what you've seen?"

"No disagreements," he said, standing slowly. It had been a long night. "One addition, though." He pressed a key and a photo appeared in place of the map. "This is a weapons magazine outside Kaechon, north of Pyongyang. That's the headquarters of the First Air Combat Command, and the magazine is located near an air base. We've had it marked as a WMD storage site for quite some time."

The satellite photo showed a rectangular area with a grid of paved roads inside a three-layered fence. In the center of each square of the grid was an oblong mound, artificially flat on one end. There were several dozen such mounds, guarded not only by the fence but pillboxes at the gate and each corner of the fence. "This was taken last year. It's been assessed as a chemical weapons site storing free-fall chemical ordnance."

He hit a key, and a new photo appeared. It showed the same installation, but now a group of armored vehicles were clustered near the entrance, and half a dozen trucks were spaced neatly along one line of mounds.

"The vehicles near the front by themselves could be dismissed as extra security, but there's only one reason for that many trucks to be inside."

Dougherty asked, "When was this?"

"Early morning, their time, today—nine hours ago. I first saw it about half an hour ago."

Low murmurs filled the room. Sawyer knew they were saying what he'd thought when he first saw the image. The genie was out of the bottle, but a better metaphor might be Pandora's box. Remembering the sharing agreement, Sawyer explained, "I'll be sending this to George Yeom as soon as we're done here," nodding toward the analyst.

Turning back to his boss, Sawyer added, "And this is in your in-box, along with more tasking requests."

Dougherty smiled. "I don't know what's left to use. The only thing we don't have watching North Korea is the Eye of Sauron." There were a few laughs, and he continued. "I will ask that the priorities be reviewed, since we now have confirmation of exactly what we were most afraid of."

He glanced at the clock and announced, "That's it. I'll be briefing the director in five minutes. Thanks for your hard work. We have more information, but that just means more questions."

17 August 2015
Ninth Special Forces "Ghost" Brigade
South Korea

Colonel Rhee Han-gil concentrated on where to put his feet, one step at a time. It was simple enough. He wasn't being shot at, and anything where he wasn't under fire was, to his way of thinking, simple.

But it was hot today. His adjutant had politely suggested classroom and marksmanship training instead of a timed twenty-kilometer march. After all, the temperature at noon would be thirty-two degrees Celsius, nearly ninety-two degrees Fahrenheit. Regulations said the troops had to be kept inside if it was thirty-three degrees or higher. Of course, the adjutant's real concern was Rhee. It wouldn't look good for the Ninth Special Forces Brigade's commander to collapse with heatstroke.

Okay, Rhee thought stubbornly, so he was on the high side of forty, maybe very high. But he was in excellent condition, and he believed in leading from the front. He knew his reputation: decorated combat service in the Second Korean War, then multiple tours in Afghanistan, and rapid promotion. He was one of the youngest officers ever to command a Special Forces brigade. There were rumors that he'd make general soon, but he was actually happier as a colonel. He'd seen too many energetic leaders promoted and tied to a desk, turning into sedentary lumps with hands.

He grinned. Well, that wasn't going to happen to him. Paperwork was why they invented adjutants.

He shook the sweat out of his eyes and turned to look down the line of trainees pushing uphill behind him. He grinned again. He was still out in front and he was carrying the same load as the twenty-four-year-old second lieutenant leading the platoon. These men had completed their advanced training before being assigned to the Ninth, the "Ghost" Brigade. But if they had expected to relax, Rhee had told them, forget it. Their real training was just starting. Especially with the insanity going on north of the DMZ, he needed these new troops in shape, now.

They were fourteen kilometers in on what the brigade called the "Stone Snake." Laid out in an extremely irregular oval in the rocky hills surrounding the brigade headquarters, the dirt path was worn ankle-deep in the surrounding terrain, except where stones resisted erosion and rose up to catch the unwary.

Rhee knew he was tired. The sweltering, sticky air didn't seem to have enough oxygen to sustain him, but he forced himself to think like an officer, a leader. He sent the lieutenant back along the line to check on his platoon. Were they drinking enough water? Were any of them limping?

The kid had a good spirit. The required time for finishing the Snake today was two hours, while any man who made it in an hour and forty-five minutes would get the rest of the day off. The lieutenant, in front of his men, had promised Rhee that the entire platoon would make it in less than an hour and forty-five minutes. Confident, the kid was already planning a barbecue for his men later.

So far, they were on schedule. But the junior officer had to learn that if he wanted his men to perform like that, it took more than words. They had to know their lieutenant was looking out for them. And if that was the only lesson Rhee managed to pound home on this hell march, he would consider it time and agony well spent.

"Sir," one of the trainees gasped, pointing ahead.

Rhee turned and saw the cloud of dust coming up a winding dirt road that intersected the Snake at several places. He shaded his eyes against the sun's glare. That was a jeep speeding toward them. His adjutant's voice suddenly squawked over the radio. "Sir, I'm with General Kwon."

The young officer didn't add anything else. He'd already said enough. Major General Kwon was Rhee's boss. He commanded the Republic of Korea's Special Warfare Command, the "Black Berets."

Rhee turned toward the platoon leader. "Bring them the rest of the way, Lieutenant! And I'll expect you to keep your promise!"

Using the energy he'd saved for the last few kilometers, Rhee sprinted for the jeep as it pulled up close to the Snake. He stopped just short and snapped a salute. "So it's started, sir."

It wasn't a question, just a statement of fact.

Kwon, lean and gray-haired, nodded sharply, with just the hint of a grim smile. "It has started, Colonel. And we're sending you and your Ghosts in deep."

CHAPTER FOUR
RECONNAISSANCE

18 August 2015
Sinanju, North Korea

The farmer had gladly offered a ride to Cho Ho-jin in return for gas money, a few Chinese yuan notes, and a story about a "business to the south." Travel in the people's republic was closely controlled, but the farmer didn't care about Cho's movements, not when the truck, the farmer, and the load of vegetables it carried were all illegal, making him technically subject to imprisonment or death.

But people needed to eat. The government ration was for two poor meals a day, which had been declared the official diet of the country. Only the elite were able to buy more food legally, at state-run stores with North Korean currency. The rest of the population either starved or found ways to make money in the gray economy, where the Chinese yuan and American dollar were the only currency that mattered. The official exchange rate of one hundred thirty North Korean won to one yuan was a joke, and largely ignored. The gray market rate was about four thousand to one.

The gray market in North Korea grew and sold food, provided goods from shoes to Japanese electronics, and services that ranged from haircuts to installing a tuner in your radio that would receive foreign stations. It survived, in spite of the government's efforts to either stop it or co-opt it, because the state-controlled economy could not provide the necessities of life.

So food was privately grown on government-owned land, and shipped in trucks that were registered to a government office, and sold at an open-air market that theoretically didn't exist, because government directives explicitly forbade private businesses. And as long as every petty official and every police officer got a part of the proceeds, in yuan—not won, if you please—it didn't exist.

As bad as things were in the DPRK, without the gray market they would be far worse, and that's why the government couldn't make it disappear. The officials that would have to enforce the edict made far more money from gray businesses than they ever would from the state.

As a result, much of the North Korean economy consisted of bribes. Low-ranking officials received payments and gratuities and outright kickbacks in return for favors and fudged records and customized documents. The petty officials used their gray income not only to buy goods on the gray market, but also to pay higher-level bureaucrats tribute and bribes in exchange for their protection.

Cho received an adequate, if not generous supply of foreign currency from his Russian masters. His last mission had been close enough to the Chinese border to facilitate a fresh supply for his travels south. He had enough money to move and eat, which in North Korea would be considered a major accomplishment. His current identification said he was an agricultural inspector, which provided an excuse to travel.

So the farmer, a squat, weathered peasant by the name of Park, had been delighted when the inspector had not asked for a bribe, but instead offered to help pay for the trip to the market. Cho listened attentively to the local gossip as they drove from the farming village, down National Route 1, over the Chongchon River to the edge of town.

There was plenty of gossip to listen to. Cho's status as a petty official didn't deter Park from complaining about corrupt police and idiotic rules. Lean and gray past his years, he was worried about much more than the weather and the greed of the local officials. The stories from the capital were beyond belief: buildings exploding, battles in the streets, and worst of all, contradictory and confusing orders to the officials, the populace, and even the military.

Park had a son in the army, somewhere south, and told Cho the boy's unit had received three sets of orders in the past week, from two different commanders: first to mobilize and head to another army base, then prepare for a defense of their own base, and then to leave and move south to the DMZ. When Cho pressed for the son's location or unit, Park replied that his son, an ordinary soldier, hadn't been told the unit's name for security purposes, and only officers were allowed to look at maps.

He spoke to the boy by phone once or twice a week. Like many North Koreans, both Park and his son had gray market cell phones, made in China or Japan and modified to work on the North Korean network. It wasn't cheap, Park explained, but while he had two daughters, Park Jang-su was his only son. And he was worried. The unit had received a full load of live ammunition twice, only to turn it in again each time.

It was an hour-long drive from Tongyang village to the Chongchon River Bridge. National Highway One was a reasonably well-maintained two-lane road. The morning traffic was backed up right before the bridge, and leaning out the side window, Cho could see a police vehicle parked off to one side. He suppressed the automatic flash of fear—his identity documents were in order.

The line of vehicles, mostly trucks like Park's, crawled forward and eventually Park stopped next to a policeman waving a small flag. "Bridge fee," the policeman demanded. "Ten yuan."

"As if I had ten yuan," Park groused. The farmer was already holding a few bills in his hand, but out of sight of the official. "I won't have any money until I sell this load. Why don't you come around then?"

"Because you farmers are too quick to leave, which is why I'm standing here." The policeman sounded like he'd been inconvenienced. "Seven yuan."

"Two," Park countered. "I may meet other policemen."

"Five," the officer responded, but Cho could tell he was just going through the motions.

"Three," Park said, and handed the bills he'd been holding out the window. "And my daughters will go hungry tonight."

"Why should they be different than the rest of us?" the policeman answered philosophically, waving them on.

Once over the bridge, they quickly came to a local road junction next to a canal, on the north side of town. Sinanju was a worker's community for nearby Anju town. The main industry was coal mining; the dust darkened every surface and made every crevice black. It hung in the air so that even the light became gray. Following the farmer's advice, Cho tied a cloth over his mouth, and virtually everyone Cho saw had done the same, as if they were all American Wild West bandits.

Cho helped Park unload his vegetables, not only out of gratitude, but because the farmer was still telling stories about what he'd heard from the south. He finally took his leave, and explored the market.

It wasn't large, just two rows of a dozen or so stalls lining a dirt lane in an open field, but the vendors were doing business. The dusty paths were filled with pedestrians and bicyclists. Some booths were quite elaborate, and clearly permanent. Cho bought a bowl of bean sprout rice from a vendor for breakfast, and tried to listen to the conversations around him.

More than a few were about politics and news from the capital. The shutdown of the state-controlled media had been very upsetting. Nobody listened to the official propaganda, but when it stopped, that meant something had changed. Cho had seen and studied gatherings like this a thousand times, and they were worried. The people faced uncertain times, and in the North, that meant hard times.

His Russian masters, like the North Korean populace, wanted to know what was happening. If there was actual fighting, how bad was it? Who belonged to what faction? His original orders sending him from the Chinese border south had included a long list of very important, but hard-to-answer questions. Replies to his two progress reports since then had only added more questions, and demanded to know why he wasn't already in Pyongyang.

Cho headed for the Sinanju train station, hoping to speed his progress. Normal bus service had been suspended, and he'd been forced to hitchhike, taking days instead of hours just to get this far. No reason had been given for the suspension, but Cho was seeing more and more signs of the government ceasing to provide its normal functions. Some state-owned stores and offices were closed without notice, and in one town he'd passed through, the food rations had run out, again, with no explanation. Fuel supplies were spotty, which may have been a reason for the bus cancellation.

He didn't know whether it was the passage of time or the diminishing distance from the capital, but he could only expect things to get worse.

The Sinanju train station was built to a plan common all over the North—a broad, once-white building with the obligatory portrait of the Supreme Leader at its peak. Two armed soldiers stood outside, but that was customary.

As he neared the entrance, Cho had already taken out his identity papers, certain he'd be challenged before he could buy a ticket. As one of the soldiers approached, Cho offered his papers, with a one-yuan note folded underneath. That was the customary fee to make sure there weren't any "irregularities" that might make a traveler miss his train.

To his surprise, the soldier waved the papers away, a stern expression on his face. He barked, "Go away, the station is closed."

Cho, confused, momentarily considered increasing the size of the bribe, but then realized that although there were people on the street, nobody was entering or leaving the train station. He was tempted to just turn around and leave, but he needed to get a train ticket. He ventured, "Do you know when it will be open again?"

The soldier opened his mouth to answer, but was cut off by a harsh "What's going on here?" from behind Cho.

He spun around to see a uniformed officer, which wasn't unusual, but he didn't expect it to be a major from the Korean People's Internal Security Forces. They were a paramilitary organization, and usually handled things like civil defense and traffic control. Theoretically, they could be mobilized to assist other security forces in times of crisis— like now, Cho belatedly realized.

The solder braced and saluted, and started to explain, but the major ignored him and instead simply said, "Papers," almost spitting out the word.

Cho still had his identity card and travel orders in his hand, but he palmed the one-yuan note as he gave everything else to the major. He didn't speak, but waited for the inevitable questions.

"Your business here?"

"I am returning to headquarters at Sukchon. I wanted to buy a ticket for passage there." Cho tried to keep his tone as respectful as possible. The major had a hard, almost angry expression, as if Cho's mere existence was an offense.

"This station has been closed to all civilian traffic until further notice."

"Civilian traffic? The army's taken over the railroads?"

"Why do you want to know?" the major demanded. He motioned to the soldier, who moved behind Cho. He was sure that there was an assault rifle leveled at his back.

"If you're a spy, you might try feigning ignorance to gather information useful to this country's enemies about the railroads and troop movements."

Cho didn't try to hide his fear. He didn't want to be arrested by this man. It was not only the risk of discovery as a real spy, but the certainty of more delay, possibly permanently. He didn't even have to be charged. They could simply throw him in prison for "suspicious activity" and leave him there to rot. Nobody in the North would ever come looking for him, and he wasn't foolish enough to believe the Russians would do anything.

The major was looking at him. "The announcement went out yesterday morning to all state organizations announcing the order. If you were really an agricultural inspector, you would have received word from your office."

"My apologies, Major, I really didn't know. Look at my travel orders. I've been up near Tongyang. I haven't heard from my office in almost a week." Luckily, that was all true, but would it be enough? Catching a spy, even a false one, might gain the major favor with his superiors. It would certainly be more interesting than patrolling an empty train station.

Cho studied the man. There were only two ways to go: big or not at all. But not too big, or that might invite other attention. Fumbling with his papers, he pulled out a card with more information on the agency he supposedly worked for. Under the card, he tucked three bills, two ten-yuan notes and a precious American twenty-dollar bill. If the common people used the Chinese yuan, the elite used dollars, and there were things that only dollars could buy.

"Here. This is my agency's headquarters. If I can call them, they will vouch for me. I've worked there for many years." He handed the card and the currency to the major, who took it, thankfully.

Cho could see the man's mind work again. The major now had the option of turning him in for attempted bribery, but that was extremely rare, and of course the major's superiors would confiscate the money—all of it. And turning in somebody for bribery didn't get you points in North Korea.

The major paused for only a moment, then returned the document, neatly palming the bills. "That won't be necessary. The buses are still running. You can use them to get to Sukchon."

Cho smiled and thanked the major for his help, then got away from the train station as quickly as possible. His masters would have to be patient, but he'd get to Pyongyang eventually.

19 August 2015
ROK Submarine *Jung Woon*
North Korean West Coast, Yellow Sea

They'd left Pyeongtaek the day before, timing their departure for a window when both Russian and Chinese satellites would be below the horizon. It wasn't certain that the two nations' intelligence services would inform the North of ROK naval activity, but there was no guarantee they wouldn't, either.

Colonel Rhee had chafed at the three-hour delay imposed by fleet headquarters at Busan, in spite of the urgency, just as he now chafed at the sub's ten-knot speed. Although the submarine was capable of twenty knots submerged, that speed would use up its battery too quickly, the captain had explained. High speed also increased the sub's chance of being detected, especially in the shallow waters of the Yellow Sea.

Even though the stealthy approach made sense, Rhee wanted to hurry. Things were falling apart up north. They all needed to find out what was actually occurring, for many reasons.

The government's reasons were obvious. The North was a dangerous neighbor and a possible opponent, but the ROK leadership had precious little information about the current state of affairs. Rhee's mission might give them vital clues about what was happening, or about to happen. The country could then take steps to counter any harmful actions, or at least prepare.

The military needed information on the KPA's readiness. Reports of deserted outposts and unusual operating patterns left the generals and admirals in the dark. Unstable political situations often bred military adventures, ill-advised but still destructive. And then there was the WMD issue. What was their status? While Rhee's team couldn't answer all the questions, much could be deduced from the information they brought back.

There was also the personal angle. Like almost everyone in the south, Rhee had distant relatives in North Korea, ones he'd never met, but still felt connected to. There were still many alive who'd been separated from parents and siblings in the First Korean War. The older generation was now gone, but that made the ties to those left just that much more important.

Family mattered in Korea—a lot. Even though they'd been taught all their lives that the North was an enemy, bent on their destruction or enslavement, that only applied to the regime, to the Kims and their minions. To the average South Korean, the average North Korean was a prisoner in his own country—starved and mistreated. Unification would not just end an evil regime, but liberate their families from lifetimes of suffering.

Rhee could see the impatience in the rest of his team, even in the sub's thirty three-man crew. Speculation and discussions about what might be happening had taken on a life of its own, and finally the captain had forbidden all discussion of the topic unless it related to Rhee's mission.

Rhee kept his team busy, distracting them with quizzes about the local geography or other details of the mission, with weapons drills, and even language practice. Aside from regional accents, the language in the North had changed, with slightly different pronunciations and different terms. Rhee and his men would be wearing KPA uniforms, but the game would be over if someone spoke like they'd come from Seoul.

It was a small team, just four men. Rhee had chosen Lieutenant Guk Yong-soo, the platoon leader who'd brought his men across the finish line in under an hour and forty-five minutes. The other two men, Master Sergeant Oh and Corporal Ma, were out of Guk's platoon. Oh had served two tours in Afghanistan, but the lieutenant and corporal had no combat experience.

General Kwon had first insisted that Rhee have someone else lead the mission, but when he'd realized that his colonel intended to go, and announced the rest of his team, he'd argued against any new men. "Not this first time, Colonel."

"Especially this first time, sir," Rhee had countered. "It's only going to get worse later. It always does. They're good, and they'll come back veterans."

"Make sure you come back with them, Colonel," Kwon insisted.

Guk and Ma were both thrilled to be chosen for the mission, maybe a little too thrilled in Rhee's opinion, but Master Sergeant Oh had simply nodded and gone to pre-pare his gear. Of course, the entire platoon helped them get ready, and they'd flown out for Pyeongtaek naval base later that day.

They left the sub via the lockout chamber, one at a time, first the lieutenant, then Oh, Corporal Ma, and finally Rhee. Because of the sub's moderate size, and the captain's con-siderable skill, they'd managed to close to the ten-fathom line, which would save them a lot of swimming. Rhee shook hands with the captain, thanked him for the smooth trip, and promised to be back at the rendezvous in three days. The sub would loiter along the northern coast, eavesdropping electronically and keeping her batteries topped off.

The Yellow Sea was relatively warm in August. To Rhee, it was almost like bath water, and he surfaced in total darkness. The other three were within meters, and linked up as soon as he appeared. The sub's captain had put them exactly where he was supposed to. A scan of the surface and the shoreline showed no movement and few lights. Fuel in the North was scarce, and the dark coastline beckoned.

With their bearings established, they submerged again and swam east, into enemy territory. Rhee automatically counted his kicks as he swam, checking the time, depth, and especially direction. He swam through a cool black void, with no up or down, no light except the faint glow of the watch and compass on his wrist when he uncovered them. At times, he thought he felt an eddy or surge of water from one of the other nearby swimmers, but probably not. They tried to move through the water with as little disturbance as possible. Not only did it reduce the chance of being spotted; it saved energy.

It was still over a mile to the shoreline. The seafloor shallowed very slowly, so they'd chosen to come in at high tide, to get as much cover from the water as possible. A half hour into the trip, Rhee was starting to watch the remaining time more frequently. He told himself it was to make sure he didn't overshoot, and he was mostly right.

The four came up within seconds of each other; four black bumps a hundred meters offshore. His night vision gear showed no activity on the beach, in fact, no sign of human presence at all. Guk, next to him, was making a similar scan, and gave Rhee the "all clear" sign as well. Oh and

Ma, on either side, were scanning the sea, and also saw nothing untoward.

The water was only a meter and a half deep here, and they water-crawled about half the distance before stripping off their swim fins and dashing to the shore. The beach surface was loose rock, and it was hard to move silently. The good news was that there were plenty of larger stones and boulders for cover. They quickly removed their swim gear and cached it in a rocky hollow and camouflaged it. They'd need it in a few days, but they couldn't carry scuba gear all over North Korea.

They were all in North Korean People's Army uniforms, matching their real ranks, except for Rhee, who wore a major's insignia on a commissar's uniform. If challenged, they were a patrol searching for defectors from their unit, which given the situation in the North, seemed likely. Three carried standard-issue North Korean Type 88 rifles, while Master Sergeant Oh had a KS-23 combat shotgun. They all carried a North Korean Type 66 pistol, a copy of a Russian 9mm Makarov weapon. Rhee and Guk wore theirs openly, the others had them concealed but accessible. Ma carried a SATCOM radio, and at Rhee's instruction, sent the signal reporting that they had arrived safely.

The team also carried an electronic listening station broken down into several subcomponents. After their mission was finished, they would assemble and leave the device behind. It could eavesdrop on short-range communications that usually could not be picked up by sensors in the South. Planners had selected several potential spots along their path where it could be placed. While it would almost certainly be found eventually, it would not be found quickly, and not until long after the team had left.

The beach, really a small cove, had a stream in the center leading inland. Hurrying the other three a little, Rhee led them along it. They'd landed right after evening twilight and had a lot of ground to cover during the short summer night. After making sure everyone's night vision gear was functioning, the colonel checked his watch and started east with Lieutenant Guk leading the way. They were a few minutes behind schedule, and Rhee told him to set a fast pace.

Although Rhee was confident of his choices, the four had not had a chance to train together as a team. Normally they would have practiced the entire mission in the South, or at least the critical parts of it. Instead, Rhee had kept the plan simple, using the basic skills that anyone in the Ghost Brigade was expected to have mastered—like crossing an enemy landscape at night without being detected. As they walked, Rhee listened carefully, checking their noise discipline.

The land rose smoothly and quickly became rolling wooded farmland, dotted with orchards and clumps of pine forest. Given the perennial food shortage in North Korea, every hectare of arable land was tilled, but many of these fields were idle this season, either by design or circumstance. Rhee could see hills rising in front of them. That would slow them down, but the hills would also help screen their movements, and give them a good place to observe their target.

Their goal was Chongju, fifteen kilometers to the east, a relatively short distance, but of course, they would not be following a straight path. Chongju was headquarters for the 425th Mechanized Corps, roughly equivalent to a South Korean division. His orders were to observe the corps for any unusual activity. He was to be especially alert for any signs of general mobilization, and to get a definite count of the units present. The division had several cantonments scattered around the Chongju City proper. His team would have to check each one, then be back at the beach in slightly less than seventy-two hours.

They followed the stream inland for a few kilometers. Farmland lay on either side, although there were lighted houses to the south. The stream led toward the north side of a farming village, and after checking his bearings, Guk led the team east.

They quickly reached a two-lane road and followed it to the northwest, bypassing a larger town, Choyang-ni, to the south. There was absolutely no traffic on the road, and Rhee felt like he was back in the water, moving through empty darkness. The sound of the summer insects kept it from being completely silent, but Rhee had to work at remembering this wasn't just a midnight stroll through a peaceful rural countryside.

They crossed a major highway, a two-lane paved road, and the land began to rise. Their goal for the night was a 230-meter high hill that lay to the east of Chongju and overlooked the first garrison they were supposed to observe. About nine kilometers from the beach, it was as far as they could get in the short night and still have time to set up a decent secure hiding place.

They were just over a kilometer from the shore, moving cross-country, when Guk, still in the front, suddenly gave the signal to stop and went to one knee. Rhee dropped as well, and froze in place until Guk whispered in the headset radio: "Movement. Four forward."

Rhee was fourth in line, and he moved as quietly and quickly as he could until he was next to Guk. The lieutenant didn't have to explain why he'd stopped. A group of people was crossing a field ahead of them, moving right to left. Rhee could see several adults and a gaggle of children. Based on their size, they ranged from their teens to toddlers. They were still some distance away, but they appeared to be carrying bundles and suitcases. He saw no weapons.

"Civilians going cross-country?" Guk asked.

"Heading west or northwest. They'll reach the shore soon," Rhee predicted. "I'll wager one of them has a boat, or knows where one is."

The commandos could hear the group now, speaking softly but still talking far too much if they were trying to avoid detection. They were about thirty meters away, and unless they changed their direction, would pass well ahead of Rhee's team. What bits of conversation he heard confirmed his theory that they were heading for a boat, and the lament that one had to be alive to harvest any crops.

Rhee checked his watch. This was not helping their timetable. He patted Guk's shoulder and whispered, "Good work. Keep up the pace, but there may be more." The lieutenant started out again, and Rhee let the others pass before taking his place at the rear again.

There were more, enough so that Rhee wished they'd brought a small UAV to give them an aerial view. Not only would it have allowed them to go around the singles, pairs, and families moving through the darkness, but the colonel wanted to see just how many there were. Was there a pattern? Were there so many because they were close to the coast? If the civilians were all moving away from a central point, that would be a place he wanted to investigate.

As it was, when Guk spotted someone, all they could do was stop, make sure the civilians were not heading straight for the team, and then wait for them to pass. While Rhee and the others saw signs that the civilians—now refugees, Rhee corrected himself—were being watchful, none showed any sign of detecting their presence.

Guk was steering them past one group by leaving the road and paralleling the tree line, when he stopped and called for the colonel again. It was the same words, "Four forward," but Rhee could tell something was wrong.

They hadn't shown up on Ma's night vision goggles because the bodies were cold, but Guk had spotted them by their shapes against the smooth ground. Rhee saw a jumble of bodies, large and small, and ordered "Ma, on lookout" on the headset radio.

While Corporal Ma kept watch, the other three first checked the bodies for any sign of booby traps, then gently untangled them.

It looked like a family group, two older adults, three more in their twenties, and a teen boy. All were civilians, and had been shot. Two piles of clothes and small belongings lay on the cloths that had bundled them together.

"No valuables," Oh reported.

"This was done by soldiers," Guk concluded.

"Concur. Robbed and shot," Rhee answered. "Gather any identity documents you can find."

"The soldiers didn't bother taking those," Guk commented, handing several to Rhee. His disgust was plain.

The colonel didn't expect the papers would be of much intelligence value, but the sheer fact that refugees were being murdered by soldiers, probably deserters, was important. He also carefully marked their location. These poor souls had family, here in the North and perhaps even in the South. They might have lost their lives, but Rhee would make sure they were not lost forever.

Rhee was reluctant to leave them where they lay, but there was no time for anything else. He ordered Guk on point again, and they resumed their trip through a land in upheaval.

Two kilometers from their destination, Guk halted them again. "Gun emplacement ahead."

That surprised Rhee. That hadn't been on the satellite photos. Of course, they were American satellite photos taken over a week ago. Rhee had been told during the briefings that newer ones weren't available. They might not exist, or ROK intelligence might not have asked for them. A request might have started a discussion about why they were needed, and the Americans might not have been too happy about Rhee's mission.

After Guk confirmed it was quiet, Rhee joined him and the two studied the scene ahead.

It was indeed a gun emplacement. Inside an earthen berm, Rhee could see the mass of an artillery piece. The long barrel made him think it was an antiaircraft weapon. There was no sign of its crew, presumably still asleep. The pair low-crawled forward slowly, watching for any movement, and angled a little to one side.

As the angle changed, the gun came into clearer profile, and Rhee identified it as a KS-30, a heavy 130mm antiaircraft gun. They were usually operated in batteries of four or six, and about fifty meters past the first he saw another emplacement. But still no movement.

Rhee didn't like the idea of a gun emplacement so close to where they were going to set up for the day, but the hill he'd chosen on the map was an ideal spot, and he was reluctant to give it up.

But where were the sentries? An AA battery had almost a hundred personnel, and in the field, even in friendly territory, they'd post at least one or two sentries per gun. They couldn't all be slacking off somewhere, could they?

They were falling farther behind schedule. They couldn't waste any more time on this, or the morning twilight would catch them still setting up. Maybe if they're that sloppy, they could still use the preselected location.

Rhee and Guk hurried back to the other two as quickly as stealth allowed, and with Guk keeping a dedicated watch on the battery, Rhee led them east toward the hill, a kilometer away. He relaxed a little once they were on its wooded slopes, and they quickly reached the crest. Rhee told the lieutenant to pick a spot and set up a hide, and while the other three did that, the colonel took out a night vision telescope and tripod and found a spot to study the gun emplacement.

With the elevation, he could look down and see the ring of six guns, with the fire control van in the center. Tents and ammunition storage were laid out, with the gun's prime movers and other transport parked off to the side. There were no lights, or signs of movement. The lack of any illumination could be due to proper light discipline. But no movement at all?

Guk reported the camouflaged hide was completed, and Rhee inspected their handiwork, making a few suggestions as if this was just another training exercise. The telescope was brought back to the hide and trained on the nearest cantonment, which held one of the three regiments that made up the 425th. It was farther away, but it was getting lighter, and almost to their relief, Guk reported seeing vehicles and personnel moving about.

While Guk studied the garrison, Rhee had Ma transmit another signal that they'd reached their first night's objective. He told the master sergeant to find a good spot and keep a close watch on the nearby emplacement. He was sure they'd only been lucky so far.

Ma reported "Message received," and Rhee told him to take a nap while he kept watch. It had been a long night, and he'd learned to pace himself. It was another skill to teach these men, and . . .

Master Sergeant Oh's voice came over the headset. "Sir, you need to see this."

That didn't sound good. After telling Ma to delay his nap until he returned, Rhee carefully made his way to Oh's position. It was fully light now, and any movement, even among the trees, could be seen at some distance.

As he approached, Oh handed him a pair of binoculars and simply pointed down the slope, a strange expression on his face.

There was nobody in the emplacement. Not only no movement, but no soldiers. At this hour, the battery should be lining up for breakfast, and crews should be servicing their weapons. But it appeared to be completely deserted.

There was certainly no risk of being spotted, but what was going on? Rhee didn't like surprises, especially in the middle of the DPRK, and he felt a chill. He told Oh, "Come with me."

Trying to balance speed with caution, they hurried down the slope and approached the nearest gun emplacement. At this point, Rhee had to abandon concealment, and hope that any North Korean solder he met would be below the rank of major. After that he'd find out what he could and talk his way out. But he had to know more.

The nearest of the six AA emplacements was empty. The gun appeared functional, with ready ammunition stacked nearby, but no crew. Standing on the berm surrounding the gun, Rhee scanned the emplacements to either side. They were deserted as well. Oh, his shotgun at the ready, seemed ready to shoot anything that moved, but nothing provided a target.

The fire control radar van was empty, its generator off. A few papers were scattered about, and the two collected them for any intelligence they might provide. There was still no movement. The bivouac area was about a hundred meters from the guns, centered on the mess tent. Rhee headed for the headquarters tent, set a little off from the others. Alert as they were, they didn't notice the smell until they were only a few meters away. Rhee looked over at Oh, who had the same expression on his face.

They knew what was inside, but still took care approaching the door, weapons level, then glancing inside before entering. On one side of the tent, maybe five meters on a side, was a pile of bodies, all in uniform. Bloodstains marked bullet wounds. Powder burns showed that many had been shot at close range.

Rhee ordered, "Watch the door." While Oh kept a lookout, Rhee searched the bodies. Their sidearms were gone, but he collected some documents. He counted five bodies: a captain, a staff sergeant, two sergeants, and a corporal. By rights, a captain would command this battery, with a senior lieutenant as his deputy.

The tent's contents, two cots, a camp desk, and other items, were scattered and broken. Two personal lockers lay open, their contents tumbled out. Rhee found a few more documents, then said, "Mess tent next."

They covered the distance in seconds, as if under fire, and paused for only the briefest check before going inside.

It was larger than the officer's tent, designed to feed the battery in shifts. The inside showed some signs of disorder, but Rhee ignored that, instead heading back to the cooking area while Oh watched the door again. A truck was parked alongside the tent, and it confirmed Rhee's hypothesis.

He walked back toward Oh, the master sergeant's gaze firmly outside. "Most of the food is gone. Only the heaviest items are left. They shot those that didn't want to join them, and deserted."

Oh muttered an expletive, shaking his head in disbelief, then said, "Those crazy bastards. An entire unit mutiny?" Such a thing was inconceivable in the ROK Army, much less a police state like the DPRK. "Where will they go?"

Rhee shrugged. "They could have scattered, back to their homes, but it's more likely they're headed for the Chinese border. It's only eighty kilometers from here. I'll bet there are a few trucks missing. Those bodies haven't been dead more than twelve hours. If they did this last night, maybe about the same time we landed, they could be at the border now. And who's going to stop a couple of army trucks?"

Oh's eyebrow's went up at the idea. "I pity any checkpoints they reach."

"Let's get out of here. I want to find out what's going in that garrison."

The master sergeant added, "And sooner or later, they're going to wonder why nobody here is answering phone calls. We shouldn't be here."

They almost sprinted back to the hillside. As they reached the wood line, Rhee used his tactical radio. "Pack up. We need to move away from here. I'll explain why later, but KPA units are likely to come and search this area any time now. And tell Ma to prepare the radio. I'll want to sent a message."

Guk replied immediately. "Understood. I was about to call you. You won't believe what's going on in that cantonment."

"I will now," Rhee answered.

CHAPTER FIVE
BREEZE

20 August 2015
Pyongyang, North Korea

Cho Ho-jin had scouted out the spot before darkness fell across the city. It was a government building, officially part of the Education Ministry, but now it lay in ruins after being battered by tanks and heavy artillery. It was hard to believe that the educational apparatus represented a target for either loyalists or rebels. Then again, he thought sourly, in Kim's regime there was no guarantee that the building had ever been remotely connected to education. It was just as likely to have been a state security prison or a special weapons laboratory.

The gutted concrete shell had burned out, but the ashes were still smoking. There were dozens of such ruins across Pyongyang, some much more extensive. Since reaching the capital yesterday, Cho had heard tank fire and the rattle of small arms almost constantly.

On reaching Pyongyang, he'd changed his identity from that of an agricultural inspector to a factory executive. He needn't have bothered. Government offices were closed or outright abandoned, and official commerce had virtually ceased.

He'd made a report to his handlers in Directorate S while still outside the city, describing what he could make out of the ruined structures, and even taking pictures of the smoking skyline with his Chinese cell phone. The device had been modified by the Russians with a better antenna and an encryption chip that was triggered by a special prefix when he sent a text message. It was also untraceable. Its location couldn't be fixed, even by his Russian masters, and the phone did not store messages or photos. If it was taken from him, it would tell his captors nothing of what he'd sent or received.

At Telitsyn's prompting, and with reluctance, Cho had entered Pyongyang proper, trying to scout the situation without drawing attention to himself. Fortunately, the fighting between the warring factions was such a huge distraction that nobody had questioned his coming and goings, and many citizens had eagerly shared information in the hopes he'd do the same. Slowly, Cho had built up a picture of the battle and its effects.

Every part of Pyongyang had seen fighting, with regular army, internal security, and police units fighting each other, attacking government and commercial buildings that either served as centers of political power or had been turned into military strongpoints. Casualties could only be estimated, but he was certain they were easily in the thousands—and more likely in the tens of thousands. No attempt had been made to count the dead. No one had even bothered to put out most of the fires, treat any of the wounded, or rescue those certainly buried in the shattered buildings.

Then had come Kim's broadcast.

Cho had been waiting in a food store near the edge of town, withdrawing from the danger near the city center. The proprietor was openly selling his goods at wartime prices, accepting only yuan or dollars, but he had food to sell, and he had plenty of customers. Like everyone else, Cho had come for the chance of a meal, and to learn what he could.

While he waited, the speaker mounted on the wall of the store, silent for several days, suddenly crackled to life. There was one like it in every factory, commercial establishment, and school, as well as most homes. In ordinary times these speakers played patriotic music, culturally uplifting plays, and carefully regulated news, especially about Kim Jong-un's many accomplishments.

But now they heard the Supreme Leader's voice. Instantly, silence had fallen across the little store. Everyone had stood motionless, staring at the speaker in disbelief.

Kim's short speech had been followed by a standard song, "Labor toward Self-Sufficiency"—just as if there'd been no four-day interruption. The reactions in that little store had been very strange, Cho remembered. Before Kim declared himself alive, the people waiting in line for their turn at the counter had chatted, sharing concerns and gossip and news. Afterward, they had stood in complete silence.

Later, he'd joined the others outside, sitting quietly and wolfing down his tiny portion of rice and pickled vegetables. Listening for any scraps of conversation, he noticed that the gunfire was much reduced, more an occasional staccato burst than a constant drumbeat. And by the time he finished, the sounds of combat had almost vanished entirely.

That had to have been the result of Kim's speech.

Was the military standing down, he wondered? Would the fighting in Pyongyang end?

But the people around him hadn't looked relieved. Surely, for most of them, a cease-fire was good news. And yet they had still looked troubled. Finishing their own small meals, they had drifted off in ones and twos, as though afraid of attracting attention.

Now, in the gathering dusk, Cho watched the street carefully, but Pyongyang's residents were already at home or hiding in shelters. The reactivated loudspeakers had proclaimed a nighttime curfew, but that was unnecessary. Several days of civil war had taught civilians caught up in the fighting harsh lessons. Anyone moving after dark, or worse yet, showing a light, risked becoming a target. None of the combatants had shown any concern for collateral damage.

The streets were clear and quiet. In the fading twilight, Cho picked his way into the ruined government building, choosing his path carefully, until he was in a part of the structure that was only scorched, and didn't seem in danger of collapsing.

Sitting down, safely away from observing eyes, he began composing a very long e-mail to Moscow. He had a lot of information to send Telitsyn and Malikov—the identities of some of the army and security units involved in fratricidal combat, what he'd learned about the extent of the destruction, and most importantly, Kim's speech and the reaction to it by ordinary North Koreans.

That, he thought grimly, was the key.

Before Kim spoke, Pyongyang's inhabitants had been worried about the war raging around them. Now they were worried about what came next.

CNN Special Report
"The Pyongyang Crisis"
The news anchor's image shared the screen with file video of Kim Jong-un inspecting a military unit. A brightly colored banner across the bottom read "Breaking News."

"A little over two hours ago, the Voice of Korea, North Korea's official news station, transmitted a short speech claimed to be by North Korean leader Kim Jong-un. Lasting just a little over five minutes, the speaker claimed to have been nearly caught by a 'cowardly attempt' on his life, but escaped with only minor injuries. He claimed that criminals and foreign sympathizers were attempting to disrupt the government, but that they were now being arrested, having done little damage. He called on the army and all loyal North Koreans to obey the orders of all lawful officials. He also promised another broadcast in the near future."

The image of the dictator was replaced by a bearded man in his fifties, sitting across from the anchor. "We are joined by Dr. Russell Hayes of the Brookings Institution. Doctor, you've heard the recording. Do you think it's authentic?"

Hayes nodded. "It sounded authentic. I'm sure our intelligence agencies are analyzing the voice. But I've listened to dozens of his speeches. And he's been much more public than his father or grandfather. The phraseology, the inflection, all sounded correct to me. Deception always remains a possibility with the North Koreans, but the timing also supports this broadcast's authenticity."

The anchor looked confused. "In what way?"

"If someone was going to air a fake, they could have done it much sooner, before the situation had degraded so badly. It's been five days since the bombing, and my hypothesis is that it's taken this long for Kim to recover from his 'minor' injuries and be able to speak."

"Is this the end of the coup, Doctor?"

Haynes nodded again. "Most likely, unless his security organizations are too badly damaged. The biggest question for the last five days has been whether or not Kim was dead.

That has now been answered. For three generations, North Korea's people have been conditioned to follow the Kims. And now that he's made his appearance, the plotters will have to admit they've failed."

"You've been following the reports of bloodshed in the capital and elsewhere. Will this broadcast put an end to that?"

Hayes sighed. "End the bloodshed? No, unfortunately not. It will only change its nature. I believe we'll see the rebel versus loyalist and army versus army fighting replaced by a massive wave of arrests and executions, including anyone even remotely connected to the plotters. That may go on for months."

The anchor looked genuinely shocked. "What's your estimate of the casualties so far?"

The analyst shook his head in frustration. "We've got information on Pyongyang, mostly from foreign embassies, and the dead are easily in the thousands. Several times that are wounded, but given the dismal state of North Korean hospitals, their chance of survival is based more on luck than receiving decent medical care.

"And we've got nothing from the countryside at all," Hayes continued. "Returning Western aid workers were a good source, but even though the State Department has recommended that all US citizens leave the DPRK immediately, few have, mostly because they can't. The airports and train stations are closed.

"All we can hope is that with someone in charge, the situation will stabilize, and the danger of the fighting spreading outside the North's borders will be much reduced."

The anchor summarized, "So we're likely to see a bloodbath, then a return to business as usual."

Haynes scowled but reluctantly agreed. "If Kim really is in charge, yes."

21 August 2015
Myohyang-san, North Korea

The thickly forested granite slopes of Myohyang-san, "the Mountain of Mysterious Fragrances," rose sharply in multiple peaks one hundred and twenty kilometers northwest of Pyongyang. Famous for its roaring waterfalls and the ancient Buddhist temples and hermitages built into its sheer cliffs and slopes, in more peaceful times the mountain was a magnet for travelers and hikers. In the narrow river valley below, the Kim dynasty kept its vast treasure trove of precious gifts from foreign leaders in the one hundred fifty rooms of the International Friendship Exhibition.

But there were no travelers or hikers on the mountain now. Nor were there any chattering bands of tourists snapping pictures of the armored train car given to Kim Il-sung by Mao Tse-tung, or the limousine presented by Stalin, or the gem-encrusted silver sword from Yasser Arafat.

Instead, hurriedly dug trenches and rolls of razor-edged barbed wire ringed the base of each peak. North Korean soldiers in full combat gear lined these new fortifications, manning machine guns, mortars, and carefully sited anti-tank missile launchers and guns. Tanks and heavier artillery pieces were concealed in the surrounding forests under camouflage netting. SAM teams were deployed on the upper balconies of the pyramidal Hyangsan Hotel.

From time to time, the officers and enlisted men laboring to turn the mountain and its environs into a fortified camp turned nervous glances on the looming spire of Piro Peak. Climbing nearly two thousand meters up the Chilsong Valley, it was the highest point on Myohyang-san.

These men knew they were under constant observation from that peak. The slightest misstep, the smallest mistake, was taken as proof of treason. The firing squads were kept busy around Myohyang-san. And every day, the heaped mounds of earth marking mass graves spread wider.

Buried deep within Piro Peak's layers of rock lay North Korea's National Command Redoubt, a labyrinth of concrete- and steel-lined tunnels, bunkers, storehouses, armories, and living quarters—sealed off from the world and danger by gigantic blast doors. Built over more than a decade at enormous cost and in great secrecy, the redoubt was designed as a nuclear bomb–proof shelter and command post for the Kims and their favored retainers in time of war or unrest. It contained an array of electronics, surveillance, and defense equipment that surpassed anything else in the Democratic People's Republic.

And now it was being put to the test.

Audience Chamber, National Command Redoubt

Carved out of granite six hundred meters below the summit, the Audience Chamber, already quite large, was given the illusion of even greater size by a massive mural that filled the entirety of one wall. Larger-than-life figures of Kim Il-sung and Kim Jong-il were depicted on the slopes of the mountain, exhorting vast masses of joyful, cheering soldiers and peasants. Floor-to-ceiling red silk hangings lined the other walls, covering cold gray concrete surfaces and steel doors. Ventilators on the ceiling pumped in cool, fresh-tasting air.

Kim Jong-un stood stiffly behind a podium, facing two television cameras. He wore a long black overcoat. It hid both the metal brace being used to prop him up and the thick bandages wrapped around his chest and stomach. A wig concealed the shaved patches and wound dressings on his skull. Skillfully applied makeup added color to his sallow, fleshy face.

He ignored the low murmurs from the generals and marshals in full dress uniform lined up behind him. They were nothing more than window dressing for the live, televised broadcast he planned to make—a visible sign of the control he claimed over the nation's armed forces. Most of them were new faces, a cast of less senior general officers rapidly promoted to fill the gaps torn in his inner circle by the same bomb that had almost killed him.

Kim gripped the podium as a wave of pain rippled through his body. Those who had betrayed him had come close to success. Believing him dead in the rubble of Pyongyang, the traitors and those they had duped were locked in battle with loyal troops across the whole of North Korea. Soon, though, they would learn the bitter truth. Once the people and the armed forces saw him alive and in command, the rebellion would collapse, dissolving from within in the revelation of its own lies and folly.

And then there would come a reckoning, he thought coldly. He would cleanse the nation of the traitors, their families, and other vermin. His nets would be cast widely. It was better that a million should die rather than risk leaving alive anyone who might challenge him.

Kim squinted at the clock mounted on the opposite wall and frowned. Its hands swam in and out of focus, impossible to read. "How much longer?" he muttered to the young, grim-faced officer at his side.

Colonel Sik Chol-jun was one of the few men he trusted, one of the bodyguards who had pulled him alive from the bomb-ravaged ruins of the Banquet Hall.

"Thirty minutes to your broadcast, Supreme Leader."

"Good," Kim said tightly, clenching his teeth as another wave of agony washed over him. "Then it is time for my injection."

Sik nodded crisply, raising a hand to summon the doctor waiting nervously with the small group of cameramen and sound technicians.

The doctor, a middle-aged man whose fear-filled eyes were magnified by a pair of thick spectacles, hurried to them.

"You know what is required?" Kim demanded harshly.

"Yes, Supreme Leader," the doctor said, already opening his medical kit. "Enough medication to dull the pain, but not so much that your speech patterns or thought processes are affected."

"You will prepare two injections," Kim told him, watching closely while he filled a syringe from a sealed ampule.

The doctor looked up, surprised. "But, Supreme Leader—"

"Do it."

Trembling, the doctor obeyed, filling another syringe.

Satisfied, Kim turned to Sik. "Carry on, Colonel."

Before the doctor could react, the younger officer took the first hypodermic away from him. Then, ignoring his startled squawk, Sik jabbed the needle into the doctor's own upper arm. A spot of bright red blood appeared on his shirt.

Silently, Sik handed the used syringe back to the stunned doctor, who stood wincing and rubbing at his arm.

"Now we wait, Doctor," Kim said quietly. "And if you are still alive in five minutes, you may give me that second shot."

He turned back to Sik. "Take your station in the control center, Colonel. You know my orders."

"Yes, Supreme Leader." For the first time, the young officer smiled. "Everything necessary will be done."

Security Control Center, National Command Redoubt

Colonel Sik paused just inside the control center, waiting briefly while his eyes adjusted to the dimmer light. The armed guard posted at the entrance grunted slightly, closing the heavy steel door that separated this room from the rest of the complex.

"Lock it," Sik told him.

"Yes, Comrade Colonel," the soldier said, spinning a wheel set into the door. Super-hardened bolts smoothly slid into place with an audible click.

Sik nodded, satisfied. Now it would take a powerful shaped explosive charge to break in.

Set even deeper inside the mountain, the control center was crowded with computer consoles, equipment panels, and TV monitors. Piping and electrical wiring covered almost every inch of the plain concrete walls and ceiling. Signs identified controls for the redoubt's ventilation systems, internal and external alarms, blast doors, fire suppression systems, and for an array of command-detonated minefields covering the slopes outside.

Four officers manned the various consoles, their fingers flickering on keyboards and old-fashioned switches as they monitored data, video, and audio feeds from the internal systems and from the various observation and guard posts scattered across the face of Myohyang-san.

Sik checked his watch. Fifteen minutes until Kim Jong-un went live on televisions across North Korea, announcing his survival and his determination to regain control.

"Go to maximum internal security," he ordered.

"Yes, Comrade Colonel," the senior watch officer, a major, said. He tapped a series of switches. Lights flashed red and the TV monitors showed blast doors sliding shut in corridor after corridor and room after room. One by one, the blinking red lights turned green. "All doors secured and locked."

"Activate overpressure systems."

The captain manning the ventilation panels nodded, already flicking controls.

Sik heard a low hiss. He swallowed twice, clearing his ears. Raising air pressures in the redoubt's sealed tunnels and chambers was a means of defending against outside chemical, biological, and radioactive contaminants. Toxic gases, vapors, and particles would be blown back outside, rather than sucked in through the ventilators that supplied the complex with fresh air. "Confirm that the Audience Chamber has positive pressure," he said, watching carefully.

"I confirm that," the other man replied, tapping a switch and dial in the center of one of his panels. "Ventilation System One-C is fully operational."

"Very well."

Sik turned to another captain, this one tasked with monitoring the external defense and observation posts. "Sound the general alert."

"Yes, Comrade Colonel."

Klaxons sounded three times, echoing shrilly across Myohyang-san's steep, forested slopes. Sik observed closely, checking the various TV monitors as they flicked from channel to channel. Each showed soldiers hurrying to camouflaged gun positions and surveillance posts.

"All defenses manned and ready, Comrade Colonel," the senior watch officer reported.

"Make sure," Sik told him evenly. "Sound the alert again."

Silently, the major nodded to his subordinate. Sik carried Kim Jong-un's favor and trust. No one wanted to cross him.

Outside, the klaxons blared again, sounding three more times before fading away.

Above Observation Post Nine, Piro Peak

Special Forces Captain Ro Ji-hun counted carefully. Four . . . five . . . six. He grinned in the darkness. It was time. He stretched carefully, testing each muscle. He and the eleven men under his command had spent the last seven days concealed beneath camouflage tarps in the middle of this boulder field high up on the mountain—moving as little as possible, conversing only in sign language, eating cold field rations, and always on edge against the possibility of discovery by a loyalist patrol.

He flicked on his shielded penlight, illuminating a circle of watchful, wolfish faces. "Remember the plan," he said softly. "Move fast. Move silently. Kill quickly and quietly. Understood?"

His men nodded.

"Then follow me."

Cradling his Czech-made Skorpion submachine gun, Ro quietly slithered out from under the camouflage tarp and crouched beside a massive, weathered rock. His troops joined him. Seven of them carried silenced submachine guns like his. Four were harnessed to a mesh-covered, metal cylinder slung between them.

Through narrowed eyes, he studied the observation post about one hundred meters down the slope.

It was a simple layout, just a narrow trench jackhammered out of the rock. At one end, slabs of granite and sandbags laid over the trench offered protection against shrapnel from artillery shells or bombs. This high up the mountain, no one really expected they would have to defend against an infantry attack. Four loyalist soldiers were visible, two peering through handheld binoculars at the valley floor far below and two more using more powerful, mounted scopes to scan Myohyang-san's other peaks and the surrounding airspace.

Ro glanced to the right. There, fifty meters from the observation post, a low, rounded gray hummock topped by a clump of brush marked their primary target. From the air, that mound would look like nothing more than a ripple of rock on the mountain's flank. But it was man-made, not natural.

He tapped his senior sergeant on the shoulder and pointed back to the narrow trench. "Sergeant Maeng. Take that observation post. No prisoners."

Maeng, squat, heavily muscled, and scarred, grinned back at him, showing a mouthful of bad teeth. "Yes, Comrade Captain."

The sergeant and his six men rose and headed downhill, spreading out across the slope—moving in short bounds, with three or four commandos always kneeling and positioned to fire while the others advanced.

Ro watched for a moment and then looked away, satisfied that Maeng would handle matters with his usual brutal efficiency. He signaled to the men harnessed to the metal cylinder. "Let's go!"

With the captain in the lead, they moved out from the boulder field, angling their way cautiously down toward that low gray hillock—straining against the weight they carried.

Security Control Center
One of the monitors was now switched to show the television feed from the Audience Chamber. Kim Jong-un still

stood braced behind the podium, while aides were guiding the generals and marshals who would serve as his backdrop into position.

"We have control over all circuits to Pyongyang, Hamhung, Wonsan, Kaesong, Nampo, and the other major cities," a voice reported. "Broadcast begins in one minute."

"This is a great day, comrades," Sik said quietly.

The four officers grouped around the equipment and computer consoles nodded vigorously.

A phone buzzed.

One of the watch officers picked it up. "Yes? What is it?" He listened for a moment and then turned to Sik. "Observation Post Nine reports possible movement near the Paegun Hermitage."

"I will speak with them," Sik said, stepping forward. He took the phone. "This is Colonel Sik. Report your situation."

"Sergeant Maeng here, Comrade Colonel," a gravelly voice answered. "Captain Ro and his team are in position."

"Very well. Carry on."

Sik put the phone down and shrugged at the others. "A peasant jumping at shadows. But better to be unnecessarily vigilant than caught napping, eh?"

The other officers chuckled.

"Broadcast begins . . . now!" the voice from the monitor said.

The image changed, showing a vast rippling North Korean flag. Stirring music swelled in the speakers with the crash of cymbals as the national anthem began playing.

"Attention!" Sik snapped.

The four watch officers obeyed, jumping to their feet. Behind them, the guard stiffened to attention, with his chin up and his eyes fixed on the monitor.

And Sik was in motion.

Whirling around, he punched the guard in the throat, crushing his larynx. Gasping, straining vainly for air, the soldier dropped to his knees.

Without hesitating, Sik tugged the pistol out of the dying man's holster. He flipped the safety down and continued turning—already squeezing the trigger as he came on target.

The pistol cracked four times, deafeningly loud in this confined space.

Hit in the head, each of the four watch officers went down. Blood and brains spattered across several of the screens and consoles.

Through his ringing ears, Sik heard the music fade out and looked up in time to see a stern-faced Kim Jong-un begin speaking.

The colonel smiled. The timing was perfect.

He moved to the ventilation systems control panel, found the switch marked 1-C, and flipped it. On a dial above the switch, the needle showing air pressure in the Audience Chamber began falling.

Sik picked up the phone and punched the button that would connect him to Observation Post Nine.

"OP Nine," Maeng growled.

"It is done, Sergeant," Sik told him. "Tell Captain Ro to proceed."

Without waiting for an acknowledgment, the colonel hung up and stood watching Kim Jong-un rant, promising death to every traitor and the immediate restoration of order under his unchallenged rule.

This would indeed be a great day, Sik decided.

From the time he was a small boy, the colonel had grown up believing that his father, a man he had never really known, had lived and died as a Hero of the Fatherland. Major Sik Sang-chol had been the brave commando leader who spearheaded a surprise attack on the American headquarters in Seoul. And though the raid failed to eliminate the American commander in chief, General McLaren, it had successfully sowed confusion and chaos in the enemy's high command.

As a young soldier, Sik had been determined to honor his father's memory by serving the regime with unswerving faithfulness and courage, even to the point of death if necessary. His loyalty and demonstrated skills had driven him ever higher in rank and responsibility, until at last he earned a post as one of the Supreme Leader's personal bodyguards.

And then his world collapsed around him.

One of his superiors in the Guard Command had shown him the secret files on his father's operation. It had been a suicide mission, though none of the commandos had known that. The extraction routes his father had been promised were never put into operation. Worse still was reading the evaluation attached to his father's personnel file, an evaluation in Kim Jong-il's handwriting.

MOST SECRET
Major Sik Sang-chol
Second Reconnaissance Brigade, Special Forces
    Loyalty: High
    Command ability: Acceptable
    Suitability for further advancement: Nil
    Recommendation: Expend him

From that moment, Sik Chol-jun had lived for one thing only—the chance to take revenge by killing Kim Jong-il's own son, the so-called Supreme Leader. When the bomb in the banquet hall failed to kill the tyrant, the colonel had been tempted to finish him off right there in the smoldering rubble. But too many of the other bodyguards were there with him, frantically digging through ruins. Better, Sik had thought, to stay alive and act the hero—ready to play his part in the backup plan.

This plan.

Ventilator 1-C Intake, Piro Peak

Ro watched from the clump of artificial brush that concealed the ventilator shaft, one of the dozens that fed the redoubt hundreds of meters below their feet. He saw Sergeant Maeng clamber out of the observation post trench. The noncom pumped his arm twice. That was the signal.

He turned to the soldiers squatting beside the metal cylinder. A length of flexible hose ran from the nozzle of the cylinder into a small, dark opening, shaft 1-C. Ro nodded to the commando crouched right by the opening. "Test it!"

The corporal shook out three matches and lit them together. For an instant, they flared up brightly and then went out. The smoke vanished, sucked into the shaft.

Without waiting any longer, Ro dropped to his knees and started feverishly turning the valve below the cylinder's nozzle. It began hissing, spewing its highly pressurized contents through the hose and down the ventilator shaft.

Audience Chamber, National Command Redoubt

The papers on Kim Jong-un's podium rustled, whipped by a sudden breeze. He tightened his grip on his speech, determined not to lose his place.

"I make this pledge to you, the people of our beloved fatherland. This gang of criminals and traitors, these murderers and paid mercenaries of the evil Americans and their puppets, will be destroyed! Even the memory of them will be erased from history! They will vanish like—"

A gob of spit flew from his mouth and spattered across the page.

Kim's left cheek twitched suddenly, contracting so sharply that some of his teeth were visible for an instant.

He fought to regain control, aware that his hands were trembling. The words of his printed text swam in and out of focus. "I make this pledge to you—" he repeated thickly, desperately trying to swallow the saliva and mucus clogging his mouth and throat without choking.

The air carried a trace of the faintly cloying smell of rotting fruit.

Behind him, Kim could hear the sounds of choking and retching from the assembled audience of military officers. He scowled, furious that the uniformed puppets he had made were ruining this moment. Would he have to order another round of executions so soon?

Then he groaned, thrown against the podium by a convulsion so powerful that it tore him from the brace propping him up. The wig concealing his head injuries slipped off and fell to the floor. Another spasm ripped through him, tearing open some of his wounds. Once-white bandages began to redden.

Slowly, wrapped in terrible agony, Kim turned his head. Most of those in the room with him were writhing on the floor, gagging and clutching at their throats. A few, still able to move, had ripped the red silk wall hangings down and were pounding frantically on the blast doors that sealed this chamber off from the rest of the redoubt. But they were weakening even as he watched, slumping to their knees, coughing uncontrollably as they drowned on their own saliva and secretions.

Beyond the power of speech now, Kim Jong-un lost his grip on the edge of the podium. Twitching and shaking without volition, he slid to his knees and then fell onto his stomach. More sutures ripped open. A fiery wall of pain roared through him, forcing a shrill, bubbling scream past his clenched teeth.

Millions of North Koreans and millions more around the world watched in horror and amazement as Kim Jong-un, the Supreme Leader, convulsed and writhed and groaned and tore at his clothes and bandages.

They were still watching as he died, along with most of the members of his new, handpicked regime.

Six hundred meters above the Audience Chamber, Ro listened in satisfaction as the last of the sarin nerve gas they had pumped into the ventilator shaft hissed out of the cylinder. The sound faded.

It was finished.

Chapter Six

Whirlwind

21 August 2015
Kunsan Air Base
Gunsan, South Korea

Brigadier General Tony Christopher stared at the television screen, frozen by sheer surprise and the horror of what he'd just seen. The cameras were still working, one facing the podium, and two others covering the crowd. They continued to pan slowly across the room, or zoom in and out. There was one close-up of Kim Jong-un's face that lasted at least a minute. He'd died in mid-spasm, and blood spattered his chin and the floor where he'd fell. Tony could not look away, or even close his eyes.

Everyone—the guards, the audience, and of course Kim—lay unmoving. In the back of his mind, Tony kept expecting the picture to go dark or turn to static. Did this mean the assassins controlled the television studio? That they were choosing to transmit these pictures as proof of their success? Or was there nobody left alive to hit the "off" switch? There certainly weren't cameramen moving the cameras back and forth, not in that room full of poison.

The question was enough to kick-start his frontal lobe. Shaking off the images that crowded his mind, he turned to look around him.

News of Kim Jong-un's survival had reached him yesterday, in the middle of a tour of the air bases and units in South Korea. As deputy commander of the Seventh Air Force, Tony Christopher was supposed to report to his boss on any problems that had surfaced because of the mobilization during the crisis. With the expectation that the DPRK announcement signaled the end of the crisis, he'd elected to continue the tour—the mobilization had been a good real-world test.

And he'd been especially reluctant to cancel the tour right then. The next stop on the schedule was the Eighth Fighter Wing, at Kunsan. He'd served and fought in the 35th Fighter Squadron, based at Kunsan, back in the day. He'd chosen to watch the speech in the squadron's ready room.

They all knew him, of course, not only as deputy commander of the Seventh Air Force, but by his call sign, "Saint," and his seventeen kills during his tours of duty in Korea and Iraq. As a distinguished alumnus of the squadron, a photo of a much younger Captain Christopher hung on the ready room's wall, just to the right of the squadron's emblem, a snarling black panther crouched and advancing. It showed him with one hand on the wing of his F-16, smiling, new major's insignia on his uniform, after his fifteenth kill—a "triple ace." The squadron still flew F-16s, although a much newer version than the "A" model he'd flown back then.

Standing up and turning, Tony faced the fighter pilots filling the ready room. Laid out like a small auditorium, rows of seats faced a large flat-screen display at the front, an unused podium pushed to one side. They sat, stunned, confused, and shocked by the wide-screen horror. Some didn't seem to understand what they'd seen, and he could hear questions asked in quiet voices: "What was that? Did he really just die? Was that real?" The ones that weren't talking to their comrades were looking at him or the other commanders in the front row.

Tony instinctively knew it was real. While they were all used to a stream of exaggerations and outright falsehoods from the North, a faked TV show of Kim's death would only harm the regime, at a time when he needed to show strength. He accepted the fact that Kim and most of his cabal were dead. But what happens next?

Colonel Andrew Graves, CO of the Eighth Fighter Wing, had of course escorted Tony on his tour of the base, with the commanders of the 35th and 18th Fighter Squadrons in trail. The four senior officers had taken up the center of the front row. The colonel and his two squadron commanders were now looking at him, or more properly, to him.

Everybody in the room knew exactly as much as Tony did about the death of Kim Jong-un. In fact, most of South Korea had probably been watching, or at least listening on the radio. There would be no uncertainty this time.

Tony fought to shift his thinking. Kim's survival and television appearance was supposed to restore his rule. Unwelcome as the regime was, the stability it offered was better than bloody civil war and a humanitarian crisis. Tony knew the Seventh Air Force was already planning to send units brought in as reinforcements back to their bases in CONUS and elsewhere, and to reduce operating tempos back to normal. He'd heard Colonel Benz, the Seventh's operations officer, grumbling about the havoc their alert was raising with the training and maintenance schedules.

But that was ten minutes ago. He turned to the wing commander. "Andy, please find Captain Drew and my flight crew and tell them I'll be flying back to Osan immediately."

Graves looked over at a lieutenant, who left the room at a dead run. Tony raised his voice just a little, so it could be heard throughout the room. "I won't predict what orders my boss will send out, but ignore anything in the pipeline right now about standing down. Make sure everybody's ready to fly." He paused, and the wing commander and two squadron commanders all nodded solemnly. Graves gestured to his two squadron commanders, and they left, followed by the rest of the 35th's pilots.

As the room emptied, Graves' cell phone sounded, and after listening, the colonel reported, "Your aircraft crew is preflighting now. They'll be ready in ten minutes."

"That gives us five to sit and think," Tony replied.

"The ROKs will go north," Graves stated flatly.

"Concur, but we won't unless our boss says so," Tony agreed. "The best we can do is hold the fort while the South Koreans take the rest of their country back."

The colonel asked, "Is there anything at headquarters saying the South won't succeed?"

Tony shrugged. "The only thing that could stop them is China, and as long as we don't go north, the Chinese may stay on their side of the Yalu."

Graves checked his watch and gestured toward the door. They started walking, with Christopher setting a fast pace. "And the Seventh Air Force becomes a piece on the chessboard of international politics," the colonel remarked, a few steps behind.

"An accurate, long-range, devastatingly powerful chess piece," Tony declared, smiling. They stepped out of the squadron's ops center into the bright, almost blinding heat. An air force jeep was waiting to take the general to his helicopter, and the two hopped in.

"General Carter and I have discussed what to do if the ROKs went north, with or without the US. In this case, the simplest plan is to take one hundred percent responsibility for air defense while the entire South Korean air force takes on the DPRK, which they are well qualified to do. Our AEW and other specialist aircraft provide support for their offensive from across the border, heavily escorted."

Graves nodded his understanding. Christopher continued, "That is one possible course of action, not an operational order, but you might want to think about the Wolf Pack's role in that scenario."

They reached the flight line and headed for a gray-painted UH-1N Huey near one end. As soon as the jeep came into the helicopter's view, Tony heard the engines whine and the rotors began to move.

The jeep stopped, and Graves came to attention and saluted. "Good luck, Saint."

Tony returned the salute, and answered, "Fly safe, Digger. If we do go north, get some." He had to speak up to be heard over the rising whine.

"Even if they're Chinese?" Graves asked, smiling.

"*Especially* if they're Chinese," Tony answered, and headed for the helicopter.

21 August 2015
CNN Special Report
Seoul, South Korea

Tammy Becker was tall and blonde, which made her a standout anywhere, but in Korea she towered over most citizens. They'd set her up against a backdrop of a cheering crowd. Although she was broadcasting from Seoul, it looked more like Mardi Gras, or a Super Bowl win. Lights on the camera created an illuminated circle of celebrating Koreans behind her, waving different-sized Korean flags.

"It's been over six hours since the death of Kim Jong-un, and the citywide, no, nationwide party shows no sign of slowing down!" She held the microphone close to her face, but still had to speak up to be heard over the singing and drums beating.

"I came here earlier today, before Kim's broadcast. I had planned to interview South Korean citizens on their impressions and hopes for the future right after the broadcast ended, but nobody here could have predicted how it did end.

"During the broadcast, the streets of this city of over ten million were virtually empty, and here downtown, every shop or business with a television had it on. Even outside, my crew and I could watch Kim's speech on a video screen that normally carried advertising.

"No other shows were aired. It was extraordinary for the South Korean government to allow any video transmitted from the North to be broadcast live, but given the importance of the crisis to every citizen of this tightly knit nation, the government preempted all other programming.

"Earlier in the day, I spoke with government officials who said the North Korean broadcast, whatever its content, would be followed by a rebuttal speech from the president . . ."

The noise from the crowd suddenly swelled and crashed over the reporter. The cameraman shouted something to her, and she nodded. The image spun and faced the street to show a military convoy, a camouflaged stream of trucks, then massive battle tanks on transporter vehicles, then more trucks towing artillery. Soldiers in the open backs of the trucks waved and shouted to the crowd, who responded as if the troops were already heroes.

Becker was shouting into the microphone now. "This is one reason the party's still going on. Within hours of Kim's death, military police, with some effort, cleared this major thoroughfare, the Nonhyeon-dong, and the first convoy came through."

She pointed off camera, in the direction the troops had gone. "Every convoy we've seen, and we've lost count, is headed the same way, toward the Cheongdam Bridge over the Han River, and then north." She paused again, drowned out by diesel engines and crowd noise. The sound became less random until finally it seemed like all Seoul had joined in a single song. It enveloped the crowd, and even if her viewers didn't speak Korean, they would recognize the joy and triumph in its tone.

"It's the 'Aegukga,' the South Korean national anthem." She paused, letting the music fill the microphone. As the song ended, she concluded, "The South Korean army is on the move, carrying the hearts of every citizen with them."

21 August 2015
Christian Friends of Korea Mission
Sinan, outside Pyongyang, North Korea
Kary Fowler didn't watch the broadcast. Her experience dealing with DPRK officials had been universally bad, and the last thing she wanted was to watch, or even hear over the ubiquitous loudspeakers, the dictator, the monster himself. She was a Christian woman, and would never wish for anyone's death, but she'd felt a deep disappointment when Kim's survival and upcoming speech were announced.

The news of his very public death found her outside, surveying the remains of their greenhouses and fields. One of Christian Friends' core missions was growing nutritious food to restore the physical health of the sick. Only in a land as poor as this could wholesome vegetables serve as medicine.

One of the student nurses, Moon Su-bin, found Kary inside a looted greenhouse, trying to see if it could somehow be repaired with materials from others also wrecked. "Fowler-*seonsaengnim*, the television—"

"You know I wasn't planning to watch, Moon Su-bin," Kary replied, a little sharply, but then she drew a breath and continued, "Is it over, then?"

"Over?" she exclaimed. "Fowler-*seonsaengnim*, the Supreme Leader is dead!" The young woman collapsed on the ground.

Moon Su-bin had volunteered at the clinic after her infant son died. With her husband in the army, she'd found friends and a home at the mission, and studied medicine and nutrition under Kary's guidance.

Moon had brought her infant son to the clinic after he came down with a gastrointestinal infection. In spite of all their efforts, and even using precious formula, four-month-old Ye-jun had only lasted a week. Small and sickly to begin with, the child would have had health problems even in the West, but malnutrition made him vulnerable. And it was endemic. Although in her early twenties, Ye-jun's mother would have been mistaken for a middle-schooler in the US.

Especially now, tearful and confused. Using Kim Jong-un's title instead of his name did not surprise Kary. From birth, citizens of the DPRK were taught that the Kims, the Great Leader, Kim Il-sung, his son Kim Jong-il, the Dear Leader, and now the grandson and Supreme Leader, Kim Jong-un, were the source of all knowledge, all virtue, and all power. Hated or loved, feared or admired, the idea of life without them was incomprehensible.

Kary knelt down beside the weeping woman and lifted her, hugging her and smoothing her hair, as if comforting the child she'd never had. "Tell me what happened."

It was hard for Moon to even describe what she had seen, watching on the clinic's tiny television. The words themselves seemed treasonous. It was a cheap Chinese model, with a terrible picture, but it had been clear enough, and Moon Su-bin was not sophisticated enough to ask if it had been faked, or how the deed had been done. Along with virtually all the clinic's patients and staff, she had watched their national leader die an agonizing death.

Kary struggled to understand Moon's tearful Korean, but once it was clear there was no misunderstanding, Kary's heart turned to ice. Disappointment at news of his survival did not become joy with confirmation of his death. She fought the fear that tried to fill her mind, and steadying herself, stood, and then pulled Moon to her feet. "Thank you for coming to tell me, Moon Su-bin. How is the laundry?"

"I was hanging it when the broadcast started . . ." She trailed off, and her gaze wandered as visions of Kim's death replaced the rest of her answer.

"Moon, we need that laundry dry!" Kary shook her shoulder gently, and told her, "Get it hung up as quickly as you can, and then find Ok Min-seo. She'll need help preparing dinner. Now go!" Nodding, the young woman hurried off.

Kary headed back toward her office, at one end of the clinic. She would have to keep them all busy, somehow, because she knew that most of them would be like Moon— confused and afraid. And keeping them busy would help keep her busy, too, because she was also afraid. She thought about the chaos she'd witnessed in the past week and shuddered. She hated anything to do with politics, but knew instinctively that North Korea had been rebuilt to Kim's design, with him as the keystone. How many would be crushed when it tumbled down?

The mission compound was surrounded by a low fence, more marker than a barrier, and she saw someone waiting by their front gate. It was normally left open, but since the coup attempt they'd been closing and locking it. It was a futile gesture, but they did it anyway.

Now Sergeant Choi Sung-min was waving to her, and she quickened her pace a little. Sergeant Choi was the neighborhood supervisor for the Ministry of Public Security. The ministry was responsible for traffic and catching criminals, but was also charged with searching for hints of disloyalty. They were ubiquitous and did their best to be omniscient. No occurrence was too small for their interest. Since the coup attempt, Choi had replaced his customary slate-gray patrol uniform with drab green fatigues, and carried a rifle slung over his shoulder.

In spite of the masters he served, Kary still thought of him as the local policeman. He'd caught petty criminals stealing from their gardens, and if the price of his service was a bag of vegetables or a bottle of pills, that was necessary but acceptable. He wasn't greedy, and since they'd treated his children on more than one occasion, the sergeant had come to see their usefulness.

As she unlocked the gate and opened it for him, he said, "You should leave Korea." She started to smile, because that was his customary greeting. When she'd first come to Sinan years ago, it had been a sincere, almost hostile sentiment. Even after Choi's children had recovered from whooping cough, he had persisted, almost a pro forma exhortation. She finally realized that he probably had to file weekly reports on his progress in "convincing the foreigner to leave." As long as he went through the motions, he could answer yes, and his superiors would be satisfied. And it was clear he didn't want the mission to close, not as long as she met him with a small parcel of food or medicine.

This time, instead of a near-joke, she could see he was deadly serious. After he stepped inside and she closed and locked the gate, they began walking toward one side of the compound. "Kary Fowler-*yang*, you have to leave. Mayor Song ordered me to arrest you and your entire staff yesterday, but I managed to dissuade him."

She was too shocked to reply immediately, and the sergeant explained, "Song-*dongji* received an urgent order from the party that special efforts were to be made to find and apprehend the foreign influences that were corrupting the country. There would be penalties for those who were lax."

Kary didn't try to protest her innocence. The word had no meaning here. "How did you talk him out of it?" By now they'd reached one end of the main clinic building. A canopy and a few old chairs offered rest and shade from the August sun.

Choi sat gratefully, unslinging his rifle and laying it across his knees. "I reminded him of the generous subsidy that your organization makes to the community. If your mission closed, those subsidies would stop. I also promised to redouble my surveillance of your subversive activities."

She almost laughed, but caught herself in time. The sergeant had been joking, of course, but open laughter could be a dangerous thing. "I'm very grateful, of course."

His face hardened. "But that was yesterday. The situation has now changed. There is no way to tell if your

organization,"—Choi refused to say 'Christian Friends'—
"will be able to continue to provide support, for you, or
him."

She heard the implied question, and replied, "We've
had no contact with home, or most of the other missions,
since the fifteenth of August." She was referring to the first
attempt on Kim's life, but officialdom had quickly prohib-
ited the use of words like "coup" or "assassination," as if they
could define them out of existence. If the heinous deed
needed to be referred to at all, it was by the date.

"We did receive a note from our clinic near Kaechon,"
she said hopefully. "They've had some problems, but are
coping and waiting for the crisis to pass."

"Is that your plan?" Choi asked skeptically. His tone was
kind, but it still sounded like a criticism. "Wait for it to go
away?"

"What else can we do?" Kary protested. "People are still
sick, and now we're even treating trauma patients, like that
robbery victim you brought us the other day."

"I had to. The hospital will only treat soldiers and party
officials now." Choi made a face. "Bandits, of all things, robbing people in the fields as they work. It was the first time
I've ever fired my weapon, other than the target range. One
burst in the air, and they scattered like crows."

"I'm glad you stopped them, but I'm glad you didn't
shoot them, either," she added. "Maybe they'll rethink their
behavior."

Choi shook his head. "Fowler-*yang*, they weren't the first
ones I've seen, and I hear reports of more all the time. And
you can't depend on the protection of the party or the army
anymore." He lowered his voice. "I watched the broadcast
in the mayor's office, along with many others." Choi spoke

even more softly, barely a whisper. "Song-*dongji* panicked, and others as well. He ordered our captain to mobilize the reserves, and form a militia for defense of the community. He had received word of army units mutinying. The Supreme Leader's death will only make it worse."

Reaching into a pocket of his fatigue pants, Choi showed Kary a small automatic pistol. "One of the bandits dropped this. It's a Makarov, just like my service pistol. Nine shots." He pulled the magazine out of the grip and locked the slide back, clearing the weapon. "Here." He offered it to her.

"No, I can't take it. I wouldn't know how to use it. My Christian faith . . ."

"The people you're responsible for don't share your faith, and I hope you're not planning to convert the bandits. Proselytizing without state permission is a serious offense." He smiled.

"Most of them will turn and run if you show any teeth." He paused for a moment, but could see she wasn't convinced. "Think of it as a noisemaker."

Reluctantly, she took the pistol and the magazine. Of course, he'd broken any number of laws in giving it to her, but that didn't matter much now.

And actually, she'd lied to Choi. Her father, Blake Fowler, had several guns in their home, and had encouraged his children, including young Kary, to learn how to use them. That didn't mean she liked them, and definitely didn't want to shoot anyone. There was too much killing in North Korea already.

Choi showed her how to use the safety and load and unload the pistol. He sighed with relief. "This eases my mind somewhat. And don't be afraid to put a few shots in the air. I or one of my men will come."

21 August 2015
Southwest of Chongju, North Korea

Rhee and his team were on schedule, but just barely. They'd reached a good spot for their hide, where they could overlook the third and last regiment of the 425th Mechanized Corps. They'd successfully snooped one regiment near the abandoned antiaircraft battery, then snuck in closer to Chongju town to have a look at the corps' headquarters, checked the second regiment's cantonment at the same time, and arrived at their last planned lookout before dawn that morning.

Over the past three nights and two days, they'd seen a land in chaos. The antiaircraft battery had been an early warning, as had the civilians moving at night.

From their perch overlooking the first regiment's base, they'd studied the unit and its activities. The 425th, one of the best-armed units in the DPRK army, was at war. Groups of armored vehicles headed in different directions, while trucks carried soldiers to man defensive positions visible in the distance. These were not simple roadblocks, but entrenchments that included machine guns and heavy weapons. The team could see mortar positions supporting the main defensive line. Who were they fighting?

Throughout the day, they'd taken turns, with one pair observing and recording the regiment's activities, while the other two kept watch and rested. Even in the field, Rhee had taken the opportunity to school the new men on their technique. He reminded Guk, "On the next mission, you'll be in the lead, with new men to train."

There was no sign of patrols or aerial surveillance, but the regiment was at full alert. Late in the day, a large column of armored fighting vehicles left in the direction of

Chongju, but its purpose was unknown. It had not returned by the time they left.

The commandos hadn't seen much activity in the farms or businesses during that first day, and only light traffic on the road, except for military vehicles. Rhee knew anyone using them for travel could expect to be stopped and questioned more than a few times, with uncertain results.

During the second night, they'd spotted and avoided more civilians, once the point man confirmed that's what they were, but it all cost time. The team heard gunfire once, so far away it was hard to hear distinct shots. It had lasted some little while, though. Either a prolonged skirmish or short battle.

During the second day, at their new hide, they'd surveyed the 425th's headquarters and another of its regiments, located nearby. This regiment was sending out patrols, as well as manning defensive positions. Groups of DPRK soldiers passed as close as five meters to them as the scouts lay camouflaged and completely silent. The patrols never spotted them. Rhee blessed their luck, not only for remaining undetected, but for the confidence it gave his team.

Rhee's report via SATCOM had included not only the strength and composition of the units, but that his team had witnessed several executions by firing squad inside the headquarters compound. The rifle volleys could be heard at a distance.

The third night, their second move, was a repeat of the first. The team didn't hear any more fighting that night, and reached their third and last planned hideout in good order. After making sure they were well concealed, Rhee had allowed them a little sleep. He was pleased with the team's performance. Lieutenant Guk and Corporal Ma had been nervous, almost hyperalert at first, but had quickly settled down. They demonstrated good field skills and followed Rhee's orders intelligently.

But even success presented challenges. After three nights and two days of creeping and watching, fatigue had begun to creep in. Soldiers were trained to recognize the signs, and also how to cope, but the field was never the same as training.

Even as they dug in and concealed themselves, it was clear that this regiment's base was different from the other two. Signs of a fight surrounded it, including shell craters and wrecked vehicles. The emplacements surrounding the cantonment, as well as the structures inside, were damaged, and some showed signs of fire. This regiment had been attacked.

There were no bodies visible, and the wrecks were burnt out. Rhee concluded that the fight had happened several days ago, likely before his team had arrived in the North.

The wrecked vehicles all appeared to have North Korean markings. A quick excursion to one of the outlying wrecks in morning twilight had confirmed them as belonging to the 425th. This one regiment was in revolt against the rest of its corps. So far, it appeared to be holding out.

Shortly after noon, Rhee recognized the sound of an artillery shell, but the new men were only half a beat behind the veterans in hugging the ground. The *whoosh* of the incoming shell was a fraction of a second long, ending in a distant, dull boom from the direction of the regiment's cantonment.

Other rounds followed, in clusters of four. Raising their heads, the team saw explosions inside the regiment's base. Rhee asked, "What size do you think, Lieutenant?"

"One two-twos, probably," Guk answered quickly.

"I agree. Do some map work and see if you can figure out where they're firing from." As he spoke, Rhee was watching the base. It was a random barrage, which was good, because it meant no artillery observer, tucked away in the hills with binoculars. There was no telling what else someone like that might see.

For about fifteen minutes, the base was hammered by medium artillery. Most landed inside the base, which occupied several square kilometers. It wasn't a hard target to hit. To Rhee, it showed incompetence in either not using an observer, or in using more than a few rounds for what was harassing fire. As a rule, after the first few salvos, everyone's either in a hole or dead.

Ma, the radio operator, reached over and tapped Rhee's shoulder as he watched the artillery barrage. "It's headquarters, sir. It's a recall." When Rhee didn't respond immediately, Ma said, "They're ordering us out."

Rhee shook his head. That didn't make sense. "You must have heard them wrong." He reached for the handset and Ma handed it to him. Automatically, the two switched places, with Ma on lookout while Rhee used the radio.

"We need you to get out now, Colonel." He recognized General Kwon's voice.

"Sir, there's a civil war going on between units of the 425th."

"That's not important anymore, Colonel."

Shocked, Rhee tried to form a question that didn't sound like insubordination. The general quickly explained what had happened an hour ago, and what was happening now. "The army is moving north. We are already across the border in several places, and you have a brigade to run.

126

The sub will be waiting for you, beginning at sundown." He broke the connection before Rhee could even confirm.

Rhee meant to put the handset away, but paused, motionless, his mind filled with the general's news. Kim dead. The armed forces of the Republic of Korea crossing the border. Could it be true...unification?

Everyone in the South had hoped for this day. He'd seen the army's plans for exactly this scenario—an invasion if the northern regime imploded. It was like D-Day and Christmas at once. He should feel happy, or excited, but decided there was just too much to do.

The artillery barrage had stopped, but while Rhee was telling the others about their new orders, Ma, still on lookout, reported, "Column approaching from the southeast." He said it softly, but Rhee could still hear the excitement.

Rhee ordered Ma and Oh to start packing while he and Guk studied the approaching troops. It was a classic armored attack, with a wedge of tanks in front, followed by armored troop carriers. All right, Rhee realized. The barrage hadn't been badly planned harassing fire. It was a badly timed preparatory barrage. It should have lasted longer, until the advancing troops were much closer to their objective. It was supposed to keep the defenders' heads down.

But the defenders were definitely not suppressed. Antitank emplacements with 130mm guns were firing at the armored spearhead, while antitank missiles leapt out toward the lead vehicles. The tanks started to take hits, while somewhere behind the attackers, artillery—heavy mortars from the sound—began dropping smoke and high-explosive shells onto the defenders.

Although Rhee had been ordered to leave, he found it almost impossible to look away from the fight before him.

They had a perfect vantage point from which to watch the attack. Both sides were using outdated equipment, all of Russian design, then either copied by the Chinese and sold to North Korea, or made by North Korea herself. North Korean copies of Sagger antitank missiles were blowing up Chinese copies of T-55 tanks, while Russian M-46 field guns from the Cold War blew up equally old Russian-built BTR-60 armored personnel carriers. He thought about the slaughter that would happen when his army met its antiquated, poorly trained opponent.

That's right, tear yourself apart, he thought grimly. *Fewer DPRK soldiers for us to deal with.* He took one last look, trying to note losses, and turned to help Ma and Oh with the packing. He told Guk, "Keep a sharp lookout all round."

Even as he packed, his mind tried to find a solution to their impossible orders. It was a little more than thirty kilometers to the spot on the coast where they'd cached their swim gear. He'd planned to use twilight and all night to cover that distance, swimming out to the submarine just before dawn. It would have been a hard march, but possible.

Now, they had to cover that same distance in seven hours, in full daylight, and the clock was already ticking. Softly but triumphantly, Master Sergeant Oh announced, "Finished!" He looked expectantly at the colonel.

By rights, Rhee should have huddled with the team to go over the plan. Instead, he asked Guk, "Anything moving to the northwest?" That was the direction they'd come in from earlier that morning. The battle raged to the east. Guk answered, "It's clear."

"Then let's go. I'll lead." The grove from where they'd observed the battle extended around the side of the hill and touched a gully on the other side. Moving in daylight without the night vision gear was easier and faster, but they had to pause more frequently to check for observers. Their North Korean uniforms might prevent them from getting shot at on sight, but it was better not to be seen at all.

A road behind the hill they'd used forked both north and west. They'd come in along the north fork last night. This time they'd head west, toward the coast.

It had taken fifteen minutes to get down the hill, and behind him, he could almost watch the others doing the math. This was taking too long. They reached the edge of a copse of trees, and Rhee knelt to check the terrain ahead. Master Sergeant Oh knelt close behind him and whispered, "Sir, what's the plan?"

"Don't get seen, don't get shot," Rhee answered, and scanned the road ahead with binoculars. *There. That's the plan.* "There's a vehicle at the crossroads ahead. That's our ride. Pistols ready."

Rhee stood, straightened his uniform and cap, and walked out of the copse toward the crossroads. The others followed in column, rifles slung.

The junction between the northern and western roads was garrisoned by three soldiers and a political commissar, a lieutenant, who spotted the approaching party and saluted crisply.

"Report," ordered Rhee in his best command voice, as he returned the lieutenant's salute.

"Lieutenant Kang Yong-suk, on post as ordered at 1100, no traffic, one deserter captured." The lieutenant gestured with an expression of disgust toward the back of the vehicle. A single corporal, dirty and bruised, sat in the back of a UAZ-469 utility truck, gagged, with his hands tied. "He's from the Second," the lieutenant explained, indicating the regiment that was attacking. "He was trying to slip past the checkpoint."

Rhee nodded and turned, but instead of approaching the prisoner, used the movement to conceal drawing a knife. He suddenly turned back and buried it in the lieutenant's side, just under the rib cage, and angled up. The young officer collapsed. The other scouts were farther away from their targets, and fired their silenced pistols almost simultaneously. None of the North Koreans even had a chance to ready their weapons, much less get a shot off.

After they'd searched the corpses for documents, Rhee ordered, "Put the bodies in the back." All four then climbed aboard, and with Guk at the wheel, drove over to a clump of trees and dumped the bodies.

With the evidence of their crime concealed, Guk turned the vehicle around and took the western fork in the road. Rhee navigated, while Corporal Ma and Master Sergeant Oh sat on one side in the open back of the truck, facing the astonished prisoner. They'd ignored the deserter the entire time; still bound and gagged, he had watched the team's actions with horror and fascination. He stared wide-eyed at the commandos.

Oh finished checking his pistol and met the prisoner's gaze. "Shut up."

"There's probably another checkpoint at the next junction, about seven kilometers ahead," Rhee said. "Be ready to shoot, but I'll use the lieutenant's orders and see if we can bluff our way through." After Guk nodded his understanding, Rhee repeated his instructions to the two in the back.

Rhee sat in the cab, feeling the warm air flow past him, and compared it to their covert progress before. They were covering much more ground, although at greater risk. He'd hoped to find a checkpoint and hijack a vehicle. He just hadn't expected to do it so quickly. But that had created a new question. What to do with the deserter? To Rhee, the answer was obvious.

"We're taking the prisoner with us," Rhee announced suddenly. Surprised, Guk let up on the accelerator pedal for an instant, then refocused on his task. The lieutenant paused for a moment before saying anything, which Rhee thought showed both wisdom and self-control. Rhee added, "We use the same flotation bladders we had on the equipment when we brought that ashore. We don't even have to untie his hands." *Although they probably would,* Rhee thought.

"And there's room on the submarine," Guk added, tacitly concurring. The vessel that had brought them to the coast, and would be waiting for them tonight, had room for over a dozen commandos, although a dozen would find it cramped. Five instead of four would not be a problem.

The local road, a two-lane graveled track, headed west. It was rough enough to keep their speed down, perhaps forty kilometers and hour, but it was much, much faster than walking. It crossed another road where Rhee had predicted they might run into trouble, but the junction was unoccupied, and they sped on. The next junction did have a checkpoint, but when they spotted Rhee's uniform and rank, the soldiers braced and saluted, then waved them through.

They were almost halfway to their objective. The next road junction was near the coast, and Rhee enjoyed a quiet moment as they drove. The fields in this area were tilled, and the crop of potato plants was nearing maturity. Rhee couldn't see anyone working them, though. He wondered if the farmers had fled or had been killed. He couldn't believe the crop would be wasted in this starving country. *But by the time it's ready to harvest,* Rhee reminded himself, *the South will be able to help.* Things were about to change.

A thump on the cab's roof was followed by Master Sergeant Oh's warning. "Movement on the left ahead. In the field."

"Keep up your speed," Rhee ordered, and scanned the low plants. There. He saw long shapes that might be soldiers lying in the rows of green leaves. Guk faced straight ahead as Rhee used binoculars, not only to check the left side of the road, but the right as well. Were they driving into an ambush?

He knew Oh and Ma in the back were ready for anything, but was also conscious of how exposed those two were, although the sheet metal cab offered little protection. Rhee searched the right side again. Nothing. "Be ready to floor it," he ordered.

"Understood," Guk answered. He had both hands on the wheel and was braced. They entered what Rhee thought was the kill zone, fifty meters away, and then they were past the spot.

The lieutenant had started to relax, breathing out in a long whoosh, when Rhee ordered, "Stop the truck!"

Guk stood on the brake pedal and Rhee bailed out the right-side door, shouting, "Ma, Oh!" He'd seen a flash of color and made a snap decision. As he came around the back of the truck, Rhee saw figures in the field spring up and run toward a distant wood line. Oh and Ma were already vaulting out of the truck and sprinting after them. Rhee called, "No weapons! Take them alive!"

Now behind the truck with a clear view, he could see two adults, towing a child as they ran. The man swung the boy, five or six, up into his arms and their speed increased.

The chase ended halfway across the field, where Ma tackled the slower woman. The husband hesitated, and Oh reached him, pistol drawn. He raised his hands as Ma pulled the woman to her feet. The adults were quickly searched, and their hands were bound behind them with zip ties. Oh got them started back toward the road, with Ma carrying the struggling child.

The adults were both in their late twenties. The man wore a white shirt and tie, and it was the white color in the field that had caught Rhee's eye. The woman wore a skirt and drab green blouse, and heels, which certainly had not helped her cross-country performance. As the group passed the spot where the family had lay hiding, Oh picked up a cloth bundle.

Rhee could imagine their thoughts. They had been spotted and captured by the army. Their fate was sealed. Both the woman and child were crying, fearful. The husband's expression shifted from fear to worry to anger and then fierce control.

As they reached the truck, Rhee gestured to Oh and Ma to load them in the back. The civilians' eyes widened first at the sign of the battered soldier, gagged and bound, and then gasped at the bloodstains on the truck bed. The mother, barely coherent, begged for mercy, while the man offered unspecified valuables if the woman and child were released.

Taking their cue from Rhee, the soldiers said nothing, but were as gentle as they could be getting the civilians into the truck. Rhee got in the back with them and Master Sergeant Oh. He told Ma to ride in front.

In an attempt to lower the noise level, Rhee drew his knife and cut the woman's bonds, then gestured to Oh to give her the child. The pair clung to each other, still tearful, but silent. Rhee uncapped his canteen and offered it to the woman. With only a moment's hesitation, she took a sip herself, testing it, then helped her son take a drink, then a longer one, before taking another herself. She passed it back to Rhee with an expression that combined gratitude and fear.

The truck was moving again, and Oh passed their identity documents to Rhee. They were indeed a family, and the husband was a municipal official in Chongju. They lived in town. While Rhee checked their papers, Oh searched the small bundle. He opened it for Rhee's inspection to reveal a sheaf of North Korean won, some Chinese yuan notes, a few rings, and a GPS device.

The man, silent until now, tried again to bargain with the commissar officer, almost pleading as he tried to explain why they were hiding in the field as the army vehicle passed. Rhee remained silent, and kept his expression unsympathetic. Finally, the child, exhausted, fell asleep.

The major, with his truck full of prisoners, was passed through the next and last checkpoint with a salute, and they headed toward the coast. He'd been expecting to arrive here on foot, and Rhee had to consult the map to find places where they could hide a large vehicle. A farm building a few kilometers from the shore was the most likely spot, so Rhee had Guk drive the truck as close to the shore as possible. After it was unloaded. Guk would take it alone to the chosen location, conceal it, and then come back as fast as he could.

By now it was late afternoon, but there was still time for Guk to make the trip and be back before sundown. The truck stopped and Guk and the others quickly unloaded, while Rhee kept watch and checked the map one last time. Oh and Ma led the prisoners, in single file, down toward the beach, while Rhee handed the map to Guk and said, "I'll see you soon."

Guk saluted and smiled, then jumped into the cab and roared off. Rhee hurried to join the fearful but confused captives as they picked their way across the uneven ground. While Ma and Oh watched the prisoners, Rhee kept watch toward the road. There was no traffic, and it soon disappeared from view as they descended into a gully that led to their cache.

While the two enlisted men recovered the swim gear, Rhee studied his captives, sitting on the ground. He imagined the thoughts going through their minds, but derived no pleasure from sustaining the mystery. Until Guk returned, which wouldn't be soon enough, the prisoners could not know the team's true identity.

They took turns keeping watch out to sea, as well as landward. It was almost an hour later that Ma, on lookout near the crest of a grass-covered dune, whistled and held up a thumb. Five minutes later, a winded but cheerful Lieutenant Guk tumbled down the slope and saluted, reporting, "Done."

With a sigh of relief, Rhee drew his knife and cut the ties on the now thoroughly confused prisoners. Dropping to one knee and facing the group, he said, "In spite of these uniforms, my men and I are soldiers from the South. We will be leaving soon," he pointed out to sea, "on a submarine that will meet us offshore. If you come with us, you will be safe, although you will be questioned." He didn't bother mentioning that if they didn't want to come, they couldn't be allowed to live. In the corner of his eye, he saw Guk, standing casually with his weapon at rest, but angled toward the prisoners, just in case.

Rhee could see the captives trying to reason it out. The tale sounded fantastic, but their captors were clearly not KPA soldiers. The corporal spoke up first. He'd seen these men kill North Korean troops, so it was easier for him to believe their story. "I want to go to the South." He was already marked for death, so if this was some sort of elaborate ruse, he had nothing to lose.

The woman stared at the swim gear lying on the sand. "Will this submarine take us all the way to the South?" She said it as if their destination was the moon.

Rhee nodded. "It will take about a day."

She looked over to Guk, standing nearby, who shrugged and nodded, then to her husband, who looked as befuddled as her, but he also nodded. She started crying again, but weakly, and clinging to the child in her lap. Speaking for both of them, the husband said firmly, "Yes. Please take us with you. What must we do?"

Rhee smiled. "Let's fit you all with some flotation gear, and then we'll take a swim."

CHAPTER SEVEN

MAELSTROM

22 August 2015, 6:00 p.m. EDT
CNN Headquarters
Atlanta, Georgia

The opening logo was the same one the network had used since the beginning of the crisis, a map of the Korean Peninsula with the part above the thirty-eighth parallel in jagged pieces, as if it was shattered glass. They'd modified it earlier that day, though, with the word "Liquidated" angled across the northern part in bright red letters.

The logo shrank and appeared to fall back, landing on the video wall behind CNN's leading military correspondent, Catherine Donner, sitting at a long desk. The video wall showed a constantly moving mosaic of military hardware in action, buildings on fire, carefully edited sections of the now infamous death scene, and shots of cheering crowds surrounding a tall blonde reporter.

Ms. Donner was neither tall nor blonde. Her mid-length hair was more gray than brown, and a weathered face seemed to exist only to frame her trademark green eyes.

"Welcome to this special extended edition of the War Room. I'm Cat Donner and I'm here with our panel of political experts, and we're pleased to be joined this hour by

Dr. Mark Ulrich from the Nuclear Weapons Disarmament Council. He's going to tell us about what we know, or more properly, what we don't know, about the status of North Korea's nuclear stockpile.

"Before we do that, we're coming up to the six o'clock hour here on the US East Coast, but Korea is thirteen hours ahead of us. Most of us were drinking our morning coffee when we heard about Kim Jong-un's very public death—no, assassination—by nerve gas, just as that country began its first night dealing with the incontrovertible proof of their absolute dictator's demise. Now, it's seven in the morning, a little after daybreak in Pyongyang." She turned to a bearded man in his forties sitting with her at the desk.

"Dr. Russel Hayes is from the Brookings Institution, and the author of several books on North Korea. His latest is *Criminal Kingdom*, which was published last year. Doctor, virtually everybody on the planet that has access to the Internet has seen the images. It's the first video on YouTube to get over a billion views. It's not pleasant to watch, but is there anything in that clip that you feel has been missed, or that people should be noticing?"

Hayes had obviously been prepared for the question, because he answered immediately, "Almost as important as Kim's death was the death of the others in the room, representing the upper two or three tiers of his regime—his reconstituted regime, I might add, since many of the original members were killed either in the explosion on the fifteenth, or in the violence since then."

"Is the Kim regime wiped out, then?" Donner asked.

"No, although they are obviously weakened. Even with the coup attempt on the fifteenth, Kim's faction had the advantage, because they were already in control. The next strongest group, the General Staff, had more raw power, but their lines of communication were broken at the top."

Donner prompted, "And the Korean Workers' Party was the third faction?"

Hayes nodded and answered, "They were actually the most numerous, with the most potential power. Everybody from a government economist to the street sweepers had to be a member of the party, and while technically loyal to Kim, the party organization has always been a law unto itself. Kim may have the steering wheel, but the party was everything else, from the economic engine to the infrastructure wheels to the workers in the gas tank. All three groups of course are corrupt, and are riddled with informers allied with the other two factions.

"When Kim reappeared, alive, many of the ringleaders of the other factions, who of necessity had been forced to reveal themselves, were arrested and shot. According to the refugees my contacts have interviewed, the arrests easily number in the thousands, while the executions before yesterday were in the high hundreds, all of leaders or important members of each faction."

"And now Kim's faction is leaderless as well," Donner concluded.

"Which means it's a mad scramble, with every man for himself. The diehards will remain, but anybody who can will try to get out or go to ground until the South Koreans get to them." Hayes shrugged. "There are a lot of party officials that are watching the advance of the ROK Army the way the German civilians waited for the US and Britain in World War II."

"And do the Chinese take on the role of the Russians this time?" she asked.

"No, the analogy doesn't hold," Hayes responded. "Beijing is very worried, and I wish I had a nickel for every Chinese press release reminding us that North Korea is a 'sovereign nation.' But as long as the US doesn't go north of the thirty-eighth parallel, China can't justify her own intervention.

"The challenge for the South Koreans will be to move quickly, before the giant that is China decides what it wants to do. If the PRC is presented with a fait accompli, it may simply accept Korean unification as a done deal. Because if China intervenes, then the US has to back up its ally, and unifying the two Koreas will no longer be the goal."

"What takes its place?" Donner asked.

"Avoiding a nuclear war," Hayes answered flatly.

23 August 2015, 8:00 a.m.
Pyongyang, North Korea
Cho Ho-jin ducked into the angle formed by a collapsed wall and checked the GPS on his phone. The city had been so badly torn up by the fighting that many landmarks were gone, converted into rubble that covered the streets. Choking smoke from dozens of fires had mixed with the August heat and humidity to form a permanent cloud. Visibility in places was down to a hundred meters, sometimes less.

The phone was his lifeline. He reported by voice now, no coded messages. That took too long. The signal was heavily encrypted, and he doubted that the North Korean security services, even if there were anyone watching for unauthorized cell phone use, would try to track him down in the middle of a battlefield.

Every building bore the marks of combat, and Pyongyang could join Beirut, Karbala, and Sarajevo in popular memory as urban battlefields.

Since arriving at noon yesterday, he'd identified some of the army units fighting in the city, with troops from all three sides vying for the possession of the capital. He intended to pass that information on as soon as he found a more secure place to spend the night. Roving patrols made it dangerous to use his phone in daylight, as he had to have an unobstructed view of the satellite—a little hard to do when one was scurrying from one wrecked building to another.

His last report of two days ago was one of his more revealing observations. The Ministry of State Security's troops had allied themselves with the Korean Workers' Party faction. Although rated as a paramilitary force, he'd seen them with heavy weapons and armored fighting vehicles. His last order was to "identify the Kim and KWP factions' leaders," as if he was a journalist who could ask for an interview.

The key would be to find the respective headquarters for each faction, then surreptitiously take photographs of anyone who looked to be in charge. It was impossible, of course. His handlers either had a poor grasp of the situation in the North Korean capital, or had been watching too many movies.

He'd been on the move all night, watching tracers arcing over different parts of the city. The night offered some concealment for somebody moving with purpose in a place where everyone who moved was an enemy.

His last meal had been rations looted from the backpack of a dead soldier. He'd wolfed them down while he watched a rocket barrage that fell like a river of fire. It landed somewhere to the west. Cho had no idea of the identity of the firer or the target. The canteen on the corpse's belt was only half full, and Cho was saving the last few swallows against dire need.

The Potong River lay a few blocks to the east. He'd considered heading there to refill his canteen, but the Potong and other rivers that ran through the city had become boundaries and defensive lines. Instinctively, he avoided the open ground near the water's edge. Even at night, there was too great a risk of a sniper with a night vision scope.

Many of Pyongyang's two dozen bridges were down, either collateral damage or dropped deliberately. The party faction held this side of the river, and a respectable swath of the city, but Kim's faction occupied several key buildings to the north, and in spite of attacks by both the party and the General Staff, they fiercely resisted.

With the General Staff to the east and Kim's people to the north, the party faction's headquarters had to be somewhere south or west of here. It wasn't much to go on, but he'd been living on luck so far. He'd just hoped he had a little more left.

An armored vehicle came up the street toward his position, rumbling on eight wheels across the rubble and cratered surface. Already hidden, Cho pulled back farther into the shadows and watched the soldier manning a heavy machine gun in a small turret on top. He seemed more worried about rooftop snipers than ground-level threats, because he kept looking up, and never noticed Cho. The vehicle passed, like a tiger in search of prey, and once it was out of sight, Cho left and headed one block west, and then south, keeping well away from any troops that might be dug in along the river's edge.

Cho progressed slowly, sticking close to buildings, pausing and listening as well as looking before crossing any open ground. Shortly after he started, he heard machine gun fire behind him, in the direction the troop carrier had headed, followed by more weapons fire and explosions. He judged it to be moderately close, although he'd thought the battle lines were farther north. More incentive to go south, but he fought the urge to hurry.

For most of the time, he might have been moving through an empty city. Occasionally he'd see a flash of movement as he turned a corner, or a face in a window. Many residents had fled in the afternoon after the broadcast, or during the night, with the remainder either dead, arrested, or in hiding.

There were enough bodies on many streets, either in uniform or civilian clothes, although civilian clothes didn't mark one as a noncombatant. Only very old or very young men, and women of any age, could be considered true civilians. He'd hidden from groups of heavily armed men that were not in any uniform, and even from individuals, whether they had visible weapons or not.

Moving in the morning daylight was definitely more hazardous than nighttime, and Cho became grateful for the smoky haze that cut the visibility, even though it made his eyes sting. A fine layer of dust and grit also coated his clothes and provided natural camouflage.

Cho's only goal was to work his way south and look for troop concentrations, while avoiding being seen and shot at by said troops. A lot of soldiers in one area meant some sort of base, and if it wasn't the headquarters, it might provide a clue to the headquarters' location.

Careful and cautious, he covered ground, always moving in a southerly direction. He spotted more uniformed bodies, but they appeared disturbingly fresh, the bloodstains wet. They still had their weapons, but Cho easily resisted the temptation to pick one up. There was already a good chance of him being shot on sight. Carrying a gun made it a certainty.

He'd stopped to check the bodies for water or food, which meant first checking them for booby traps. With his attention concentrated on searching for hidden grenades or other hazards, he'd failed to notice the tank turning onto the street several blocks behind him to the north. At least, that's what he'd told himself later, trying to comfort an ego badly bruised at being surprised by a tank.

The tank crew's attention may have been attracted by his movements. They may have thought the enemy soldiers were lying prone, or they simply had orders to shoot up anything suspicious. Cho's first warning was the deep cracking sound of the tank cannon, and the shell striking the building above and behind him. Luckily, the high-explosive shell didn't detonate until it was inside the structure. Enveloped in a choking cloud of smoke and dust, battered by pieces of falling brick and masonry, he hugged the ground as machine gun bullets kicked up dust around him.

He heard a scream nearby, and at first thought one of the soldiers was not dead, but then realized it was from behind him.

He turned his head to look, still keeping as low as possible, and saw an opening in the building where the shell had blown the wall out. He could see into the ground floor and the basement below it. There was movement in the basement level, and people, and he heard more cries, of pain and fear.

The tank's diesel engine and the sound of its treads were getting louder. In half a moment, the remaining smoke would clear and the tank crew's aim would improve significantly. Cho considered playing dead, but was worried that he didn't appear dead enough. He decided the basement represented a better option, at least in the short term.

He low-crawled backward, covering the five meters in what seemed to be a few swift movements, and half-slid backward down a pile of sloping debris into the basement. The dimness of the basement was enhanced by the cloud of cement dust that hung in the air. Unlike the outside, there was nowhere for it to go, and it divided the room into brilliant dust-filled sunbeams and opaque shadows.

Cho scrambled out of the light toward a dark corner and had to stop short, because it was occupied. A middle-aged woman hugged two children, while an older woman sat leaning against the wall. They were covered with dust, but he could see blood on one of the children's arms, and on the mother's shoulder—a lot of blood there.

Out of the sunlight, his eyes quickly adjusted and he could see two more people, a young couple, in another corner, both as far away from the new opening as possible. He agreed with their strategy and headed for a clear spot next to the wall.

The family near him and the couple in the corner looked at the newcomer suspiciously. Cho ignored them and hunkered down in the corner, moving a few pieces of masonry to make more room.

The machine gun fire had stopped, and he heard the tank's engine as it ground ahead. Once it was past, he'd have to . . .

The tank had stopped again. It was much closer than before. And then he heard voices. He searched his memory. In that fleeting glimpse of the tank firing at him, had there been infantry following behind it?

He looked around the room more carefully. It appeared to be an office, with a few old metal desks, filing cabinets, and obligatory posters on the wall. Paper and scraps of paper littered the floor. Everything was layered with dust and grime, which made it hard to see any detail in the dim light.

There. A door, in the center of the same wall they crouched against. He almost leapt over the woman in his haste, and began shifting the debris that blocked it. He tried to be quiet, but every piece of rubble he moved caused others to fall. To Cho, it sounded like an avalanche.

"What are you doing?" the older child, a girl of maybe ten, asked curiously. Her high, piping voice pierced the dark and dust.

Cho, struggling to free the door, hissed, "Quiet, child!" He gestured with his head toward the opening above. The girl didn't understand, but the mother did, and told her daughter to hush. She then struggled to her feet and gathered her family. Moving must have been painful for her, but by the time Cho was through the half-open door, they hurried after him.

Cho's only thought was to get away from the opening to the street. The door had led them into a basement hallway, pitch dark. He was still trying to choose which direction to go when a loud *WHAM* echoed from behind him, followed immediately by another *WHAM* a few moments later that staggered him. The family group let out small shrieks of surprise and fear, and Cho decided the direction he was facing would have to do.

The hallway was clear, and they all stumbled along. His outstretched hand felt a corner in the wall, and he followed it, the family close behind. He paused for a moment to listen for any sounds of pursuit, but there were none.

The mother asked in a whisper, "Are they following?"

After a long pause, Cho answered, "No." And then after another pause, added, "They probably think two grenades are enough." *They aren't paying me enough for this.*

"Thank you for saving us," the mother said, and the older woman offered her thanks as well.

Cho shook his head—a silly gesture in the pitch dark—and replied, "I saved myself. You just followed."

"A wise man shows his back," the grandmother quoted. It was an old Korean folk saying that praised leading by example, with his followers behind.

Cho sighed, but they had common purpose, to survive and get out of this building. He took out his phone. The dim light from the screen was more than enough to navigate by, and he wanted to use the phone's GPS to make sure they moved in the proper direction, but there was no signal this deep in the shattered building.

"What is that?" the girl asked curiously. Few North Koreans owned such elaborate cell phones.

"Something I stole." Cho didn't want her asking more questions, and in this chaos, stealing wasn't necessarily a crime.

Cho used the phone's light cautiously, illuminating a passage briefly and then hiding it before leading his small entourage forward to the next corner or junction in the hallway. The mother followed behind, supported by her daughter. The other child, a boy of five or six, clung silently to his grandmother's skirt, ignoring a deep gash on one arm.

They followed one hallway that led to a larger passage, headed east–west. There were stairs at the west end leading up, but the steps were blocked by debris. East led back toward the street where he'd seen the tank. As he reluctantly turned to backtrack his route, the mother said one word, "Please," and sank to her knees.

He heard the exhaustion and pain in her voice, and answered, "Rest. I'll find a path out of here."

"Thank you. What is your name?" Koreans were sticklers for proper introductions, and he automatically answered, "I am Cho Ho-jin, *ajumma*." He used a form of address reserved

for mothers and "mature" women. Calling a twenty something office girl "*ajumma*" would have gotten him slapped.

Even though she was in pain, she said formally, "I am Cheon
Ji-hyo. This is my mother, Gam Sook-ja, and my children, Go
Shin-chang and Go Shin-ha," pointing to the girl and the boy.
The girl bowed. Cheon asked, "There was another couple in
the room with us. Did you see what happened to them?"

Cho shrugged, and winced at the pain in his back. He'd
had a rough day. "They didn't come out behind you," he
answered. He left unspoken the conclusion that they'd been
caught in the grenade blasts. "Did you know them?"

"No. We never learned their names." She sighed sadly
and settled herself more comfortably. "We will rest and wait
for your return." Her voice was weak.

Cho nodded and started to head east, but the girl, Go
Shin-chang, began to follow him. He stopped and motioned
for her to go back. "Stay here with your mother, child."

"No. I'm quiet, and if something happens to you, we
need to know." *She'll probably take the phone*, he thought, *but if
I'm dead, who would I call?*

He couldn't argue with her logic. They would die in
this place if they didn't find an exit. "All right, but stay back
some distance." She nodded, and they set out. She did stay
back, three or four meters, and her footsteps were light.
They navigated by sound, using the light from his phone
sparingly. Cho was beginning to worry about the battery
charge. He'd been using it heavily.

After about twenty-five meters, they came to a large
cross-passage, equal in width to the one they were in. He
turned south, and came into what looked like the main
entrance. Although the doors could be opened from the
inside, someone had chained them shut.

The two found a fire axe on the wall and tried to break the lock, without success, but searching the offices, they found a coat rack with an iron upright. Using it like a crowbar, Cho was able to twist the chain until the lock broke. Clearing the chain away, he cautiously opened the door, which led up to a small lobby and the main exit to the street. He didn't open the outer door, but did look through the nearly opaque glass. He could see no movement, and it was quiet.

With the young girl in front, they hurried back to the other three. Gam Sook-ja, the grandmother, held the boy in her lap while the mother leaned against her shoulder, asleep. It took some care and effort to rouse her, and even a gentle shake on the uninjured shoulder caused her sharp pain. It took both Cho and the woman's daughter to get her upright, and they moved at the best pace they could.

They had to half-lift the mother up the steps, and Cho had to stop the grandmother from just walking outside. Leaning Cheon against the wall, with Go Shin-chang keeping her from collapsing, Cho motioned the others into a corner, and after taking another look through the glass, opened the door just enough to look down the street, toward the street where the tank had passed.

With one direction clear, he opened the other door slightly and made sure that direction, to the west, was clear as well. He stepped outside.

The sunlight, even filtered by smoke and dust, was more than welcome. He watched and listened carefully while the others emerged, and reported to them, "There is fighting in the distance, but I can't hear any nearby. Where will you go now?"

Go Shin-chang answered for them. "There is a foreigner living west of here, just outside the city. She runs a clinic.

Our neighbors went there when they were sick. It's a mission, with food and medicine. They can treat my mother and brother, and your back as well."

"My back?" Cho's back was sore, but that was understandable. A wall had fallen on him.

The girl took a step to his side and reached around to touch him, below his shoulder blade. She showed him a fingertip wet and red. "You're bleeding in three places." After a pause, she added, "Please come with us."

Maybe that wall had some sharp corners. His orders took him south, but if west led to the chance of medical attention, that was an acceptable detour. Nodding agreement, Cho took the mother's uninjured arm and put it over his shoulder, then faced west.

Besides, the mother wouldn't last the day without some sort of medical care. She could die from blood loss and dehydration, and the boy needed stitches and antiseptic, or he would eventually lose the arm, and his life.

Cho's hatred of North Korea did not extend to the general population. Only a fool blamed a farmer for the king's crime. His father, Cho Hyun-jae, had been executed by the Kims for failing to win a war they started. Cho's family had been punished beyond reason for this "offense," as if losing his father wasn't punishment enough. That was the first of many reasons that he had for hating the DPRK government.

Not that he was fond of his Russian employers. They'd fed and educated him, but only as a tool. He'd given good service, but now their orders were absurd. Were they ready to use him up?

Their slow progress had brought them close to a cross street, and rather than stop carrying the mother, he told Go

Shin-chang to scout the intersection, and what to look for. The girl ran ahead.

He hoped the mission wasn't far.

23 August 2015, 7:30 p.m. local time
Christian Friends of Korea Mission
Sinan, outside Pyongyang

Kary Fowler heard the shout from Kwan all the way in the kitchen. "Fowler-*seonsaengnim,* come quick!" Kwan, alert but hobbled with a broken ankle, had volunteered to watch the front gate and serve as general lookout.

Others outside repeated the call, and she motioned to some inside as she left the dining hall. Whatever was going on out there, it sounded like Kwan needed reinforcements.

Thank heaven she hadn't heard any pistol shots. She'd loaned Kwan Sergeant Choi's gun, not only because he had sentry duty, but because he'd served in the army and might actually use it, if need be.

She burst out the front door of the dining hall, but had to clear the office building to see the gate clearly. She rounded the corner at speed and, glancing back, was relieved to see two other women in her trail.

The gate was still closed, and Kwan was pointing down the road. In the twilight, she could see a knot of people trudging unsteadily toward the mission's gate. She hadn't slowed down, and he opened the gate before she reached it.

She turned onto the road and hurried toward the group. She could tell they needed help just from the way they walked—exhausted, barely lifting a foot before putting it down again. As she got closer, she could see darker patches in the dirt and grime that covered them.

She called behind, to people still in the compound. "Ok, get a stretcher!"

An older woman was in front, leading a glassy-eyed little boy. A few steps behind was a girl, and a young man with an older woman on his back in a fireman's carry. The girl saw Kary come out the gate and ran to meet her, calling, "*Ajumma*, please help us, my mother, my brother . . ."

Kary ran past the girl, then the woman and boy, and reached up for the mother. She could only hope the wound wasn't as bad as it looked, because the upper part of her garment on that side was dark with blood. Even in the sunset's light, the woman, perhaps a little over thirty, was dangerously pale. The man, his face streaked with dirt and perspiration, kept walking as Kary examined his passenger.

She was still alive, although her pulse was fast and weak. Lifting the corner of her bloody garment, Kary could see a round hole. She'd seen enough bullet wounds in the past few days, and could only guess what it had done to the bones in her shoulder. There would be a much messier wound in the front, although resting on her savior's shoulder may have staunched the bleeding somewhat.

Two of her helpers arrived with the stretcher, and positioning it behind the pair, they gently leaned the woman back, and then level, before setting off at speed for the dispensary. The man nodded and wearily said "Thank you" before falling, first to his knees, and then face-first onto the road. His back was bloodstained as well, and the girl, pointing, said, "His name is Cho. He's hurt, too."

Kary called for another stretcher, then told the girl to follow the others with her mother. Taking Cho's hand, she knelt down next to him and waited for help.

Chapter Eight

Unleashed

23 August 2015
Special Warfare Command, ROK Army Headquarters
Seoul, South Korea

Rhee paused briefly to adjust his uniform and made sure his black beret was snug under his belt. His right shoulder protested the quick movements, but he ignored the pain, and once satisfied, strode into the outer office. Marching to the aide's desk, Rhee snapped to attention and barked, "Colonel Rhee, Commander, Ninth Special Forces Brigade, reporting as ordered."

There was no need for the aide to use the intercom; everyone in the office heard Rhee, including Major General Kwon.

"Ah, excellent, Colonel, come in," Kwon remarked as he stepped out of his office. Rhee attempted to render a snappy sharp salute as soon as his superior appeared, but he wasn't able to get his shoulder to fully comply, nor mask the slight twinge on his face. The general looked intently at Rhee as he returned the salute. He'd seen the subtle facial expression and the favored right shoulder. Pointing to the offending limb, he asked, "What did you do to yourself this time?"

Embarrassed, Rhee stretched his shoulder out as he replied. "It was a bumpy transfer to the helicopter, sir. The seas were rough and I was unceremoniously jerked off the submarine's deck. I much prefer jumping into the ocean from a helicopter. Being reeled in felt too much like being a fish—very disconcerting."

Kwon laughed at Rhee's explanation. The colonel had a well-earned reputation for a dry, eccentric sense of humor. "Well, I'll try not to have you dangle on a line like some halibut in the future," teased Kwon. Then more seriously, "But it couldn't be helped this time. We have a momentous task on our hands, Colonel, and I have a special job for your Ghosts. Please, come in to my office."

Rhee followed the general, who gestured to one of the large chairs in a back corner of the room, away from the desk. An enlisted steward brought up the rear with a beverage tray, offering a cup of tea, first to Kwon, then Rhee. "Would you care for some tea or coffee, Colonel?" asked the sergeant.

"Tea would be splendid. Thank you."

Kwon sat down and sipped his tea, waiting for the sergeant to depart and close the door. "I read your preliminary report, Colonel, several times, in fact. I found it . . . difficult to believe."

Rhee nodded. "I'm sympathetic to your doubts, sir. I was there, I witnessed the regiments of the 425th Mechanized Corps fighting each other, and I'm still struggling to grasp what I saw. It was most bizarre."

"I think we'd better get used to the bizarre, Colonel Rhee. It will be with us for some time. I assume you saw a recording of the Supreme Leader's death?"

"Yes, sir. I watched it on the submarine. The beast got only what he deserved."

"Be that as it may, that well-executed assassination caught us completely off guard. We had already started to stand units down after Kim's radio announcement, and we have to undo all that, and quickly." Kwon rose abruptly and started pacing. "Any further information from your prisoners? Particularly this Pung Jin-Ho?"

"No, sir. Pung is a low-level party official, assigned to the Korean Workers' Party municipal staff at Chongju. He knows nothing of military value. The only insight of any importance is his knowledge that there are three main factions involved in the fighting: the Kim family, the Korean Workers' Party, and the General Staff.

"He believes the Kim family's assets are the weakest of the three, but they are more concentrated around Pyongyang and that makes them still dangerous. From what the American intelligence reports indicate, the KWP and General Staff factions are doing most of the fighting right now. According to our other guest, Corporal Bak, the 425th was split between the KWP and General Staff factions. I think it's safe to say that the entire North is in complete chaos right now."

"A chaos that could spread and consume the entire peninsula if we don't handle this correctly," remarked Kwon. Rhee watched as his general paced in silence. He had never seen him this somber before. Kwon walked as if there were a heavy load on his shoulders. Suddenly, Rhee felt excitement building within him. Were they actually going to do what he had only dared dream about? He shifted his weight in the chair, struggling to keep his composure, to contain the hope that was welling inside him.

"Yes, Colonel," Kwon answered without even looking in Rhee's direction. "President An authorized Operation

Unity this morning. We are going to reunite our people. After nearly seven decades, we will be whole once more."

Rhee felt like shouting, but he managed to restrain himself, simply asking, "What do you want me to do, sir?"

"You can begin by stuffing that unbridled optimism of yours back into your rucksack, Colonel," chided Kwon with a smug grin on his face. "This operation, even under the most favorable of circumstances, isn't going to be quick, easy, or inexpensive. Our nation is embarking on a task that is going to take us decades to complete. But . . . if we fail at the onset, it will take far longer and cost us dearly."

"They're our kin, sir," Rhee replied firmly. "Held hostage by criminals. Liberating them is worth every drop of blood spilled, every won spent."

"Hmmm, I'm not so sure the younger generation shares your burning conviction, Colonel. But still, the majority of our people believe as you do. That is why we're moving forward. Come over to the map."

Rhee jumped out of the chair and joined Kwon by the large map of the Korean Peninsula on the wall.

The general pointed toward several areas along the thirty-eighth parallel as he spoke. "Elements of the First and Third Armies have already crossed the DMZ along the three major avenues of approach and are heading north. We moved slowly at first, but it soon became obvious that the KPA Forward Army corps have all pulled back. To assist in picking up the pace, I've assigned the First, Seventh, and Thirteenth Special Forces Brigades to scout ahead and clear the way of any left-behind obstacles."

Rhee looked at the map and saw unit markers some twenty kilometers past the DMZ along the Kaesong-Munsan approach to the west, the Chorwon approach down the middle, and the east coast approach along the eastern seaboard. It was very strange, looking at the map and seeing markers for ROK Army units streaming into the DPRK. The general was right; Rhee better get used to the bizarre.

"I'm keeping the special mission units behind to guard against infiltration by DPRK Reconnaissance Bureau teams and to pick up any high-ranking officials if they attempt to escape the fighting to the north," Kwon continued. "Needless to say, we are going to have a colossal humanitarian problem on our hands, the refugees will be flowing like water over a falls. As for you, Colonel, I've saved the really hard job for your Ghosts."

Rhee's left eyebrow cocked up with curiosity, nothing the general had described thus far sounded particularly easy. There was a lot of territory to cover, and very few men to do it. None of the special forces units had even a thousand men in them, and their area of responsibility would only grow as the ROK army pushed northward. Rhee wasn't sure if he should feel honored or concerned.

"We've been ordered to initiate Operation Gangrim— the securing of as much of the DPRK weapons of mass destruction inventory as possible. The Third, Ninth, and Eleventh brigades will take this task on," ordered Kwon. Operation Gangrim was named after the Korean mythological hero, Gangrim Doryeong, who captured the king of the underworld. Capturing the North's WMDs would be at least as difficult, if not more so.

Rhee frowned. He was very familiar with the Gangrim plan, but the units the general had listed were less than adequate. He opened his mouth to speak, but Kwon beat him to it. "Yes, Colonel, I'm well aware the OPLAN calls for at least four brigades to execute this mission, but we didn't anticipate the Kim regime would come crashing down so fast, nor that we would be able move so quickly. Our plans needed to be adjusted."

The Korean colonel heard the sharp edge in Kwon's voice and realized that the man had had a similar conversation before . . . and lost. It was time for Rhee to salute smartly and do the best he could, with what he had. "Understood, sir. What are my orders?"

The professional response helped to ease the general's manner. Kwon may have been expecting an argument. "I've had the target list thinned out, since we'll be shorthanded for this mission. All the known and suspected facilities near the DMZ will be handled by the advancing First and Third Army units. Your Ninth Special Forces Brigade will tackle the big facilities on the west coast. The Third will go up the center, and the Eleventh will cover the facilities on the east coast."

Rhee whistled softly. He now understood what Kwon had meant when he said he was saving the "really hard job" for the Ninth Ghost Brigade. Circling the area to the north of Pyongyang with his finger, Rhee half stated, half asked, "So, my unit will be responsible for the major nuclear facilities as well as the chemical weapons depots to the south of the capital."

"Exactly."

Rhee swept his hand over the area on the map. "These sites are the ones we know about or suspect, sir. How are we to deal with the estimated numerous unknown sites? My resources will be limited. I certainly won't be able to go hunting for them."

"Once we have command of the skies, we'll be able to send in reconnaissance aircraft to begin large area searches.

They will provide likely locations for your men to investigate and secure as necessary. We have no illusions about getting all of the WMDs, Colonel. Our goal is to secure as much as we can."

Taking a deep breath, Rhee nodded and said, "We will do our best, sir."

"I'm hoping elements of the Third Brigade will be able to link up with you before you get to the nuclear facilities, but I'd be lying if I said that was a likely prospect."

Staring at the map, Rhee barely heard the general's last sentence. He looked at his diverse and, unfortunately, spread-out target set. This was going to be a bastard of a job. Turning back toward Kwon, he asked, "I'm assuming we'll be inserted by air?"

"Yes, Colonel. But it will have to be a phased deployment; the Fifth Tactical Airlift Wing only has sufficient lift capacity to deploy one brigade at a time. Yours will be first, followed by the Eleventh, and then the Third. Unfortunately, the insertion won't be quite as covert as you're normally accustomed to.

"Due to the size of the units involved, the deployment schedule, and the urgency of the situation, we're just going to blast on in. Given the confusion and degradation to the North's air defense network, we believe we can deliver you before they can react. However, there will be a fighter and SAM sweep just ahead of the C-130s. Just in case," Kwon concluded.

The general's last statement did not encourage Rhee one bit. Intentionally giving up the element of surprise ran counter to everything he'd been taught. He knew the ROK Air Force was short of tactical transports, but this was more than a mere inconvenience. If the insertion was challenged,

Rhee could lose hundreds of his men before they even hit the ground. The operation was getting uglier and more complex with each passing moment.

Grasping for straws, Rhee asked, "What about asking the Americans for help?"

Kwon shook his head sternly. "General Fascione and the American ambassador briefed the president, defense minister, and the Joint Chiefs of Staff yesterday. The US has publicly declared this to be an internal Korean issue. They won't deploy any forces north of the DMZ, or violate DPRK territorial waters."

"China," Rhee stated bluntly.

"Of course," answered Kwon. "The Americans are hoping that by keeping their forces south of the DMZ, and dropping broad hints, the Chinese will stay north of the Yalu."

"An interesting theory," observed Rhee with growing frustration. "I don't think it's very likely, given the refugee buildup on the Chinese border, but I can appreciate the Americans' caution."

"Don't be too hard on General Fascione. He's a soldier like us and has to follow orders. From what I saw, he didn't appear pleased with the idea, either. He will move as many units as he can forward to the DMZ to take over the defensive positions, allowing our troops to head north. He's also requested additional units to reinforce the current standing US force. With luck, a strong US presence will deter the Chinese, or at least force them to think about it first. We can use that time. This is a meaningful compromise, Colonel."

Rhee nodded slightly, feeling a little ashamed. He'd served with many US military personnel over his career and the vast majority had been honorable people, willing to help defend the Republic of Korea. And in the last war, many American comrades died during those cold battles. Soldiers he could trust—politicians, not so much. "When do we leave, sir?"

"I need your brigade ready to move out by 1700 tomorrow. You'll be dropped just after nightfall. This is, by far, the most difficult assignment I've given anyone in my career. I'm giving it to you because your brigade is the best. I'm confident you'll get the job done."

"Nothing is impossible, sir," replied Rhee, quoting the ROK Special Forces motto. He then snapped to attention and rendered honors before departing.

Personnel Support Office, ROK Army Headquarters
Seoul, South Korea

Rhee walked the halls of the army headquarters building on autopilot, his mind preoccupied with all the preparations that he and his men had to make, and quickly. Drop zone locations, unit deployments, weapons fit, logistics, and numerous other operational considerations all fought for attention in his brain. The size of the operation alone would strain his limited staff; the severe time constraint would only complicate the process. They had just over a day to pull everything together and execute. "Nothing is impossible," he muttered to himself.

The Korean colonel was just passing an open office door when his thought processes were abruptly derailed by the sound of a voice. He stopped suddenly and spun around looking for whoever was talking. The man was speaking in English. He *knew* that voice. Peeking into the office, he saw an American army officer talking to one of the admin clerks. The man turned his head sideways—Rhee lunged toward him.

"Little! Kevin Little!" he exclaimed.

Little turned to face the enthusiastic greeter. Confused, he had no time to react before a lithe Korean Special Forces officer plowed into him. When the man finally looked up, Little saw that Cheshire cat–like grin.

"Rhee! Rhee, you son of a bitch! How the hell are you?" Little cried with excitement as he gave his friend a bear of a hug and slapped him repeatedly on the back.

"I am well, my friend, very well. When did you get back in country?"

"I arrived about three weeks ago. I haven't been in country even a month, and the DPRK goes nuts! I think Korea is trying to tell me something," joked Little.

"Nonsense, Little-*ssi*! My motherland will always welcome you warmly." Looking around the office, Rhee saw many confused faces; some glared on with disapproval. He'd certainly overstepped the bounds of normal military etiquette, but they didn't understand. The bond between him and Little had been forged in combat during the last war. The American officer was closer to him than his own brother. Still, Rhee's senior rank required him to display the requisite discipline and decorum while in the presence of more junior Korean soldiers.

"Do you have a moment for tea? Or coffee?" he asked.

"I'm as busy as a one-armed paper hanger right now, but for you, I'll make the time," replied Little.

Rhee and Little quickly adjourned to the cafeteria to begin catching up on nearly a quarter of a century of absence. Little had transferred out of South Korea in late 1990 as things were heating up in Iraq. Small-unit leaders with combat experience were in high demand, and with the People's

Republic of China keeping the lid on the DPRK, the US presence in South Korea was drawn down to deal with the new threat. And like so many other military members from different countries, duty always got in the way of staying in touch, and the two drifted apart.

Kevin pulled out a chair and plopped down, tossing his cover onto the table. Rhee was doing the same when Little pointed to the black beret. "So when did you get drawn into the Special Forces?"

"Soon after the war," Rhee replied, and then took a sip of tea. "I was told that I had shown promise and was encouraged to join."

"Encouraged? Or drafted?" winked Little with a smile.

"Technically, drafting is a form of encouragement, Colonel Little. I merely showed good judgment by accepting their offer." Both men laughed heartily. God, how Little had missed talking to this man.

"How's your Korean? Is your grammar still terrible?"

"I'm brushing up," Kevin admitted, a little defensively, "but who taught me grammar in the first place?"

"I'm a soldier, not a language teacher," Rhee joked.

"You certainly seem to have done well for yourself," said Kevin, pointing to Rhee's collar devices.

"Yes, indeed. I'm a commanding officer of a Special Forces brigade. The Ninth, the Ghosts." There was a note of pride in Rhee's voice as he brandished his unit's patch. "And what about you, my friend, what have you been up to all these years?"

Little shrugged. "Three tours in Iraq, two in Afghanistan; you know, the usual for a career officer."

"That's a lot of time in war zones, and presumably in combat," remarked Rhee carefully. "I don't mean to offend you, my friend, but why are you still a colonel? When you left Korea you were already a captain."

The American smiled weakly and shrugged again. "Some of the higher-ups felt I had been promoted a little too quickly during the last Korean crisis, that I needed to have more time in grade. I lacked the normal experience of a well-rounded army officer, or so I was told. Those battle-field promotions put a serious damper on my career during peacetime. I almost didn't make colonel."

"That is absurd and unjustified!" growled Rhee. "You earned those promotions by your deeds. You did very well during that war."

"*We* did very well, Rhee. It wasn't just me," countered Little. "Besides, my new job will hopefully make the necessary course correction, I'm the new commanding officer of the Eighth Army's headquarters battalion."

Rhee winced. "Being exiled to 'admin hell' is not my idea of a get-well tour. You deserve better, Kevin."

"Well, in this current situation, I may be more helpful as an admin weenie." Little looked around the room to see if anyone was paying attention to them, then leaning forward said, "I'm sure you're aware that we aren't going north with the ROK Army."

"Yes, I was just informed by my general. I can appreciate your country's concern about China, but I don't think it will matter in the end. They'll come south as soon as they see us making appreciable gains."

Little nodded his agreement. "You aren't the only one who thinks that, but our government doesn't want to give the Chinese an excuse. As it is, I have to bring the reinforce-ments USFK wants in batches. That's why I'm here today, on a Sunday, to get the paperwork squared away for the lead units of the Twenty-Fifth Infantry Division to arrive in country by midweek."

Rhee took a deep breath. The North Korean civil war was the long-awaited opportunity for reunification that he and others had yearned for, and now their longtime ally was getting cold feet. Frustration swelled in him, an emotion that his friend was sympathetic to. Looking at his watch, Rhee knew he had to get going. There was a lot of planning that still needed doing before they began Operation Gangrim. Grabbing his black beret, Rhee stood, paused, and then leaned over the table.

"Kevin, there is one issue that I think your country could be of great service to us. Your people have far more experience dealing with mass refugee situations than the Republic of Korea; you have the knowledge and resources to deal with the wave of humanity that is coming. Do you think it would be possible for the United States to take on the responsibility of handling the humanitarian crisis? That would allow my country to send more combat units north."

Little hesitated, considering the Korean's request. Yeah, the US could do it, but would the government buy off on it? There was only one way to find out. Rising, he answered, "Yeah, Rhee, we could help handle the refugee issue. We'd need to get General Fascione on board, but I don't think that'll be a problem. Getting both our governments to agree to this, well, that may take some doing. But I can easily tweak the arrival schedule to get military police, medical, and engineering units here first. Let me bring it up with my boss and see what I can do. In the meantime, be careful my friend, and don't get all shot up like last time."

Rhee, feigning bewilderment, smiled, and said, "I really don't know what you're talking about, Colonel Little."

23 August 2015
Presidential Office
Beijing, People's Republic of China

It had already been a long day for President Wen Kun, and the Ministry of State Security, Second Bureau's depressing report on the disaster in the DPRK was making it even longer. The idiotic North Koreans had flung themselves headlong into a gruesome civil war, and China had little ability to influence the outcome. That is, of course, unless the People's Republic of China wanted to interfere militarily.

The People's Liberation Army had presented an invasion plan to the Central Military Commission earlier that afternoon, but it had been received coolly. Many remembered the last time the country got involved with a war on the Korean Peninsula. Did China really want to put that millstone back around its neck?

When the tide of the Second Korean War had turned decisively against the DPRK, the United States approached China to assist in bringing the conflict to an end. The Chinese Communist Party leadership was hesitant at first, but the economic and technological concessions offered by the US and South Korea were enticing. And it didn't hurt that the dragon would get a chance to poke the Russian bear in the nose...hard. In the end, the politburo decided to accept the role of peacekeepers, and with the help of the US Air Force, moved the first troops into North Korea.

At first, the mission proceeded as planned. The KPA was disarmed and its units withdrew north of the DMZ. For the first year, everyone's focus was on the basic humanitarian needs of the North Korean people. Preventing mass starvation proved to be an expensive proposition. As time wore on, China found itself committing more troops and money to help maintain the peace and to rebuild the basic infrastructure damaged during the war. Repairs consistently took longer and cost more than expected. The US and South Korea kept their word, but the economic benefits of the open markets was soon outweighed by the costs of their "occupation."

After five years, China had become weary of babysitting the grotesquely inefficient and needy Democratic People's Republic of Korea. The United Nations and several humanitarian organizations had provided some assistance, but China found itself paying the majority of the bill overseeing a demanding and ungrateful charge. Desperate to get the burden off its back, but wanting to maintain the status quo, the CCP decided to put another Kim back on the throne. In 1995, China announced that the twelve-year-old Kim Jong-un would be the next "Great Successor," when he attained the age of twenty-eight. Until then, his aunt, Kim Jong-il's younger sister, Kim Kyong-hui, and her husband, Jang Song-thaek, would act as regents and guide the young Kim as he was groomed for the top leadership position.

Jang was a known quantity in China; he was a dependable ally and wasn't too expensive. As the vice chairman of the National Defense Commission, he held considerable influence in the Korean Workers' Party, in addition to his new position as regent. Still, there was some tension with other senior KWP members who felt he had sold his country out for a cushy Chinese job.

To maintain their position, Jang and his wife literally bought the military's loyalty by rebuilding the KPA with Chinese materiel. They then secretly poured massive resources into ballistic missile development and research into weapons of mass destruction. After witnessing the results of Operation Desert Storm, Jang knew that even a rebuilt People's Army would be no match for the high-tech ground and air forces of the US and Republic of Korea. The DPRK would need an ace in the hole to prevent them from losing yet another war. They needed an effective deterrence. They needed nuclear weapons.

North Korea's failed nuclear test in 2006 was a rude awakening for the Chinese. They were just as surprised as everyone else. Jang quietly reassured his allies that the weapons were defensive only, to keep the imperialists at bay while he hoped to mold North Korea's economy along the lines of the Chinese model. Placated, the Chinese offered lukewarm support to Jang while warning him to slow the pace of development—the threat of nuclear weapons alone would be enough to keep the US south of the DMZ. By the time of the successful nuclear test in 2009, the genie was out of the bottle. There was little China could do then.

In the fall of 2010, Kim Jong-un took his initial steps toward succession when he was appointed the vice chairman of the Central Military Commission. At the end of 2011, he was declared the "Supreme Leader" and commander of the KPA. Finally, in April 2012, Kim was elevated to the ultimate position as First Secretary of the Workers' Party of Korea—twenty-two years after the Second Korean War had ended, another Kim had come to power.

Initially, everything seemed to proceed smoothly. Kim talked about altering North Korea's economy along Chinese lines, he seemed open to negotiations with the South, and he wasn't quite the blowhard that his father had been. The

Chinese initially thought Jang had done a good job preparing the boy for his role, and that he would be easy to manipulate. China would be able to influence the DPRK's future without having to foot the bill. Then the wheels fell off the apple cart.

In December 2013, Kim Jong-un had his uncle arrested and executed for treason. Kim's aunt then suddenly disappeared from the pubic view and was rumored to be either dead or in a vegetative state following a stroke after she learned of her husband's fate. Scores of senior party officials were then purged, executed for high treason. Most were either related to Jang or to the traitors who had betrayed Kim Jong-un's father. The young Kim then proceeded to put those loyal to him in positions of power.

Now, Kim Jong-un was dead, and the DPRK had plunged headfirst into a vicious civil war.

A knock at the door pulled Wen from his gloomy recollections. An aide entered the room and marched quickly toward the Chinese leader, carrying a folder. "Comrade President, I have the PLA intelligence report you requested on the Republic of Korea Army's movements."

"And?"

"The initial reports have been verified. South Korean troops have crossed the Demilitarized Zone and are proceeding north."

Wen let out an exasperated sigh; he knew this would happen. Damn those stupid North Korean fools! "What about the American army units?" he asked.

"Elements of the Eighth Army have advanced to the DMZ, but they have not crossed. They appear to be replacing the ROK Army units that have entered the DPRK."

"A wise move," Wen replied cynically. "By keeping to their long-held view that this is an internal Korean problem, they make it more difficult for us to become involved."

"But, Comrade President, we can't have a unified Korea allied with the Americans on our borders," objected the aide.

"I am well aware of our stated position!" snapped Wen. "But have you considered the damage comprehensive economic sanctions will have on us if we intervene militarily? Or what that black hole to our south will cost us to invade and hold? Not just for five years like last time, but possibly decades!"

Wen paused to compose himself. Ranting at a junior aide would not accomplish anything. Taking a deep breath, he looked up at the stunned young man and said, "Inform the commanders of the rocket forces, army, air force, and navy to put their units on alert. Then schedule an emergency CMC meeting for this evening. We have much to consider."

23 August 2015
Foreign Intelligence Service Headquarters
Moscow, Russia

Pavel Telitsyn closed the anonymous e-mail account with an angry stab of his finger. Nothing! Cho Ho-jin was well past due on his next scheduled report. The last one was now nearly two days old, and it had been very alarming. The factions struggling for control were indiscriminately shooting anything that moved. Civilian casualties were horrendous and the damage Cho described in Pyongyang was reminiscent of the battle histories from the Great Patriotic War that Telitsyn had read in school. But there the comparison ended. There was no clear understanding as to what faction a particular military unit was allied with, or even if a unit's loyalty was all that firm—Telitsyn suspected some military leaders traded their unit's services to the highest bidder.

The picture Cho had painted was one of unmitigated chaos, with no direction or strategy behind the fighting—attrition of the enemy's forces appeared to be the only discernable goal. He had also warned his superior that it was getting harder and harder to find the information Moscow wanted. Cho doubted many in North Korea could truly be sure who was ultimately in charge of the various factions.

Anger bubbled within Telitsyn. He had to resign himself to the fact that he had probably lost an extremely valuable asset. And for what? He wanted to lash out at those fools on the security council. They had to know there was virtually no chance of obtaining the information they said they so desperately needed.

And if by some miracle the Foreign Intelligence Service had managed to obtain the information, what could they have done with it? There were very few combat units in the Eastern Military District that could be mobilized and moved quickly. With only one railway line leading up to the Tumannaya River, the Russian army couldn't hope to transport anything more than a token force to the nineteen-kilometer-long border. Idiots!

The spymaster took a deep breath; there was no point in delaying this any longer. He grabbed his secure phone and dialed his superior's direct line. The phone was picked up on the second ring.

"Deputy Director Malikov."

"Sir, it's Telitsyn. I regret to inform you that our North Korean agent has missed another scheduled communications period. This makes two days with no contact. It is my belief that he has probably been killed in the line of duty."

"Really? And what makes you so confident that he has given his life for Mother Russia? Couldn't he have just as well deserted, comrade?" Malikov's voice was cold, uncaring.

Telitsyn was furious, but he bit his tongue. He wouldn't get anywhere by screaming at his boss. "Sir, Cho went to Pyongyang as ordered. He made several reports and each time the navigation function on his satellite phone put him within one hundred meters of where he said he was. We sent him into a damn Stalingrad! The odds were very much against him surviving for long in that hellhole!"

Malikov audibly sighed on the other end. "Calm yourself, Pavel Ramonovich. I understand your frustration over losing a valuable asset, but our duty is to follow orders—whether we agree with those orders or not is irrelevant. Regardless, it appears that we no longer have direct human insight into what is happening in the DPRK. I will inform the director. And Pavel, my condolences on the loss of your agent."

"Thank you, sir," replied Telitsyn tersely. He knew the deputy director's sympathies were without sentiment, merely a pro forma response. The click in the receiver announced the end of the phone call.

Hanging up, Telitsyn opened one of the bottom desk drawers and took out a bottle of vodka. Pouring a small shot, the Russian raised the glass, a salute to a fallen comrade, and gulped the fiery liquid down. Returning the bottle to the drawer, Telitsyn went back to work.

23 August 2015
33rd Infantry Division, IV Corps, Headquarters
Pyongyang, North Korea
"The headquarters for the Kim faction is here, Comrade General. In the remains of the Korean Workers' Party

Central Committee complex banquet hall," Ro Ji-hun said, pointing to the location on the Pyongyang city map. The special ops captain smiled in the dim light. "This has, of course, incensed the KWP faction greatly and they've already attempted two frontal assaults."

"Both failed, I'm sure," remarked Tae, shaking his head. The rubble from the bombed building would offer excellent defensive positions. Troops attacking from the front would literally have to crawl over the shattered walls and columns, exposing them to concentrated machine gun fire from multiple locations. Any attempt would undoubtedly end in slaughter. Tae was content with that outcome. The Kim faction would expend valuable ammunition and take some casualties, while the KWP faction was bled white by their foolish charges.

"Yes, sir. It was a poor use of their soldiers and accomplished nothing." Ro almost sounded sorry for the slain KWP troops. "However, our reconnaissance indicates the KWP is massing additional units for yet another attempt over here, at the Mansudae Assembly Hall."

Tae smiled. "Do we know when this attack is to begin? It would make for an excellent diversion for our forces."

"Unfortunately, we do not know exactly when the KWP faction will make their next move. But I have men in position monitoring their troops' every action. We may get as much as a thirty minute advance warning, but that is probably the best we can do."

"You've done well, Captain," complimented Tae, pleased with Ro's report. The Korean general now had all the location data he needed to plan an assault on what was left of the Pyongyang Defense Command, the mainstay of the Kim faction's forces. Tae would still need some reinforcements from

Vice Marshal Koh, but a strong flanking attack would crush the Kim loyalists. The General Staff would then only have to conduct mop-up operations to finish off the remaining isolated pockets of resistance. Once the city was secured, the army could declare itself in charge and consolidate its holdings over the rest of the country. If all went well, the fighting would be over in a week, and the city would be theirs.

"Thank you, Comrade General," replied a delighted Ro. General Tae Seok-won rarely gave compliments.

"Do you have anything else to report, Captain?"

"Just one thing, sir. It's an unsubstantiated rumor, from a single prisoner, but I believe it is sufficiently important to bring it to your attention."

"Very well, continue."

"The prisoner stated that Vice Marshal Choe Ryong-hae is still alive and was spirited away from the city early this morning. He didn't know Choe's destination, only that it was to the north."

Tae's jaw hardened. This would be incredibly bad news if the claim was true. Choe Ryong-hae was the second most powerful man in the DPRK, and a close ally to the Kim family. Choe's second son was married to Kim Yo-jong, Kim Jong-un's younger sister, and this made Choe the closest thing to an heir apparent. If he had escaped the General Staff's closing pincer, he could become a rallying point for other Kim loyalists. That was unacceptable.

"Do you believe this man? Is he still alive?" Tae asked quietly.

"It is hard to say, Comrade General. He was attempting to bargain the information for his life. It could be nothing more than complete fiction. However, he is still alive and can be interrogated at your convenience."

"But if his story is true, then we have a serious problem on our hands."

"Yes, sir. That is why I thought it best to inform you."

"A wise decision, Captain Ro. Well, we need to—"

"General Tae! General Tae!" called out the excited voice of Captain Ryeon, the general's aide.

"In here, Captain," shouted Tae tersely. The interruption was not welcomed.

Ryeon burst into the command post; the man looked shocked. Tae's emotions changed from annoyance to concern. Ryeon was not a man to be easily shaken. "What is it, Captain?" asked the general more calmly.

"Comrade General, I have message from Vice Marshal Koh. The imperialist's puppets have crossed the demilitarized zone. There are reports of incursions all along our border."

It was Tae's turn to be astounded. How could the fascists just stroll across the border? Two of the four Forward Army corps was supposed to have remained behind in defensive positions to deter the Americans and South Koreans from even considering crossing the DMZ. The news was disastrous.

"How did this happen?" growled Tae with frustration. "Why didn't the First and Second Corps engage the enemy?"

Ryeon swallowed hard. He was well aware of his general's temper. The captain could see he was already on a slow boil. "Sir, apparently all four corps withdrew. Some of the units that Vice Marshal Koh believed were loyal to the General Staff have gone over to the KWP faction. There is heavy fighting at Wonsan."

Tae rubbed his face with both hands. This was completely unexpected. Koh had repeatedly assured him that they needn't be concerned about their rear. Now they had imperialist forces climbing up their backside. If they weren't stopped, they would soon encircle his IV Corps. And while the fascists wouldn't intentionally side with the Kim forces, he would still have to deploy troops to defend his rear. This would seriously compromise his ability to execute the attack against the Kim faction. Tae suddenly realized he didn't have a week to secure the city; at best he had three days.

The general took a deep breath, composing himself. They would have to make drastic changes to their plan. "Comrades, we can no longer afford the luxury of a conventional attack against the Kim loyalists. We have to move much faster if we are to secure the city and prepare our defenses against the imperialists. Captain Ryeon, prepare the troops for an assault with special weapons.

"Ensure all personnel have chemical weapons defense gear, and have Major Eun bring special shells to the Thirty-Third Division's artillery regiment. We'll lay down a barrage of gas shells on both the Kim faction and the KWP forces, followed up with regular suppression fire as the infantry executes a shock attack. I want this attack to take place as quickly as possible. Now go."

"Yes, Comrade General!" shouted Ryeon, departing hastily. There was much to do before the attack could begin, and Tae's patience was already thin.

Tae then turned back to Ro. "Captain, I want you to extract every scrap of information from this prisoner, and then we need to verify if what he is said is true. I need to know if Choe is still alive. Is that clear?"

Chapter Nine

The Murder of Pyongyang

24 August 2015, 07:45 local time
US Eighth Army Headquarters, Yongsan Garrison
Seoul, South Korea

People unfamiliar with the military often thought that since Colonel Kevin Little commanded the headquarters of the Eighth Army in Korea, that meant he was in charge of the entire Eighth Army. They did not understand that although a colonel was a senior officer, a colonel typically commanded a battalion of maybe a thousand to two thousand people. Or they might not understand exactly how big an army is. The Eighth Army consisted of several divisions, which in turn were composed of several brigades, and each brigade contained several battalions, with each battalion commanded by a colonel.

The battalion that Kevin Little commanded was a special one in the Eighth Army's organization. The headquarters battalion took care of Lieutenant General Robert Tracy's command group, and all the headquarters' communications, intelligence, and logistics staff. It provided security personnel, everyone's transportation, and everything else they needed, from tents to printer paper. Although not a combat command, which was what every colonel wanted, a badly run headquarters battalion could disrupt the entire Eighth Army—not that Kevin would ever let such a horrible thing happen.

Little had seen his share of fighting in the Second Korean War and in Iraq and Afghanistan. He already had command experience as a lieutenant, captain, and major. Being assigned to command the headquarters battalion was not a bad thing. It meant that he was being groomed for larger responsibilities, and higher rank.

Because the headquarters revolved around the general's schedule, and Kevin helped manage that schedule, he was able to carve out fifteen minutes when he knew the general would listen to his proposal. He just didn't know if the general would agree.

General Tracy's first intelligence brief of the day was at 0730, with his entire staff, and by promising to take over part of the usually half-hour presentation from the intelligence officer, Kevin got a chance to make his pitch. He was almost sure that raising the priority of certain supplies meant for the intelligence section wouldn't get him in trouble with the IG. Probably. Besides, it was for a good cause.

Colonel Muñoz, the G2, or intelligence officer, covered the air and naval situation quickly, and then went on to detail what they knew of the different faction's troop movements, which wasn't very much. The only unusual addition was a section on the progress of ROK troops in their advance north.

It was an unusual advance, of rushes forward of ten or more kilometers, then pauses while a KPA unit was scouted, not only on its position and strength, but its allegiance, and whether it intended to fight or surrender. Belligerent Northern attitudes often changed as attack helicopters or fighter-bombers orbited nearby, waiting for the end of negotiations.

"Indeed, General, the real problem is proving to be logistics. Many of the roads are crowded with refugees, and prisoners coming south are taking up transport and security troops that are needed elsewhere." Colonel Muñoz pointed to the map display, thick with arrows and unit symbols north of the now-moot DMZ. "Although the eastern part of the peninsula is weakly held, the terrain is so mountainous that the drain on the ROK logistics was too much, and they have shifted most of their effort over to the west."

"That's the real prize anyway," General Tracy observed. "All the big fighting is around Pyongyang. The majority of the factions' remaining strength is concentrated there. I'd encircle the whole area, then see who wanted to deal with me. The trick is to do it quickly, while the Chinese are still deciding what they want to do."

It was now 0740, and Muñoz knew he was edging into Kevin's allotted time. He looked over to Kevin Little, sitting to one side in the area usually reserved for briefers. The general followed his gaze, and spotted Kevin. "Colonel Little, are you giving our G2 a hand?" he asked, smiling.

"I'd like to give you a little more detail on the refugee and prisoner situation, sir, and propose something that would speed the ROK advance." As he spoke, he walked toward the podium, and Muñoz gave him a controller like relay racers passing a baton.

Kevin pressed a button and a bar chart appeared. "These are the figures for the refugees already housed in the six camps the ROK government has established. They're already overcrowded." He pressed another control. "This map shows their locations, and the ROK Army units assigned to run them."

The next slide was another bar chart, labeled "Projected Increase in Refugees." Little started to speak, but Tracy cut him off. "You don't have to convince me there's a problem, Kevin. Give me the short answer. How bad is it going to get?"

"People are going to start dying soon, mostly from diseases they contract in the camps. They're malnourished to start with, and weak from the trip south, and many are bringing sicknesses we haven't seen in the South or the US in decades: tuberculosis, diphtheria, dysentery, and malaria. Most haven't been vaccinated. And it could spread outside the camps, because so many Southerners are coming there looking for relatives."

"So you want to send US medical units to assist the ROK forces?" Tracy asked. "I don't see a problem with that. It's a good idea, Kevin. I'll make it happen."

"It's only the first step, sir," Kevin continued. "We have a lot of troops over here that are at a high state of readiness, in case the Chinese come across the border, and we've got reinforcements arriving from the US all the time. If the Chinese don't intervene, or until they do, our troops have little to do but wait."

He paused, and clicked the controller several times. "This is a list of American units I recommend taking over the existing refugee camps from the ROKs. They'll also set up more places for the ones still coming."

Tracy was studying the list while his chief of staff took notes. Kevin pressed his point. "The switch frees up a lot of South Korean troops—military police, engineers, and additional infantry units—to go north. Our armor and artillery units won't be involved in this, so they're ready to move, and they are what the Southerners would need most if the Chinese intervened."

The chief of staff, Colonel Page, asked, "What if the Chinese do come south? We'd have a lot of our people tied up taking care of civilians. I agree armor and artillery would be a priority, but if we're dealing with the Chinese, one thing we will definitely need is numbers."

General Tracy nodded. "And the ROK units in the north will be spread out all over creation trying to occupy the country."

Kevin smiled. He'd thought about that question. "The ROKs are mobilizing reserve units as fast as they can and sending them north as garrison troops. If the Chinese attack, we let the reserve units take our place."

Tracy smiled. "The Blue House should like this. They get more units for the advance, and if the balloon does go up, we still go north."

Colonel Page wasn't convinced. "We will be moving quite a few troops out of garrison to positions just below the border. What will the Chinese make of that?"

"We'll let the press watch. Public affairs will have full access," Kevin replied.

Tracy looked on approvingly, and picked up where Kevin had stopped. "And the troops will have something useful to do, helping people instead of waiting for something we hope doesn't happen. And maybe all those war hawks who want to send us north right now, which would definitely cause the Chinese to jump in, will quit quarterbacking from the bleachers."

The general smiled broadly. "Well done, Kevin. This gives a boost to the South Koreans, it's good for our troops, and it will help the Korean civilians; heaven knows they can use it. We'll call it Operation Backstop, and I know the perfect man to run it."

Kevin felt a cold hand close around his heart. He didn't respond right away. He couldn't think of anything that would prevent the inevitable, and the general just nodded slowly. "Backstop is your baby, Colonel. You're the man to run it. Turn the battalion over to your deputy. Tell Jane it's her chance to shine."

24 August 2015, 8:00 a.m. local time
Christian Friends of Korea Mission
Sinan, outside Pyongyang

Sergeant Choi came by again that morning, he said on the orders of Mayor Song, to look for "deserters or other criminals." Two militia soldiers, wearing red armbands and awkwardly carrying automatic rifles, had accompanied the sergeant, but Choi honored Kary's request that they remain at the front gate while the sergeant made his inspection.

She recognized one of the soldiers as a local shopkeeper, and didn't trust either one's competency with firearms, or not to steal something if they could.

Choi made a point of looking everywhere. First the office building, which also had quarters for the CFK staff and a chapel, then the dining hall, with its kitchen and storehouse. The policeman had been polite, allowing the mission's business to continue as he searched, sharing gossip and what rumors he thought were worth repeating. They were all local rumors, though. All state-controlled media were off the air, and if anybody had a bootleg radio, they weren't advertising it.

There was no need to talk about the fighting in the city. The whole town could hear the near-constant rumble of artillery and tank cannon, which at irregular intervals would crescendo and then fall in volume, but remained thankfully distant.

The biggest news was still the mayor's reaction to the fighting. The day after Kim died, Mayor Song had ordered, "that for security reasons Pyongyang residents fleeing the city are to be housed at the Greatness of Labor municipal hall." The building was one of the largest in town, and served as a meeting place or a theater for socially uplifting entertainment. Officially, they were supposed to be fed and given medical care, but Kary had heard—not from Choi— that the refugees had nothing but bare floors and a thin soup, served once a day.

The last building to inspect was the clinic and dispensary. Choi said, "I'm supposed to inquire about Cheon Ji-hyo and her family that arrived the other day. They must join the others in the Greatness of Labor hall when you think they are able to be moved."

And which one does the mayor think is the greatest threat? The mother, grandmother, or the two children? But Kary didn't say that aloud. "She's still recovering from the first surgery. She needs at least one more operation, and then at least a week in bed."

"And the man that brought them in, Cho?"

"I sewed up four deep lacerations in his back. He lost a lot of blood. He may be up tomorrow."

"His papers are in order, but as soon as he's mobile he'll be required to volunteer for the local militia."

Kary nodded. "I'm sure he will be happy to do his duty."

The sergeant didn't question her judgment, or press for too many details. The mayor suffered the mission's existence because she provided medical care the town of Sinan couldn't. And while he had ordered Choi to take any healthy outsiders to the municipal hall, every person she housed and fed was one less for him to deal with.

Choi ran down the list of other patients at the clinic. They had ten beds, and eight were occupied. Cheon, her family, and Cho were five of the eight who had fled the city, while the other three were locals. Cheon was the worst trauma patient, and the worst local citizen was Rang Gi-taek, in his fifties, who was fighting pneumonia and losing.

With the hospitals closed to all but the party and the army, Kary's clinic offered the best medical care in the area, both for the locals and refugees from the city. She would have been swamped, but only people who knew about the mission came there.

But as proud as she was to be helping, she also seethed inside at the limits the regime had placed on her organization. She could have done so much more, for people who needed so much and asked for so little. And there were so many she'd lost. Kary had become very familiar with Korean funeral customs.

Standing by the front gate, ready to leave after his fifteen-minute tour, he said, "You are a good woman, Fowler-*seonsaengnim*, but you should get out of Korea."

"I can't leave," she insisted in her best Korean.

Choi looked over at the two militiamen, and moved a few steps back into the compound, away from the gate. Lowering his voice, for a moment Kary thought he was going to give her another pistol. Instead, he said, "The mayor has declared that this place is not part of Sinan, and is not to be protected. He explicitly ordered me not to respond to any calls for help from here." He nodded solemnly at her shocked expression, and added, "I will disobey that order if I can, but he actually thinks this place is one of the secret bases our enemies will use to launch the final attack on Pyongyang." He smiled, but there was no humor in it.

As he walked away, the two soldiers following, she sighed. He probably was giving her good advice. She knew that. He had her best interests at heart. When he'd inspected their storeroom and its meager contents, tucked neatly in one corner, he'd just shaken his head and closed the door. He hadn't even taken a tin of food.

With Choi's thankfully short visit out of the way, she'd headed back to her office, via the clinic. She made the rounds as often as she could. Even if there was little she could give them, at least she could keep close tabs on their progress.

As she entered the long room, this time without the sergeant, volunteers and the patients' family members greeted her quietly. Kary walked down the center aisle, between the double row of beds, speaking with any patients who were awake and checking everyone's vitals. Few were as sick as she'd told Sergeant Choi, except possibly Cheon Ji-hyo.

The woman was mending slowly, getting by on minimal doses of the clinic's painkillers and antibiotics. One or both of her kids were always on one side of the bed, her mother Gam Sook-ja on the other.

Kary couldn't look at Cheon without feeling a little pride. She'd done more surgeries lately than she'd ever imagined, and Cheon Ji-hyo's shoulder had been by far the most difficult. Bullet and bone fragments had torn through the muscles, but guided by divine hands, she'd repaired the torn muscles and stopped the bleeding. In a few days, Kary would have to go back in to see if she'd . . .

"Fowler-*seonsaengnim.*" Cho Ho-jin had left his bed and was standing politely nearby. "May we speak?"

Kary had done a fair amount of stitching on Cho's back. She tried to remember the Korean word for "quilt." He was pale, and obviously sore, but he'd been upright since yesterday.

"I haven't examined you today yet. Do you feel well? If you laid down . . ."

"Perhaps in your office, or outside."

She nodded. "Outside then. There's a little breeze." They walked to the "patio" and sat, shaded by the awning. Cho removed a T-shirt several sizes too large for him and turned in the chair so she could sit next to him and examine her stitching. He gave her a little while to work.

The four lacerations varied from one relatively deep puncture a centimeter across, to a ragged slash that had some width as well as depth. Bruising was already turning his back into a patchwork of blues and black, but thankfully none of the wounds showed signs of redness or swelling.

As she replaced the dressings, Kary said, "You are a genuine hero, Cho Ho-jin. Cheon Ji-hyo owes you her life."

"As you said yesterday, but I just got her here. Your care saved her. But let this hero give you some advice. You must leave this place. Right away."

"That isn't the first time I've heard that advice, and not even the first time today."

"It's good advice."

She spread her hands helplessly. "I can't. People need us. If I had left, who would have treated you or Cheon?" After a pause, she added, "Besides, it's over a hundred kilometers to the border with the South, and just as far to the northern border with China."

"A hundred and thirty to the South and a hundred and eighty to China. I checked."

"Should I walk? What about the patients? Their families? What would we—"

Cho cut her off. He spoke quietly, but with great intensity. "Questions can be answered, problems solved. The journey is long and perilous. Not everyone reaches their destination. But there are many who have set out, because to stay was even more dangerous. To sit here and hope puts too much trust in your god."

"I cannot leave these people," Kary said with such finality that Cho knew the matter was closed. She rose to leave, but Cho put his arm out to stop her, and winced at the motion.

"One other thing, Fowler-*seonsaengnim*. I am very grateful for your care. I have little to offer in payment, but . . ." He paused and removed his cell phone and offered it to her. "It's much better than most of the phones around here. It has a satellite capability, and is hard for the authorities to trace."

Surprised but intrigued, Kary took the device. Cho could see the wheels turning. She asked carefully, "Is this the type of phone an agricultural inspector needs for his work?"

He smiled. "No, it is not. But don't ask me what I use it for. I don't know if you'd like the answer. But I'm sure you'd like to call your family back in America . . ."

Her face lit up, and she said, "Yes! That would be amazing!" Excited, and unfamiliar with the device, she couldn't dial it at first, and Cho entered the number for her. Surprisingly, it was a Korean phone number.

"My good friend Anita is in our mission in Sinanju. She has a satellite phone, too," she explained to Cho, then focused her attention on the phone. "Hello, Anita, it's Kary!"

Not wanting to listen in on her conversation, Cho nodded and decided to take a short walk. Yesterday he'd walked up and down three times inside the clinic, on Kary's orders, and today he felt up to walking around the compound.

A low wall surrounded what used to be six buildings, but now was only three. Behind the office, clinic, and dining hall were the remains of three greenhouses. Wooden frames and plastic sheeting hadn't been much of a barrier to looters. He couldn't tell when it had happened, but it didn't really matter. The three buildings, of light wooden construction, wouldn't stop even a casual intruder. All that work lost. He could imagine her sadness at their destruction.

Cho realized he cared about these people and their foreign benefactor. Perhaps it was all the effort he'd expended getting Cheon Ji-hyo and her family here. He wanted them to be safe.

It was hot. He'd meant to circle all the way around the compound, but a wave of weakness overcame him, and his back started to complain, so halfway through his circuit, he turned toward the clinic. Once inside, he lay down carefully on his stomach. Exhausted, he fell asleep.

Sharp pain woke Cho when he tried to roll over in his sleep. Automatically, he felt for his one possession, the cell phone, and remembered he'd loaned it to Fowler. Standing gingerly, he discovered he actually felt rested, although still sore. He'd been asleep a little over an hour.

The patio was empty, and now in full sun in the middle afternoon. Listening, the sounds of battle to the east seemed louder, but still distant.

Walking slowly, he headed for the middle building. The first door in the long hall was labeled in both English and Hangul as "Office." It stood half-open, and he could see her in a wooden chair, head cradled in her hands.

At the sound of his footsteps, she turned to face the door. She had been crying, a lot. Cho had meant to ask for the phone, but stopped with the first word half-formed.

After a moment, he spoke softly, "Can you tell me what's wrong? Is there anything I can do?"

"Oh, no, there's nothing," she answered, forcing a cheerful tone. She reached to one side of her desk, retrieved the cell phone, and turned to hand it to him. It looked like she was ready to burst into tears again, at any minute.

She is carrying this entire place on her shoulders. Cho wanted to do something, anything for her. As he took the phone, he said, "Even if I can't help, I can listen." Cho gently lowered himself into the only other chair in the room. He tried to adopt a relaxed pose, but as his back touched the chair, he winced and quickly sat forward.

The motion bordered on the comic, and Kary smiled, which improved her appearance. She sighed, and explained sadly, "When I called Anita to ask about the mission there, she told me it was gone, stripped bare by refugees headed for the Chinese border—except very few are getting across. The Chinese have lined the border with soldiers. They're shooting people who try to sneak across." She sounded horrified and disgusted at the injustice of it.

"So now there are huge squatters' camps all along the Chinese border, thousands of people with no food or water. They've already started to die of thirst and disease.

"And Anita is under house arrest! The local officials blame her for the deaths. They say her mission is supposed to be feeding the refugees—all of them!" She took a breath and tried to sound positive. "But she's alive, and praying for help."

It's what Cho might have expected, if he'd taken time to think about it. But that didn't make it any better. "I'm sorry that your friend—"

"But the news isn't all bad," Kary interrupted. "The South Korean army crossed the thirty eighth parallel two days ago, on the twenty-second, not even a full day after Kim died. They're advancing quickly, and Pyongyang is their main objective. All we have to do is hang on a little bit longer."

The news stunned Cho. He'd never really thought about a unified Korea. In his life, it had been enough to punish the Kim regime, to make them pay for what they'd done to his family. He'd never imagined the fatherland actually disappearing, being absorbed into a new whole.

He didn't know what such a place would be like.

Cho found a quiet spot and used the phone to search the news reports. Media reports, especially in wartime, were unreliable, but it was clear that the Southerners were coming, and in strength. There were many photographs of them in Kaesong, a large DPRK city on the west coast, just north of the border, and fighting at the bridge over the Ryesong River, maybe ten kilometers to the north of that. Enemy scouts would be well forward of that.

But were they the enemy?

He didn't trust the South Korean government any more than his Russian handlers or the Chinese. And as for the South's American allies, he'd always thought of them as powerful enemies, as well as the South's protectors. As far as his politics went, he wasn't really for anything, but there were a lot of things he was against.

Helping Cheon Ji-hyo and her family had been one of the first positive things he'd done in a long time. This was something to work for.

The South's goal was Pyongyang, of course. The Kaesong-Pyongyang highway would lead them straight here. Cho considered their progress. The Southerners would have—probably already had—complete air superiority. Any concentrations of KPA resistance would be pounded from the air and then smashed or bypassed. And the KPA was rotten, poorly equipped, and ineptly led. He had seen that with his own eyes. And now the North's military was splintered and weakened by civil war. The real question was how long they'd last before collapsing completely.

At highway speeds, Southern troops could be here in half a day, but realistically, it might be less than a week, or much more. Or parachute troops might land here tonight.

He went to tell Kary Fowler what he'd discovered. They couldn't tell anyone else, of course. There would be too many questions about how they'd found out. But he'd change his advice. In a few more days, everything might be very different. He couldn't imagine what life in a unified Korea would be like, but for once there was cause for hope. Until then, he'd do whatever he could to keep this place, and the people here, safe.

For a brief moment, Cho thought about calling his Russian handler. Pavel Telitsyn was probably worried about him. The man had shown Cho some kindness, but either Telitsyn or his superiors had ordered him to Pyongyang—essentially a death sentence.

He was expendable in their eyes. If he called in now, they would only demand he go back and obtain the information they wanted or die trying. So be it. They had given him his final mission, and as far as he was concerned, he'd fulfilled it to the best of his ability. Now he had a new assignment, to do what he could to keep these people alive.

Contented, he went to see if Kwan, who was supposed to be keeping watch, had fallen asleep again.

The fighting in the city had been heavy all afternoon, if the rumbling was any indication. Even though they were outside the city proper, Cho could hear the difference between the deeper sound of artillery and the sharp crack of tank cannon. There was plenty of both. The other patients said it was the loudest and longest battle they'd heard.

Cho had coped with his worries by joining Kwan on lookout duty. Even with the meager rations, his strength was returning, although it would be weeks before his back was completely healed. Fowler said she'd take the stiches out in a few days, as long as he promised to take it easy. Laughing, Cho had promised to stay away from any battles.

Now, Cho tried to gauge not only the intensity of the fighting, but whether it was getting any closer. It was impossible to tell. Then he saw someone with a rifle running toward the mission. He tensed for a moment, but he spotted the red armband of a militiaman.

Cho found Kary in the kitchen. She had started preparing the evening meal with Ok Min-seo. "Fowler-*seonsaengnim*, a messenger has brought word that several people from the city are being sent here. He says they are very sick."

She furrowed her brow. "I thought people from the city were supposed to be taken to the municipal hall."

"The messenger also said that the mayor won't let them into the hall, because they might spread disease, and ordered them brought here."

She put down the knife and wiped her hands. "I'll be there in a moment. I'll examine them outside. Please make sure everyone else stays inside. And don't you touch them either," she said sharply.

Cho hurried out of the kitchen, shooing a few curious folk inside. He was still telling them it was "Fowler-*seonsaengnim*'s orders" when he spotted six militiamen carrying loaded stretchers. Kary came out of the dispensary gloved and masked, and told Cho to bring several spare pallets from the beds to the east side of the dispensary, in the shade. Moon Su-bin helped him find and carry them outside, and by the time the stretcher-bearers arrived, the two had set up places for the patients to lie down.

There were three of them, a man and woman in their twenties or early thirties, and an older man, all in civilian clothes. The young man lay quietly, but the woman was coughing and retching. The older man was unconscious, and his breathing was shallow.

Kary tossed a pair of gloves to Moon, and to Cho as well, then knelt down to examine the woman. She was struggling to breathe, and Cho could see her eyes were watering, and mucous was streaming from her nose.

They didn't have a portable respirator, but Kary sent Moon back inside for their oxygen bottle. She spoke to the woman, who was wide-eyed with confusion or fear. As she spoke, she placed her hand on the patient's forehead. "No fever," she remarked out loud, "but she's soaked with sweat."

Moon returned with the oxygen bottle. Kary placed the mask over the woman's mouth. The woman calmed, but couldn't lie still. Her arms and legs spasmed and twitched, even as her expression softened.

While Moon held the mask, Kary examined the woman for other symptoms or wounds, but announced "No trauma," with a combination of relief and curiosity.

"How are her pupils?" Cho asked.

Surprised by the question, Kary answered, "Both pinpoint and unresponsive."

Cho's insides tightened, and chills ran through him. "Look for inflammation in her nose and mouth," he instructed.

Kary used a penlight, then confirmed his suspicion. "Bright red, almost like a burn." She stood quickly and turned to face Cho. "What is this?" she demanded.

"Nerve gas, probably sarin," Cho answered. "Absorbed through the skin or inhaled," he gestured to the female victim, "which is likely what she did."

Cho could see the diagnosis shocked Kary, but she stayed focused, probably because she had patients to take care of. She asked, "Is there any treatment that you know of, other than atropine, administered immediately?"

Cho shook his head sadly. "No, at this point it's just supportive care. But they probably still have the chemical on their clothes or skin. If so, they're still absorbing the toxin, increasing their dosage. They have to be decontaminated immediately, along with anything they have touched." He held up a gloved hand. "Your instincts were good. We can't touch them directly. The good news is soap and water—lots of both—breaks the chemical down. Their outer clothing should be buried."

Moon reported, "Fowler-*seonsaengnim*, this one is dead." She was pointing to the younger man.

Kary nodded sadly. "We'll decontaminate him as well." For a Korean funeral, bathing the deceased was the first step in preparing the body anyway. She turned to Cho. "Will you please instruct the militia soldiers while I tend to my patients?"

While Kary gave orders to her helpers, Cho explained to the militiamen how to decontaminate the stretchers and anything else the patients had touched, and what symptoms to watch for.

He also told them to note any shells or rockets that did not explode with their customary force, or that seemed to give off smoke or vapor. They were so rattled by the words "nerve gas" that he had to repeat his instructions twice, and he wasn't sure they would remember any of it.

She was waiting for him after he sent the militiamen off. "Those men are afraid," she observed.

"They have every right to be," Cho answered. "They have neither the knowledge nor the materials to protect themselves, or this town."

"How long does nerve gas last?" she asked.

"Sarin is 'nonpersistent.' It breaks down after several hours, although pockets in sheltered areas can remain dangerous longer. Sunlight and water causes the gas molecule to break up. It's hot today, which will speed the process, but it also makes the chemical more active, more lethal, until it does. Other types of nerve gas are 'persistent.' Their effects can last for weeks or months. If someone has used chemical weapons in the fighting, then part of Pyongyang, probably a large part of the city, is poisoned."

"Why a large part?" she asked.

"Because nerve gas is an area weapon. Using only a few shells or rockets accomplishes nothing."

"Someday I hope you will tell me how you know so much about sarin, and about your phone."

"When we have the time, Fowler-*seonsaengnim*, you may ask me any question you wish, and I will tell you the truth."

They were almost at the entrance to the clinic when Cho suddenly stopped walking. "Fowler-*seonsaengnim*," he said firmly, "we must leave this place. Now. Immediately." Cho's tone was urgent, almost frantic.

"Are we in danger here? Can the gas drift that far?" she asked.

"Not from the center of the city," Cho answered, "but from western edge, yes. And the fighting will spread," he added. "Parts of Pyongyang are now impassible. The combatants will have to fight elsewhere."

The look of fear on Kary's face told Cho she understood the threat. Like the other horrors of war, civilians always suffered far more than the soldiers.

"But my patients, the staff . . ."

"Anyone who breathes is at risk. The whole town should get as far away from the city as possible."

"Then go," she said. "You're recovered enough. The stiches can come out . . ."

"No," he said firmly. "Not without Cheon Ji-hyo and her family. I can't leave them after all the effort to get them here. And I won't leave without Moon Su-bin, or you."

"But they need me here."

"You have to be alive to help them. And we might meet one or two people on our way that could use your skills."

Cho could see that she was weakening, and felt a surge of hope. Cho pressed his point, mind racing as he proposed a plan. "We do it right away—this instant. Tell your staff and patients to gather their families here."

"But the neighborhood monitors will find out. They'll never allow it."

Cho shook his head in disagreement. "Didn't you say Sergeant Choi was in charge of this neighborhood? Considering what you've told me, he'll probably help us load the trucks."

"What trucks?" she asked.

"The ones I'm going to get from the town's collective, 'on the orders of Song-*dongji*'"

"But . . ."

"Right now, those panicked militiamen are spreading news of the nerve gas through the town. The mayor and his officials will be so terrified that by the time he understands what's going on, we will be gone."

She remained silent, considering his plan. Her face was a mask, and his fears grew that she'd say no. Finally, Kary reluctantly nodded. "All right. I'll get us organized here, but I'm sending Moon Su-bin with you. Her cousin Ja Joon-ho works at the collective's motor pool, and he can drive."

Cho walked off at a brisk pace with Moon in tow. Kary had placed her trust in a surprisingly knowledgeable stranger with a mysterious background. She said a quick prayer for their success and ran into the clinic. It only took a few minutes to tell everyone what they were doing. It really wasn't a detailed plan. Most nodded, willing to trust her—in fact, willing to trust her with their lives.

Messengers ran off to gather families. By now, word of the desperately sick patients that had just arrived was spreading through the town, overlapping with the stories about the nerve gas. She proposed that, if questioned, people were coming to the clinic "to check on their family members."

Once the staff was moving, Kary took the time to speak with each of her patients. Gam Sook-ja, Cheon Ji-hyo, and the other patients from Pyongang were eager to leave. They had no ties to Sinan, and had already suffered in the fighting. Now their home was poisoned. They couldn't go back for some time.

The other patients were also willing, except for Rang Gi-taek. He was barely conscious, and one of his grandchildren spoke on his behalf. "We were preparing to take him home anyway. We will do it now." If it was possible, Koreans near death were brought home, not only for comfort in their last hours, but so that their spirits would be rooted to the place where they had lived, and not become lost.

There was precious little food and medical supplies to take, and Kary knew that eventually they would have lost it to looters, or seen it destroyed when her mission was engulfed in fighting. It might be enough to keep them alive until they reached the advancing Southern army.

Thoughts about armies caused her to step outside and listen to the sounds of the fighting. To her newly experienced ears, the shelling and gunfire seemed no closer, but intense. She often compared it with the sounds of a summer thunderstorm. She prayed it would remain distant.

Families began arriving in ones and twos and threes, and they were told to wait in the clinic. Some of them were telling wild tales about the fighting in the capital, or what was happening elsewhere in Sinan. None of the news was good, and Kary saw justifiable fear start to become unreasonable panic, to the point where she told Ok Min-seo, the cook, to put every able-bodied soul to work at anything she could think of.

With no immediate crises apparent, Kary took a few minutes to gather a few personal items from her quarters and the office. She wanted to take the Bible from the chapel. It had been a gift from her family, but she weighed its worth against the danger of being discovered with "religious items." Standing in the chapel, considering, she heard the sound of truck engines.

She ran outside to see two, then three trucks turn off the road into the mission. She waved them around back, behind the dining hall, and ran in between the buildings to meet them there. Cho and Moon were in the first one, a blue stake truck that had been fitted with wooden sides, then a military-looking flatbed, and then another stake truck that might have been white, a long time ago.

She ran up to the cab as Cho stopped with a screech that hinted at badly needed brake work. As he climbed down, she said "Three? How . . ."

"There was almost nobody there. Ja"—Cho pointed to a young man getting out of the second cab—"was the senior person at the motor pool. The city government is in chaos. They've received orders that Sinan is to become a 'fortress against the counterrevolutionaries,' whoever they are."

"Most of the city officials have fled." The different but familiar voice belonged to Sergeant Choi, getting out of the passenger's side of the second truck. He ignored her surprised expression. "I'm glad to see you're finally taking my advice, Kary Fowler- *seonsaengnim.*"

Dumbstruck, Kary could only nod, and Choi continued. "Song Kwang-sik," the sergeant almost spat out the mayor's name, "has taken his family and six of the militia as an escort and headed for the Chinese border. Most of the town officials are following his example." Kary noted that Choi hadn't used the customary *"dongji"* title when referring to the mayor, which made the use of his name almost an insult.

People had come out of the clinic and the other buildings to look at the new arrivals, and Choi said, "Military units are en route to occupy the town and set up defensive works. We don't have any time to spare. Any civilians left here will be drafted either as militia or laborers. Come on, I'll help you get loaded."

The patients and supplies were put on first, split between the three vehicles, and then the others began to board, to find the trucks already had some passengers. Choi explained, "My niece and her husband and children are on the last truck. Other citizens of Sinan also want to go with you. You should have enough space for everyone; in fact you have to, because as far as I know, these are the last three working vehicles in town."

He saw her start to ask a question, and held out a hand, forestalling her. "I'm not coming. I have family here that can't be moved, and with the mayor and the others gone, I'm now the senior official. I'll do what I can to keep everyone still here safe. But I have a parting gift."

He handed Kary an official-looking form. "One of the mayor's last official acts was to issue himself travel orders allowing him and his companions to travel freely anywhere in the country." He smiled. "My niece's husband was in charge of drafting the document and accidentally made a second copy, which, in his haste, the mayor also signed."

Almost in tears, Kary reached to hug Choi but he stepped quickly back. "The mayor and I have been trying to get you to leave since the day you arrived. I'm sure he'd approve. Now get out of here, as quickly as you can."

The convoy pulled out, heading west, away from both Sinan and Pyongyang. Cho drove the lead truck with Kary on the passenger's side, and she leaned as far as she could out the window, keeping the now-empty mission in sight for as long as she could. As familiar as it had been to her, she was now terrified of forgetting what it looked like, and she studied and memorized everything she could, until it passed behind a hill and out of sight. Once it was gone, she finally let the tears come.

CHAPTER TEN
NIGHTMARE

24 August 2015, 1545 local time
Operation Backstop Headquarters, Munsan Refugee Camp
Outside Dongducheon, South Korea

They'd barely set up the command post, but Operation Backstop was in full swing, with Kevin letting his new deputy, Lieutenant Colonel Shin Sung-mo, manage the handover of the six existing camps from the ROK Army to American units. That part was going smoothly, but problems were already cropping up.

Some of the refugees refused to believe that they couldn't bribe the personnel that managed the camps, for one. They could not imagine a system where one couldn't buy a place at the head of the line.

That was almost comic compared to the biggest problem: the difficulty of getting the civilians properly immunized. Most didn't trust the government to give them good health care (unless they could buy it through graft), and Kevin was spending more time than he'd like organizing classes in basic health practices, with a minor in civics.

And Southern civilians were becoming a problem as well. The camp administrators were recording names and other personal data on the Northern refugees as fast as they could, but the South Koreans weren't waiting patiently, and even if they did wait, it wasn't at home. Excited and hopeful civilians pestered the staff or tried to get into the camp by any means possible to search for northern relatives or northerners who might be from the same place as their relatives.

Some civilians had received word by various means that their relatives were coming, and sometimes even where they were headed. Many were convinced that their relations were inside the camp, waiting for a happy reunion. When they didn't get an immediate answer from Kevin's staff, they simply found a spot nearby and waited, creating a second "camp" outside the first.

Kevin was supposed to verbally report to General Tracy once a day. He had planned to make his first call this evening, so when one of the staff told him the general was calling, he knew it had to be news.

"Kevin, turn to CNN." Like any headquarters, a TV screen was always on, with the volume muted. Theirs was set to a Korean news station, and Kevin told his staff to switch the channel.

He didn't even need to hear the announcer. A red banner across the bottom edge flashed, "Chemical Weapons Used in North Korean Civil War." Most of the staff came over to watch the report, and Kevin stepped away from the crowd. "Then it's been confirmed?"

Tracy sighed. "Yes. We've gotten scattered but consistent cell phone and Internet traffic out of Pyongyang—or more correctly, from the outskirts of Pyongyang—that someone's using what looks like nerve gas. It was likely artillery or rockets, since we haven't seen much air activity, or, thank heaven, missile launches. There are reports of heavy casualties, but no numbers." His tone changed, and he ordered, "Effective immediately, screen everyone coming out of the North for traces of any chemical agent."

Kevin automatically answered, "Yes, sir." They'd already been watching for symptoms and doing spot checks with detection strips, just in case, but this changed everything. They'd have to set up decontamination stations . . .

"And make sure all your people have their gear handy and are properly briefed, Colonel. You're still getting organized, but we can't discount the threat of a missile attack with a chemical warhead."

"Understood, sir," Kevin agreed emphatically. "And we will have to teach the civilians what to do. The medics have plenty of atropine."

"Then what are your first impressions, Colonel?"

"Major Kae took me on a tour. He commands the infantry company taking care of the refugees here. He needs a battalion. I'll need at least that. A lot of the civilians are still celebrating that they're out of North Korea and not dead. And they're getting decent meals. But there's some serious culture shock. There are problems to solve, but we can make it work. But my prediction about the number of refugees was off, sir."

"How far off?" Tracy asked.

"By a factor of two or three, at the very least," Kevin answered. "It's not just those who make it across the border on their own anymore. The South Korean army is sending empty supply trucks back loaded with refugees and prisoners. Whole villages and KPA units are being transported south. Major Kae says the army's policy is to remove anyone along their route of advance so they don't pose a security threat to the army's rear, but that's a pretty flimsy excuse."

Tracy was sympathetic. "I can understand why. They've watched their relatives suffer for a long time. But I agree. You can't support half the population of North Korea."

"Sir, I'm hoping you can take this up the chain and we can get the government to change the ROK Army's orders. I've got twelve thousand–plus in the Munsan camp alone, and at the rate they're coming, I'll need three times the number of camps we have now."

"That's a valid point. I'll speak to my Korean counterpart, and send it up to Combined Forces as well. Good luck."

Tracy had signed off like he was sending Kevin into combat, but Kevin understood the general's meaning. His own life wasn't in danger, but lives were at stake, as well as the reputation of the US Army. He wasn't going to take his assignment lightly.

He hung up and headed back to the far-too-large group surrounding the television. The volume was up, so he could hear the broadcast, even though the crowd was three deep and he could only see half the screen. The anchor was interviewing a senator from one of the Western states.

". . . about the Chinese reaction if American forces go into North Korea?"

"If we stopped worrying about what China, Russia, and the rest of the world thought, we would already be in Pyongyang. Letting the South Koreans do it alone is a typical half-measure for this administration."

The senator thundered, "Does anybody in the White House or the Pentagon remember that when China invaded Korea sixty-five years ago, they *lost*? I bet the Chinese remember."

He paused to draw a breath. "We've had US troops in South Korea for sixty-five years, and fought two wars there.

Now, when they're needed to finish the job, the president gets cold feet. The South Koreans have made it plain they'd welcome our participation."

"The Chinese ambassador . . ."

"Of *course* the Chinese don't want us involved. They're watching a smaller version of their own sick political system collapse, right on their front doorstep. Democracy is winning, and the president's leaving our troops on the sidelines. My bill will force the . . ."

"I think that's enough of a break," Kevin said softly, but the colonel's voice carried clearly. In ten seconds, the group had scattered, with the last straggler pausing only long enough to mute the broadcast.

25 August 2015, 0550 local time
Ninth Ghost Brigade Forward Headquarters
Near Sariwon, North Korea

Like the motto, special operations forces train to do the impossible. They can lay in hiding near hostile forces, reporting on enemy operations for days at a time without being discovered. They can thread their way through opposing units and attack a command post or key part of their adversary's defenses, opening the way for friendly forces to attack with a much better chance of winning.

For most nations, special operations missions are few and far between, and a country's special operations forces might have only one or two teams on a mission at one time—unless you were South Korea. In the event of a war with the North, the ROK Army had designed Operation Gangrim to swiftly attack over a hundred bases and installations across North Korea with special warfare troops. Their orders were to either capture or destroy the weapons of mass destruction before they could be used. It had a very tight timeline.

Nobody in the South had any illusions about Kim's willingness to use WMDs against either the ROK Army or the cities in the South. North Korea was known to have large stocks of chemical weapons, a dozen or so nuclear weapons, and possibly even biological agents. Leaving even one depot in the hands of the regime could cause untold destruction and pointless slaughter. Rhee and the other brigade commanders understood that Gangrim was strategic, both in scope and effect.

Only the ROK's Special Forces soldiers had the skills to operate independently behind the battle lines in small groups. But add to that was the complexity of managing many such missions at the same time. Rhee had thirty-seven known and potential WMD targets to strike in his sector, one of three covering North Korea. They were installations with suspected or confirmed stocks of WMD agents, delivery systems like heavy artillery or ballistic missiles, or both.

His field headquarters was outside the city of Sariwon, deep in Northern territory, about halfway between Pyongyang and the advancing ROK forces. The base had been inserted by air and was supplied by near constant helicopter deliveries of fuel and ammunition, and served as a staging base for ten-man teams that were airlifted to different targets.

Gangrim had been designed for wartime, and assumed an organized opposing army. The DPRK civil war worked to their advantage in some ways, for instance, the lack of air opposition. In other ways, though, it was a greater problem. The unstable, almost unreadable political situation meant there were many actors who could choose to use WMDs. At least one already had.

The use of nerve gas in Pyongyang meant that the other combatants would likely follow suit, if they could. There was no time for subtlety. Command of the air allowed the helicopters to operate unmolested, and urgency demanded that concealment be sacrificed in the name of speed. So far, the risks had paid off.

Rhee spent more time in the air then on the ground. Accompanying WMD specialists that cataloged and removed any weapons that were found, he inspected each installation after it was captured, and interviewed the team leader about the assault. In peacetime, the team's after-action report would be thoroughly studied and the findings distributed to the rest of the brigade. That might come later, but for the moment Rhee had to evaluate each leader's job and decide whether there were lessons to be learned. Rhee also had to judge the team's readiness to move on to another target, often just hours later.

He was returning from another inspection, with the Ninth's headquarters in sight through the side window of his helicopter. The Ghosts' machines were Korean-built Surions that had replaced the old American-built UH-1s. The Surion was faster, and had an advanced "glass cockpit." The ones operated by his Ghosts had special modifications, including muffled blades and engine noise, special sensors, and protective countermeasures. His command bird was fitted with extra communications gear and a worktable that served as a flat-screen map display.

Rhee was working while they flew, assigning newly available teams to targets, when the copilot reported, "Colonel, I've got the team leader at Bongmu. Enemy forces are greater than expected. He reports they are getting ready to transport some of the ammunition from the depot. Brigade HQ is already tasking UAVs for air support, but he can't wait. He intends to attack immediately."

"How far?" Rhee asked the copilot over the headset. He could have asked to speak with the team leader, but the leader hadn't asked for permission to attack. He'd just reported the changed situation.

He heard the copilot answer "Eighteen minutes."

"Do it, Lieutenant." Rhee was already dialing up the Bongmu site on the map display, and felt the machine turn and accelerate. The floor also dropped away, then rose and fell again as the pilots followed the uneven terrain. They might have air superiority, but there was no sense taking chances, either from a stray fighter or antiaircraft emplacement.

The pilot managed the actual flying, just meters over the ground or the treetops, while the copilot navigated and watched for threats or obstructions ahead of them. They weren't maneuvering violently, but it paid to be belted in. This near dawn, they could have flown using visible light, but they kept their night vision goggles on. Obstacles had better contrast.

Rhee studied the analysis of the Bongmu weapons depot. Artillery shells with nerve gas, according to the intelligence they had, for divisional and corps artillery. The garrison was supposed to be about a company of about a hundred men, which meant only a third or so on duty at any given time. The ten-man squad would have had no problems with a force of that size. But if someone were moving WMD ammunition, there would be additional security. How much?

The swaying motion of the helicopter distracted Rhee for a moment. He wasn't prone to motion sickness, thank goodness, but he took a moment to look up and settle his inner ear. Master Sergeant Oh, his comrade from his first mission into the North, sat across the cabin from him, securely belted in. Oh had strained his right shoulder on his second raid during Gangrim, and had been assigned to light duty until it recovered. Rhee could relate to that. Rather than send him to the rear, which Oh had loudly but respectfully resisted, Rhee had chosen him as his personal escort.

Oh could still shoot a pistol, but the sergeant's primary task was to watch the colonel's back in the field. Rhee always carried both a K5 pistol and K7 submachine gun, so as long as he wasn't blindsided, he could take care of himself.

"One minute out."

Rhee acknowledged the copilot's message and checked his gear. "We're being met," the copilot reported, which told Rhee the landing zone was secure and the fight at Bongmu was over.

The helicopter set down in the clear space in front of the depot's gate. The compound was relatively small, maybe five hundred meters square enclosed in double-layered fencing. A guard tower at each corner was anchored by a bunker built into its base. A few wooden buildings inside the wire were backed with several rows of angular concrete structures. Rhee knew each would have a heavy door and contain several hundred artillery shells loaded with chemical warfare agents. Outside the fence, the ground had been cleared, and kept clear, for a hundred meters all around. Beyond that was a ragged wood line.

The towers and a few of the buildings showed marks from the combat, and numerous trails of smoke curled and merged into a haze that filled the air and stung his eyes.

Rhee didn't see anyone in protective gear, so he assumed it was just smoke. He also noted the blackened hulks of two armored vehicles. Those were not listed as part of the depot's garrison.

Lieutenant Gung Ji-han waited nearby on one knee. It was light enough to see his expression, and Rhee knew the news wouldn't be good.

As the cabin door opened and Rhee stepped out, Gung stood and saluted solemnly. "Mission failure, sir. At least two large trucks left the compound during our attack. An early estimate is at least eight pallets of 152mm ammunition were on them." He pointed to a road that ran past the depot. "They were headed north. My UAV controller is trying to locate them now."

"Casualties?" Rhee asked.

"Four of my team are wounded. Three are mobile, but Corporal Park has two bullets in the chest and my medic's fighting to keep him alive. The medevac helicopter is en route. At least thirty KPA dead, with another fifty-plus prisoners and wounded. We know there are stragglers in the woods, but we don't know their intention."

Rhee nodded acknowledgment. Many North Korean soldiers had used combat as an excuse to desert, but others simply became separated during the action and might still be motivated to fight. "All right, elaborate," he ordered.

Gung kept it short. "The trucks were already here when we landed, along with another company of troops and the two fighting vehicles. We called for UAV support, but their ETA was too long. We could see the trucks were preparing to leave, so we attacked."

Rhee nodded his understanding. It was a difficult situation—two or three times the expected odds, and facing the immediate prospect of losing control of the WMDs. "I would have chosen to attack as well," Rhee encouraged the lieutenant.

But it was still a loss. Forty percent casualties and they had not stopped the trucks, after all that. And Gung's team would have to be rebuilt before they could take on another mission. He'd get a detailed debrief of the combat later, but for the moment, he would endorse the lieutenant's decision.

Gung seemed to take some reassurance from Rhee's statement, but there was a lot to do. "Where are your people now?" Rhee asked.

"My medic's with Corporal Park, the UAV controller's looking for the trucks, two are guarding the prisoners, two more are searching the woods, and the last two are checking the buildings for stragglers and documents."

"All right, Lieutenant. Make sure your UAV controller transmits the data on the trucks to brigade. I'm going to get you some help. You can't provide security with only six effectives. They'll . . ."

A dirt-streaked trooper ran up and saluted the pair. Rhee recognized him as one of Gung's team, but couldn't remember his name. He was winded, and the soldier's expression held bad news. "In the woods," he reported between breaths, pointing. "Bodies. Lots of them."

Rhee said, "Show us," and they followed the soldier back at something just less than a dead run. They slowed at the wood line, moving along a path through thick brush and young trees. About ten meters into the woods, the smell reached them, and they all gagged at the stench of rot and decay.

Another ten meters brought them to the scene. A stream ran through the woods, although in August there was no water in it. The V-shaped gully, about two meters deep and two meters across, was choked with bodies. Rhee could see civilians in work clothes, soldiers in DPRK uniforms, the bright colors of both women's and children's clothing. His mind flashed back to the bodies he and Oh found murdered and robbed what seemed like a long time ago. If that was a crime, what was this?

Gung had turned away and was clutching a tree, vomiting and shaking with reaction. Oh had tears in his eyes. Their guide was on one knee, and appeared to be praying.

Rhee Han-gil felt the weight of his command more than he ever had. It was his job to know, and he forced himself to walk over to the edge. From that angle, he got a better view of the depth of the gully, and could see the corpses jumbled together. The ones toward the bottom were discolored from decay, and he tried to guess the number of dead. His mind rebelled, but there were at least a hundred, maybe twice that number.

His stomach churned, not just from the stench, but the thought of so much pointless death. A crime like this *should* reek, he decided. It should foul the air and rise until the heavens were repelled. What about the men who did this? Did they carry the smell with them?

Rhee's emotions collapsed from a whirl of different feelings into a tight knot of anger. He ordered brusquely, "With me," and strode quickly down the path, back the way they'd come and toward the depot. Lieutenant Gung, still wiping his mouth, followed with the others.

As they emerged from the woods, without breaking stride, Rhee asked, "Where are the prisoners?"

Gung answered, "We put the enlisted men in their barracks, and the officers and noncoms in two empty ammunition bunkers."

"The officers, then."

The soldier left to return to his duties, while the lieutenant increased his pace to take the lead. As they entered the camp, another trooper ran up to the group. He was heading for the lieutenant, but stopped when he saw the colonel, bracing and saluting crisply. "Sir, Private Geun Seo-bin."

Rhee returned his salute. This soldier wasn't as distraught as the first, but obviously had disturbing news. "Report."

"Sirs, I think you should see what we found in the officers' quarters." He pointed to a wooden structure next to the headquarters building. Rhee was in no mood for distractions, but the trooper's expression was earnest and grim. The North Korean officers weren't going anywhere.

It was only a few meters to the small building. The door was intact and the walls unmarked. There had been no fighting here. A short corridor led to four doors, two to a side. All four had evidently been locked, because they were now kicked in.

Private Geun led them to the first door on the right. "This is the commander's quarters," he explained. Rhee saw something that reminded him of a poor student's dormitory room. A bed, little more than a cot, occupied the opposite wall, while a desk and battered chair stood next to a window on the left. The drawers had all been pulled out and their contents dumped in the search for documents. The wall to the right was filled by a wardrobe, ransacked, and two wooden footlockers, side by side. Both had been padlocked, but the hasps were now broken. The private walked straight over to the nearest footlocker and opened the lid.

Rhee and the lieutenant could see bundles of currency, watches, cell phones, and other electronic devices. A metal circle that might hold keys was strung with rings. The colonel reached over and opened the second locker. Its contents were identical.

There could be no mystery where it had come from. Rhee had actually felt his anger begin to subside as they inspected the officers' quarters, but at the sight of the looted wealth, it returned and flared into a white-hot rage.

Wordlessly, Rhee turned and headed back outside. Gung and Master Sergeant Oh hurried to follow him. "Which bunker are the officers in?" the colonel demanded.

Still trying to catch up, Gung answered, "Number four, in the back row."

Each bunker was a little larger than a two-car garage, made of roughly cast concrete, with a wide metal door. The uneven surface was unpainted and weathered, the only marking a large black number on the gray-painted door. While the other two readied their weapons, Lieutenant Gung opened the latch. "We broke the one on the inside, so they couldn't get out," he explained.

Gung had to pull hard to swing the heavy door open. The space inside was much smaller than its outer size would indicate. About four meters square, the bare walls and floor were harshly lit by a single fluorescent fixture. There was room for four or six pallets of artillery ammunition, but it was empty.

Four men sat on the floor, against the side or rear walls. They didn't rise or do more than turn their heads toward Rhee and the others. Rhee could see that while they were disheveled, none were wounded.

One looked older than the others, and was a captain, according to his collar tabs. Rhee asked Gung, "Is this one the senior officer?"

"The depot commander," Gung confirmed. "We captured him trying to escape into the woods."

Rhee and the others still held their weapons at the ready, and he motioned with the muzzle, pointed toward the captain. "You. Get up."

The North Korean pointedly ignored the order, turning his face away from Rhee, but Rhee lunged forward and grabbed the front of the man's fatigue shirt and dragged him out of the room as if he was a bag of potatoes—a small bag. As Rhee stepped outside, he ordered Gung, "Shut it."

Using both hands, Rhee roughly pulled the man upright, then slammed him back into the side of the bunker. "The bodies in the woods." Rhee spat out the words, not bothering to phrase it as a question.

"I don't know . . ." was as far as the captain got before Rhee jammed his forearm into the other's throat. Rhee held it there, watching the prisoner weakly struggle, until he could bottle up the anger again, and stepped back. The North Korean fell to his knees, gasping and rubbing his throat.

"Tell me." Rhee wasn't wasting words.

Coughing and rubbing his throat, the captain looked to either side. A lieutenant stood to one side, weapon not leveled, but ready. A sergeant stood farther back, watching the woods but also quite capable of shooting him, if he made a break toward that direction. Their expressions did not have the fury of the colonel, but they looked more than willing to kill.

Rhee started to move, but the captain forestalled him by speaking quickly. "Our orders were to kill anyone who approached the depot, or who we thought was trying to go south, or any deserters."

"Did your orders include robbing them?"

"They didn't need it anymore," the captain answered.

The anger in Rhee's chest filled him like cold liquor, burning even as it chilled. Without thinking, he drew his pistol and racked the slide.

"Colonel, *stop!*" The shout caught Rhee with the pistol's muzzle inches from the captain's forehead. He kept the weapon pointed at the officer, but turned his head to see Master Sergeant Oh, walking quickly toward them. "Don't do it, sir."

Rhee swallowed hard, and looked at the piece of human filth in front of him. Oh's shout was unheard of, a serious breach of military discipline, and it was that as much as his words that had made the colonel pause.

"He's a prisoner, sir. It's not worth your career." Oh spoke softly, but his tone was a little different than one a noncom would use addressing a colonel. They were also comrades, who served together and trusted each other completely.

His mind processed the sergeant's words, and Rhee realized he didn't need to kill the North Korean anymore. The fury drained away, leaving him almost weak for a moment. He turned to the lieutenant and ordered, "Put this *gesekida* back in his hole."

Gung, looking both horrified and relieved, motioned with the muzzle of his K7. The prisoner slowly stood and walked back toward the front of the bunker, Gung three paces behind.

Holstering his pistol, Rhee sighed and said softly, "Thank you, Master Sergeant. I lost control, and was a fool."

"You were closer to him than I was, that's all, Colonel," Oh answered. He added, "We need you, sir."

Gung returned and stood silently until Rhee noticed him. "The prisoner is secure, Colonel." He said it so carefully that Rhee knew the lieutenant was almost as traumatized as the North Korean.

Rhee gathered his thoughts. "Before we were interrupted, I was going to get you some additional security while we moved the remaining WMDs out, then we'd abandon this place. Now that's changed. We're going to hold it. I'll bring in regular infantry as well as an additional team from the Ninth, and specialists to take out the WMDs, per normal procedure. And I'm going to bring in investigators from the Judge Advocate General. You are not to remove the prisoners until I say so."

"You want them to remain here?" the lieutenant confirmed. Standard operating procedure was to get the prisoners out of the way as soon as possible, usually on the same aircraft that brought in the WMD and ordnance disposal experts.

"That's right. Use them, especially that *shipcenchi* of a captain and the other officers, to remove the bodies from the ravine. That will take quite a while, and I'm sure the JAG investigators will want to take them into custody after that. With luck, they'll die in front of a firing squad."

25 August 2015, 9:00 a.m. local time
Near Chaeryong, North Korea

It didn't look like a gas station, but the farmer they bribed with the last of Cho's yuan notes insisted that if anyone had gasoline, it would be the restaurant north of the Baesok train station. He'd been quite precise, and even given Cho a map and a note.

"For that much money, he should have filled the tanks with his blood," Cho grumbled as they approached the location.

"I think you did well to get any information at all," Kary remarked, "much less a place where we can get fuel for three trucks." She sounded optimistic. Cho reserved judgment, watching the fuel gauge. They'd had to siphon fuel from the other two trucks to keep the flatbed going, and if they couldn't find fuel somewhere, they'd all be walking.

Traffic was light, and three trucks in company should have attracted more attention, but there were few people about, and the military units they'd passed on the road had ignored them, headed either north or south at speed. The country looked empty. They were still about a hundred kilometers from the southern border by road. The advancing South Korean army was closer, maybe half that distance. Kary wondered how many people had left their homes to go south or just avoid the fighting.

They'd been stopped twice at checkpoints, but Mayor Song's paperwork and a story about orders to take an American woman south had been enough to get them through, along with a few bills as bribes. North Korea might be in upheaval, but people always needed money.

Kary, comparing the farmer's map with the landscape, announced, "Here." They turned off a two-lane macadam road onto gravel. The restaurant, if that's what it was, sat alone a hundred meters off the main road, surrounded by cultivated fields. Most held ripening crops, although more than a few were fallow. It was a low, one-story building, but large enough, with thankfully plenty of space for the three trucks to park.

It also seemed to be abandoned. There were no other vehicles nearby, nobody outside or visible through the windows, and no smoke coming from the kitchen's chimney in the back. Painted a faded yellow, the sign in Hangul under the obligatory photo of the Supreme Leader simply read "Good Food."

Picking up a small medical bag, Kary said, "I'll check on my patients while you see if anyone's home."

Cho put a hand on her arm and asked, "Why don't you come with me? That farmer kept glancing at you while he dickered with me. A beautiful, exotic American woman might help with the negotiations."

Kary nodded, but was a little flustered. She hadn't paid any attention to her appearance in a long time. And Cho was smiling as he said it. Was he joking? What if he wasn't?

As the two got out of the truck, others hopped out from the other two cabs and the back. Moon Su-bin and her cousin Ja Joon-ho were in the second truck, and Kary told them to keep everyone close while they looked for gas.

A thick man in his mid-forties stepped out of the front door and looked over the group. "We're closed," he said harshly.

Cho nodded his understanding, but approached and offered him a paper. "I have a note from Do Han-il."

The man pursed his lips, and took the note Cho offered. He asked, "Is he getting any business at that run-down appliance shop?"

Did he glance in Kary's direction? *He has to be curious about who I am*, she thought.

"He was a farmer when I talked to him," Cho answered.

"All right." The proprietor seemed satisfied. "I might have enough for all three trucks, but it will cost you."

"I have the money."

"Let's see it."

Cho showed him the corner of a single American twenty-dollar bill. "Let's see the gasoline," he responded.

The man stepped back inside, and came out with a twenty-liter plastic jerry can. "One bill, one can."

"We need six cans. Two bills."

"Five is all I have. Four bills." He definitely looked in her direction. Kary wasn't thrilled at being a negotiating tool, but it was for a good cause. And she was glad Cho was handling the negotiations. She'd learned how to dicker well enough, but lacked a lifetime of experience.

"We'll take them all. Two bills."

The gasoline dealer remarked, "Why do I get the idea you only have two bills?"

"Forty US dollars is going to be worth a lot, unless you've got South Korean won," Cho countered. "Yuan notes will be worthless after the South Korean army gets here." He pointed south. "They'll be coming up that road tomorrow or the next day."

The man shrugged. "Then why not just wait?"

"We've got injured and sick people," Cho explained. "We can't wait."

"And the Southern army is really coming?"

Cho took out his satphone and called up pictures and maps that showed the progress of the ROK forces.

"All right, I'm convinced. Four cans for your two bills, and that's my final offer."

They were on their way twenty minutes later. Grateful for the gasoline, nobody had asked about food. As Cho started their truck, Kary leaned over and tapped the gas gauge, hoping it was stuck. It was up from near empty, but read just a little over half full. "It should be enough," she said hopefully.

"It has to be," Cho answered, "since I'm now out of both Chinese and American currency."

"I'll repay you," Kary assured him.

He waved it off. "Don't be silly. It was the Russians' money, anyway." After a short pause, Cho asked, "Have you given any more thought to calling your father?"

Kary shrugged, hoping Cho would let the question pass, but he pressed his point. "You said he was a very powerful man in the American government."

"Yes," she answered simply, but did not elaborate. She knew where the national security advisor fit into the US government, but she'd remained willfully ignorant of his exact duties. After a pause, she added, "He's retired now, anyway. He's head of a foundation somewhere."

Cho sighed, and she could hear his frustration. They'd driven through the night, talking to keep each other awake. Cho had kept his promise. She'd asked her questions about who Cho Ho-jin really was, and after getting over her surprise, learned about his youth and the reasons for spying for the Russians.

That had led to stories about her growing up with a famous father, who'd been gone too much and whose business seemed to be imposing American power on the rest of the world.

Her generation had grown up with armed conflicts on the television news every night, and she hated the images of shattered families and wounded innocents. Unlike many around her, the people suffering on the screen were never foreign or strange to her. They needed her help, and at the earliest possible age, she'd joined Christian Friends, already experienced from work she'd done with refugees during summer breaks from college.

Driving at night, with no light but the dashboard and headlights in front of them, it had been easy to talk, to tell

Cho about things she hadn't spoken of in years, and later of things she barely admitted to herself. Cho had also been open with her, glad to have someone to trust after many years of being more than just alone.

"When was the last time you spoke with your father?" Cho asked in a noncommittal tone.

"A few months ago. Early June, on his birthday."

"I wish I could do that. I don't have many memories of my father. Like yours, his duties kept him away from us, but I remember my mother being very happy when he was home, and his plans for me. He never returned from the war. Once it was clear the North had lost, he was simply arrested and shot as a traitor. There's no grave that we know of. He's lost to us forever."

Kary could feel the weight of his arguments, but procrastinated. "He's been out of the government for twenty years. And I've always been the one pushing him away. I'd thought about reconciling with him when I went home for my next visit, but I can't just phone him up and say, 'Hi, I need your help.'"

Cho shrugged. "Maybe it's different in America, but in Korea, you go to family first. Families fight with each other, and do foolish things, but they are still family. And the help isn't for you personally."

His final point made her reluctance look selfish. *Swallow your pride, girl.*

By now she had learned how to operate Cho's phone properly, and she dialed her dad's number in Indiana. It was late there, but her father often stayed up into the small hours.

It only rang twice. He was awake. "Blake Fowler here." His tone was cautious. She didn't know what his caller ID said, but it would not be a familiar number.

"Dad? It's Kary."

"Kary? Thank God. Where are you? Are you safe?"

"I'm still in North Korea, but we've left the mission and we're heading south. I've got some injured people with me and we hope to reach the South Korean army later today."

"But you're not hurt?" he said hopefully.

"No, Dad, I'm fine, but we have patients with us who were gassed. A friend thinks it was something called 'sarin.'" She looked over to Cho, who did not speak English, but confirmed her pronunciation. "Somebody used a lot of it in the fighting in Pyongyang. There are so many dead, Dad."

"I'd heard that, but we still don't have a clear picture of what went on in the capital. Would you be willing to describe what you saw to someone I know?"

Irritation flared inside her. All he could see was the big picture. "Dad, I've got three trucks full of injured and wounded, who haven't eaten anything since yesterday morning . . ." She felt a hand on her shoulder, and Cho's gentle pressure calmed her, reminding her of why she was calling. He didn't pat it or try to soothe her. She might have lashed out at him if he'd done anything like that.

"Dad, I'm sorry. I'm tired and scared, and some of my patients might not last the day." She paused, and then added, "And yes, I'll talk to anyone you want. The world should know what's happening there."

"And I'll talk to some friends I have in Korea. Where are you, exactly?"

She told him, using the phone's map, where she and their ragged convoy were and their planned route. "The South Korean army is somewhere ahead of us. We don't know about any Northern soldiers."

"I'll tell the ROK government where you are and that you need urgent medical assistance. At a minimum, I can make sure they know you're not an enemy unit. With a little luck, you will be met. And Kary, anything you can tell us about what happened in Pyongyang will be a huge help to everyone, not just in the US, but in Korea as well. There haven't been a lot of eyewitnesses." He sounded very grateful that she was one of them.

"Just tell anyone you can to send everything they can."

"All right, Kary, let me hang up and start making some phone calls. Stay safe, and can you please call me later today, to let me know how you are?"

"I promise, Dad, I'll call later today." Suddenly, she was reluctant to end the call. "Dad, I'm so sorry I haven't called before. If you're mad at me, I'll understand."

"I won't deny I've been worried, but all I am right now is very, very happy. Let me make these phone calls and get things moving. I love you, Kary."

"I love you too, Dad. I'll call you soon."

She sat quietly, crying again, and patted Cho's arm in thanks.

CHAPTER ELEVEN

EXODUS

26 August 2015, 1300 local time
Operation Backstop Headquarters, Munsan Refugee Camp
Outside Dongducheon, South Korea

They talked while they ate, her first decent meal in a day and a half, according to what he'd been told. Wearing a plain blouse and skirt, with her hair tied back, she looked tired, but spoke forcefully. "Cho Ho-jin should be released immediately. He has been detained without charges." If she was enjoying the food, she didn't say so.

"Miss Fowler, my deputy, Lieutenant Colonel Shin, says that Cho is on their intelligence watch list. Did you know he's the son of the DPRK general who led their army in the last war? Shin's recommendation was that Cho be turned over to their intelligence people until his status is resolved."

"Colonel Little, I can 'resolve his status' right now." She repeated the phrase as if it was as stupid as it was vague. "I know all about his father, who was shot for losing the war, by the way. Cho hated the Kim regime and worked as a spy for the Russians. Here." She rummaged in her bag and removed an electronic device, handing it to the colonel.

Kevin, more than a little surprised, and absorbing the new information, studied what looked like a top-quality satellite smartphone.

Kary explained, "Cho gave it to me just before we arrived. He knew he would be searched if he was arrested, and the phone would have been taken from him. We used it to find out about the South Korean army's advance, and to navigate our way here, and to call my father. According to Cho, it uses special encryption and is hard to track."

"Why would a Russian spy help you?" Kevin asked.

"He's not a spy anymore," Kary asserted. "He quit after the Russians sent him on a suicide mission into Pyongyang." The colonel did not look convinced, and she explained. "The Kim regime executed his father and seized his family's possessions. His mother died penniless while he was still a child, and he had to live on the street until the Russians recruited him. He doesn't love the Russians any more than the Kims, but they gave him the chance to strike back at the people who'd hurt his family. But Kim is gone now, so there's no reason for him to continue."

"Miss Fowler, people don't just 'quit'—"

"He saved a woman's life after she was severely wounded, by bringing her to my clinic. That's how we met. He was wounded himself."

"That's laudable, but the Russians —"

Adding another bargaining chip, she said, "He was the one who recognized the nerve gas attack, and told me the best way to treat the victims."

"The South Korean security —"

"He was the one who got us out of Sinan before we were caught up in the fighting, and he was the one who convinced me to call my father. And I know my father wants me to report what I know about the gas attack. What I know, I learned from Mr. Cho. He knows much more than I do, and

I doubt if he'll want to talk while under arrest." That was her final, and most valuable chip.

They'd eaten lunch in the colonel's "conference room," a tent with screened sides that provided shade and a little privacy, away from the busy headquarters tent. While staff cleared away their trays, Kevin used the time to consider her request.

Kevin had heard of Kary Fowler even before she'd arrived, from a message coming down through General Fascione's headquarters, but originating much higher up the chain. It warned of gas victims arriving in a three-truck convoy and their desperate need for medical attention.

They'd been spotted by ROK scouts north of Kaesong and given an MP escort straight to the Munsan camp. Everyone in the convoy who required treatment was hospitalized immediately.

That's where he had found Kary Fowler, in the hospital, a small but forceful woman in her mid-thirties, discussing her patients with the medical staff. She'd refused to speak with the colonel until she was satisfied with her patients' care, and then had immediately turned to Kevin and demanded her companion Cho's release.

She was an extraordinary woman. It wasn't the largest single group of refugees that had arrived, but it was large enough, with some seriously injured, and she hadn't lost anyone. And there were gas victims. And a spy. Or an ex-spy?

"Colonel, can you help me, or is there someone else I should be talking to? I'm grateful for lunch, but if they move Cho . . ."

Kevin realized he had been sitting silently for too long. "Miss Fowler, I'll take your request up the chain of command, but the best I think we can do is get him transferred to our custody, here in the camp. Is that satisfactory?"

She answered "Yes!" gratefully, almost joyously, and watched while he contacted Shin and gave the necessary orders. "I've already told Eighth Army intelligence about your arrival. Please make sure Mr. Cho is willing to share what he's seen in Pyongyang. We're interviewing anyone who's been near the capital, but I suspect his account will be especially valuable."

"Will they bring him here?" she asked.

"Yes. He can stay here at Munsan, but I'll need someone to monitor him on a frequent basis. I could place him in your custody, but that could make your return to the US complicated."

"What return? I'm not going anywhere. Those are my patients, and . . ."

"I think the doctors can properly supervise their care."

"These people won't trust the doctors. They won't even understand that they're getting proper care. They've never had it before."

That got Kevin's attention. The senior medical officer had briefed him on "cultural differences" between the staff and the refugees, and had already mentioned the same issue.

Fowler continued, "You wouldn't believe the state of public health in the North. One of the first things I had to do was organize classes in basic health practices and nutrition. None of them have been vaccinated—"

"Miss Fowler, would you like a job?" interrupted Little.

Surprised, she remained silent for half a moment, and gave the colonel a look that said that as far as she was concerned, the jury was still out. "What kind of a job?" she asked cautiously.

"My assistant. Ombudsman for the refugees. Health educator. I'll give you a dozen blank badges and you can make up a new title every day. I need help, Miss Fowler, if I want to do these people any good. You know what needs to be done, and you speak fluent Korean."

"I sound like a Northerner," she complained.

"All the better. The refugees will listen to you, and the Southerners will listen because you're helping their new countrymen. You can start by organizing those health classes you talked about. We've got six camps right—"

"Six!" she exclaimed.

"Yes, six, and all are badly overcrowded. Three new camps are being set up, and they should begin taking some of our overflow in a few days, as well as new arrivals."

Fowler sat back in her chair, looking like she'd been poleaxed. "You really do need help," she said.

"I'll take that as a 'yes.' I'll get you quarters with the female officers and some clean fatigues . . ."

"No." She said firmly. "No uniforms."

"No offense, Miss Fowler . . ."

"Please, call me Kary."

"Wouldn't you like a change of clothes?"

She smiled, imagining her bedraggled appearance, but insisted. "You're right, but no military clothing. I'll get some scrubs from the hospital."

"Whatever you want," Kevin replied cheerfully. "It's my custom to tour the camp at 1700. Would you like to accompany me?"

26 August 2015
Hwangju Air Base
North Korea

It had been a big operation. Hwangju Air Base housed a regiment of Russian-built MiG-21 Fishbed interceptors. The type first entered Soviet service in 1959, and had been out of the Russian inventory for almost thirty years, but they were still flying in the Korean People's Air Force.

Or had been, before the air base had been hit hard by the ROK Air Force. The antiaircraft defenses—outdated radars, guns, and missiles—had been ruthlessly flattened before a second wave of attackers used smart bombs on the concrete shelters and open revetments that housed the fighters themselves. The strikers had also destroyed the control tower, the maintenance hangars, the fuel system, and anything else to do with airfield operations.

Hwangju existed to protect another nearby installation, nestled against a low mountain some thirty kilometers to the northeast. Sangwon housed a brigade of the North Korean Strategic Rocket Forces, equipped with Rodong-1 ballistic missiles. They were capable of reaching any part of South Korea, and even parts of Japan.

The sounds of the explosions at the air base were still echoing when Surion helicopters, carrying a full company of SOF troopers, stormed the Sangwon base. Gunships covered them, and fighters orbiting high overhead covered the gunships.

Although the garrison, maintenance, and other parts of the brigade were housed in ordinary structures, the brigade's reason for existence, its six missile launchers, were sheltered in tunnels that had been driven into the rocky slope. Farther back, in caverns blasted inside the mountain, were the missile magazines, with possibly thirty or more missiles. Some of them might be fitted with nuclear warheads.

The missile base had been hit on the first day of the Southern advance, but only enough to collapse the doors that led to the tunnels, and of course destroy the garrison and its antiaircraft defenses. If the launchers couldn't leave the tunnels, they were not an immediate danger. And even if the missiles weren't protected by their rocky stronghold, the South couldn't risk destroying them until they were sure of what was in there. That's why Rhee's men were needed.

Only one ten-man team had landed by helicopter near the base, and had noisily attacked, still causing a fair amount of damage. Meanwhile, the platoon's three other teams landed some distance away before dawn and, approaching on foot, had come in from the other side, achieving total surprise.

Their targets were the entrances to several smaller tunnels used by the missile brigade's personnel to enter the tunnel complex. Once inside, the teams would have to fight their way down narrow rock tunnels against an unknown number of defenders, while doing as little damage as possible to the facility. And they had virtually no information on the layout of the chambers beyond the entrances.

In addition to the risks associated with armed defenders in tight spaces, any conventionally armed missiles would have seven-hundred-kilogram explosive warheads, and all the missiles were fueled with two corrosive chemicals: red fuming nitric acid and hydrazine. Since the missiles were not filled with fuel until just before launch, large quantities of those deadly chemicals had to be stored somewhere inside.

Every officer in the Ghost Brigade had begged to be given the assignment. General Kwon had personally forbidden Rhee from leading the attack. The colonel satisfied himself with riding in his command helicopter, coordinating with the air force units supporting the attack, while Captain Ji, one of his best company commanders, ran the actual assault. Rhee's other job was to keep General Kwon and the rest of the brass happy with situation reports. Captain Ji had other things to do.

Rhee's men quickly secured the parts of Sangwon that were outside the mountain. His helicopter landed, along with more machines carrying a reserve infantry company. They would gather prisoners and search the smoking ruins for anything of intelligence value. He could expect no word from Ji's force while they were deep inside the mountain. The rock blocked all radio communications from inside.

After fifteen minutes had passed with no word from inside the mountain, Rhee sent the rest of his SOF troopers inside as reinforcements, and prevented himself from worrying by supervising the eager but inexperienced reserve company commander.

After another ten minutes, a runner emerged and reported, "All secure, sir. Captain Ji reports no sign of special weapons."

Shaking his head, Rhee reported to Kwon, then ordered, "Take me to Captain Ji."

The personnel access into the mountain was two meters wide, with armored doors that were scarred where Ji's men had burned the locks away. Rhee followed the hurrying trooper down a pale green tunnel deep into the rock. Florescent fixtures provided enough illumination, but also highlighted a layer of haze near the ceiling.

It stung Rhee's eyes, and he could taste gun smoke and the acrid tang of flash-bang grenades. Ji's men had gone in with a triple load of flash-bangs, and tactics for clearing a confined area devoid of friendlies encouraged their use.

He could have traced Ji's progress by the trail he'd left. Scorch marks, bullet scars, and KPA corpses punctuated the tunnels, and they passed several doors and passages leading in other directions, labeled but still mysterious and still a little threatening. Master Sergeant Oh had returned to his own team, and Rhee missed having someone watching his back.

It took almost ten minutes to reach Ji, who was in a very wide, industrial-looking tunnel with tracks running along the center of the floor. Ji saluted when Rhee appeared. "All parts of the facility secured. Nine wounded, two seriously."

Nearly thirty percent wounded, Rhee thought. *A hard fight.* Rhee returned the salute, and responded, "But no WMDs?"

Captain Ji motioned to a sergeant. "Here's my specialist."

The sergeant came to attention. "Sergeant Sin Soo-ro, Colonel." He pointed behind him to a large door in the tunnel side. It was open, with rails from the main tunnel curving inside. "Our first count is thirteen missiles." He pointed to the opposite side of the tunnel and another open door. "The warheads are stored there, and we count nine. Their markings and configuration are consistent with conventional high explosives. No sign of chemical warheads or nuclear devices."

Rhee took the time to look into both storage areas. The missile magazine was a vast space, especially considering it had been painfully hollowed out at enormous cost. It could hold twice as many missiles as they'd found. Steel supports networked the walls and ceiling. A crane system overhead allowed the missiles to be moved. Even without their warheads, and without fuel, they still weighed several tons and were fourteen meters long.

The empty missiles could be placed on platforms and then moved on rails. They would be taken to the other space and joined to a warhead, then moved again to a launcher and fueled. To Rhee's immense relief, none of the missiles had been mated to a warhead, much less moved to a launcher.

But he could hear the disappointment in Captain Ji's report, and felt it himself. Outside again, he gave a more complete report to General Kwon. "We're still collecting documents, and intelligence can tell us if they ever were here, but I can confirm there are none here now."

"This was the last potential nuclear site in your zone of operations, Colonel. So far, Gangrim has found none. I don't know whether to be relieved or worried. Do you have any recommendations?"

"I'm going with the 'worried' option, General. They could all be in a single location, under tight control," Rhee suggested. "We just haven't found it yet. There are still more facilities north of Pyongyang, but it is assumed there will be considerably more resistance."

"That's possible, but it's also equally possible that weapons have been dispersed, so they can't be captured all at once." The general paused, and added, "We won't gain insight hashing over old arguments. At this point, intelligence becomes even more important. We have to become detectives as well as soldiers."

"Understood, sir."

"One other thing I can tell you about, now that Sangwon is secure. I've chosen a commander for the Bongmu garrison, Colonel Ham Seung-min. You won't know him. He's been recalled from retirement. He's in excellent health, and has command experience."

Rhee was both delighted and a little dismayed. He'd essentially been commanding two bases, with two very different missions. The operation at Bongmu was still going on, of course. It would take weeks for the investigators and forensic scientists to remove the bodies and attempt to identify them.

Lieutenant Gung and his team, except for the badly wounded Corporal Park, had asked to stay and help provide security for the site.

Rhee had agreed. They were out of the fight anyway, and the colonel understood why they wanted to remain. But they weren't going to do the job by themselves. A company of reserve infantry had arrived yesterday evening, and another was due to arrive soon.

Rhee had insisted that Gung remain in command, especially of reserve troops still shaking the rust off. But that situation was uncomfortable, especially in rank-conscious Korean society. Then they'd received new orders about the refugees: Don't ship them south anymore. Feed them and keep them there. A mission of that size was beyond even Gung's capabilities.

But Rhee couldn't suppress his misgivings. The general had made it a point to tell Rhee that Colonel Ham was in "excellent health." He asked, "Exactly how old is the colonel?"

"Sixty-seven," General Kwon answered." "He's not the only officer being recalled, either. If we want to take our country back, we will need everyone's help. And his last assignment was in the supply corps. The colonel will arrive at Bongmu by noon, along with another company of infantry."

"And a lot of rations," Rhee added. "Last night, they already had civilians gathering nearby. More will come."

"It's easier to ship the food up there than bring them south, feed them, and eventually send them back north. If you can spare enough time to be relieved, that will be his problem, not yours."

26 August 2015, 2130 local time
Operation Backstop Headquarters, Munsan Refugee Camp
Outside Dongducheon, South Korea

Cho Ho-jin found Kary back at her "office" in the headquarters tent. Although there were always people working, it was quieter after the dinner hour, and it gave her time to think and plan for the next day.

Kary's office consisted of a table with two folding chairs. A cardboard box under the table held a few items she worked with and several hard-copy printouts she still had to read more carefully. Her badge of authority, a cell phone with Kevin Little's number already loaded, lay on the corner of the desk. As sparse as her workspace was, it was prime real estate. Colonel Little's office was just a few feet away.

She sat with two pads of paper on her lap. One had a list of tasks that needed to be done right away, and the second listed things that had to be done before the first list could be dealt with. She was tired, overstimulated, and wrung out. It was a different kind of tired than her recent all-night drive south with Cho.

But she also felt happy, and relaxed in a way she hadn't felt since the coup in the North had begun. Barring stray missiles or rogue dinosaurs, she was physically safe, the people she was taking care of were safe, and she could work to make things better.

And her latest phone call with her father had gone very well. It was her third or fourth, and while she was telling him about the camp and her work, he was telling her about her cousin's wedding plans. It was several months off, and she might be able to attend.

She knew other people talked to their families like that all the time, but her anger at her father, turned sideways, had kept her away from the family member closest to her. Kary could be stubborn. She understood that part of her personality. She had Cho to thank for breaking the logjam.

The words on the paper swam, and she shook her head to clear it. At some point, she'd have to go back to the tent she shared with three other women and sleep, but her mind whirled with thoughts that needed to be captured before they flew away. Then she could rest.

Cho came into the tent. She waved and offered him the other chair. Sitting, he reported, "Cheon Ji-hyo just came out of surgery. I spoke with the doctors, and they said there was very little work left for them to do." His smile broadened. "Gam Sook-ja and the children said to thank Fowler-*seonsangnim* for saving their mother's life again."

Kary sniffed. "And of course, you had nothing to do with that."

Cho ignored her. "I helped Gam put the kids to bed, and came to find you."

"I wish I could have been in the surgery. Did they have to . . ."

Cho held out a hand. "I deliberately did not ask for details. The surgeon is looking forward to speaking with you tomorrow, and he will tell you everything, using words I would not understand. He was impressed. He thinks you are wasted as the camp's ombudsman."

Kary laughed and swept one arm around her. "And give up all this?" She added, "It's a shock, coming from one small clinic, but we can do so much to help these people."

"And I want to help. Which I won't be able to do if I have to take that civics class you're setting up."

"It's not all day, and they need it. You need it. The North Koreans have lived three generations surrounded by lies. Plus you can tell me how well it's working."

"So now I'm spying for you," he smiled. "I suppose I can do that."

She shook her head and gestured vigorously. "No, don't even joke like that."

He nodded. "My apologies. Force of habit." Then his expression became serious. "I do need to speak with you about something else, but not here."

Standing, Kary tossed the two writing pads on the desk, then reconsidered and retrieved them, along with the cell phone. "Lead on."

Outside, the area was lit by overhead lights that reminded her of the streetlights back home. They followed a bare earth path that served as Main Street for the Backstop headquarters area, walking from one pool of light to the next.

Beyond one row of tents, they could see the Munsan camp proper. Over twelve thousand people were crammed in an area meant originally for eight. Even some distance from the camp, the many voices blended into a constant hum that might fade at night, but never went away.

It had cooled, although the air remained humid, so it was only warm instead of sweltering. Other Backstop personnel sat outside or walked and chatted. The serenity of it was still novel to Kary, removing a weight she didn't know she'd been carrying.

Curiosity made her want to ask what he needed to talk about, but she trusted Cho to tell her when the time came.

The Munsan camp had been set up in what had been farmland, and the pair quickly came to the edge of what was bare earth and turned into cultivated crops. It was some sort of grain, but she couldn't tell what type in the dark. Clouds blocked the moon and much of the starlight, and in the rural darkness, she could barely see his face.

He continued to walk, leading her along a two-lane road for some time, until she could see that they were truly alone.

"Do you still have the pistol?"

Surprised, she answered "Yes" automatically. While Cho had of course been searched after his arrest, she and the other refugees and their belongings had not been searched. "It's in my footlocker in my quarters tent. It's locked, of course."

"Could I please have it?"

"What for?" It was a stupid question, and before Cho could answer, she quickly added, "Why do you need it? Do you think the Russians will try to kill you? Here?"

"No, not the Russians, or the South Korean NIS. This is not about espionage." He sighed, and explained, "Walking around, I've seen some things in the camp that . . . concern me."

He pointed back toward the camp. "All those people have been thrown together, and they are busy setting up a new society modeled after the only one they know. While you want to help, others want to prey on them. A lot of people left the North, all kinds, and some of them are undoubtedly criminals."

"But why do this?" she asked. "Tell the South Korean authorities what you saw. It might put you in a better light."

Cho disagreed. "*If* the authorities listen. And it's only hints and suspicions, but I believe there are some in Munsan who were used to living off the work of others. Many will see this as a chance to make a fresh start. Others will keep to their old ways."

Kary nodded, understanding. "This is a fresh start for you, isn't it? You've done what you wanted. Cheon and her family and the others from Sinan are safe. I don't know what ex-spies are supposed to do. Shouldn't you be getting plastic surgery or new fingerprints or something?"

Cho laughed at the idea. "I don't think that's what happens. I wish I knew. I don't know what the North will become, or what it's like to live in the South. Besides, I don't want to go anywhere. Here is where I'm needed the most."

"Hey, that's my line," she responded.

"You're a good teacher," he replied. "I'll stay and help you, as long as you'll have me."

Cho had said that with some feeling, and Kary thought about that as they turned around and headed back.

It took about fifteen minutes or so to reach the cluster of tents used by female personnel. It was roped off and clearly marked with signs in several different languages, all saying "No men after 2200!" Below that, somebody had written in marker "How about 2215?"

While Cho waited, she hurried to her tent. Two women, both army officers, were reading, while her fourth room-mate was absent. Squatting down and unlocking the foot-locker next to her bed, Kary rummaged under her few clothes and other possessions for the pistol. Wrapping it in a spare pair of scrub pants, she closed and locked the lid, then hurried out.

Even though she'd agreed to give him the weapon, she was still troubled. If someone was shot by Cho, that was her responsibility. Cho wasn't a violent person, but she knew he was capable of shooting someone if he had to. And should she even have a weapon, or allow Cho to have it? She was sure the army would discourage civilians from having them, but she also believed that if she'd asked the colonel for permission, he might have allowed her to keep it—reluctantly—but certainly not a North Korean civilian, who had been a spy for the Russians.

It wasn't a long trip back to where Cho was waiting, and her worries must have shown in her expression, because as she passed him the bundle, he asked, "Please, trust me."

"I do," she said, and her worries vanished.

CHAPTER TWELVE
SHOCK AND AWE

27 August 2015, 0530 local time
East Coast Fleet Flagship *Great Leader*
20 NM Northeast of Wonsan Airport, North Korea

Vice Admiral Gong Kyeong-pyo looked back at the dark silhouettes as his "armada" sailed in three long columns toward its objective. Never before had so many ships of the Korean People's Army Navy sailed together in such a massive formation. He felt immense pride as more shadows became visible against the slowly brightening sky. Twilight was in full bloom, the eastern sky glowing a deep crimson. Dawn would peek over the horizon in another half hour, and then their attack would begin.

The admiral considered it a small piece of good fortune that all his ships were still together after their three-hour transit in the dark. It was the only good news he'd had for some time. Four days earlier, South Korean forces had bombed the submarine bases at Mayang-do and Chaho. Fourteen of the East Coast Fleet's Type 033 Romeo-class submarines were either sunk or severely damaged, along with many of their infiltration midget submarines. The following day, the imperialist puppet's ground troops seized the naval base at Changjon. What had initially started out as an internal revolution had now become a three-way fight—only the third party had much more weight to throw around. Both the General Staff and KWP factions' strength had already been weakened, and would continue to do so with each passing day as the two sides engaged in vicious battles.

The fascists were taking advantage of the DPRK's internal crisis to pick the meat off their bones. That was why the General Staff committee had approved the amphibious assault at Wonsan. They had to quickly defeat the Korean Workers' Party forces there and then establish a strong defensive line against the approaching invaders. Given the last reported Southern rate of advance, the imperialists would reach Wonsan in only a few days.

The east coast's mountainous terrain was slowing the Southern forces a little, but intelligence reports put ROK Army scouts at the outskirts of Tongchon and Hoeyang. Senior naval officers had pushed hard for the amphibious assault, even though they acknowledged it was a risky plan. If the General Staff followed their own more conservative approach, they would find themselves squeezed between the KWP and the fascists. The committee chose the lesser of the two evils.

"Comrade Vice Admiral," announced Senior Captain Song Dong-shin as he walked on to the frigate's bridge wing. "We are approaching the turn point. Distance to turn is five kilometers. The only contact we hold is a surface surveillance radar on the southeast coast of Ryo-do."

Gong grunted. The radar on the large island outside the entrance to the harbor was expected. Reconnaissance Bureau sniper troops had watched as the radar, and its accompanying missile battery, were emplaced on the island—moved from one of the coast defense sites near Wonsan. It was the only seaborne defense that the KWP faction had; the patrol boats berthed at the Munchon naval base had all been scuttled by their crews.

"Very well, Song. Order the gunboats to proceed. Their orders are to support the sniper troops in neutralizing the missile battery. Then deploy the missile squadron to port, just in case the imperialists show up."

"At once, Comrade Vice Admiral!"

Gong raised his binoculars and surveyed his fleet again—almost fifty ships. It would be more accurate to call them "boats," as only a handful of the vessels displaced more than one hundred tons. Flashing lights began flickering astern. His orders were being sent out. Soon the Soju-class missile boats would peel off to port and screen the fleet from any enemy approaching from the south. At the same time, the two gunboats were to head straight for the missile battery.

Their small guns had little chance of silencing the battery, but they would provide the necessary diversion to allow the concealed sniper troops to attack and eliminate the radar, the missile launchers, and their crews. It was unfortunate that the two old veteran ships would likely be destroyed in the process, but their loss would not be in vain. A klaxon sounded behind him; the flagship was going to battle stations.

Special Patrol Craft 1001
West Side of Ryo-Do

The battered man leaned on the silent radar repeater for support. His body ached every time he moved. He stared out the bridge window, still wishing he had died with his crew. The captain also felt ashamed that he hadn't been able to carry out his orders to scuttle his ship. The newly modified missile patrol craft had been docked across the harbor, undergoing repairs to one of the diesel engines and other systems. He didn't receive the order directly. Their communication system was down, but he did notice the other patrol boats starting to settle at their berths, and the smoke rising from the boats stored on shore. Before he could pass the word, KWP troops had stormed aboard and started shooting. Every last member of his crew was executed and he was severely beaten, but left alive. They needed him.

"So what do you think of our strategy, Comrade Captain?" asked the political commissar. He wore the rank of major, but Captain Hak had no idea what his name was.

"I'm not your comrade, Major," Hak spat out defiantly.

"No, I suppose not," retorted the short, scrawny young man. His arrogant smile grated the captain. "But you haven't answered my question."

"Hiding behind an island is for lesser vessels," scoffed Hak. "This ship was built for speed and stealth. She was designed to dart in undetected, fire her missiles, and dart out. You waste her best attributes sitting here in the shallows behind a rock."

Special Patrol Craft 1001 was one of three surface effect ships in the North Korean navy, a high-speed patrol craft that rode on a cushion of air, reducing her drag in the water. Her hull was shaped to reduce her radar cross-section, but the added guns and other equipment on her deck largely negated any benefit.

"Perhaps, Captain. But even a cheetah stays low, hiding in the tall grass, pouncing only when its prey is within reach. We'll use your ship's speed, but only when our targets are in sight."

"And then you will die," Hak observed confidently.

The political commissar was losing patience with this fool. The only reason Hak was alive was so he could direct the special patrol craft with its four Kh-35, or SS-N-25, anti-ship missiles into position and fire them. After that, the major had no further use for him.

"Comrade Major!" interrupted a sergeant. "The missile battery command post reports two contacts approaching at high speed."

"See, Captain. Now it begins." That irritating smile again. "Please get us ready to attack."

Surface Action Group Alpha
Republic of Korea Ship *Choi Young*, DDG 981
40 NM Southeast of Wonsan Airport

Captain Park watched the large flat-panel display with amazement. If anyone had told him the Korean People's Navy could put forty-seven ships into a single formation, and sail under full EMCON, he would have dismissed them as an imbecile. But there it was, right before him. Three long columns of ships moving, more or less, in a straight line and not a single radar was emitting. "Astounding," he whispered quietly.

The video feed from the Super Lynx's FLIR sensor turret allowed Park to keep a close eye on the enemy fleet while keeping himself radar silent. The North Korean ships had just finished executing a turn to starboard. It wasn't pretty, but they all managed to stay in formation. There was no doubt now; they were heading for Wonsan. Judging by the infrared video, there were at least two dozen amphibious ships. The North Korean General Staff had apparently learned a thing or two from the US Navy; they were attempting to flank their opponent from the sea. Park found himself begrudgingly impressed.

"Captain, the four patrol craft that broke off from the main formation have been identified as Osa I–type missile boats. They're establishing a screen approximately five nautical miles off the formation's port side," reported the tactical action officer.

Park glanced at the main plot; the SAG still had plenty of distance before coming into radar range of this new screen, should they begin transmitting. "Very well, TAO. We'll remain on this course for a little longer. Have the other two ships gone to general quarters?"

"Yes, sir, all ships are at battle stations, with radars and weapons warmed up and in standby."

The captain grunted his acknowledgment.

Great Leader

"Comrade Vice Admiral, all ships have completed the turn," reported Song.

"Excellent, Senior Captain!" smiled Gong, pleased that everything seemed to be going as planned. "Have the bombardment squadron assume their position at the head of the formation. Stand by to execute the rocket barrage. Also alert the hovercraft and light landing craft to prepare to assault the beach."

"Yes, sir."

Within moments, the eight Chaho-class attack craft passed by the flagship to port and assumed a line-abreast formation ahead of the fleet. Each boat was armed with a BM-21 rocket launcher that would salvo forty 122mm rockets in a single burst. The concentrated barrage was to be launched just as the hovercraft reached the beach. The slower Nampo light landing craft would immediately follow, along with the six Chong-jin–class gunboats providing dedicated naval gunfire support. Three larger Hantae-class landing ships would bring up the rear, with half of the troops and the twelve main battle tanks.

The fifteen Kongbang hovercraft carried two battalions of Reconnaissance Bureau amphibious sniper troops, or North Korean special operations forces. The beach had a low grade and an unobstructed approach to the Wonsan airport. The hovercraft would be able to run right up to the closest buildings before discharging the sniper troops. Their first task would be to establish a beachhead for the slower light and medium landing craft that would follow. If all went well, over 2,100 troops and a dozen tanks would be dumped behind the KWP defensive positions. The amphibious troops would be in a perfect position to roll up the seaward flank, just as units from the First Corps conducted a general assault along the entire defensive perimeter on the landward side.

"Admiral! Missile alert!" shouted Song.

Gong burst through the bridge to the starboard wing and saw the four bright flashes in the early morning sky as the missiles were launched from Ryo-do. He hoped the two gunboats saw the flashes as well; otherwise they'd be dead in a little over two minutes. The admiral shook his head; there was nothing he could do to help them. He needed to concentrate on getting the troops ashore.

"Senior Captain, signal the fleet, all ahead flank! Energize radars!"

Special Patrol Craft 1001

Hak saw the bright glare from the missiles' booster rockets as they rose from the island. Shaking his head he mumbled,

"Idiots." They'd just wasted half of their firepower by launching an attack on what were undoubtedly decoy ships. The politically reliable KWP soldiers didn't seem to understand what was happening; at least he hoped that was the case.

"Ah, see Captain! My comrades have already begun the attack. It is time for us to move out," squealed the major. Hak almost laughed at the man's naïveté.

"Very well," acknowledged the captain. "Helmsman, ahead two-thirds, steer course one zero zero."

The young soldier looked down at the control panel, his eyes darting back and forth as he tried to find the throttle. Grumbling, Hak walked over, followed closely by the political commissar. Pointing to a lever, Hak said, "This. Move it up two notches."

As the ship began to move, the loudspeaker suddenly blared, "MULTIPLE RADAR EMISSIONS, BEARING IS TO THE LEFT, FIVE DEGREES."

"There are our targets, Captain, as expected," smirked the major.

Choi Young, DDG 981

"Captain! Missiles have been launched from Ryo-do. They are *not* heading in our direction! And we have numerous ESM hits on surface search radars, all coming from the DPRK fleet."

Park looked up and saw the four missile icons as they moved slowly from the island. They were Russian Styx variants, or perhaps KN-01 cruise missiles. Either way, they were slow, high fliers, easy targets. But most importantly, they weren't coming toward his ships. Still, someone had just launched missiles and the large formation had lit off all their sensors, and that changed everything. "Stand by to energize radars!"

Great Leader

As soon as the boosters cut out and fell away, Gong lost sight of the missiles in the darkness. Flashes from near the horizon meant the two gunboats were firing their guns and chaff launchers. Silently he urged them on. Thirty seconds later, two bright flashes suddenly bloomed. At least two missiles had hit, and flames could now be seen dancing along the darkened skyline. Turning back toward the island, Gong saw a glowing line of fire along the coast of Ryo-do. Raising his binoculars, he could see the launchers were burning furiously. An explosion or two later, and the command vehicle was engulfed as well. Satisfied, Gong watched as the hovercraft screamed by his frigate at forty-five knots.

Special Patrol Craft 1001

"Energize the surface search radar," ordered Hak. The KPW soldier looked at the major, awaiting confirmation of the order.

"Is that wise, Captain?" asked the commissar. His hand hovered near his holster.

"If you want to shoot missiles, then we don't have a choice," lied Hak.

"Very well. Energize the radar, Sergeant." The soldier looked around for the transmit button. Completely frustrated, Hak walked over and pushed the man out of the way, turned on the radar, and put his face on the viewing hood.

After a few sweeps he barked, "Firing bearing, green one zero, range thirteen kilometers."

"What kind of foolishness is this, Captain?" yelled the major as he pulled his pistol. "What do you mean by green?"

Hak rolled his eyes. The man was utterly clueless. He screamed, "Green! As in starboard! To your right!" The captain raised his right hand to emphasize his point. "The firing bearing is right one zero degrees, firing range is one three kilometers! Have your men enter that data in the fire control computer and quickly. You don't have much time before they figure out what is going on and shoot missiles at us!"

The political commissar hesitated, then nodded curtly to the phone talker, who passed the firing data to the missile control console. Moments later the soldier reported, "Missile firing data entered."

"Fire!" shouted Hak.

Great Leader

"Comrade Vice Admiral, we have a surface search radar close by, bearing green zero zero seven degrees" reported Song. The vice admiral marched over to the frigate's radar repeater and looked along that bearing. A faint blob showed briefly. He knew exactly what he was looking at.

"Urgent missile attack!" commanded Gong. "Firing bearing, green zero zero seven degrees, range one zero kilometers. Fire four missiles!"

The two North Korean combatants fired almost simultaneously, with four missiles leaping from each ship's launch tubes. The missiles climbed rapidly, jettisoned their boosters, and dropped just as quickly back down to low altitude, skimming the water's surface. It took only forty seconds for the missiles to cover the distance between the two ships.

Gong watched with fascination as the four missiles launched from the hostile patrol craft passed just in front of the Najin-class frigate's bow. The seekers soon activated, but not before they had passed—they never had a chance to see the target.

Special Patrol Craft 1001

Hak eyed the major as the commissar watched the missiles fly off toward the fleet. The KWP commissar waited impatiently for the expected glorious result, but there were no explosions. Enraged, the major turned and roared, "How could we possibly miss all of those ships? You intentionally sent them off in the wrong direction!"

The angry man lunged toward Hak and struck him across the face with his pistol grip. The captain was thrown to the floor, dazed.

"You shall die for your treason!" snarled the major.

The North Korean captain struggled to regain his senses from the blow. Once his vision came back into focus, he saw the crimson-hued face of the political commissar. Then Hak started laughing. It was the last thing the major heard.

Great Leader

Gong looked on with smug satisfaction. Two of the missiles had slammed into the surface effect ship, essentially disintegrating it. Looking through his binoculars, all that remained was a pool of burning fuel on the water, dotted with bits of floating debris. Now there would be nothing to stop him from putting the troops ashore.

Choi Young, **DDG 981**

"Missile alert! Active seekers bearing two nine zero. Missiles identified as SS-N-25s," shouted the ESM operator.

Park's head snapped back toward the master display; four bearing lines pointed in the direction of the incoming weapons. "How did . . ." The captain shook his head; there would be time to ask questions later, assuming they survived. For now, he had to act.

"Energize all radars! Weapons are released! Engage surface and air targets."

Great Leader

"Comrade Vice Admiral," Song cried. "Multiple hostile radars bearing red one six one!"

Gong raced to the port bridge wing and stared aft. On the horizon he could see one glowing flash after another. Missiles were being launched. "No!" he growled.

Spinning about he yelled at Song, "Order the missile squadron to engage! All ships, missile alert to port!" As Song began repeating the orders over the radio, Gong looked back to see the Soju missile boats already peeling away. He could only hope there weren't many ships in the imperialist's formation, otherwise they would all be dead.

The Soju missile boats began shooting their elderly Russian Styx missiles. One after another, each missile leapt from the launcher and arced skyward. There was nothing else to do but wait. It could be several minutes before the missiles would appear over the horizon.

Choi Young, DDG 981

"Missile alert! The Osa missile boats have launched," yelled the TAO. There was fear in the man's voice.

Park saw the sixteen new radar tracks, the icons showing the missiles' location as they sped toward his ships. They had somehow walked right into a trap. Park knew his SAG was in real trouble. Even though the Styx missiles were less capable, there were more of them and they were closer. "Engage Styx missiles with SM-2! Have *Yangmanchun* prepare to engage with Sea Sparrow! All ships stand by with countermeasures!"

The KDX-II destroyer's forward vertical launcher erupted in flames as SM-2 surface-to-air missiles thundered out of their launch cells and raced toward their targets. Moments later, two explosions marked the deaths of a Styx missile. More SM-2s were launched, but this time the intercept was a lot closer.

Park watched as his flagship downed six Styx missiles in rapid succession. Now, *Yangmanchun* began firing her shorter-ranged Sea Sparrows. Confident that the threat from the older antiship missiles was being dealt with, Park turned his attention back to the newer SS-N-25 Switchblade missiles that had been fired earlier, but from further away. His formation was in an optimum position to deal with the Styx attack, but not so well against the more modern threat. Specifically, the least capable ship, *Masan*, an *Ulsan*-class frigate, was the closest to the incoming attack. She had no missile defenses and most of her guns were manually aimed. They would be next to useless against a small sea-skimming target.

"Bridge, CIC, signal hard left rudder, new course two four five. All ahead flank. Execute immediately," barked Park over the intercom. By changing course to the left, he hoped to unmask his aft director in time to get a shot off. If not, he needed to bring his point defense gun to bear, just in case. It was going to be close.

As the three ships started their turn, the SS-N-25 missiles cleared the horizon, their seekers looking for a target. *Choi Young* fired another two SM-2s, but only her forward director had a clear line of sight. *Yangmanchun* was out of the fight, her directors blocked by the flagship, but the KDX-I destroyer began popping chaff to try and lure the missiles away from the formation.

One of the SM-2s faithfully guided in and destroyed an antiship missile—splash one. But by this time, one of them was now heading directly to *Choi Young*; the other two had locked onto *Masan*. Park ordered the RAM operator to fire two rolling airframe missiles at *Masan*'s assailants, then engage the one missile homing in on his ship. At a distance of half a mile, one of the RAM missiles locked onto the Switchblade's infrared signature, homed in, and exploded—splash two.

Masan was not so fortunate. The point defense missiles couldn't turn fast enough to catch the crossing targets as they flew by. The frigate's guns had opened up, and tracers were streaming from all along the hull. One of the SS-N-25s was hit and detonated a hundred meters from the ship, pelting the hull and superstructure with high-speed fragments—splash three. But it was the fourth missile that killed her. It hit the frigate right at the waterline, burrowed deep inside her, and detonated. The force of the blast ripped the hull apart and broke the ship's back. *Masan* was split in two. With both parts engulfed in fire, she slowly began to sink.

Great Leader

Gong knew the missiles were close when all four Soju missile boats suddenly exploded, bursting into flames. The fleet began firing all its guns in the general direction of the attacking wave, but there was little hope they'd do much good. Then explosions started dotting the port and center columns. The smaller gunboats simply disappeared after the massive blast, vaporized.

The 30mm Gatling guns on the frigate began roaring as they spewed projectiles toward the oncoming Harpoon missiles. One was hit and pitched into the sea, but another plowed into the hull amidships. The shock threw Gong to the deck. The lights flashed and then went out, as all electrical power was lost. The mortally wounded ship began leaning to port. The sound of fire raging below decks could be heard on the bridge. *Great Leader* was dying.

The admiral pulled himself up and struggled to the port bridge wing. Many of his ships were on fire, sinking; some were just gone, burning fuel marking their last known position. Then Gong saw the three Hantae-class landing ships. All had been hit. One had already capsized and another was being consumed by a firestorm. The South Korean onslaught of twenty-four Harpoons had ripped the heart out of his fleet.

27 August 2015, 1:00 p.m. local time
August 1st Building, Ministry of National Defense Compound
Beijing, People's Republic of China
The eleven members of the Central Military Commission sat in complete silence, awestruck by what they were hearing. An army senior colonel from the Second General Staff Department's Second Bureau was wrapping up the intelligence assessment on the North Korea situation. The news was all bad.

"Late this morning, elements of the ROK Third Army overran the General Staff faction's defenses at Sariwon," said the senior colonel as he pointed to the large map display. "Resistance was limited, as the South Koreans had an overwhelming advantage in numbers and airpower. As of noon today, South Korean forces had penetrated over one hundred kilometers into DPRK territory in the west, and nearly seventy kilometers along the eastern coast. At their current rate of advance, both Pyongyang and Wonsan will fall in the next two to three days."

President Wen sat quietly while the other members debated amongst themselves. This was the CMC's sixth meeting in the last four days, and there was a growing consensus that China had to do something—but exactly what still eluded them.

"Senior Colonel," injected the PLAN commander. "You say Wonsan could be taken by the South Koreans rather quickly. What about that General Staff amphibious attack force you told us about yesterday? Were they successful in landing and flanking the KWP positions?"

The senior army officer took a deep breath. What he was about to say wouldn't go over well. "Admiral, the intelligence information is only a few hours old, and there is still considerable analysis to be done, but the initial estimate is that the General Staff faction landed only about half of their troops. The rest were lost when a ROK Navy missile strike inflicted severe casualties on the attack force.

"Of the four dozen ships and small craft in the fleet, approximately one-third was sunk outright. Some of the larger ships suffered heavy damage, and may have sunk as well. And while the DPRK special forces were landed and inflicted considerable casualties on the KWP units, neither the General Staff nor the KWP has a strong hold on Wonsan. Neither will be able to stop the ROK First Army from taking the port. As for the East Coast Fleet, it has sustained excessive losses and has ceased to be a viable force."

"What about the North Korean air force?" demanded the PLAAF's top general.

"The ROK Air Force has near complete command of the skies," answered the senior colonel. "Any DPRK aircraft that manages to get airborne is soon intercepted and shot down. The South Koreans appear to have an extremely good knowledge of the airspace. A Y-8 electronic intelligence aircraft that we sent to collect tactical radio traffic off of Pyongyang was intercepted by six ROK F-16s and escorted to the border. The intercept was very professional. The lead pilot even asked our aircraft to leave politely, in passable Mandarin."

"They're acting like it's their airspace!" complained the air force commander.

"And the Americans must be helping them. Their E-3 aircraft are orbiting just across the DMZ," added the minister of national defense. The debate was going nowhere. Wen had had enough.

"Yes, Comrades," he interrupted. "The Americans are providing support to the ROK forces, support that is in full compliance with their defense pact. Have you even bothered to notice that every single last American unit is south of the DMZ?"

"But, Comrade Chairman, the Americans have been bringing in a steady stream of reinforcements for the last four days. They are merely buying time," protested the commander of the Rocket Forces, China's missile force.

"And what are they doing with those reinforcements, General Zhao?" demanded Wen. His irritation was growing. "The Americans have taken over managing the humanitarian crisis for the ROK government! So not only are they abiding meticulously to their defensive agreement, but they are also providing an incredibly useful service to the Korean people. If you don't realize the incredibly awkward position this puts us in, then you need to wake up!"

"Comrade Chairman, it has always been our policy that we wouldn't accept a unified Korea allied with the United States on our border," said General Fang, one of the CMC's two vice chairmen.

"Yes, General, that policy has served us well while there *was* a North Korea. It was designed to prevent the South Koreans and the Americans from attacking an allied, sovereign state." Wen stood up, looking intently at the general officers seated around the table. "But that state has collapsed, by its peoples' own actions, so where does that leave us?

"Many of you have recommended we invade North Korea to stabilize the country. But which faction do we align with to justify our entry into this civil war? Or is it your intention to merely annex the territory? Wouldn't this defeat the purpose of our policy? We'd be sharing a border with an extremely hostile South Korea that would be even more closely aligned with the United States, as well as every other Asian nation. And then there is the inevitable and dangerous outcome to us becoming involved: once our forces head south, the Americans will come north.

"My point is simply this, comrades. Do we really intend to risk a war with the United States over that dung heap that was North Korea? At the very least we put our economic future at considerable peril; at worse, we put the very existence of China as we know it on the chopping block."

Wen saw a number of the senior officers at the table nodding their agreement. The minister of national defense saw it as well. Sighing, he asked, "What is your intention, Comrade Chairman?"

"We will send our army in, but under the guise of humanitarian assistance. We'll set up refugee camps, bring in food and medical supplies and personnel, but the camps will be on Korean territory. To establish a proper defensive perimeter, we'll advance fifty kilometers across the border. We may have to move further to ensure a safe operating environment for aid workers, but we'll limit our advance for now.

"I expect the Americans will surge northward the moment they realize we've crossed the Yalu. We must exercise due caution to not provoke them, or the South Koreans if possible."

"What about the North Koreans?" inquired Defense Minister Yu.

A cynical smile popped on the president's face. "We retain the right of self-defense, Comrade Minister. If they fire on us, we will eliminate the threat."

"I understand your wisdom now. Thank you, Comrade Chairman," said the relieved general.

"One last thing," added Wen. "Any territory we take will be used as a bargaining chip when this unpleasant crisis is over. We *will* be part of the discussion about what transpires on the Korean Peninsula."

27 August 2015
Munsan Refugee Camp
Outside Dongducheon, South Korea

It was easy to stay concealed. The grassy path was filled with "tent-to-tent" people. Cho had no problem keeping his target in sight, while at the same time blending in with the throng of humanity that had filled the refugee camp. Besides, he was confident he knew where the individual was going.

When Cho first saw him two days earlier, an itch started between his shoulder blades. Nothing seemed right about the way the middle-aged man walked and talked, and he seemed very well supplied with American bills. Then yesterday, Cho had watched as the man bullied a young Korean girl. A passing military police patrol caused him to release her and disappear behind the tents. Cho discretely followed the young woman and listened in to her complaints to her father and mother. As he suspected, the man was "recruiting" for a prostitution ring. Then he heard the name: Jeon Yong-ha.

Finding where Jeon spent his time was elementary tradecraft for a seasoned spy. Now that Cho had verified the information he'd obtained was accurate, he spent the rest of the afternoon reconnoitering the area. Looking for avenues of escape, personal guards, and possible traps. By the time Cho finished, he was almost late for dinner with Fowler-*nim*. He found being around her refreshing; her concern for others was so unlike everything he'd experienced in his life. Being around her gave him purpose and hope. He'd discovered that he would do anything to make her happy.

It was well past ten at night when a darkly dressed and masked Cho crept back to Jeon's tent. As he expected, there was only a single guard outside. The man was an amateur, a simple-minded thug. A small group of young women walked past the tent, catching the guard's eye; he stared at them with desire. The man stared a little too long; he never knew what hit him.

Cho pulled the unconscious body into the tent and bound his hands and feet with duct tape. A strip wrapped around his head a couple of times and covering his mouth would keep him quiet. Cho then adjusted the bandana covering his face and took the guard's position out front, intentionally staying in the dark shadows. Half an hour later Jeon came swaggering back with another guard and a young woman in tow. She didn't look very happy, probably because Jeon was being rather rough. He didn't even bother greeting his "guard," and signaled for the other man to hold open the flap while Jeon threw the young woman inside.

"Now, bitch, we'll see if you're any good. And if you so much as squeak, the first person to die will be your mother!" he growled menacingly.

Suddenly there was a loud thud behind him as the guard who came back with Jeon fell face-first to the floor. "You fool! What kind of imbecile are you? Now get up—"

The sharp *clack* of a round being racked into a gun's chamber interrupted Jeon's tirade. He turned slowly to see a disguised Cho leveling a pistol squarely between his eyes. "Now, Jeon Yong-ha, I suggest you sit down, quietly. If you so much as squeak, well, I don't think I need to tell you who will be the first person to die, do I?"

The stunned Jeon staggered back to a camp chair and sat down. His eyes were wide as saucers. Cho threw the roll of duct tape to the woman. "Bind his hands and legs to the chair. Make sure he is secured firmly, his right hand first."

Confused, the woman took the tape and began wrapping Jeon's wrists and forearms. She used a lot of tape. Jeon slowly shifted his eyes toward the woman, but Cho immediately snapped his fingers to regain his undivided attention. "I wouldn't recommend doing something so foolish, Jeon Yong-ha. I wouldn't miss at this range." Cho emphasized his point by assuming a marksman's stance. Jeon swallowed hard. The unknown intruder had foreseen his move.

It wasn't long before the woman stood and said, "I'm finished." Then more fearfully, "What will you do to me?"

"Excellent," said Cho as he quickly inspected her work. Jeon was completely immobilized. Reaching for the tape, Cho finally answered her question as he put a strip over

Jeon's mouth. "I won't do anything to you, miss." Cho used the proper Korean word for a younger woman, but spoke with a Southerner's accent. No need to make it easy for Jeon, in case he tried to identify Cho later. "But I would greatly appreciate it if you would go and find an American military police patrol and bring them here. I'm sure they would be most interested in Jeon's activities."

The woman's expression was one of surprise. Cho's answer was completely unexpected. She carefully made her way to the exit, but before departing whispered, "Thank you, sir." Cho nodded slightly, acknowledging her gratitude. As soon as the woman disappeared, Cho bound and gagged the other unconscious guard with duct tape and then went over to Jeon's locked footlocker. He shook his head with disapproval. The padlock was a joke. He had it open in seconds. Cho dumped the contents onto the cot. There were several weapons, a couple of ledger books, and lots of American money.

"You really should be more careful with your important business documents, " Cho teased as he looked through one of the ledger books. It contained a lists of his prostitutes and patrons, as well as transactions with several drug dealers. "Yes, the Americans will be most interested in all this." Jeon grunted in frustration as Cho looked on with distain.

The young woman soon returned leading a squad of MPs. Cho observed them from a distance as the Americans went in and discovered all the gifts he had left out. He was particularly pleased when he heard the sharp yelp from Jeon as an MP peeled the tape off his mouth. Moments later the Americans escorted the ringleader and his two guards away. Cho doubted he'd be seeing Jeon Yong-ha any time in the near future.

It was nearly midnight when Cho returned to Kary's office. She was still there, typing away on her laptop, trying to figure out how to order medical supplies with the US Army logistics system. Her frustrated muttering told him the system was still winning—for the moment.

Quietly he entered and placed the pistol on the desk. His stealthy approach startled her. "Oh! You're back!"

"Of course, mission accomplished. Here's your pistol."

Kary eyed first the handgun, then Cho. "You . . . you didn't shoot anyone, did you?"

"Absolutely not! I know you'd frown on such a thing," replied Cho with feigned injury. "I merely used the weapon as my culminating argument in a moral debate. That's all." He took the pistol and wrapped it in a scarf she'd brought, and tucked it out of sight.

"Uh-huh," she responded. The skeptical look on her face showed she wasn't buying his explanation.

"I can assure you, Fowler-*seonsaengnim*, no one was physically injured in tonight's activities. Although, several egos were completely crushed," remarked Cho with a broad grin. Teasing Kary was a newly acquired pleasure for him; he found that he liked the way her nose wrinkled when she was slightly annoyed.

Kary frowned and raised her finger preparing to deliver a reprimand, when she was interrupted by a large yawn. She hadn't realized just how tired she was.

Cho looked on with concern. "Shouldn't you be asleep? You've been struggling with this program since before I left, and you've already had several very late nights this week. You need to rest."

"And you're trying to change the subject," Kary protested, but her thin smile betrayed her appreciation. "But whoever came up with this program is a sadist!"

"I believe that is a mandatory trait for all computer programmers, everywhere," declared Cho while stretching. "Anyway, I'm going to bed, and I hope you will too . . . soon."

"I won't be long. And thank you, Ho-jin *oppa*."

Cho bowed slightly, gratified by Kary's use of the term of endearment, *oppa*. It could be translated as "big brother." She trusted him, and that simple acknowledgment warmed his heart.

27 August 2015
White House Situation Room
Washington, DC

General Fascione struggled not to yawn while he briefed the president. It wasn't that the information he was providing was inconsequential or boring; it was just that the last several days had been very long, and he was running out of gas. "And even though the ROK Army is starting to face more organized resistance from KPA units, they still anticipate securing Pyongyang within the next three days—five at the most."

"What about China, General? Is there any indication from your end that the PRC intends to intervene?" President James Wyman was a worried man. The sudden collapse of the Kim regime had caught America unprepared, and the reduced US military presence wouldn't be able to do much about a full-blown Chinese invasion.

"So far, Mr. President, they are staying massed on the border. They've sent in a reconnaissance flight or two, and I wouldn't be surprised if some of their SOF people are in North Korea, but they've largely stuck to their side of the Yalu. The CMC is probably still trying to figure out what the best course of action is. This crisis took them by surprise as well, perhaps more so, since they had senior contacts in country."

Wyman nodded. "I've spoken with President Wen, General, and he didn't sound like a happy man. He was uncomfortable with our movement of troops and aircraft to the Republic of Korea. I reassured him that our reinforcements have been tailored toward helping South Koreans manage the huge inflow of refugees. I suspect the success of the ROK Army is not sitting well in Beijing."

"Understandable. We'd be just as uneasy if there were a civil war in Mexico and a foreign country was sending in military forces. I know it's not a great analogy, but it does capture how the Chinese feel about this. Do you have any other questions, Mr. President?"

"Just one, General. You mentioned the ROK Army has started an Operation Gang . . . Gang . . ." Wyman started thumbing through his notes

"Gangrim, sir. It's a contingency plan by their special operations forces to locate and seize as much of the North Korean WMD stockpile as they can. So far they've done pretty well with the forward chemical weapons storage bunkers. The North had a lot of gas hanging around, not that this is a surprise."

"I'm more concerned with Kim's nuclear weapons, General."

"Yes, Mr. President, I thought you would be." Fascione smiled politely. He could understand the president's higher priority about the nukes; chemical weapons would only affect those on the Korean Peninsula. "From what little I've heard, the ROK commandos haven't found anything yet."

"I see," stated Wyman. His expression showed his displeasure. "General, I'm not very happy with this arrangement.

I'd like to have a US observer as part of this Operation Gangrim."

Fascione took a deep breath. He'd have to word his answer carefully. A US general just didn't say no to his commander in chief lightly. "That may be difficult to arrange, Mr. President."

"I understand it's a sensitive topic, General. Give the South Koreans as much latitude as you can in approving our observer. Suggest someone they know and trust, and then do some light arm-twisting. It's in both our best interests to find those nuclear weapons, and we can lend more 'quiet' assistance if we have someone on the ground, as it were."

The general nodded. "I understand, sir. I'll do my best to get someone directly involved." Suddenly, the general's face changed from uneasiness to confidence. "And I think I know just the soldier for the job."

28 August 2015, 12:30 a.m. local time
Munsan Refugee Camp
Outside Dongducheon, South Korea
Kary laid dozing on her desk. Her stamina had all but vanished. She was abruptly jarred to consciousness when Cho's cell phone started buzzing in her back pocket. Initially she thought it was her father, given the time difference, but a quick look at the number showed it was her friend Anita. "Hello," Kary answered.

"Kary . . . Kary, it's me, Anita." Kary heard the excitement and fear in her friend's voice. She was now fully awake.

"Anita, what's wrong?"

"Kary, there are Chinese soldiers everywhere. They started coming through our camp a few minutes ago. There are hundreds of them, Kary, on the Korean side of the border."

"What?" exclaimed Kary. "Anita, are you sure?"

"Absolutely, Kary. There are tanks, trucks, and other vehicles pouring through our camp right —"

"Anita? Anita?" Kary shouted. She looked at the phone's screen. "Signal Lost" it said. The connection had been broken.

Chapter Thirteen

Precipice

28 August 2015, 7:05 a.m. EDT
Democratic People's Republic of Korea UN Mission
New York, New York

The United States had never had diplomatic relations with North Korea, but the country did have a seat at the United Nations. The diplomatic mission that supported the DPRK representative to the United Nations was located in Manhattan, on East Forty-Fourth Street, near the East River. In the past, it had sometimes served as an informal, unofficial link between the two countries.

There was no sign marking the location of the DPRK mission, just a steel door at street level in a pale brick office building. Credit unions, restaurants, hotels, and other diplomatic missions crowded against it and each other in the commercial district.

Lieutenant Joe Vitale led the Emergency Service Unit for Lower Manhattan, and he hoped adrenaline could substitute for sleep, at least for another fifteen minutes. It had been a busy night. Federal agencies had piled onto his operation like he was giving away toasters—State, FBI, Homeland Security, even the CIA. The New York City Police Department was used to interagency operations, but it all took time. If he'd had his choice, they would have done this last night.

It had to happen quickly. He was in the lead van, with two more behind. As his convoy turned onto East Forty-Third, units blocked the incoming lanes off First and Second Avenues. Another unit was already covering the building's parking garage.

A few startled pedestrians watched his assault team boil out of the van, but uniforms coming out of the second vehicle shooed them down the street, toward the corners, and made sure nobody else entered the area.

His team wired a charge to the door in moments, then waited impatiently for the "all clear" from the uniformed officers. Joe took that moment to check the big picture. His people were properly set, the investigators were standing by in the third van—well, okay, they were trying to watch, leaning out the side windows, but they were far enough back.

His headset radio buzzed with static for a moment, and the sergeant reported. "Clear, Joe."

Vitale gave the command and plastic explosive along the hinge edge of the door detonated, sending the door clattering inside. It was made of steel, and they didn't have time for half measures. The lieutenant was second in line, maybe twenty feet from the door, and even with the lead man holding a ballistic blanket, Vitale could feel the pressure wave ripple over him. The noise and blast reminded him of a flash-bang, but they were well back and tight against the wall.

They went in at a run, down a short corridor to a second steel door, just as stout as the first, and locked. They'd been expecting this, and Vitale called, "Breacher up!" then stepped back to let the man work. In fact, he kept right on backing up as the demo expert prepared the charge.

Passing the word on his headset, he stepped outside, but stopped just past the entrance. The corridor would channel the blast. He'd be safe around the corner.

His demo expert was by definition the last man out of the corridor, but Joe still took one last look down the hall before pulling his head back and signaling again. This time the blast was not as bad, although hearing protection could only do so much.

The second door led into a large office complex. Joe found himself standing in a reception area, facing an empty desk. The walls were decorated with the North Korean flag, and photos of the three Kims were mixed with colorful shots of laughing children in traditional Korean clothing. The room was filled with a light gray haze that stung his eyes. There was nobody in sight.

His assault team was already pouring through the door. They knew the basic layout of the mission, based on the builder's records, and Vitale stepped back and tried to be the big picture guy while the other six team members broke left and right.

Less than a minute later, he heard "Got one. Bringing him out" over the headset radio. Two team members emerged from the left-hand corridor almost dragging a handcuffed Korean, in his mid-fifties. Vitale didn't even have to use the photo guide they'd assembled.

"Ambassador Soon Yeo-rim, I presume?"

Soon had not come willingly, and his rumpled appearance was not improved by his expression. Bright red with outrage, he shouted, "This is a diplomatic mission. The UN—"

Vitale tried to suppress a broad smile, almost succeeding. "The UN voted yesterday to disestablish the North Korean seat in the assembly. I'm sorry if you didn't know, but according to the UN Secretariat, you haven't been answering your phones for several days."

The ambassador hardly listened. "You have no right to arrest me! I have diplomatic immunity!"

"You're not under arrest, Ambassador. Since the US has no diplomatic relations with your country, and the reason for your presence no longer exists, you and your staff have been declared persona non grata. You're in protective custody until we can return you all to North Korea, if there's any of it left."

His headset earpiece crackled. "Lieutenant, we've got some more. Two people, shredding documents."

"Have them join us," Vitale ordered cheerfully, then continued addressing Soon. "We also received word from a credible source that there might be illegal materials here, possibly including drugs or counterfeit currency. I have a warrant that allows us to search this establishment for evidence, including documents regarding such activity. There's also the matter of over one hundred twenty thousand dollars in unpaid parking tickets."

Two more Koreans appeared, a man and woman in their late thirties. Using the photo guide they'd prepared, Vitale identified them as one of the cultural attachés and his wife. Although handcuffed, they walked in under their own power, in time to hear the last part of Vitale's speech. Their expressions shifted from worried to terrified, especially when they saw how furious Ambassador Soon was.

"Please, we wish to defect!" the woman said. Her husband, looking downcast, simply nodded agreement.

Soon looked like he wanted to say something to them, but by now had gained control of his anger. He was still furious, but remained silent.

29 August 2015, 1000 local time
Taedongmun Park
Pyongyang, North Korea

General Tae Seok-won watched through binoculars from a spot near the edge of the park. Two people had shown up. Jeup Do-bin was thin, even for a North Korean, and his lined face made him looked over sixty, although he was probably younger. His hair was only lightly threaded with silver. Jeup had been a deputy intelligence minister under the Kim regime, but had joined the party faction early on. Tae knew he'd become one of their most effective military commanders.

The other party faction representative was a woman, Lee Su-mi. General Tae knew of her. She headed the Pyongyang "Workers' Union," which had little overt power as a labor union, but massive influence throughout the party bureaucracy. She was younger than Jeup, perhaps forty, and had a broad, almost square face. It didn't look like she smiled a lot.

The fact that Tae faced two people instead of one meant that the party faction was divided, unable to agree on a single leader or a single policy. It would make his task twice as hard.

General Tae had waited in his vehicle, a conspicuously unarmed and open-topped GAZ jeep, until the party representatives had entered the plaza. There had been no agreement on how they would arrive, or who would come. Or even that they would arrive unarmed. Tae wore his sidearm. The others, although in civilian clothes, had plenty of places they could conceal a pistol. Lee Su-mi wore a *hanbok*, the high-waisted flowing traditional Korean dress that Kim had decreed women should wear, and she could hide a grenade launcher under that.

Lee walked a little in front, so she must be the nominal leader, but either Jeup wouldn't acknowledge her lead, or the faction didn't trust her negotiating skills. Tae could accept that. Trust was in especially short supply these days.

When the two were about the same distance from the pavilion as the spot where Tae's jeep was parked, he stepped out and motioned to his aide. The vehicle roared off, and Tae went to meet them, reaching the first steps almost the same instant they did.

Taedongmun Park lay on the north and west side of the Taedong River. Technically, it was party faction territory, and Tae had chosen the area for the meeting based partly on that point. He wanted the meeting, and was willing to come to them.

He'd chosen a pavilion near the water, originally meant to shade dignitaries during public events, including water displays. Without any walls or interior structures, it was completely open. He was sure there would be observers from the party faction watching for any sign of treachery, just like the men he had on his side of the river.

The pavilion had sustained some damage. The colorful tile floor was littered with rubble, and he'd noticed scorch marks on the steps. But while there might be a few holes in the roof, the structure was sound.

The general stepped gratefully into the shade and walked toward the center, stopping a few meters away from the other two. "Thank you for meeting with me," Tae began in a polite tone.

"Get on with it," Lee said harshly. "You asked for a cease-fire. You asked for us to meet here with only an hour's notice. What is so urgent?"

Tae refused to be irritated. "Do you have somewhere else you need to be, Lee-*dongmu?*" Tae used one of the words that translated as "comrade." Under the Kims' rule, they had replaced most of the other terms and honorifics Koreans traditionally had used. This particular word implied equal or lower social standing.

"Stop wasting my time!" Lee insisted. She looked at the opposite riverbank, as if she was checking for snipers. They were there, of course, but she'd never spot them.

"Don't worry. The cease-fire will last for at least another hour," Tae replied, "and hopefully longer than that. The Chinese have crossed the border in strength."

"My grandmother knows that," Lee replied coldly, "and she's been dead for twenty years. Did you know the Southerners have crossed the border?"

Tae bit back his immediate reply, and forced himself to ignore the insult. *Stay on topic.* "Then why are we fighting each other? Foreign forces have invaded our country, and we are making their job easier."

Lee looked as if the last thing she wanted to do was to join forces, but Jeup Do-bin spoke for the first time, asking, "What do you propose?" Lee shot her colleague a sharp look, but remained silent.

"Complete integration of both forces. Existing commanders retain in place up through battalion level. Brigade and higher commands distributed equally to both sides. I command, with one of your people as my deputy. One of your people can also have command of the unified artillery. We ration the supply—"

"And you have support of the rest of the General Staff?" Lee interrupted.

"I am the senior officer of what remains of the General Staff."

"Your ranks have thinned somewhat," Jeup remarked.

"But we are still more numerous than you."

"We occupy most of the Kim faction's territory now."

"After we destroyed their leadership with our rocket attack," Tae responded. He didn't need to mention that the rockets had been armed with nerve gas. It was a gentle reminder that he'd done it once. He'd let them wonder if he could do it again.

Lee scowled and asked, "Why should you have command of the combined forces?"

Tae smiled, and almost laughed. "Because I'm a professional soldier. Because you allowed survivors of the Kim leadership to escape to the north while your troops were looting their headquarters." He saw their surprised expressions and nodded. "We have many sources of information."

"You think you would do a better job?"

"I already am," Tae replied forcefully. "I'm looking at the overall situation, and I understand that if we immediately join our forces and reorient our defenses, we *may* be able to hold off the South Koreans, come to terms with them, and then present the Chinese with a unified force. Hopefully, the Chinese army will then withdraw without a fight."

"Work *with* the Southerners?" Jeup asked, astounded. "That's completely unacceptable."

Lee Su-mi vigorously nodded her complete agreement. "It's treason!"

"Against who?" The general looked at them, suddenly unsure of their grip on reality. He took a few steps, pacing back and forth, and finally turned back to face them. "What would you do?"

Lee looked over to her negotiating partner, and Juep explained. "Our military staff has discussed the problem, and we are not opposed to a nonaggression pact with the

General Staff. We then meet the Chinese threat to the north, while you hold off the southern invasion. We turn the city into a fortress, and make them pay for every meter with a hundred enemy soldiers. Faced with unacceptable casualties, the invaders will come to terms."

"That isn't a plan," Tae retorted. "It's wishful thinking. And to what end? Do you think the Southerners will let us restore our country? The Kim dynasty is shattered. The entire mechanism of government has been torn apart, and can never be restored.

"And with which of us will they negotiate?" Tae continued, his tone sharper. "The Southerners will be here first. I'll be fighting long before you will. They will wear me down until my troops simply can't fight back. Do you expect us to fight while you sit and watch?"

Lee asked, "What price would you sell our country for, to gain the South's cooperation against the Chinese?" Her expression indicated that she thought just discussing the idea was treason.

"What terms would I ask for from the Southerners?" Tae asked as if considering it for the first time. "We place ourselves under their military authority. They supply us with munitions, food, and fuel. They provide air cover during our operations against the Chinese." He shrugged. "Some of their artillery wouldn't hurt. We agree to set up a caretaker government under martial law in that part of the country we still control. With a nonaggression pact, of course."

"Martial law?" Lee spat angrily. "You mean a military junta with you in charge. You'd be nothing more than a puppet for the South, just as the South is a tool of the Americans."

Tae felt as if he was dealing with a two-year-old. "That is what's *possible*, whatever labels you want to use." Almost pleading, he argued, "Face reality. Now that China has intervened, the Americans will join the Southerners, intent on first wiping us out, then pushing back the Chinese. The entire country will become a battlefield, and we will just be part of the rubble.

"A negotiated settlement with the South gives us at least some control over our fate. We have a little time before the two sides meet and engulf us. Let's join forces and get the best deal we can, while we still can."

Jeup looked to Lee, and Tae could see her calculating, weighing risks and payoffs, but only for half a moment. Remarking almost casually, "This is pointless," she turned and walked back the way she'd come. After she'd taken a few steps, Jeup followed, with one last glance at the general.

Sighing, Tae stood, watching the two leave, wondering what words would have changed her mind, or if it was even possible. Now he had to . . .

The two had reached the edge of the pavilion, and Lee made a quick cutting gesture with her right hand, at waist level. Tae threw himself sideways, toward a pillar, but most importantly leaving the space he'd previously occupied. He saw a heavy-caliber bullet strike the floor where he had been standing, and heard a deep *crack* from a second round passing much too close to his head.

Tae dodged again, this time running full tilt, heading out, changing direction every five steps or so. There were at least two shooters, and . . .

Something struck his back, just below the left shoulder blade, hard. The vest absorbed most of it, but the pain of the blow warned he was moving too slowly. The general had reached the edge of the steps that led out of the pavilion. Out there, without the partial cover of the pillars, he'd be an easy target. They might be able to get a head shot.

At the edge of the steps, at a dead run, Tae launched himself into the air, hoping the only direction the snipers weren't expecting him to go was up. Below and ahead, the ground sloped down to the water, and as he came down, he tucked in, like his parachute instructor had taught him so long ago.

He landed with a roll. Timing it almost correctly, he stumbled a little as he stood, but kept moving toward the river. He saw another bullet strike the ground nearby, as if he needed any more incentive. Then he heard a different sound, almost a howl, from above him.

Stretched full length, Tae hit the water. The weight of the vest seemed to triple and pulled him down, but he wanted to get away from the surface. The bottom sloped gently, and he turned sharply right to parallel the river's bank.

He'd barely had time to inhale before going under, and had begun to push up, intending to take a breath, when the water above him turned to froth and rapid-fire booms echoed in his ears. The water carried dozens of concussions to him, although thankfully with reduced intensity.

Tae stayed down until death above the surface was a better choice than drowning. He was in water shallow enough to kneel, and he brought his head out. With his helmet still on, he hoped he looked like a turtle. He gratefully gulped air and looked around.

The last salvoes had evidently landed, because although the air still echoed with explosions, there was no sound of incoming shells. Bitter, choking smoke filled his nose and mouth. It was impossible to see anything from his position, but that was understandable.

He'd had every piece of artillery in his force zeroed in on that pavilion and the area around it. Mortars, the 122s, his three remaining 152s, and of course the multiple rocket launchers had all been organized to deliver a time-on target barrage if Tae gave the signal. It turned out the signal had been him dodging and running.

He heard the sound of an engine, and turned to see his troops on the far bank starting a motor in a small boat.

Snipers were for sissies.

29 August 2015, 1130 local time
Seventh Air Force Headquarters
Osan Air Base, South Korea

Tony Christopher was hurrying, but he still got to the conference room late. More properly, the general had already started, which made him late no matter when he arrived. "My apologies, sir," Tony said as he took a chair next to Lieutenant General Randall Carter, commander of the Seventh Air Force.

"That's okay, Tony. I only called you nine minutes ago." Besides the general, Kevin could see other members of the Seventh's staff in the room.

The conference room's lights were lowered, and Carter and his staff were facing a large flat-screen display on one wall. It showed the middle part of the Korean Peninsula, with Seoul near the bottom edge. It was filled with tactical symbols, but Tony didn't get a chance to sort them out.

As Tony took his seat, General Carter ordered, "Ben, start it over again," and the briefer nodded. The image froze and flickered as the different symbols shifted position. "Watch the upper right corner," Carter suggested.

The briefer, an officer on the Seventh's operations staff, explained, "This is taken straight from their Air and Missile Defense Cell. The Koreans use feeds from our stuff as well as their own sensors, so we share the fused image. We're running at one-to-one time," the briefer said, pointing to the upper right corner of the window.

Tony noted that the recording's start time was only twenty-one minutes ago. A small white square appeared in North Korean territory, north of Pyongyang, then quickly changed to a red diamond. "One of the missile warning satellites picked it up first, then cued everyone else. The Koreans had Aegis ships on both sides, we had an E-3 Sentry here,"—he pointed to a spot just off the North Korean coast—"as well as land-based warning radars belonging to both countries south of the DMZ—I mean the thirty-eighth parallel," he corrected. The infamous Demilitarized Zone was definitely militarized now, with the Korean army streaming northward through it. Originally the buffer between North and South Korea, the term no longer held any meaning.

"None of the Aegis ships were able to engage. The geometry wasn't even close." The red diamond moved rapidly, compared to the tracks of friendly aircraft on the display. A label appeared, reading "Scud," which was a liquid-fueled ballistic missile, one of the most numerous in the DPRK inventory. It was carried and fired from a mobile launcher. A number below the label showed its speed. The value almost shimmered as it rapidly changed, steadily increasing. The missile was still in its boost phase.

A curved line appeared, perhaps thirty seconds after launch, leading from the missile symbol to an oval that included Seoul and its western suburbs.

"This is when the South Koreans hit the sirens. Seoul has been holding drills every day since the crisis started, but they only had two minutes between the alarm and calculated impact."

Other lines came up from locations in the south and joined at the symbol, changing colors. "The ROKs had two batteries in position to engage. White means they're tracking, yellow means they have a firing solution, and red means they're engaging."

Missile symbols moved along the lines toward the diamond, a pair from each battery. They seemed to crawl, and Tony urged them on, as if this wasn't a recording.

The ellipse around Seoul had grown for a while, then shrunk and shifted as the missile's motor burned out and it began to arc over the top of its trajectory. The oval's center crept slowly north and west, away from the center of the city.

Then the plot fell apart. The red diamond disappeared, and several new contacts clustered near the place, shifting back and forth from white to red. The lines connecting the interceptor missiles to their original target had disappeared, then reappeared, with lines connecting each interceptor to different targets. They shifted from one to another, but never steadied up.

"Decoys?" Tony muttered to himself, as the interceptors and their target merged and disappeared from the display.

The briefer reported, "South Korea is still using the PAC-2, while we have the upgraded PAC-3, but we still might have missed, even if our people had been in position to shoot. Nobody thought the DPRK had decoys on any of their stuff, let alone an old missile like the Scud. The Missile Defense Cell will begin analyzing the engagement immediately, of course, but as bad as the threat was before, it just got a little worse."

General Carter asked, "What news from the impact site?"

"It's too soon. Many of the first responders are still en route. It obviously wasn't a nuclear weapon, and there are no reports of gas or other chemicals, yet. But even if it was a conventional warhead, that's almost a metric ton of explosives. Although with the decoys, the warhead is probably a little smaller, say three-quarters of a ton. That'll still make a hell of a divot."

The briefer pointed to a spot northwest of the city center. "It landed in a suburb called Goyang. They may have been aiming at Gimpo Airport, to the south, but if that's the case, they're really bad shots, because that's way outside the missile's CEP. In any case, although Goyang is a suburb, it's heavily built up, filled with high-rise apartments."

As the lights came back up, General Carter observed, "Ever since the Chinese crossed the border, Washington's been in a tailspin, while we waited for the other shoe to drop."

The general held up a hard copy message. "I was just handed this, and people, the boot has hit the floor. This is a flash precedence message to all PACOM units authorizing us to enter former North Korean territory, in coordination with our ROK allies, and assist them in eliminating DPRK military resistance. Priority is any WMD sites, but any KPA target is fair game."

Then he added, "Of course, this is Washington. They gave us no guidance on what to do about the Chinese, so standard self-defense rules apply. I'll go back up the chain and ask for more clarity on the rules of engagement, but for the moment I'm interpreting 'self-defense' to include Chinese attacks on South Korean forces."

He stood up and the rest of the staff rose as well. "Let's go help our friends take back their country."

29 August 2015, 1200 local time
Near Chungwha, North Korea

Kevin Little was too fascinated by the landscape to pay any attention to his stomach. He was thankful that the last few minutes had been over relatively flat terrain, although the pilots probably felt terribly exposed. This entire area had supposedly been taken by South Korean troops, but they weren't taking any chances.

And it had been a fight. Any flat land in the North was either settled or farmed, and Kevin could see plumes of smoke coming up from different points in the middle distance. Cultivated fields had been torn up by vehicles and craters from bombs or shells.

Closer in, he could pick out individual buildings and other structures that had been damaged or outright flattened. Only a few were still burning, so every column of smoke really meant ten or twenty buildings destroyed.

He could tell that a lot of it had been by airpower. According to his South Korean counterpart, the ROKs had adopted a blitzkrieg style of warfare, with planes smashing any organized resistance with a blizzard of ordnance. Helicopter gunships then supported the advancing ground troops, quickly overrunning the still-recovering resistance.

Or the ROK scouts would accept their surrender. That was happening a lot lately. Soldiers without a government don't fight well. Occasionally, the ROK forces had even been contacted by radio before they reached an area, with terms for a peaceful surrender discussed. Sometimes, it worked out.

Historians would describe the ROK advance across the thirty-eighth parallel the same way they talked about Patton's charge into France in 1944, or Desert Storm in 1991, with many of the same problems. Without enemy resistance, transport capacity becomes the limit to movement.

As they flew north, Tony saw every road choked with vehicles, moving north or south. The DPRK's flimsy road network was operating well past capacity. If he'd had to drive to his destination, a distance of perhaps seventy or eighty miles, it likely would have taken days.

"Colonel," the pilot announced, "ten klicks." Kevin acknowledged the report and looked forward at a line of low hills. Of course, the Surion helicopter was much lower, and Kevin remembered to keep his eyes outside as the floor of the helicopter surged under him.

The machine climbed slightly to follow a two-lane road that led more or less north through the hills, and Kevin looked out at the heavily wooded hillsides and the bustling traffic below. The vehicles were almost entirely ROK Army, but he could see occasional civilian North Korean cars and trucks, as well as a lot of people on foot.

Cruise speed for a Surion helicopter was well over a hundred miles an hour, and the aircraft burst out from the gap into a wide valley. Over his headset Kevin heard the copilot request clearance and landing instructions, and just moments later they were slowing.

Of course, they didn't have to descend very far to land, and Kevin unbuckled while the crew chief slid open the side door and hopped to the ground. He came to attention and saluted as Kevin stepped out, as did a lieutenant waiting with a jeep near the pad.

The officer seemed to straighten still further as Little approached. "Lieutenant Bin Jae-moo, sir, Second Battalion, Ghost Brigade. The colonel is at the forward observation post," he reported, pointing to the top of the ridge.

Kevin returned the salute and climbed into the jeep. Bin started it with a roar and headed for a dirt track that climbed sharply. Raw earth and freshly cut brush showed where it had been made passable. To his credit, the young lieutenant did not try to set any speed records, or impress Kevin with his driving skills.

"Colonel Rhee says you two served together in the last war," Bin ventured.

"We were together for most of it," Kevin confirmed.

He was reluctant to say more, but the lieutenant pressed him. "The colonel says you saved his life."

"We saved each other's lives," Kevin responded. "More than once." The lieutenant was curious, and would have happily listened to any war story Kevin told, but the colonel needed to focus on the now.

Kevin had been having flashbacks of the fighting since he'd arrived in Korea. The crisis, then meeting Rhee after so long, had brought all the memories rushing back, both good and bad. He didn't fight his recollections, but he didn't encourage them, either.

This was still Korea, but a very different war. And this time he wasn't some junior officer, trying to run a platoon or a company. Kevin felt the weight of his rank. Any mistakes he made now would impose a far greater penalty on others instead of himself.

Bin followed the trail up for almost ten minutes, and while the area was supposed to be secure, Kevin kept his carbine close by. Dense woods came right up to the edge of the road, and could have hidden anyone or anything.

The Korean lieutenant parked the jeep below the crest of the ridge, and readied his own weapon before leading Kevin into the trees. The still air was filled with green light filtering through the leaves. Quietly threading their way past denser clumps of brush and fallen branches, they reached the ridgeline quickly, then descended the other side.

Rhee's observation post was a horizontal crease on the northern side of the hill, about twenty meters below the crest. It had been improved and hidden so well that Kevin was only meters from the spot before he could tell where the natural vegetation ended and the camouflage began. He had to step in and down. They'd deepened the fold until the forward edge of the dugout was chest-high.

Kevin Little's old comrade was busy observing the terrain with a set of tripod-mounted artillery scopes, dictating, while an enlisted man took notes. Another soldier operated a tripod-mounted video camera with a long lens pointed at the city, while another tripod held a laser rangefinder, ready for use. Behind them was a rack for their rifles, probably taken from a personnel carrier, and a map table. In the corner, two soldier-technicians were working on a complex communications center.

The ridgeline they were perched on was the last high ground between the ROK forces and Pyongyang. The North Korean capital straddled the Taedong River, which twisted and snaked across a wide plain. Built-up areas were intermixed with cultivated fields right up to the city limits. Pyongyang itself still had a dramatic skyline, although Kevin knew at least a few of the taller buildings had collapsed from damage, or been deliberately brought down.

Smoke enclosed the city in a dirty gray dome, fed by countless fires. Certainly nobody had tried to actually put any of them out, and Kevin could see whole blocks blackened, and others still burning, charred clusters adding to the overall haze.

Lieutenant Bin handed Kevin a pair of binoculars, but the city limits were at least ten kilometers away. The magnified image gave him a little more detail, but the heat haze and smoke prevented him from seeing much. He spotted a burning tank in a crossroads near the outskirts, and what were probably entrenchments in some open ground. It was too far to see if the trenches were occupied.

That made Kevin think of Rhee's more powerful binoculars. He lowered the glasses and turned to see Rhee watching him, smiling broadly. The Korean colonel was happy, almost euphoric.

"In at the finish? That's great!" Rhee offered his hand and they shook hands warmly. "Welcome to the end of the Kim regime, Colonel Little!"

Rhee pointed out toward the plain. "I've got eight teams spread out around the southern edge of the city, observing and reporting. They've encountered a few armed deserters, but all the organized military forces are inside the city.

"And they're still fighting each other!" Rhee grabbed Kevin's shoulder in excitement. "All the observers report small-arms and artillery fire continuing inside the city."

"When will you take the city?" Kevin didn't even use the word "attempt" in his question. Success was a foregone conclusion.

Rhee frowned. "Tomorrow morning, maybe ten hundred by the time everyone regroups and reloads, but I don't think we should wait. We should go now!"

"Do you have the troops?" Kevin was more than surprised. He hadn't seen any camps or staging areas on his flight north.

Rhee nodded, still smiling. "Units are already moving through this ridgeline to jumping-off positions for tomorrow's attack. Others are coming in from the open ground to our west. We have the lead elements of several battalions of mechanized infantry already in position; the rest of each unit is moving up. I say 'don't stop.' Just keep moving forward."

"Without a plan?" Kevin asked. They couldn't have had the time needed to develop a proper operations plan, especially to take a city. Urban fighting could destroy an army. Buildings, especially ruined ones, made excellent fortifications. Just ask the Germans about Stalingrad.

"We divide the city into sectors using the street map. I don't know if I've told you this, but I memorized the layout of this place years ago." He pointed toward Pyongyang. "In my mind, I've spent as much time there as I have in Seoul.

"We can have the troops in each sector deal with their own opposition, with helicopter gunships in support. They drive straight for the city center. I've already picked sector commanders, and as new units arrive, we use them as reinforcements, or send them into one of the empty sectors, always in strength. My teams have identified landing zones all over the outskirts of the city. We can bring in infantry units by helicopter right up to the edge of the battle.

"And the US Air Force is in the fight now!" Rhee continued happily. "Combined with our own aircraft, we don't have to wait for artillery. I know US Army gunships are flying north. They'll be able to add their firepower soon as well."

Rhee gestured toward the city. "Look at them. They're disorganized, and we know they're understrength and badly supplied. Do you still think we should wait?"

"What are you waiting for, then?" Kevin asked.

"I submitted my plan to General Kwon earlier today. He's taking it to headquarters right now, and he's pretty persuasive."

29 August 2015, 2:00 p.m. local time,
August 1st Building, Ministry of National Defense Compound
Beijing, People's Republic of China

"Exactly what is the range of a Hwaseong-5 missile?" President Wen asked the defense minister. China's Central Military Commission had quickly gathered for an urgent meeting after hearing the news about the missile attack on Seoul.

Defense Minister Yu's response was qualified. "It's a copy of the old Soviet R-17. The Americans call it the Scud B, and Second Bureau's always assumed the range was similar, about three hundred kilometers. But if the North Koreans have added decoys . . ."

"Still, that barely crosses our border, if it was fired from the same position as they did today." The PLAAF commander was dismissive. "And it was a conventional warhead."

"This time," the defense minister countered. "One scenario the intelligence people have suggested was that this was a 'live test.' The DPRK has never fired a ballistic missile operationally. Previous missile firings were always carefully planned and rehearsed for weeks ahead of time. They were more for propaganda than training. Now that they've done it once in real-world conditions, they'll go back and correct any problems before firing missiles with nuclear or chemical warheads."

That got their attention. The defense minister pressed his point. "And it's not about just the old R-17. That's relatively short-ranged. Their Nodong reaches over a thousand kilometers and can hit Beijing. The Musudan has a range four times that, and can reach almost every place in China except the westernmost parts of Xinjiang and Tibet. The Taepodong goes even further, to Tibet and India.

"I wouldn't waste a long-range missile on a test. They were able to pick Seoul because it was within range. And they missed. I imagine they're working to fix that problem."

"Do we have any idea how many missiles or what types the North Koreans have left?" the air force commander asked.

The defense minister started to answer, but the navy commander interjected, "More importantly, who controls the nuclear warheads? Have the South Koreans captured any?"

President Wen cut in. "If they'd captured any, and especially if they thought they'd found all of them, we would have heard about it. The South Koreans would be thumping their chests and shouting the news."

Yu pressed a key on the controller. A map of Korea appeared. An irregular red line crossed the peninsula, and the map was dotted with symbols. "The line shows the farthest we know that South Korean units have advanced. It's safe to assume that these sites behind that line have been captured and examined." He used a light pointer to highlight different installations in the area north of Pyongyang.

"The capital is the ROK's current goal, and is certainly a major objective, but three-quarters of the country lies north of that, with dozens of sites that haven't been touched. The circles mark known chemical weapons locations, the triangles nuclear sites. The Second Bureau says the confidence level of these locations is moderate to high." The minister smiled. "But the head of the Second Bureau also took pains to remind me of the obvious fact that any of these weapons could be moved, so his confidence level is perhaps not as high as it once was."

The defense minister put the controller down and turned to face Wen. "This is why, Comrade Chairman, fifty kilometers across the border is not nearly enough! We have a responsibility to remove the threat these weapons pose to China. We have the forces already in position, and now we have starting points across the Yalu."

"We've seen exactly one missile launched, and it was aimed at Seoul," the navy commander insisted.

"Can you promise that they will all be aimed at Seoul?" the defense minister retorted. "Until a few hours ago, a ballistic missile attack was only a possibility. Now it is a reality, and what's left as a possibility? In this chaos, there is no guarantee that whoever controls those weapons, and we have no idea who they are," he added, "will not lash out in many directions, including ours. Is our trust of North Korea strong enough to accept that risk?"

Nobody had an answer for that. President Wen surveyed the group, but whether afraid to speak, or out of ideas, they were silent. Then he looked over at the army commander. He knew the general well. In his younger years, Wen had been a political commissar in the ground forces and they had served together several times. "General Shu, you've been silent. Your troops would be making the advance. I'd like to hear your thoughts."

Shu didn't answer right away, but after a moment, he shrugged and said, "I fervently hope the chance of some North Korean faction firing any kind of missile toward us is small, but right now, the risk is as high as it's ever going to be. I've been trying to imagine our fate in the eyes of the nation if we let something as horrible as that occur."

The army general let that sink in, then added, "And if the land we occupy now will be used as a bargaining chip later, then I'd like as big a chip as possible."

Wen didn't ask for a show of hands. He ordered the defense minister, "The fifty-kilometer limitation is removed. Advance as far into DPRK territory as necessary to ensure the safety of our citizens."

CHAPTER FOURTEEN
SECOND BATTLE OF PYONGYANG

30 August 2015, 1430 local time
Headquarters, IV Corps
Pyongyang, North Korea

Tae stared at the map in stark disbelief. The picture it presented was devastating. The general looked slowly over at his aide. Tae's next orders would spell either survival or doom. He had to know if he was seeing an exact representation of their situation. With a low but steady voice, Tae demanded, "Is this information accurate, Major Ryeon?"

The newly promoted North Korean officer was caked in dirt; a fresh wound on his forehead was covered with a field dressing. He looked worn out and hungry, but it was his crestfallen expression that drove home what he had to say. "I'm sorry, Comrade General, but the intelligence from our Second and Third Corps colleagues has been verified by our cyber warfare soldiers. The map is unfortunately accurate. Pyongyang is almost completely surrounded by imperialist forces."

Tae almost growled as he threw the map to the floor. He knew this was coming, but it didn't make accepting the humiliating reality any easier. He paced around the bunker, rubbing his sore shoulder. Those blind KWP fools had ruined their best chance of organizing a proper defense of the city. Tae had very few options left to him, and none had even a poor chance of success. He knew what he had to do, but the soldier in him found it repulsive. The general suddenly felt very tired.

"There is one more thing, General," said Ryeon quietly. "I regret to inform you that Lieutenant General Yoo Ryang-ho is dead. He was killed in an artillery attack on his headquarters earlier this afternoon. Colonel Mok has taken command of the Third Corps."

Tae nodded silently, his stern face disguising the pain he felt. He couldn't afford to lose Yoo, not now, not after the warring factions had finally pulled together.

It was the day after the disastrous meeting with Lee and Jeup that a runner approached Tae's position waving a white flag. The message was simple. A senior military member of the Korean Workers' Party faction asked to meet Tae at the place and time of his choosing to discuss terms for a truce. Tae's reply was equally simple—same location, one hour.

When he arrived at the Taedongmun Park plaza, he saw a single man standing in the open. The man was wearing a Korean People's Army uniform, an encouraging beginning. As Tae approached, he soon recognized the individual as a classmate and colleague: Lieutenant General Yoo Ryang-ho. Tae hid his surprise as he continued picking a path through the rubble his people had created only the day before. He was careful to scan the area as he walked, the botched double-cross still fresh in his mind. But Yoo was the closest thing to a good friend a senior North Korean military officer could hope to have. Tae hoped this was still the case.

"Greetings, General Tae," spoke Yoo as he rendered a snappy salute.

"Greetings to you as well, Comrade Lieutenant General," replied Tae. After returning the honor, he added, "I'm pleased to see you are still alive, Yoo-*dongmu.*"

"Thank you, sir." Yoo approached Tae slowly, arms up, hands open. "I regret the foolish actions of my political leaders yesterday. The military council was not consulted on their plan. I would have cautioned them not to underestimate you, and that you rarely do things in a small way."

Tae had to laugh; Yoo always had a way with words. "I suppose a battalion-level artillery barrage could be considered excessive by some."

"Perhaps," Yoo smiled as he stopped less than a meter from Tae. "Nonetheless, it was quite effective. I am here to listen to your proposal."

General Tae was momentarily surprised. That Yoo was here didn't change the fact that the KWP faction was fractured. Could this man speak for them? He had to know. "Do you have authority to negotiate, Comrade Lieutenant General? What about the Korean Workers' Party leadership?"

"I am authorized to conclude a truce with you, if I believe it is in our best interest. As for the 'political leadership,' those ignorant fools will no longer interfere with military matters."

Tae nodded. He understood Yoo's explanation to mean the party's leaders were either dead or imprisoned. He really didn't care, as long as they were out of the way. "Very well, Yoo-*dongmu.* Here is my proposal."

Fighting a bad case of déjà vu, Tae described his plan to merge the military forces of the two factions and establish a defensive line against the South Koreans and the Americans to the south and the Chinese to the north. Initially, he skipped the part about negotiating a truce with the US and South Korea, and then together pushing the Chinese out.

He decided that breaking the news slowly would have a better chance of success.

Yoo listened without saying anything, but as soon as Tae finished, he asked, "Tell me, Comrade General. Do you truly believe we can hold out against the imperialists? I'm sure you're aware that they are outside the city, just beyond those hills." Yoo pointed southward.

Alarm bells went off in Tae's mind. Yoo's question, under normal circumstances, would be considered treasonous, punishable by death. Tae didn't know if Yoo was opening an avenue to discuss surrendering to the ROK and US forces, or verifying Tae's suspected lack of commitment to the DPRK. The easily seen movements of Yoo's arm could have been a signal. Was his "friend" about to end his life? Tae's intuition fought back the fear and told him to stay put, so he stood his ground—there was no crack of a rifle, no explosion. He was still alive.

He sighed deeply before answering Yoo. "No, my friend, I do not believe we can keep the imperialists at bay for more than a day or two. This is the terrible irony of a civil war; all casualties are doubled, all ammunition expenditure is doubled, all the damage to our country is doubled.

"We have worn ourselves out to the point that we are now outnumbered and outgunned by a technologically superior foe. The best I can hope for is to put up enough resistance to get the fascists to think twice about trying to take the city. Then I'll present our terms. If I'm successful, perhaps we will have help in defending against the Chinese."

Yoo nodded; he seemed resigned to Tae's assessment. "Not exactly a recipe for victory, is it?"

Tae chuckled again. "Only if you're trying to make a bitter stew."

A pained look flashed on Yoo's face. "I . . . I find it unbearable that I failed to protect my country. That I had a role in its destruction."

"We can discuss who is to blame later, Yoo-*dongmu*," countered Tae. "Right now, I need your help to save what is left of our home."

Coming to attention, Yoo saluted once again. "I accept your terms, Comrade General. What are your orders?"

Amidst the rubble, the two men embraced.

"Sir, what are your orders?" Ryeon's question jerked Tae back to reality. He didn't have the luxury to mourn the loss of a fine soldier and friend. That would have to wait. Grabbing the map off the floor, Tae motioned for his staff and unit commanders to assemble around him.

"Unit status, Major," barked Tae with confidence. His men were exhausted, at the edge of human endurance; they needed to draw strength from him for the coming battle.

"Per your orders, sir, the remnants of the 815th Mechanized Infantry Corps and two understrength brigades from the 820th Armored Corps have moved north to shore up the badly damaged 425th. With the exception of one understrength armor battalion, most of the Pokpung-ho and Chonma-ho main battle tanks have been sent to defend against the Chinese advance.

"The remaining units of the 820th have been distributed between the center and flanks to support each of the infantry divisions. All tanks are in prepared positions and camouflaged against aerial reconnaissance. We have five near full-strength infantry divisions, one at each front and one in reserve," concluded Ryeon.

Tae nodded as his aide pointed to the unit locations on the map. "What's our tank strength?" he asked.

Dejected, Major Ryeon looked downward and swallowed hard. The rest of the staff didn't look much better. "We can only field 207 tanks, mostly older Chinese Type 88s and Type 69s. A great number of our armored vehicles are damaged or have broken down and require a repair facility. And we are extremely short on fuel and ammunition, sir. The unpleasant fact is that most of the tanks don't have full fuel tanks or ammunition loads."

Tae fought the urge to laugh. It was either that or cry; the situation was beyond absurd. The pitiful number of older Chinese tanks, with their rifled 105mm guns, was hopelessly outmatched. They *might* be able to scratch the paint on the vastly superior K1A2 and K2 tanks that would lead the ROK assault. His only hope was that the South Koreans didn't have enough shells to kill all of his tanks. "It will have to do, Major. Use some of the damaged tanks as decoys; they can still serve a purpose by absorbing South Korean ordnance."

"Yes, sir, Comrade General."

"Comrades," blared Tae as he turned toward the fatigued assembly. "Make sure your men are well entrenched. Keep your heads down until after the rocket barrage, then let go with everything you have. Hold your positions for as long as you possibly can, then fall back to the next defensive line. I expect every man to fight hard and well, but understand this; I will not condone any suicide charges."

The general walked along the line of his commanders, looking each one in the eye as he spoke. "The simple truth of the matter is that we are too weak to win this fight. Our goal is to make it as hard as we possibly can for the Southerners to enter the city. We want them to stop and think about the casualties they'd suffer if they tried to take it. Once we have their attention, I'll go out and present our terms. Understood?"

There was an awkward silence as the twenty-four men looked at Tae with a stunned expression. Never before had a general officer said there was no hope of victory. Never before had a general officer expressed concern for the health and well being of his men. They all had been taught from a young age that life was a gift from the state, to be used by the state as it saw fit. If a man was called to sacrifice his life for the benefit of the state, he was to do so gladly. General Tae's words were unlike anything they'd heard before, and ironically troubling. They just didn't know how to respond. Finally, Major Ryeon blurted out, "Yes, sir!" The others followed immediately.

"Very well. To your posts, Comrades," ordered Tae.

Ninth Ghost Brigade Field Headquarters
12 KM South of Pyongyang, North Korea

Rhee looked through his artillery scope at Pyongyang; the smoke from the interdiction barrage earlier had long since cleared. There was no sign of fighting, or movement, in the city, at least the part he could observe. The attack on the North Korean capital was still an hour away; it had taken General Kwon longer than he'd anticipated getting permission, and more delay getting all the units coordinated and in place. The US combat units had to catch up with the tactical situation, then given their assignments in the battle plan. More people take longer to orientate and move— a simple fact of military science. Nonetheless, the delay grated Rhee; the North Koreans were up to something. He could feel it.

"Colonel, here is the latest UAV report," said an SOF private, offering a folder.

Rhee snatched the document and began reading it. The barrage had failed to stop the traffic on the Yanggak Bridge, one of the last remaining major spans on the Taedong River, and KPA troops and tanks had moved across, taking up prepared positions right in front of him. The South Koreans could have continued the bombardment, or hit the bridge with airdropped munitions, but they needed that bridge. He frowned, shook his head, and grunted; maybe this wouldn't be as easy as he first thought.

"What's wrong, Rhee?" asked Kevin. He saw the grimace on his friend's face and knew the news wasn't good.

"It would seem, Colonel Little, that some enterprising individual has managed to convince the two sides that fighting us would be preferable to each other. It looks like KWP faction forces have crossed the Taedong River and assumed defensive positions alongside the General Staff faction."

Rhee handed Kevin the report. The American's Hangul wasn't that great, but the pictures said all that needed to be said. Rhee was right. A lot of tanks and men had crossed the river, which could only mean that a truce had been arranged. The other photos showed numerous built-up areas just outside the city limits that looked like revetments. Most were camouflaged, but some were more hastily put together than others. He could see what looked like tanks in some of the revetments; he suspected there were more in the others.

Numerous makeshift bunkers dotted the landscape in and around the tanks. Each probably held a heavy machine gun, or possibly an ATGM crew, with overlapping fields of fire. Whoever was in charge knew what he was doing.

Kevin passed the report back to Rhee. "That is a very respectable defensive perimeter, Colonel. This won't be a cakewalk."

"Agreed, Colonel Little-*ssi*," replied Rhee. There was a hint of frustration in his voice. "Nevertheless, General Kwon in his note says the attack will go on as planned." The Korean colonel pointed to a cover memo at the front of the report.

"The Chinese have taken Taechon, and are moving south very quickly. We cannot delay in taking Pyongyang. Kwon said additional air support would be provided, but that is the best that can be done."

"Well then...humph," grunted Kevin as he stood up, "I guess we'd better get ready."

"Yes, indeed. I trust you brought your personal protective ensemble?"

Kevin winced at the thought of having to put on the nuclear, biological, and chemical protective gear. It was a hot, stuffy day, and the NBC gear would only make it worse—a lot worse. "Yes, I brought it. What MOPP level are we going to?"

"Level two. For now," Rhee answered. "All three factions have used chemical weapons against each other. I seriously doubt they'll have any objections to using them on us."

IV Corps Command Observation Post
Pyongyang Koryo Hotel
The floor shook violently, and the air became filled with dust from the powerful shock. A large aircraft bomb had gone off right in front of the Pyongyang Koryo Hotel that Tae was using as a forward observation post. Originally a Kim family showpiece for foreign visitors, the twin-tower, high-rise hotel had been heavily damaged during the earlier

fighting. Now the rubble provided excellent protection for Tae and his staff as they watched the battle unfold from the vantage point of an eighth-floor suite.

After picking himself off the floor, Tae took a quick look around at his men. None of them appeared injured, but their ears would ring for several more hours. Gathering his binoculars, the general went back to the wall lined with sandbags and stared out to the south—he should be able to see them any moment now. The preparatory bombardment by aircraft and artillery had been impressively intense. Tae was briefly envious of the amazing firepower he had just witnessed. But now that it had slackened off, the ROK Army would begin their assault. Major Ryeon stumbled up beside his general and leaned against the sandbags. He wiped a fresh layer of dust from his face.

"That was uncomfortably close, sir," he remarked.

"Yes, it was, Major. And no, I won't move to the bunker," replied Tae with a smirk.

"Comrade General, we cannot afford to lose you."

Tae kept grinning, but never took his eyes from the binoculars. "I appreciate your sentiments, Major, but I have to see what is happening myself. The timing of our actions depends on it. I cannot direct a battle from a hole in the ground!"

"Yes, sir," mumbled Ryeon.

"Stop acting like a *halmeoni*, it's unbecoming a soldier of your rank." Tae smiled as he teased his aide, calling him a grandmother. The lightheartedness ended quickly, though, his expression becoming more serious. "Any reports on casualties from the bombardment?" he asked.

"Not yet, General. I can only hope that the imperialists attacked many of the decoy positions."

Tae grunted his acknowledgment. Then turning to face Ryeon he inquired, "And the special weapons?"

"All special weapons have been removed from the artillery units and placed in secure storage in the rear, per your orders."

The general sensed the uneasiness in Ryeon's voice; Tae knew his order had not been popular. "I understand your reluctance to follow that order, Major Ryeon, as well as some of the other unit commanders. But it was essential that there be no possibility of a misunderstanding or error. The use of special weapons would severely complicate our negotiations."

"There has been some grumbling, Comrade General," admitted Ryeon. "If I may ask, sir, why don't you want to use the special weapons? It would make our defense far more robust."

"We need to push our Southern kinsmen, and their American allies, back through traditional means. This will have a far greater impact on their confidence. And while special weapons would likely kill more of their soldiers, it would also anger them. I want them to be careful, not incensed. Besides, using chemical weapons would only delay the inevitable. Pyongyang cannot be held indefinitely. It's to everybody's advantage if we end this without a protracted battle. Ahh . . ." Tae pointed to a wall of smoke forming along the city's outskirts.

"Our guests are coming. Alert all units. And remind the rocket artillery commanders to fire their rounds quickly and then abandon their launchers. The Americans' reputation for rapid, accurate counter-battery fire is well justified. Our artillery crews will have precious little time to do their job."

"Yes, Comrade General, at once!"

Ninth Ghost Brigade Field Headquarters
12 KM South of Pyongyang, North Korea

The heavy smoke from the obscuration fire blocked Rhee's view of Pyongyang; he could only hope it was having the same effect on the city's defenders. Looking closely, he could see the lead elements of the 13th Mechanized Infantry Division moving quickly over the open field. So far, there was no response from the unified KPA units.

"Anything from the teams?" he asked impatiently, walking over to the digital map display. Ghost Brigade had inserted four reconnaissance teams inside the city two days earlier, strategically positioned to observe the movements of KPA personnel and vehicles. Well hidden amongst the rubble, they had a commanding view of the southern approaches to Pyongyang, and their reports had provided crucial intelligence that complimented the UAV information.

"No, sir," answered Lieutenant Guk, staring at the secure data display. "Last report was no further movement detected."

Kevin scanned the area with his binoculars. K2 Black Panther tanks were in the lead, followed close behind by a second wave with K1A2 tanks and K21 infantry fighting vehicles. Moving at forty kilometers per hour, it would take them only eighteen minutes to reach the city's outskirts. The K2 tanks were closing fast on the smoke; but the North Koreans remained silent. The American colonel shook his head. "I don't get it, Rhee. Back in the day, they would have started firing by now. I didn't think the KPA had changed their battle tactics all that much."

Rhee shrugged. "Perhaps they are very low on ammunition."

"I don't buy that. If you let the enemy get too close, you won't have time to shoot more than a few rounds before he's on top of you. It doesn't make sense to save ammo if you get overrun."

Suddenly, Kevin saw smoke trails rising up from the north-northeast—a lot of them. "Holy shit!" he yelled. Rhee looked up and watched as hundreds of rockets sailed skyward. The secure radio then abruptly squawked to life. "Gulf Niner Hotel Zero One, this is Gulf Niner Tango Six Two, incoming artillery rockets. I repeat, incoming artillery rockets."

IV Corps Command Observation Post
Pyongyang Koryo Hotel

General Tae watched with satisfaction as the initial barrage of over one thousand rockets spewed out from Yanggakdo Stadium. Located on Yanggak Island, in the middle of the Taedong River, the large stadium concealed four battalions of BM-11 and BM-24 rocket launchers in its tunnels and sheltered parking areas. Now completely covered in smoke from the rocket motors, Tae hoped the crews had abandoned their launchers quickly. They wouldn't have time to reload.

The rockets began exploding around the South Korean armor units, throwing columns of flame and smoke skyward. He briefly allowed himself a moment of smug pride. No doubt the imperialists would be wondering how his battered army could pull off such an attack without the aid of an active sensor or radio. He savored the irony of the low-tech method used by Captain Ro and his special forces team. The commandos had dug themselves into the hills to the northeast of the invader's position, patiently waiting until their lead elements were aligned with a preselected landmark, marking their location. Ro then signaled it was time to begin the attack with a simple mirror and sunlight.

"Major, order the Seventeenth Armor Brigade to advance on the flanks. Antitank missile crews are to follow behind. Artillery, stand by to engage the follow-on units!"

Ninth Ghost Brigade Field Headquarters

The staccato of exploding rockets sounded like popcorn in a pan. The heat and smoke from the detonations blocked both visual and infrared sensors; Rhee couldn't see a thing for the interference. Behind him he heard the rapid firing of howitzers—ROK and US Army 155mm self-propelled artillery were about to rain steel on the KPA's parade. One didn't need a counter-battery radar to see where the massive barrage had originated.

Lieutenant Guk waved excitedly for his commander, and both Rhee and Kevin hurried over to the communications tent. Guk didn't even bother to explain; he just hit the mike key and said, "Gulf Niner Tango Seven Four, this is Gulf Niner Hotel Zero One, repeat your last."

"Gulf Niner Hotel Zero One, this is Gulf Niner Tango Seven Four. I have hostile movers, Papa Hotel, company strength, on the left flank."

Rhee shook his head; things were getting ugly. Then Guk pointed to the notepad where he had scribbled the first message and held up six, then two fingers—team Six Two was making a similar report. *Damn it!* cursed Rhee silently.

Grabbing the radio mike, he switched to the main attack frequency and barked, "All units, this is Gulf Niner Hotel Zero One. Hold hostile movers, Papa Hotel, company strength, on both flanks. I repeat hostile movers, Papa Hotel, company strength, on both flanks."

The radio net burst into furious activity as the advancing armor units started looking for the enemy tanks. Kevin saw the worry on Rhee's face; the earlier bravado had long been erased. "Pokpung-ho main battle tanks?" he asked.

"Yes, Colonel Little. We've walked right into a hornet's nest," remarked Rhee. Then turning to his ISR team he shouted, "Get a UAV in there. Now! I need to see what's going on!"

Running across Pyongyang's ruined outskirts, the K2 tanks had formed defensive wedges, while the K21 IFVs stayed in two parallel columns, their guns trained outward. The K1A2 tanks branched out along the flanks, keeping a sharp eye out for the KPA tanks reportedly coming their way—behind them lay eighteen disabled or destroyed armored vehicles. The wall of smoke was thick, with fires raging all around them from both sides' artillery barrages. But at the far ends of the wall, several streams of white smoke flew out from the dense haze. The smoke grenades billowed a thick cloud, obscuring what was behind from both visual and infrared sensors. The Pokpung-ho tanks were making their entry.

Streaking out of the white curtain came fifteen tanks, seven on the left flank, eight on the right. They immediately adjusted their turrets to line up with their targets and opened fire. The 125mm smoothbore guns fired armorpiercing sabot rounds that had little chance of penetrating the front glacis armor of a South Korean tank, but the tungsten darts easily pierced the sides. Six ROK tanks were killed almost immediately, but not before they had returned fire. South Korean AH-1F helicopter gunships had also joined the fray, firing TOW antitank missiles. In less than a minute, all fifteen of the KPA vehicles, their best tanks, were obliterated. But it was just enough time.

While the ROK armor concentrated on the Pokpung-ho tanks, two dozen Reconnaissance Bureau antitank missile teams ran out of the smoke curtains, dropped to the ground, aimed their missiles, and fired. Their Soviet AT-4 Spigot missiles would have little chance of hurting the tanks that were now rushing toward them head-on. Instead, they targeted the far more vulnerable IFVs. Holding their ground while .50-cal machine guns bullets and 40mm cannon rounds kicked dirt and rubble into the air around them, the teams focused solely on guiding their missiles, hitting eight K21 armored personnel carriers. The missiles' HEAT warheads shot hot molten metal through the hulls, killing the vehicles and many of their occupants. Still more in each vehicle were wounded. The North Korean missile teams had no chance to celebrate their success, as they were ferociously beaten back with heavy casualties.

Moments later, the lead Black Panther tanks plunged through the thick smoke. As soon as they emerged on the other side, North Korean Type 69 and Type 88 tanks began firing. Their efforts were futile. As the solid shot bounced off the ROK tanks, they began firing self-sharpening armor-piercing sabot rounds that sliced through their older foes even after passing through sandbags and broken concrete. The Chinese-made tanks quickly burst into flames once hit, often exploding their ammunition and blowing their turrets high into the air.

Some of the hidden ATGM teams attempted shots at the speeding K2s, but the tank's active protection system intercepted any missile that managed to get close. With the origin of the missile tracked by the millimeter wave radar, a high-explosive round would follow immediately thereafter, eliminating the missile launcher's crew.

As the other vehicles popped out into the clear, the IFVs deployed, putting down a withering fire while dismounting the onboard infantry. Some of the North Korean AT-3 Sagger missile crews managed to hit a ROK armored vehicle, but these were few. Fewer still were the number of vehicles disabled or killed. Helicopter gunships flew low along the North Korean line, launching high-velocity rockets and strafing with 20mm Gatling guns. The intense barrage forced the North Korean soldiers to keep their heads down, suppressing their fire. This allowed the ROK infantry to storm the now-exposed positions and destroy them one after another. The KPA front line was collapsing rapidly.

IV Corps Command Observation Post
Pyongyang Koryo Hotel

Even though Tae intellectually understood that the enemy's assault would quickly overrun his first defensive line, watching it happen was entirely different. His troops were completely outclassed, and yet they had succeeded in bloodying one of the imperialist puppet's best units. He could see ghostly images of the vaunted Black Panther tanks burning through the haze. Tae nodded his approval; his men had done well. Now it was time to pull back.

"Major Ryeon, have the mortar batteries lay down suppression fire on the lead imperialist forces. Order all frontline units to fall back to the second defensive line." Tae paused and quietly rebuked himself, he had to stop thinking like this. The old propaganda won't help him achieve his goals. And while shedding the habits of decades wouldn't come easily, he had to start setting the example for the rest of his men.

"And have the Twenty-Third Artillery Brigade fire their barrage on the follow-on ROK units. Start in close and walk the salvoes toward the hills. Four rounds per gun, then have the crews go to their shelters."

"Yes, sir, at once."

"Oh, and Major, order the surface-to-air missile troops to engage any helicopter that gets within range. They've roamed the skies freely long enough."

Ninth Ghost Brigade Field Headquarters

Rhee's jaw tightened with each tank and IFV that was hit. His body was tense with pent-up frustration. Even when he looked through his spotting binoculars, he didn't seem able to stand still. Kevin noted his friend's agitation with empathy; he felt it as well. In the last war, he and Rhee were the ones down on the battlefield, fighting on the front lines. This time, their positions and responsibilities pushed them toward the rear, to directing the forces in combat. As if sensing Kevin's thoughts, Rhee quietly muttered, "I should be down there. I can't tell what's going on so far away, and with all the smoke."

"That's not your job, Colonel," Kevin chided. "And in the thick of it, you'd see less than you could from up here."

Little was stating the obvious. Rhee shot him an annoyed glare, but it subsided quickly. His American colleague was also entirely correct. "You could at least be more sympathetic, Colonel Little."

"That's not my job either," replied Kevin sarcastically. Another loud rumble echoed from the direction of Pyongyang. A large cloud of smoke and flames reached skyward. Something big had just exploded.

"That was one of our helicopter gunships," lamented Rhee.

Kevin looked through his binoculars toward the city. It was hard to make anything out, but the occasional flash and explosion told him the fighting was still going on strong.

"Is it me, or have the North Koreans recently become more stubborn?" he asked.

Rhee nodded his agreement. "Yes, they seem to be more determined to fight now. They're not running or surrendering like they did earlier."

"That suggests a good commander is calling the shots."

"Agreed. Unfortunately for us, he appears to be quite competent. The other corps commanders on both flanks have reported similar stiff resistance."

"Colonel Rhee!" shouted Guk from the comms tent. "Team Seven Four reports the KPA units are withdrawing, moving back to a second line of prepared positions. The team lead says the troops are withdrawing in good order. They're not running away."

"Pass the information on, Lieutenant," ordered Rhee, shaking his head. "Use the primary frequency. We need to let the lead units know the KPA isn't done fighting just yet."

No sooner had Rhee given the order than another round of North Korean artillery began landing on the advancing infantry divisions. And just as before, ROK and US artillery let loose with an intense counter-barrage.

"No, they're not done fighting yet," repeated Rhee.

IV Corps Command Observation Post
Pyongyang Koryo Hotel

Tae stood motionless and watched the fighting for hours. His men were putting up a good fight, but with each passing moment, ROK Army units pushed closer and closer to the Taedong River. He knew his men were on the verge of exhaustion, as he could now see imperialist infantry advancing unimpeded from building to building from his observation post some three kilometers away. It was only a matter of time before his units simply collapsed.

To the southeast he could see some of his tanks valiantly engaging South Korean K1A2s. It was pointless; their guns simply couldn't penetrate the Southern tanks' advanced armor. One by one, the old Chinese tanks were gunned down. As Tae looked further to the east, he saw what was left of the Tower of the Juche Idea. A monument to the Kim concept of political, economic, and military self-reliance, it had been shattered, just like his country.

Here he was, fighting a losing battle to convince the imperialists that it would be better for them to join forces. Tae needed to ally his forces with those of his state's former enemies to the south, to fight their former communist allies to the north. He was fighting because he needed the South to help him preserve what was left of his country. The irony couldn't have been more bitter.

"Comrade General," interrupted Major Ryeon. "Colonel Mok reports that his units have taken over thirty-three percent casualties and that they are almost out of ammunition. Other commanders have made similar reports of high casualties and low ammunition. Most of our tanks have been destroyed, and those that are left have few shells, if any."

Tae sighed deeply. They had done all that they could, all that was possible. Now he had to save what was left of his men and hope it had been enough. "Signal all units to retreat as planned. Have the mortar batteries lay down smoke to cover the withdrawal. Tell the engineers to drop the two spans on the Yanggak Bridge."

Ryeon saluted smartly, then departed at a run to pass on the general's orders. Soon Tae saw puffs of white smoke bloom on the river's southern banks. Hundreds of boats and rafts then appeared as the survivors made their way slowly across the Taedong. In the waning twilight, bright orange and yellow bursts of light flickered along the two causeways of the Yanggak Bridge. Through his binoculars, Tae saw that major portions of both had been destroyed. It was now impassable. If the imperialists wanted to cross over the river, they'd have to bring up bridging units. That would take time, and they would be vulnerable—another point in Tae's favor.

"Sir, all your orders have been carried out," reported Ryeon.

"Very good, Major."

The young officer paused; he still found it difficult to question the intent of a general officer. But curiosity finally got the better of him. "Comrade General, what do we do now?"

Tae turned and smiled. "Now we wait, Major Ryeon. We let the Southerners and the Americans take stock of their situation. And give them the opportunity to consider the prospect of taking this city by force, street by street, building by building. Then, in the morning, we'll present them with another option."

CHAPTER FIFTEEN

PARLEY

31 August 2015, 0535 local time
Taedong River Bank
Pyongyang, North Korea

The shadows darted from one mound of rubble to the next, careful not to expose themselves to the light growing slowly in the east. The streets were littered with the remains of buildings, tanks, and soldiers. A pall of smoke from many sources promised a dim, gray day.

The intense battle yesterday had come to an unexpectedly quick end as soon as the surviving KPA units had withdrawn across the Taedong River. Like someone throwing a light switch, the fighting had simply been turned off. And with the exception of an occasional rifle crack, the night had become strangely quiet. It was as if the North Koreans had all disappeared.

From his command post in the hills to the south, Colonel Rhee Han-gil had watched the orderly evacuation of the DPRK troops via a UAV video feed. The KPA soldiers were not running. They took turns firing and moving back, always facing the enemy.

This was no rout, but a well-planned and executed retreat. The commanding general, whoever he was, was a skillful individual. Rhee found himself begrudgingly impressed and worried at the same time.

Along with the other senior officers, he'd expected the North Koreans to mount a hold-at-all costs defense. Instead, the KPA had made a fighting withdrawal, trading space for ROK casualties, while keeping their own forces relatively intact. Whoever was in charge knew how to run a retreat.

With a good commander directing the KPA forces, the fight to take the rest of Pyongyang would be much more costly. Especially as it looked like the last bridge across the Taedong River had just been destroyed.

Rhee and Little were both hunched over the UAV monitor, trying to see just how badly the Yanggak Bridge was damaged. The two colonels feared the worst as they studied the display, desperately wishing for a clearer picture. But there was so much smoke and dust in the air it was impossible to make anything out. Frustrated, Rhee went back to using his night vision binoculars. They weren't any better. Suddenly, an annoying buzz sounded from the comms tent.

"Colonel," shouted Guk. "It's General Kwon on the secure line, sir."

Rhee hurried back over to the tent and grabbed the encrypted satellite phone. "Colonel Rhee here, sir."

"Colonel, I want you to head down to the Taedong River and survey the bridges. I need to know if any have even a remote chance of being usable. The UAVs aren't good enough for a detailed damage assessment. I need close visual inspection, from the ground . . . tonight."

"Of course, General. We'll leave immediately."

"Excellent. And keep your eyes open for potential locations that can support pontoon bridges. We may have to use them if the bridge isn't an option." Kwon didn't sound happy at the idea. The Taedong was a big river. Laying a pontoon bridge under fire from a hostile shore would be slow and costly.

"Yes, sir," Rhee replied. Then after a short pause he added, "General, if I may ask, how did the other corps do?"

The gruff sigh told Rhee all he needed to know. "Not as well as we had hoped, Colonel. The First Army's Seventh Corps barely got into the city proper before being bogged down; the same for the Third Army's Fifth Corps. Your sector is the only one that made its planned goals, but you and I both know why."

"The river," answered Rhee, nodding. The KPA troops had evacuated the area just before they blew up the bridges. The ROK troops had gained ground quickly, but, with further progress blocked by the river, it had no value.

"Exactly. We need to get across the Taedong, and quickly."

"I'm not looking forward to what happens when we do."

"Yes, Colonel, I know bypassing the city makes more military sense, but there are the political aspects. Taking the city will break the back of the KPA resistance. So find me a way across that river! Kwon out."

Rhee put the phone down, turned back to Kevin, and queried, "Colonel Little, would you care to join me and my team for a stroll along the Taedong?"

"Sounds like fun," Kevin answered, straightening up from the UAV station. "When do we leave?"

"Now."

It had taken the evening and most of the night to reach the riverbank. Now Kevin ran, stooped over, to the remains of a burnt-out building and threw his back up against the charred brickwork. Everywhere he looked, he saw the signs of a pitched battle. The blackened hulks of KPA tanks and shattered bunkers lined the shores of the Taedong River. Unmoving figures in both sides' uniforms lay in close proximity to the still-smoldering ruins. The wounded had been recovered soon after the fighting had stopped, but they hadn't had the opportunity to remove the dead.

He saw Rhee hold up his hand, signaling the four men behind him to stop. The South Korean colonel scanned the area ahead with his night vision goggles and then waved them forward. The observation site was less than a hundred meters away. The Yanggak Bridge was the second structure Rhee's recon team had been assigned to inspect; the first, the Chungsong Bridge to the west, was a total loss. Kevin had little hope this next one would be any better, but they still had to get close enough to assess the damage with their own eyes. Other teams from the Ninth Special Forces Brigade were surveying the four remaining bridges to the northeast. Listening in on their reports to Kwon wasn't encouraging. Most of the bridges across the Taedong River were unserviceable, wrecked beyond repair. They'd have to be completely rebuilt.

The five men stayed low as they scurried toward their first planned survey site, a small peninsula a couple hundred meters from the bridge. Actually, there were two bridges. The first was a steel-framed railroad bridge, and the second a reinforced concrete, multilane highway span beside it. Either would meet the army's needs. The railroad bridge was in front, from the team's viewpoint. Rhee stayed low as he ran along the rocky shoreline. His chosen path kept them close to the water's edge; he didn't want to be seen by either friend or foe.

From everything Rhee could see, there wasn't a hostile soldier in sight. The UAV above them hadn't seen anyone on or near the shore on Yanggak Island, nearly four hundred meters away. Their portable UAV monitor showed only hotspots from the fires still burning in the destroyed stadium.

But even if there were no enemy soldiers in sight, Rhee was equally concerned about the friendly units nearby. Even though the ROK 25th Infantry Division had been informed his team would be in the area, the colonel suspected the troops would be more than a little trigger-happy after the battle. And there were always a few who never got the word. As the division's defensive perimeter was just a mere eighty meters away, he felt it prudent to stay out of sight. He didn't want to risk being fired at by friendly units.

As the group approached the peninsula, Kevin saw the mound they had spotted in the satellite imagery rising up out of the water. It was actually a pile of gravel, stored there temporarily for the concrete plant a couple hundred meters to the west. The gravel was dumped in a loose "L" shape, giving them cover from the friendly forces to the south. They had also chosen the mound because it was a few meters taller than either bridge's deck. Crawling up the nine-meter rise of loose aggregate proved to be a bit of a workout, but once at the crest, they had a good view of both bridges—well, at least the southern part.

The Yanggak Bridge had two separate sections. They could see the spans that reached from the southern shore to the island. A second set of bridges linked the island to the rest of Pyongyang, but they were hidden behind the island itself.

Rhee pulled out his night vision binoculars and began a sweep, while Kevin and the other team members assembled a laser rangefinder with an integral GPS receiver. The equipment would take the exact measurements needed to construct a detailed computer rendering of the railroad and highway portions of the bridge.

"No contacts," Rhee reported.

Kevin was already scanning the closest structure. He sighed heavily; the railroad bridge was not an option. "Rhee, the four center spans on the railroad bridge are completely destroyed—gone. We can cross that one off our list."

"What about the highway bridge?" asked the Korean colonel, a note of irritation in his voice.

"Looking now," Kevin replied. From this vantage point, they had a decent, but not unobstructed view of the highway bridge. Fortunately, it was just a little taller, allowing Kevin to see the spans through the railroad bridge's steel framework. What he saw was more encouraging. "It looks like they concentrated their explosives on the center two spans. The other four look untouched."

"What's their condition?" requested Rhee as he continued his safety scan.

"I can't tell for certain, but they're not completely dropped. I can still see some intact pavement. They're definitely damaged; I just can't say how badly from here. We should be able to get a better view from the second survey site."

"Understood," said Rhee, then briefly turning his head toward his team demanded, "Corporal, status on the measurements."

"Give us two more minutes and we'll be done with the railroad bridge, sir. We'll have to do the measurements on the highway bridge from site two."

Before Rhee could acknowledge the report, Little interrupted with a whispered, "What the hell is that?"

"Where?" shot back Rhee.

"Straight across the river. Just up the hill from the construction site, on the shoreline."

Rhee quickly repositioned his night vision binoculars and saw two, then four very bright heat sources. They were moving slowly down the hill. When he lowered the binoculars, he could see them as well—bright pinpoints that left afterimages. "Flares?" he murmured incredulously.

"That's what they look like to me, too. But why would anyone want to use flares, especially after a large battle?"

"Perhaps because they want to be seen," Rhee remarked dryly.

Kevin rolled his eyes. "Obviously, Colonel. But *why* do they want to be seen?"

Rhee shrugged; he didn't have a good answer for that. Both men watched the bright orbs as they moved steadily toward the shoreline.

"It looks like they're headed down to the river," observed Kevin.

Suddenly, his radio headset crackled to life. "X-Ray Two Romeo Zero One, this is Alpha Three Sierra Two Seven. UAV holds multiple contacts approaching the shore of Yanggak Island. Contacts appear to be heading for the dock. Over."

"Alpha Three Sierra Two Seven, this is X-Ray Two Romeo Zero One, we have a visual on contacts as well. Do you have an estimate on their numbers? Over."

Rhee motioned for the portable display; he wanted to see the UAV video feed himself.

"Can't tell for certain. The contacts appear to be using flares. They're partially blinding the UAV's IR sensor. Estimate six to eight individuals."

Rhee and Kevin looked at the small screen. Shimmering balls of light filled the display. Fleeting images, no more than shadows, were obviously people, but it was impossible to see how many.

One thing was certain: the procession was heading for the makeshift pier used by the construction company. A small motorboat was tied to the dock.

When the group carrying the flares finally reached the dock, two of the lights appeared to get on the boat, while the other two stayed put and started waving in the air. Rhee watched as the boat pulled away from the dock, swung its bow around, and headed toward the south bank—toward them. Puzzled, Little looked over to see his friend was just as confused. What they were seeing just didn't make a whole lot of sense. Rhee shook his head and keyed his mike. "Alpha Three Sierra Two Seven, this is X-Ray Two Romeo Zero One. The boat has left the dock and is moving toward the south bank. Can you give me an estimated landing position?"

"X-Ray Two Romeo Zero One, this is Alpha Three Sierra Two Seven. Our best guess is that it is heading to the concrete plant—one hundred eighty meters to your southwest."

"Roger. Inform General Kwon we are moving to intercept," announced Rhee as he signaled his men. They had already packed up the rangefinder and laptop and were ready to move out. "Gentlemen, it looks like we'll be having visitors. We don't know their intent, but it's clear they want us to see them. Therefore, we will exercise restraint. Do not fire unless you see a clear and immediate danger to the team, understood?"

"Yes, sir!" they responded.

"All right then, let's go see what this is all about."

Tae emerged from the wrecked administrative building with Major Ryeon at his side; four Reconnaissance Bureau soldiers followed close behind them. Each of the special operations commandos held an emergency signal flare high in the air. As they marched across the courtyard, General Tae got his first close look at the ruined Yanggakdo Stadium some fifty meters to his left. In the growing light, he could see that it had been completely devastated by ROK and American artillery. He had to respect the enemy's capabilities; he was also pleased that his assessment had been correct. His rather unusual orders had saved the lives of many of his rocket artillery troops. Tae's demonstrated concern for his men's well-being had rippled through the ranks like wildfire. His behavior was unlike any North Korean general, and because of that, he enjoyed the soldiers' complete loyalty. Should his plan succeed, he would need it.

Taking up a diamond formation with Tae and Ryeon in the middle, the six men headed down to a dock and a small motorboat. Uneasy with being out in the open, Ryeon fidgeted as they walked, constantly looking skyward.

"Calm yourself, Major," admonished Tae. "I'm quite certain their unmanned vehicles saw us the moment we left the building. If they wanted us dead, we wouldn't have gotten ten meters."

"Yes, Comrade General," mumbled an unconvinced Ryeon. The young major was still struggling with his general's unorthodox tactics. They deviated from everything Ryeon had been taught. When the general described how they would use flares during their walk to the construction dock, Ryeon briefly considered that his superior had lost his mind.

Tae chuckled at his aide's discomfort. The general shared his aide's uneasy feelings—the older man just hid them better. "I understand your misgivings, Ryeon Jae-gon, but by using the flares, we make our presence and movements, how should I say it, blindingly obvious? The Americans call this kind of behavior 'over the top,' and it should make them curious. I fully expect to be met after we cross the river."

"My apologies, General," Ryeon replied sheepishly. "I confess that I'm still having difficulties adjusting to our current situation."

The general burst out laughing. "So am I, Major, so am I. But the world has changed, and either we accept that change and adapt, or we die."

The two men walked the rest of the way to the dock in silence. Ryeon kept looking skyward in a vain attempt to spot a loitering UAV, just in case Tae was wrong.

Once they reached the boat, Tae, Ryeon, and two of the commandos boarded. A Reconnaissance Bureau soldier untied the line, and the boat slowly pulled away from the dock. As an added precaution, Tae ordered the two soldiers on the dock to begin waving their flares—just in case the Americans had somehow missed them earlier. The boat swung around and began its short journey to the concrete plant dock on the south side of the Taedong River. The general insisted the boat proceed slowly, again to make it clear this wasn't a raid of some sort. He scanned the area by the concrete plant with his binoculars. He didn't see anyone, not that he expected to. His reception committee would remain hidden until the very last moment. At least, that's what he would do in their place.

As the motorboat made its way to the other shore, Tae went over in his mind what he would say once his party was confronted. He kept reminding himself there could be no provocative statements, no threats—just simple facts, delivered professionally.

Initially, Tae thought he and Ryeon should be in their dress uniforms. But upon further reflection, he decided that wouldn't be appropriate. The Democratic People's Republic of Korea was no more, thus the uniform had no basis and its presence would only serve as an irritant to the South Koreans and Americans. No, he and his aide would wear their combat fatigues. Even though the uniforms were soiled with dirt and sweat, their best chance at a truce demanded the meeting be between soldiers. A shiny political ornament would be completely out of place.

The engine throttled back and the boat coasted the last few meters, bumping up gently against the dock's pilings. One of the commandos threw his flare into the river, jumped on to the dock, and secured the line to the bow. The second commando followed, looped the stern line around a cleat, and then assisted Tae out of the small craft. Once all four men were on the dock, the Reconnaissance Bureau soldiers assumed a protective position in front of the general, weapons raised.

"Lower your weapons!" barked Tae. "We are not here to fight! Get it through your thick skulls our mission is to secure a truce with our *former* enemies, so we can fight off the Chinese. I will not tolerate any action, even a defensive one, which might ruin our chances of success. Is that clear?"

The two commandos hesitated, then slowly lowered their assault rifles. Their expressions exposed the struggle they had fighting deep-rooted instincts. Seeing the edgy look on their faces, Tae said, "I know what I'm telling you conflicts with everything you've been trained for. I understand that. But the simple fact of the matter is, none of us were trained to deal with our country falling apart. Follow my orders and we will succeed in preserving our land. The future government will be different, of that I am sure, but this is still our home. And we must protect it from foreign invaders."

Tae then turned and strode off the dock and up the ramp toward the road. Silently, he wondered just how far they would get before being challenged. When they reached the road, Tae stopped, looked around, and motioned for his party to form a line. Then, in a loud voice he ordered, "Raise your weapons, remove the magazines, and clear the chambers."

The commandos slowly lifted their assault rifles, carefully removed the magazines, and placed them in their tactical belts. The soldiers then cleared the chambers, showing the weapons were now completely disarmed.

"Sling arms," commanded Tae. In an almost drill-like fashion, the men placed their weapons over their right shoulders. The general nodded and ordered, "Forward, march."

They had barely taken ten steps when a loud voice sounded out from the mound of sand and gravel. "That is far enough. Halt and identify yourself."

Tae grinned as he signaled the group to stop. They'd gotten about as far as he expected. Clearing his throat, he shouted, "I am General Tae Seok-won, commander of the Korean People's Army. I'm here to discuss terms for the surrender of Pyongyang."

After Tae's announcement, the North Korean contingent stood quietly, waiting for a response. When it didn't come, Tae called out again, "Did you hear me? I said I'm here to discuss terms for the surrender of Pyongyang."

Behind a small heap of sand, Rhee stood in stunned silence; his expression was one of complete amazement. This was absolutely the last thing he expected to hear. Pointing over his shoulder, he said in English, "The man says he's General Tae Seok-won. He wants to discuss terms for the surrender of Pyongyang."

Kevin was equally shocked, but whispered, "I heard him! My Korean's not that bad." After a moment, the American urged, "Answer him, Rhee!"

"How do you respond to that?" exclaimed Rhee in a hushed, but intense voice.

"You can start by acknowledging his presence," instructed Kevin. "I'll try and find out if this guy is really Tae."

Both of them knew from intelligence briefings that Tae was a senior member of the General Staff faction. The most recent reports had listed him as the likely commander of the troops in the capital. Before the coup began, the general had commanded the DPRK's Chemical Directorate, and intelligence had linked him to the sarin gas attack in Pyongyang. While Rhee gathered his thoughts, Kevin got on the radio.

Finally, Rhee turned in the direction of the North Korean party and shouted, "Yes, General, I heard you. I'm just a little surprised by your offer."

Tae smiled. His plan appeared to have worked. The South Korean's delayed reply suggested his confusion was genuine; Tae could only hope that an equal bewilderment had started to percolate up the chain of command. "Yes, I'm sure you are," remarked the general. "However, I'm not accustomed to negotiating with a pile of rock. Show yourselves. You know my men's weapons have been rendered safe."

Rhee turned back toward Kevin. There was a faint smile on his face. "Well, he certainly sounds like a general."

"If you don't wish to discuss my terms, we can just go back to fighting each other. My men are more than willing to make your visit to Pyongyang very interesting," shouted Tae. There was a note of annoyance in his voice.

"Yep, that's a general," observed Kevin. "And he's getting pissed."

Rhee exhaled sharply. "I suppose we should go out and hear what he has to say."

"That would be the sensible thing to do."

"I suppose I should salute him too," grumbled Rhee. Kevin just shrugged his shoulders.

After taking another deep breath, Rhee instructed his team, "Follow my lead, weapons ready." He then counted to three with his fingers. Once he reached three, the Korean colonel slowly walked out from behind the mound. Kevin and the other team members followed.

Tae saw five men suddenly appear to his left, their weapons raised. He signaled his people to stand fast and spoke quietly, "Stay at ease. If they wanted to kill us, we would already be dead."

Rhee approached the North Koreans cautiously. Kevin stayed to his left, while the three commandos fanned out to the right. They walked slowly, careful not to do anything that could be interpreted as a hostile act, and stopped some ten meters from Tae. Lowering his weapon, Rhee came to attention and rendered a smart salute. Kevin followed suit. Pleasantly surprised, Tae returned the honor.

"I see you are well disciplined," commented the general. "I assume I'm in the presence of a ROK Special Forces unit?"

"You would be correct, sir," answered Rhee. "I am Colonel Rhee Han-gil, commander, Ninth Special Forces Brigade. This is Colonel Kevin Little, US Eighth Army."

Tae bowed slightly and pointed to his right. "This is my aide, Major Ryeon Jae-gon. My security guards are Reconnaissance Bureau soldiers." Ryeon rendered a salute once the general mentioned his name.

Rhee returned the salute and then looked closely at the two commandos; they were just as uneasy about the meeting as he was. From his earliest days in the ROK Army, Rhee had been taught to despise the Reconnaissance Bureau. Their skill and ruthlessness was well known and feared. Still, Rhee recognized these men were peers of a sort and deserving of respect. He bowed lightly in their direction. They reciprocated his acknowledgment.

"You said you wanted to discuss terms for the surrender of Pyongyang, General. I'm listening," Rhee stated firmly.

"Yes, Colonel, but in truth, it's more than just Pyongyang. If my terms are accepted, I'll order all units loyal to the General Staff and Korean Workers' Party, throughout the country, to cease hostilities against Republic of Korea and American forces. I'll also order the surrender of all weapons of mass destruction possessed by both groups to ROK or American units."

Rhee's mind whirled. The general was offering an opportunity to end the fighting between the Korean peoples. But there was still the issue of his terms. Forcing himself to speak calmly, he replied, "That is a very attractive offer, General. What are your demands?"

Tae frowned. "'Demands' is a very undiplomatic word, Colonel. I prefer to call them 'conditions.'"

"Of course, sir. What are your conditions?" solicited Rhee as politely as he could. His curiosity grew with Tae's measured response. Diplomatic niceties were rarely a matter of concern to a North Korean general officer.

Walking slowly toward Rhee, Tae offered him a hand-written document as he began what was obviously a well-rehearsed statement.

"First, the Republic of Korea officially pledges to take control of the former Democratic People's Republic of Korea's territory.

"Second, the ROK government, along with international support, begins immediate relief efforts to provide food and medical assistance to our citizens.

"Third, the ROK government preserves the Korean People's Army's organization and command structure. I am to be granted *temporary* authority as commander in chief; however, I will place myself under the authority of the ROK chairman of the Joint Chiefs of Staff, and the chief of staff of the army.

"Fourth, the ROK government provides the KPA with ammunition, food, and fuel so that we can defend our land."

Glancing at the paper as Tae ran down the list, Rhee saw they were exactly as Tae had said. The first two were givens, but the last two would be a major problem for the Joint Chiefs of Staff, not to mention the Blue House.

"Your first two conditions will happen as a matter of course, General," responded Rhee carefully. "However, I do not understand the purpose of the last two."

"I have very good reasons for those conditions, Colonel," Tae answered calmly, but his tone was forceful. "If the Republic of Korea wishes to reunify the peninsula, then the population and the military of what was the Democratic People's Republic of Korea must join with those in the South. Uniting against a common enemy will do that faster than anything else. We love our country just as much as you do yours.

"Furthermore, my men would rather die fighting a hopeless cause than become prisoners, scorned and shamed for doing their duty. I trust our actions as of late have made that very clear."

As Rhee listened to the general's passionate rebuttal, he suddenly grasped the purpose of their fierce defense earlier. "General Tae, are you telling me that yesterday's fighting was a message? A demonstration of your resolve to be treated as equals?"

Tae smiled. "Precisely, Colonel Rhee. We had to show we are willing to fight to the bitter end. If your government wishes to reunify the peninsula, we must have a say in how that will be done."

Rhee nodded his understanding; a military force was the first and most obvious form of a state's existence. Tae's argument was reasonable. But the heavy casualties both sides had suffered, just to get his message across, angered Rhee. It was typical North Korean behavior. Forcing himself to remain calm, he took a deep breath and asked, "And the second reason?"

"You'll need my men to help fight the Chinese," Tae replied.

Rhee reacted to Tae's claim with suspicion. "Once your forces surrender, there will be no need to fight them. The Chinese have officially said they were only concerned about the lack of control of the DPRK's weapons of mass destruction. This ceases to be an issue once you transfer control to us."

"Don't be naïve, Colonel," scolded Tae. "China will not quietly tolerate a unified Korea on their border. The only way they'll leave is if we push them out. And for that, you'll need the forces at my command."

The last part caused a chill to run up Rhee's spine. While General Tae's assertion was unsettling, Rhee knew he was right. He'd heard Kwon and other senior officers discussing their prospects of fighting both the Chinese and the remaining KPA forces. They were not optimistic.

After a pause, Rhee announced, "I understand your conditions, General. However, I must discuss them with my superiors. I'll return shortly."

"By all means, Colonel. We'll wait. We have nothing better to do."

Rhee turned to leave, but caught himself in mid-stride and looked back at the North Korean general. "I'm curious, General Tae. We know chemical weapons have been used during the fighting here earlier. We were fully expecting you to use them against our assault. I'm sure you still have some in your possession, don't you?"

"Of course," Tae grinned. "I have an ample supply of special rockets and shells."

"Why didn't you use them, then?"

"Would you have been willing to listen to me if I had? I wanted to make a point, Colonel, not create a blood enemy."

"I see. Please excuse me." Rhee saluted, then motioned to Little as he started walking away. The American was close behind him. As they passed by the corporal, he held out a tablet for Rhee. The colonel took it, looked at the display, and passed it to Kevin. Little raised the tablet and looked at a stock NIS photo of General Tae Seok-won.

"Same guy," remarked Kevin as he handed the tablet back.

"I concur. He is who he says he is. That is an encouraging beginning."

They stopped a short distance away, but well out of earshot of the North Koreans. Rhee radioed headquarters and urgently requested that he speak to General Kwon. It didn't take long before the general was on the net.

Rhee explained the situation and confirmed the North Korean general's identity. He then listed Tae's conditions, and his justifications for them. Kwon listened quietly as Rhee concluded his report. "Finally, Tae claims that he has an ample supply of chemical weapons that he deliberately chose not to use against us."

"Do you believe him?" Kwon asked.

"We both know how many empty depots my men found; I'd have to say I do."

Rhee heard his general curse loudly. "This makes no damn sense, Colonel! No sense at all! Why fight so hard, and then offer to surrender? Is he trying to put us off guard so they can counterattack?"

"That would be hard to do without bridges, General," argued Rhee. "As a barrier, the Taedong River works both ways. Honestly, sir, I think Tae is being truthful, as hard as that may be to imagine."

"You mean to tell me that you actually believe this criminal? This filthy communist?"

Rhee had been expecting this. General Kwon was old school. He was famous for his fierce determination, and equally infamous for his hatred of the Kim regime.

"There wasn't the usual communist bluster, sir. He never mentioned reestablishing party rule even once. In truth, General, I agree with his reasoning."

"Colonel Rhee, the man has used chemical weapons on his own people!" objected Kwon.

"All three factions have used chemical weapons, sir," Rhee countered. "If we're going to reject the surrender of every senior North Korean officer that used WMDs during the civil war, then we should prepare for a long, costly fight, one we could very well lose."

A soft laugh suddenly echoed in the earpiece. Once it stopped, there was a sharp sigh, followed by, "All right, Colonel, what do you recommend?"

"I recommend we accept his terms, sir," Rhee stated frankly.

"You understand that this is a political hand grenade," remarked Kwon. "How do you expect me to sell this up the chain of command?"

Rhee smiled. Kwon was at least listening. "Simply point out that we will achieve our goals. Pyongyang is taken ahead of schedule, and with far fewer casualties than we estimated. The Blue House will love that. And if the rest of the KPA units obey Tae, then the fighting between our armed forces will be over throughout the rest of the country. We get our hands on more WMDs—a lot more, since Tae almost certainly knows about caches that we didn't even have a clue existed. Maybe that will be enough to get the Chinese to back off.

"But most importantly, sir, accepting Tae's terms give us the best chance at achieving reunification in a reasonably peaceful fashion. Sir, we can't throw this opportunity away because of decades-old hostility. The healing has to begin some time . . . why not now?"

Kwon was quiet at first; Rhee knew his boss was thinking over his subordinate's words carefully. Finally, after another sigh, Kwon lamented, "You realize we could both be court-martialed for treason. Committing our government to an alliance with the enemy."

"I see nothing treasonous about allying ourselves with other *Koreans*, sir. However, if we're convicted, I'll gladly take the upper bunk."

The general burst out laughing; the quip was typical Rhee. "All right, you rogue, I'll endorse your recommendation to General Yeon. You go and stop the civil war."

Tae waited patiently as the South Korean colonel was obviously having an animated conversation with this superior. After several long minutes, the two colonels started walking back toward Tae and his men. The general's anxiousness grew with each step, but he waited for Rhee to come to a stop. Then calmly, Tae asked, "Well, Colonel Rhee Han-gil, what will it be?"

Rhee stepped forward and offered his hand. "We accept your terms, General."

31 August 2015, 0830 local time
US Forces Korea Headquarters, Yongsan Garrison
Seoul, South Korea

General Thomas Fascione sat silently at the head of the conference room table. The USFK chief of staff, Major General O'Rourke, and deputy, General Park Joon-ho, were seated next to him; both men fidgeted in discomfort as General Yeon Min-soo, the ROK Army chief of staff, ranted in a fierce tirade—the man was livid.

"How dare that man obligate us to a truce without proper consultation from the president! And Kwon—he should have known better! This is typical Special Forces behavior; they think they can operate outside the rules that apply to everyone else!"

Fascione stood up abruptly. His face betrayed his irritation. "I really don't understand what the problem is, General Yeon. Based on everything I've been told, Colonel Rhee's actions achieved what was in the best interests of the Republic of Korea—no, correction, the new unified Korea."

Yeon's face became tighter as he restrained himself from looking up at the towering American general. "He's a colonel, General Fascione, and he doesn't have the authority to commit the Republic of Korea to a truce with the likes of that criminal Tae! Nor does General Kwon! The idea of integrating the KPA into our military structure, even if Tae is willing to place himself under our command, is simply unacceptable."

"Perhaps I'm just an 'Ugly American' who doesn't appreciate the Confucian hierarchy that your culture finds so endearing, General," began Fascione, his nostrils flaring. "But from where I come from, the mission comes first! Your government is entitled to make its own decisions on how to deal with the former KPA troops, of course. But if I were you, I'd suggest not repeating the same mistakes we made in Iraq with the de-Baathification policy. We're still paying for that bonehead maneuver."

30 August 2015, 9:30 p.m.
CNN Headquarters
Atlanta, Georgia

The screen was filled with a sea of multicolored lanterns flowing down the street. In the background were several large floats depicting various images of Buddha. South Korean flags waved everywhere, and the sound of firecrackers could be heard echoing in the background. Given the size and festiveness of the throng, one could be forgiven thinking it was New Year's Day, or even the Buddha birthday celebration. It was neither; the official announcement from the Blue House of Pyongyang's capitulation had been made only thirty minutes earlier. The spontaneous rejoicing was the emotional outpouring of a people that had waited decades for this moment—the reunification of Korea.

Sitting at her news anchor desk, Catherine Donner watched in awe as thousands of Koreans sang, shouted, or chanted their joy in downtown Seoul. As soon as the video clip was done, she turned toward the camera and began reading her script.

"All of Seoul, a city of ten million, erupted into celebration immediately after President An Kye-nam announced that the North Korean capital of Pyongyang had been captured by ROK Army units during the early morning hours. YouTube and other social media outlets show similar celebrations throughout the Republic of Korea. In essence, the country is throwing one great big party, and not without justification.

"After nearly seventy years, and two wars, the divided halves of Korea are becoming one. And while the *beginning* of the reunification process is indeed a cause for festivities, it is only the start of what will undoubtedly be a lengthy, and arduous integration, particularly since these two countries have long harbored hostile feelings toward each other.

"While there will unquestionably be bumps along the road, President An's opening remarks that the Republic of Korea will not make the same mistakes that America did in Iraq, was an encouraging and refreshing start. Still, there are reports of continued fighting between the former Korean People's Army and Chinese army units to the north of Pyongyang. State Department officials declined to make any comments, stating that negotiations were continuing with Beijing."

Chapter Sixteen
Reaction

2 September 2015, 1:00 p.m. local time
Munsan Refugee Camp
Outside Dongducheon, South Korea

"Are we prisoners here?" Ye Dong-soo didn't waste any time. The big, weathered farmer had been appointed by the rapidly growing crowd outside Kary's tent as their spokesman, not that they needed him to articulate their position. They all wanted to go home.

There was no way to answer Ye's question directly. "Yes" was untrue, and "no" would be treated as a denial of what seemed obvious to him.

He was frustrated, heading for angry, but Kary tried her best to answer emotion with reason. "If you go north, the army will stop you at the border. The government has declared all of the former DPRK as a war zone. They have a huge problem taking care of the people that are still there, and deserting KPA soldiers are preying on civilians. And where there was fighting, there are damaged roads and unexploded shells . . ."

Ye hardly listened. "We heard all that yesterday, from the general in that long-winded speech! But Pyongyang has surrendered. There may be fighting in the north, but our village is well south of there. We are trapped here, while the Southern army loots and burns our homes!"

Kary was surprised at the accusation. "That's simply—"

"We've seen the pictures on the broadcasts. Whole streets in Chorwon were on fire!"

"That's from the fighting," she insisted.

"Nobody's putting out the fires. We have to get back to protect our homes. And my crops should be harvested."

She persisted. "There's no transport to take you back. Every truck in the army is taking soldiers or supplies north."

"That's a lie!' he countered angrily. "There's a whole row of trucks at the base, right next to the camp. Give them to us, if you don't want to do it yourselves." Ye was almost pleading now.

"The motor pool?" Kary asked. "They aren't mine to give. Besides, how many can each one hold? Fifteen? Twenty? How many people are in this camp? When it's finally time for you to return, the army will send hundreds of trucks."

He didn't look convinced. She tried a different tack. "Please, Ye Dong-soo-*ssi*, you know I'm helping people reunite with their relatives here in the South. Individuals and families are leaving the camps every day."

"Yes, a handful at a time," Ye argued. "The trucks would be quicker." He threw up his hands in frustration. "Walking would be quicker."

"It's what I can do," Kary insisted. "Colonel Little said my job was to care for you and your countrymen—food, shelter, better medical care than you've ever had. And I've added more: classes for the children, and any adults willing to go."

"Propaganda," Ye grumbled. But he was calming down. "Everyone here took terrible risks to come south because a civil war is no place for a family. We are grateful for what you have given to us, but it's time to go home!" His emotions boiled up again, and he slapped the table for emphasis.

"I will meet with the Korean army commander right away, and ask him what can be done to speed up the process." Kary sighed. "At the very least, he can give me—and you—a timeline and progress reports. Maybe he could come back and explain exactly what they are doing."

"No! No more speeches!" Ye insisted.

"When I find out, can I count on you to pass on what I do learn?"

Ye scowled. "You know where I'll be," he answered, and stalked out of Kary's tent.

Others of her staff were waiting their turn to see her, but Kary told them to wait for half a moment while she stood and went over to the table where they kept a pot of coffee brewing. It was relatively fresh, and much better than the Chinese instant coffee most in the North drank.

The last two days had been an emotional roller coaster, and she could only hope that the ride was bottoming out. The victory in Pyongyang had been welcomed in Munsan, if not celebrated as wildly as nearby Dongducheon, or Seoul, or really every city in the South.

Alcoholic beverages were discouraged in the Munsan camp, and that may have also dampened the celebrations, but people from the North had a different context. They had been brought up being taught that South Korea was an enemy, and now its army had invaded and conquered their capital city. Even Northerners who hated the Kims felt conflicted. They certainly didn't feel liberated.

The news media didn't help her cause, describing the "collapse" of DPRK resistance and heavy KPA casualties, or announcing that the front lines were now north of the capital. Too many government officials, egged on by eager reporters, had already declared victory. Even when confronted with news about the Chinese invasion, they predicted that their all-powerful army would drive them out of "United Korea."

Within hours, some people in the camps had simply left, walking out the same way that they walked in. They were inevitably picked up by ROK military police near the border and returned to Munsan; sometimes the worse for wear.

The same thing was happening to South Koreans who headed north to look for relatives, but Southern citizens were just told to go home, not taken to a camp where the disgruntled could gather and reinforce each other's frustration.

Less than twenty-four hours after the fall of Pyongyang was announced, Kary's tent had received a steady stream of people wanting to leave, and asking if she could please arrange transportation back north. There were so many helicopters and trucks and airplanes going in that direction. Certainly there was room for a few passengers.

Kary had appealed to Little's deputy for help. In all the chaos it was hard to find a point of contact with the South Korean army, now once again in charge of Munsan and the other refugee camps. The new reserve colonel had been sympathetic and helpful. He'd even called a meeting to explain to everyone why they had to remain at Munsan, at least for the foreseeable future. Food supplies in the north were problematic, and he couldn't guarantee their security. No, he couldn't give them a definite date when they could go home.

It hadn't gone well.

And today it was even worse. Munsan offered shelter, food, and many other positive things. But it was also crowded, uncomfortable, and smelly. People had to stand in long lines for anything worthwhile, and even with the classes Kary had organized, there was little to do. Those things were acceptable if the alternative was living in a war zone, but the war was almost over, wasn't it?

She sat back down and one of the staff came over with a question. The children needed a playground. Could space be found? Kary was pretty sure she could get the city leaders in Dongducheon to contribute some equipment.

Another reported there were still incidents of food hoarding. It was understandable that people so used to scarcity would want to have some food reserved if the situation changed—or if they were planning to make a trip, Kary realized.

But there were few places in camp where food could be stored that were even close to being sanitary. Not only had there been incidents of food poisoning, but insects and even rats had appeared. How could she give people confidence in their food supply? And were the times of hardship really over?

As the afternoon progressed, she listened to the problems the staffers posed and either resolved them or, more usually, added them to a list, Kary watched the clock. Not only was her stomach complaining, the evening meal was only served until 1930.

She was missing Cho again. He spent a lot of time on errands for her, or the camp commander, who had found him useful. The South Korean officer openly admired someone who had worked against the Kim regime directly. There was no longer any talk of him being arrested.

Kary usually waited for Cho Ho-jin to appear before going together to dinner. She also often found him waiting near the ladies' quarters when she came out in the morning. At meals, he asked questions about governments and laws, or life and work in the South and faraway America. In return, he fed her tidbits of camp gossip. Many made her laugh, while others helped her understand the life of a refugee.

By 1910, she gave up waiting for him and headed for the mess tent. She made it a point to eat what everyone else did. She needed to see that the camp's residents were being properly fed.

The tent was full of people eating, and there were still a fair number waiting to be fed. She got in line, picking up a tray. Maybe it was good that she'd come in so late. The mess line had been open for over two hours, and the cooks weren't keeping the serving area as clean as it should be. And they were running short . . .

She heard a commotion over at the far end of the mess tent, and then a gunshot. Her heart froze. She dropped her tray and headed in that direction.

Or tried to. Most of the people in the tent were running away from the source of the noise. Only her height allowed her to dodge and push upstream against a river of humanity. As she got closer, she could see some sort of fight had broken out, a dozen or more men, young and old, punching and wrestling. It wasn't clear what they were fighting about, and she couldn't see anyone with a pistol, or any other weapons.

She had to stop it, somehow, and was trying to figure out how when a phalanx of soldiers, in body armor and carrying batons instead of rifles, ran in the front gate of the camp.

In wedge formation, they pushed their way through anyone that didn't get out of their way fast enough, and drove straight into the center of the scuffle.

Teams of soldiers began pulling individuals out of the fight. While two men immobilized a combatant, another zip-tied his hands, blindfolded him, and turned the now helpless prisoner over to other soldiers, who had roared up in a truck.

It was brutal, but efficient. Kary wondered how long they had trained . . .

Something pricked the back of her neck. As she automatically tried to step forward, away from the irritation, a callused hand materialized around her throat. It firmly held her against the sharpness, and squeezed just hard enough to threaten her windpipe without preventing her from breathing.

"Don't speak." She tried to pull away and the hand tightened more. It felt like it was made of stone. Her movements also jostled her assailant's other arm, and she felt a sharp pain on the back of her neck. "This knife is very sharp. Turn around."

To reinforce the order, the hand slid out to her shoulder and spun her a half circle. It pushed her roughly forward. "We're going out the front gate." Still in shock, and hardly given time to understand, she complied, or more accurately, didn't resist.

She half stumbled and began walking. The knife and the hand holding it dropped down to her upper back, while the other hand relaxed its grip, but stayed firmly on her shoulder.

Frightened, almost numb, she looked at the people around her, but their attention was on the fight and the soldiers breaking it up. The knife, if that's what it was, enforced her silence. A few people glanced in her direction, and presumably saw whoever was close behind her, but had no reaction.

After a few steps, she asked, "Why . . ."

The hand pinched her shoulder, hard. He pushed her roughly and they began walking more quickly. "I said, do not speak!" the voice said harshly. "Save it for the motor pool. You are going to sign out all four trucks for this evening."

It was Ye Dong-soo. She'd spoken to him long enough that afternoon to recognize his voice. They were walking quickly, almost to the front gate and the Korean army base outside. Other people were nearby, but almost everyone's attention was still drawn to the fight. It was starting to get dark, too.

"They're stopping civilians at the border." She'd said as much that morning. Wasn't he listening? The shock and paralysis of the surprise was passing, but fueled by adrenaline, her mind was racing. Could she persuade him to let her go? Could she yell for help somehow without getting stabbed? People were passing by them all the time. Why didn't they notice?

At least he didn't squeeze her throat this time. "You are coming with us. If we are stopped, you're going to tell them that the army has given us permission to return home. I'm sure you will be able to convince them," he added almost brightly.

She looked at the people walking by. Everyone was heading toward the altercation in the mess tent. She thought about winking or making some sort of weird expression. After all, Ye was behind her. He wouldn't see it. But their first reaction would be to ask her what was wrong. That wouldn't help her at all, and would just involve someone else.

Then she saw Cho Ho-jin. He'd just turned the corner and was heading toward them, walking quickly. He was some distance ahead, but they were still close to the camp. He had to pass by her to go in the front gate.

But what could she say? Did he have the pistol with him? No. She remembered it was back in her footlocker.

"We don't have any paperwork to take the trucks, or to cross the border." Cho was only meters away.

"I'm sure you can talk us through. The people at the motor pool will listen to you." She tried to look straight ahead, and not at Cho.

Then he passed them without even looking in her direction, heading toward the commotion with everyone else. How many tall American women were in this camp, anyway? Was he too distracted to notice them?

Her heart sank and her legs seemed to lose their strength. His sudden appearance had meant salvation, but he'd passed by. More afraid now, she thought furiously. *Keep Ye talking.*

"What about drivers?" she asked, trying a practical approach.

"They're already waiting near the motor pool," Ye answered. "We'll be moving in minutes, and loaded..."

Ye's reply ended with a strangled "Gurk!" His hand on her shoulder tightened, then was torn loose. The motion pulled her around, and she saw Cho standing behind and to one side of the farmer. He had one hand on the front of Ye's throat, pulling him back hard, so that he fell backwards over Cho's outstretched leg. Cho was twisting his upper body as he pulled Ye down, literally throwing all his weight into the movement.

Her kidnapper, surprised and wide-eyed, landed hard enough to knock the wind out of him. Cho then delivered a vicious kick to the side of Ye's head, and the farmer went limp.

Kary realized she was screaming, as much out of surprise and reaction to Cho's fierce attack as she was from fear. She forced herself to stop, as those around her, including several ROK soldiers, saw what had happened. Ye and his alarmingly large knife were quickly taken into custody, while Cho promised to bring Kary to the provost's office as soon as she'd had some time to recover.

She shivered, swallowing hard, and found Cho was supporting her, one arm around her waist and the other under an elbow. She did feel a little unsteady.

Cho was almost frantic. "Are you all right? Did you get cut anywhere?" Even as she tried to answer the question, Cho swung her around to check her back and neck for injuries.

"What about your throat?" he asked, studying her throat and then her shoulder. "Does it hurt anywhere?" He was holding her by her shoulders, his face full of concern.

Without thinking, she hugged him, hard, wrapping both arms around him and burying her face in his neck. She wasn't crying, not exactly. It was half for support—no, it was all for support, and right now he was an iron pillar. "I thought you didn't see me," she said after a moment.

His arms were around her now, too. "I would never walk past you. You're easy to find, especially in a crowd of Koreans." That made her laugh, a little, and she eased her grip to something less desperate.

"Your expression was completely blank," he explained. That was my first clue. And that *nappeun nom* was right behind you. You'd never let someone get that close."

"Really?" she remarked, looking at the two of them. They both laughed, and realized that a small crowd surrounded them. As they released each other and she stood straighter, she heard cheers and questions. The *ajummas* all wanted to make sure she was unharmed, and everyone congratulated Cho on his neat takedown of her assailant.

She realized that she was still holding Cho's hand, but was reluctant to let go. She was also a little embarrassed. Public displays of affection in Korea were usually limited to hand-holding, or a quick peck on the cheek. Embraces like theirs often earned a scolding from more conservative citizens, but under the circumstances, allowances could be made.

Cho also noticed her holding his hand, but made no move to break away. He smiled and said, "If you're all right, you should go to the provost's office."

"Please come with me?" she asked.

3 September 2015, 0410 local time
Seventh Air Force Headquarters
Osan Air Base, South Korea

The Seventh Air Force was now fighting a round-the-clock war. Lieutenant General Randall Carter and his deputy, Brigadier General Tony Christopher, had agreed long ago that at least one of them would be in the ops center at all times. With advanced sensors and night vision gear for pilots, nighttime was just another operational environment. In fact, it was a little safer than flying during the day, with a lower risk of visually aimed potshots. And the air was smoother, without the thermals from daytime heating.

And it didn't help that Washington was thirteen hours behind Seoul. The message Tony was reading had been sent at three in the afternoon, Washington time.

He'd already sent word to wake the general. They were supposed to be getting at least six hours of sleep out of every twenty-four, but it was a goal they didn't always reach. For something like this, the boss had to be told right away.

General Carter hurried in, still shaking off sleep. Both he and Tony had quarters in the same building as the ops center. "Flash precedence?" he asked.

"The Chinese rejected the latest note," Tony explained, handing Carter the hard copy. "All of a sudden, Pyongyang falling doesn't seem like such a big deal."

"It does change one's perspective," Carter remarked as he read the message, then took the time to read it again while Tony waited silently. "At least they're giving us decent ROEs for the Chinese. Beijing is going to regret this," the general predicted.

"They can still cause a lot of problems," Tony replied with caution.

"But they can't justify taking and holding Korean territory, at least not easily in this day and age, and we can cause problems for them as well." Carter said the last part in a very positive way. Turning, he looked at the unit status board and pointed. "What are the Nineteenth and Twenty-Seventh doing?"

Both squadrons were equipped with F-22 Raptors and had been among the first reinforcements the Seventh Air Force had received, along with a flock of transports and aerial tankers.

"No changes, General. Rotating escorts for the E-3C AWACS and E-8C JSTARS aircraft, four reconnaissance sorties later today, and the rest on standby." With total air superiority, the Raptors had little to do, but that could all change quickly.

"Reinforce the escorts from pairs to four-ship formations, and have the rest of the aircraft in the squadrons come up to alert plus fifteen at 0900. Send that out now, then tell the mission planning cell to double the escorts on all missions that will be anywhere north of Kaechon at 0900 or later."

Tony made notes as the general spoke, nodded, and then simply looked at his boss.

The general was apologetic. "I'm sorry, Saint. I can't tell you much, but you might want to look up 'horizontal escalation.' And between now and then, you and I are going to sit here and think of every dirty trick the Chinese could play on us, and what we can do to stop it."

3 September 2015, 8:30 p.m. EDT
CNN Special Report
The wall behind the news anchor displayed a map of the South China Sea, framed by China on the north, Vietnam to the west, the Philippines to the east, and Malaysia far to the south. The blue oblong was dotted with small islands and archipelagos, and on the network's map, two of the islands, both in the east near the Philippines, were highlighted by glowing red boxes. Insets showed close-ups of a triangular atoll and US warships steaming in formation. A scrolling banner across the bottom of the page read, "Naval Confrontation in the South China Sea—US and China Ready to Fight?"

"We're breaking into our evening coverage to tell you about this latest development in the ongoing faceoff between China and the United States. Only hours after Beijing flatly refused to discuss their advance into the former North Korea, US Marines landed on a small island, not really even an island. It's a tropical atoll called Scarborough Shoal, after a British ship that ran aground on it in the late 1700s.

"US Navy warships showed up early this morning local time and began escorting Chinese-flagged fishing boats out of the area. Those that refused were boarded. The 'Notice to Airmen and Mariners' posted by the US government declared an exclusion zone around the entire area while the US and Philippine Navy conducted 'joint maritime security operations.'" The anchor read the text verbatim, but without any understanding.

"With us this evening is Dr. Eric Anderson from the Naval War College, a widely published expert on China and the long-running South China Sea dispute, to put this action in context."

Anderson was slim, well dressed, and evidently used to being interviewed. He didn't waste time or words. "The waters around Scarborough Shoal are being heavily fished by the PRC, Taiwan, and the Philippines. The atoll lies 530 miles from the nearest Chinese territory, and 130 miles from the Philippines.

"The exclusion zone bars other ships, including Chinese and Taiwanese vessels, from the area, and will allow the Philippine fishermen to operate without fear of harassment by the Chinese Coast Guard or other PRC paramilitary ships. That's been a real problem for them."

He paused for a moment. "It's a minor economic hit for China, but a big boost for the Philippines, an important American ally in the region."

The anchor asked, "Is there a lot of fishing around the Spratly Islands, where the second exclusion zone was declared?"

Anderson nodded. "Some, and also the possibility of oil or mineral deposits. They've never been properly explored or developed because China, the Philippines, and others have been squabbling over them for decades.

"Lately, China's been expanding the islands in the Spratly archipelago, adding airstrips and radar stations in what the international community calls 'disputed territory.' Beijing is trying to claim squatter's rights, but that only works if the other side, like the Philippines, is weaker.

"The US is guaranteeing that the Philippines will have full access to the resources in those two areas while shutting the Chinese completely out. It shows that America, which so far remained impartial in these territorial disputes, will now come down hard on the side of its allies. It also reminds China that the US Navy is still . . ."

The anchor held up a hand while she listened to her earpiece. "Dr. Anderson, my producer says the Chinese ambassador to the UN has just released an official statement. He's sending it to me now."

She turned to read the flat-screen display to one side. After a moment she reported, "It's not very long. They condemn the 'unlawful seizure,' and so on, then say they will not be intimidated, and threaten 'grave consequences.'"

Facing her guest, she asked, "What do you think that means, Doctor?"

"It means we're playing on a different level now."

4 September 2015, 9:00 a.m. local time
August 1st Building, Ministry of National Defense Compound
Beijing, People's Republic of China

President Wen asked the question flatly. "How much more do we stand to lose?"

The foreign minister, already apologetic, answered, "I can't say, Comrade Chairman. We didn't believe the Americans would react that strongly, or quickly. My analysts are studying US official statements and other sources, trying to understand what they missed."

"Maybe the US president has been reading Sun Tzu," added Defense Minister Yu. "Our possessions in the South China Sea were vulnerable. They used them to send us a message."

Wen responded, "A message, a reminder, or a threat?"

"That depends on how we wish to view it," the defense minister answered. "But the Americans don't want to fight us any more than we want to fight them."

"But they are fully involved now, as you correctly predicted they would be. But with the fall of Pyongyang and the surrender of KPA units to ROK or US forces, the situation has changed, and not to our advantage."

The defense minister reminded them all, "This isn't about that capital or the Korean People's Army; it's about nuclear weapons in the former DPRK. We haven't found any in the territory we've occupied—none. And we've heard nothing from the Americans or the South Koreans, so it is likely they haven't found any either."

"Comrade Chairman, our troops are near Dong-an and Yak-san, only ten kilometers from the Yongbyon nuclear facility. Our best chances of finding nuclear weapons is there. We must seize the facility before we even begin to consider a cease-fire."

"Even if it means firing on South Korean forces, General?" asked Wen. "The intelligence reports suggest the South Koreans are now supporting the former KPA units, providing them with provisions and ammunition. What if our soldiers come in contact with ROK Army units? Are we now to engage them as well?"

"If we move quickly, that may not be necessary, Comrade Chairman," answered the defense minister. "The advance of US and ROK army forces has slowed, due to the need to organize and supply former KPA units. If we get across the Chongchon River, and then stop, establishing a defensive line from the coastline through Anju to Tokchon, we maximize our chances of finding the nuclear weapons, while minimizing the possibility of an altercation between our forces and the Americans and their ROK ally."

Wen frowned as he considered Yu's suggestion. After a brief moment, he nodded slowly and said, "Unless we wish to change our goal, we must continue."

Several CMC members shook their heads; the defense minister repeated strongly, "The security of China against a nuclear attack is paramount."

The president stood. "Then that's it." He ordered the foreign minister, "We must make every effort to remind the world that we are doing this on behalf of all Asia. We will not rest until the Kim's nuclear stockpile is found and destroyed."

CHAPTER SEVENTEEN

JUGGERNAUT

4 September 2015, 1500 local time
Third Army Field Headquarters
Outside Taedong, North Korea

General Tae Seok-won and his battle staff were engulfed by a sea of ROK uniforms. The North Koreans wore camouflage fatigues, just like the other officers and soldiers at Sohn's forward headquarters. To a civilian, they might have looked the same, but Tae knew that they stood out vividly. The two green colors were different, one darker, the other brighter, and the brown had a reddish tone that contrasted when he stood next to one of the Southerners. It had distracted Tae a little at first, marking him and his men as outsiders, but he was trying to rise above it. He hoped Sohn and the others could get used to it as well.

Sohn had placed his headquarters at Taedong, ten to fifteen miles west of the capital, because the highways were still intact. The South Korean general and his staff were meeting in an open-sided tent. Whether by accident or design, the map table they used faced away from Pyongyang. Tae knew that if he turned to the southeast, he could mark the city's position by the gray cloud that hung over it. From their position on the city outskirts, he could see the highway, carrying their troops northwest.

The Battle of Pyongyang was over. Now the two armies had to adjust from fighting each other to working together to face the oncoming Chinese. The capital city's highways had been torn up by fighting long before the South Korean army had arrived, and that battered network now had to support thousands of vehicles and ten times that many men, with their supplies. The first order of business was repositioning both armies along a new defensive line north of the city.

The first task Sohn's engineers had been assigned, even before restoring electric power or repairing the water system in Pyongyang, was clearing the roads that led out of the city. Youth Hero Highway led west toward Taedong, while Sochon Street led north. Both avenues were completely choked with military traffic pulling out of the city, and movement was frustratingly low.

Everything capable of moving and fighting was being sent north to establish a new defensive position near Sukchon and Sunchon. By the time disparate ROK and KPA troops got there, they had to be ready to fight again, but this time on the same side. Tae and his officers found themselves sharing information with the Southerners that would have gotten them shot just a few weeks earlier: radio procedures, weapons and ammunition inventories, unit strengths. Tae also found he needed more and more resources from Sohn's forces as additional KPA units declared their loyalty. Fuel and food were the biggest concern, of course, but they also needed artillery. Most of Tae's had been destroyed in the fighting at Pyongyang.

But there were other, more sensitive issues, such as the investigators that had been "interviewing" his men. "If you want my soldiers to work with yours, they can't be afraid they'll be thrown into prison," Tae demanded.

The intelligence colonel on Sohn's staff countered, "Some of the men you command were party officials, responsible for human rights violations, or other criminal activity. A lot of them aren't even soldiers. They're still wearing civilian clothes."

Tae bristled at the phrase "criminal activity," but waited for the colonel to finish. "Immediately after the fifteenth of August, the government issued a general order for all able-bodied men, most of whom were reservists anyway, to be mobilized. Regardless of the clothes they wear, they are soldiers under my command."

The colonel didn't back down. "Your own role in the Kim regime is still under investigation as well, General," he threatened.

"Then perhaps the best thing for my men and I is to defend Pyongyang against whatever Chinese units break through your defenses. Your men can stay outside the city limits."

General Sohn shook his head. "That isn't what we agreed to."

"Neither was criminal prosecution of my troops," Tae responded sharply. "I'm adding a new condition: blanket amnesty for all the men under my command. It never occurred to me that you would allow this type of thing, but if you are, then we will remain in Pyongyang and you can do without my eight full divisions of veteran soldiers."

The colonel actually laughed. "That's the best place for them! They'd crack and run as soon as the Chinese opened fire."

"That's enough, Colonel," snapped Sohn.

Tae laughed. "Really, Colonel? Then please explain how these soldiers— outnumbered, hungry, low on ammunition, and surrounded—held against a full-fledged frontal assault by your best troops. And have you forgotten that I already have many other troops already fighting the Chinese?"

Tae was answering the colonel's insult, but he made sure to include the general and the rest of his staff in his reply. He then turned to address Sohn directly. "My men are fighting for their homes now, and if they survive to go home, they deserve to live free of revenge."

General Sohn nodded. "Agreed."

5 September 2015, 0115 local time
Anju Bridge, Chongchon River
Anju, North Korea

They came in low from the southwest as fast as they dared, only slowing once they neared their objective. They were in a hurry.

Rhee wasn't in his personal helicopter this time, but a stock machine of the Ninth Brigade, along with the rest of his five-man team. It had been a short ride, only seventy-five kilometers from their new base outside Pyongyang to Anju, or more specifically to a bridge just west of the city, over the Chongchon River.

He used the ride to work on replacing their top cover. While they had prepped and loaded for the mission, they'd been able to watch a live video feed from a Searcher UAV that they'd sent north of Anju. Chinese troops were coming south, at speed, and the Ninth Brigade was using the UAV to search for the advancing PLA units. Unfortunately, it may have found them, because ten minutes after Rhee's team took off, the UAV's signal ceased.

Whether it was to hostile action or some operational accident was impossible to tell. The controllers had lost time while they confirmed that the vehicle was truly gone before launching a replacement. Unfortunately, the UAV was built for endurance, not speed. The Israeli-made UAV, about the size of a Piper Cub private aircraft, traveled just about as slowly. In fact, their Surion helicopters were faster. The UAV would be on station some time after they arrived, but it wasn't there yet.

As they flew north, Rhee had weighed their options. The Chinese were advancing faster than threatening weather, and he needed to know where they were. In theory, loss of their reconnaissance could be used to justify a mission abort, or at least a delay, but he decided against it. There was no time to reset and start over.

Gangrim Phase II was well underway. Rhee and his Ghosts were once more tracking down North Korean WMDs, this time north of Pyongyang. And with the detailed information from General Tae, they'd seized a number of bunkers that neither the South Korean NIS nor American intelligence knew of. But the intervention of the Chinese had almost doubled their workload. Instead of just removing the threat of chemical or nuclear attack, they now had to also slow the advance of the Chinese army.

The weight of the Chinese advance was coming down the western side of the Korean Peninsula, along a coastal plain some sixty kilometers wide. From that point east, the land rose and became hilly, then downright mountainous— definitely not good ground for armored vehicles. In fact, that kind of terrain would slow any type of unit. Besides, Pyongyang was in the western part of the DPRK, and the distance to the former North Korean capital from the Chinese border was shortest on the west.

While the western coast was relatively flat, it was threaded with rivers that flowed from the mountains westward to the coast. The Chongchon River ran east to west right across the coastal plan. Half a kilometer wide in spots, it made a perfect defensive barrier.

And there were a lot of other smaller rivers and bridges. South Korean and US aircraft and special operations teams were dropping them ahead of the advancing Chinese as fast as they could.

Or at least, they had been. ROK aircraft had already destroyed three of the four bridges across the Chongchon near Anju, but they'd lost two F-16s on the last raid. Accustomed to complete air supremacy, the ROK Air Force had cut some corners, in the interest of speed. The strikers had been sent out without escorts, and had run in to a Chinese offensive fighter sweep, a flight of J-11 Flankers looking for trouble. Surprised in mid-strike, the F-16s had lost two of their number before escaping.

Chinese fighters venturing that far south told everyone that the days of unopposed air operations were over. It also hinted that the Chinese were very interested in that part of the Korean landscape.

That's when Rhee Han-gil's Ghost Brigade got the mission, barely seven hours earlier. The last bridge over the Chongchon River was his target. The ROK Air Force would stay busy, hitting nearby targets, but with more precautions.

Luckily, Rhee's plan was simple, largely because there was no time for anything fancy. A South Korean navy sub in the Korea Bay would launch Hyunmoo cruise missiles. They were stealthy and smart enough to follow the river valley from the coast all the way up to the bridge. They were guided by GPS signals, and were accurate enough for most targets, but the concrete piers that supported the Anju Bridge were only a few meters across, and they were very strong.

Rhee and his team would get close to the bridge and set up a differential GPS transmitter. It would provide a ground reference for the missiles' navigation systems, reducing their miss distance from several meters to a few centimeters—less than two inches.

His team would sneak in, set up the transmitter, calibrate it for their location, wait for the boom, and then sneak out. With a little luck, they wouldn't even be seen, much less have to fight. Rhee was more than happy to let the navy do the heavy lifting this time.

They had clear weather, and relatively smooth air. The helicopter's radar warning receiver remained silent, and they arrived at the insertion point only fifty minutes after taking off. Rhee was mindful of the short distance back to friendly forces. The united Korean armies needed time to regroup.

Rhee was the first man out, followed by Lieutenant Guk, then the two corporals and finally Master Sergeant Oh, carrying the real-time differential GPS transmitter. Weighing about twenty kilos, and the size of a large backpack, the only tricky thing about using it was telling the transmitter its precise geographic position.

To guide missiles within centimeters of the target, the transmitter had to be placed just as precisely. They would use laser rangefinders to feed distances into the device, which already had a very accurate map loaded in its memory. While Oh and his assistant, Corporal Dae, took measurements and typed the results into a laptop computer, Rhee,

Guk, and the other corporal, Ban, would make sure they weren't disturbed. Unless there was a hardware problem, they'd need ten minutes. When it was ready, they would send a signal via satellite, and the sub, loitering at periscope depth, would launch six missiles. A few minutes later, the Anju Bridge would be history.

Of course, nothing was ever that simple. The city of Anju, on the southern bank of the river, was suspected to be one of the last strongholds of the Kim faction. Intelligence estimates suggested that at least a division was holed up in the city. And the only high ground in the area was a pair of low hills on the river's south bank, barely four kilometers west of the city. That's where they had to place the transmitter.

They'd landed as planned, a little over a klick from their destination, and the helicopter departed, going to a loiter spot farther south where it would wait.

In spite of the clear weather and a half moon, they were using night vision goggles. The river was on their left, a few hundred meters wide. Lieutenant Guk, on point, led them across dry rice paddies, using every bit of the meager cover. The low-lying land near the river was all farmed, with only an occasional tree or row of bushes separating one field from the next.

They could hear insects, and even the plop of a fish jumping occasionally, but nothing of human origin. Most honest folk were asleep at this hour, and the fighting discouraged casual travel at night.

They were in single file, a few meters between each man. They made little sound, and spoke only to warn of possible threats or to give an all clear. Rhee had even turned down the volume on his headset radio.

There were a just few lights ahead on the left, which marked a village to the west of Anju, named Unhak-ri.

Unfortunately, it sat on top of the nearest of the two hills that overlooked the bridge, and Rhee's team carefully worked their way past the settlement, heading for the eastern hill, which was a little closer to their target, anyway.

The burst of fire, and then another one, made the five drop and freeze as one man. Guk's voice reported softly, "I can't see the source, but it's ahead of us, toward the bridge." There were no signs of bullet strikes near them, but Rhee had the team sound off, just to be sure. Everyone was fine.

Rhee tried to imagine what the circumstances were up ahead. Was the Kim faction fighting with the now united KPA? Were there deserters or bandits ahead, preying on civilians?

They listened for a moment, then Rhee gave the all clear and they began moving forward again. Another single shot, maybe from a pistol, caused them to stop once more, but there was still no sign of the shooter, or that they were even the target. Rhee ruled out accidental discharge as a possibility. Then a cascade of fire from several weapons removed all doubt. There was a firefight ahead of them.

Caution dictated they slow and be more vigilant, but necessity hurried them along. The only certainty was that people ahead of them were shooting at something. Hopefully, the night vision gear, keyed to heat emissions, would spot them before they saw Rhee's Ghosts.

The bulk of the second hill lay ahead of them, a dark mound blocking the stars to the east. There were no buildings on it, and it was not cultivated, just covered with low scrub and saplings not worth cutting down for firewood.

"Three forward," Rhee said from the third position. Moving past Corporal Ban, he found Guk about ten meters ahead, prone, goggles up, using night vision binoculars. Rhee quietly approached and went prone as well. Without speaking, Guk offered the colonel his binoculars and pointed to a spot two-thirds of the way up the hill. Rhee flipped up his own night vision gear and adjusted the binoculars.

Unlike his goggles, which sensed heat, the binoculars amplified the existing light, as well as magnifying the image. Bracing his elbows, Rhee followed the lieutenant's cue and searched the hillside.

Movement caught his eye, and he saw someone come up to a kneeling position, fire, and then drop down again. It was a short burst, and he was firing up the hill, away from the river. What was he shooting at?

There was another shot, this time from the pistol again, but it wasn't quite a pistol. And then a different person fired, but remaining prone.

Rhee lowered the binoculars and turned his head to see Guk watching him. "Sir, we need that hill." It was obvious, but the lieutenant was confirming the logical conclusion that followed from that fact.

There weren't supposed to be any friendlies in this area. "Take Dae and swing south until you can go up from the back. I'll bring the others in from here. Tell me when you're ready."

Guk took Corporal Dae and headed off, while Rhee called the other two team members forward into line-abreast formation. He used the binoculars to study the hillside, not only to watch for any reaction to Guk's movements, but also to try and get some sort of clue about who was fighting whom. *So much for sneaking in,* he thought.

Rhee heard a "Ready" over his headset, and answered, "Moving."

Corporal Ban was the team sniper, and had set up his DSR-50, a heavy .50-caliber sniper rifle. It was fitted with a powerful night vision sight, and he'd provide overwatch while his two comrades moved up.

As soon as Rhee heard Guk's radio signal, he advanced, staying low, eyes on the hill, rushing to the best cover he could find. A beat after the colonel stopped, Oh moved up, then it was Dae's turn to displace forward while Rhee had his glasses trained on the hillside.

They'd practiced the tactic so much it was almost instinctive. Each could pick a piece of cover that gave his comrades good places to go when it was their turn to move. Whenever he was stationary, Rhee studied the combatants and watched the clock. The ROK Air Force raids would keep any Chinese fighters occupied for a while, but Rhee wanted his team done and gone before the Chinese got a chance to notice anything else.

There were several shooters on each side. One group was armed with automatic rifles, and Rhee was pretty sure now that strange pistol shot he'd heard before was some sort of silenced assault rifle. That implied special operations forces. Before everything came apart in the DPRK, the North had plenty of SOF troops.

And he'd bet at least one of the sides was allied with the Kim faction. That made the other group at least a nominal ally, but there was no guarantee that they'd be friends. And he didn't have time to sort out who was who.

They were getting close, perhaps two hundred meters from the hill, when Guk reported, "We've found a body. It's Chinese."

That brought him up short. The others with Rhee had heard the report as well, and he signed for them to remain in place. "Confirm Chinese," Rhee transmitted.

Guk responded immediately. "Digital pattern fatigues, weapon is a suppressed QBZ-03."

Chinese weapon, Chinese uniform. The pieces fell into place instantly. Pathfinders, sent to seize and hold a strategic chokepoint, like a bridge, were a tactic as old as war. And the others must be Kim faction troops guarding the bridge.

"Engage the Chinese," Rhee ordered. "Self-defense only against the other side."

Rhee had barely finished speaking before Ban's rifle boomed. Even with a muzzle brake and a suppressor, it sounded like a thunderclap. Rhee kept the glasses to his face long enough to see what was likely a Chinese soldier fall, and brought his own weapon up to cover Ban as he hurriedly shifted position forward. Oh was firing as well.

It was another two bounds before they saw any return fire, coming from the Chinese positions. It struck close to Rhee, who was in front, but Ban's rifle boomed again and Rhee heard Ban report, "Target down." The Kim side of the firefight was silent, but Rhee could hear the fire from his men, and Guk reported, "Engaged, two down."

They kept moving forward, up the hill slope, team members staying low and bringing a lethal crossfire down on anyone that shot back.

Finally, they were near the crest, and Rhee saw a dead Chinese soldier, one of Ban's victims, given the size of the hole in his chest. He switched back and forth between the IR goggles and the night vision binoculars, looking for enemies. All the nearby heat sources belonged to his men or freshly dead Chinese.

Guk's voice warned, "Coming in from your right," and the lieutenant and Corporal Dae joined the other three.

Corporal Dae reported, "Sir, while we were working our way up the hill, I got word the UAV is on station." Dae was the team's radioman and UAV controller.

Now that the long-delayed vehicle was on station, Rhee could only smile. "Look for the Chinese. Send it up the highway." While Dae did that, the rest of the team stayed low and kept a wary eye down the hill.

A few moments later, a voice called out, "Yellow Five." At least it was in Korean.

While the rest of his team took cover and searched for targets, Rhee called back, "I don't know the countersign. There are nine dead Chinese soldiers over here. Are there more?" Ban was still moving, looking for a clear angle, but Oh and Dae both reported that they had targets.

There was no immediate response, and Rhee added, "Do you have wounded? We have a medic."

The voice answered, "Identify yourselves."

Rhee wasn't going to lie. "ROK Army. We're here to blow up the bridge. Will you agree to a truce? We don't have to fight."

"We're supposed to guard the bridge."

"The Chinese are coming soon, before daybreak if those bodies tell us anything." Rhee was beginning to feel silly, holding a conversation with someone twenty meters away in the dark. The clock was ticking, but he really didn't want to kill other Koreans if he didn't have to. He repeated, "Will you agree to a truce?"

After a short pause, the voice responded, "Truce." He didn't sound pleased, but stood and took two steps forward. In his goggles, Rhee could see a figure in fatigues. He was holding an assault rifle, but it was pointed down.

Hoping that if they were double-crossers, they were also bad shots, he stood, moving slowly, and said, "Colonel Rhee Han-gil, ROK Special Forces."

"Captain Tak Ho-rim, DPRK Reconnaissance Bureau."
Tak didn't mention allegiance to any faction, but it didn't
really matter. "Where's the rest of your team?" Tak asked.

"They are ready to stand down, if your men are as well."

Tak sighed. "There's nothing to fight about—at the
moment," he added.

The two sides rose to their feet slowly, weapons lowered,
but everyone seemed reluctant to sling them. "We have two
men wounded," Tak announced.

Rhee motioned to Corporal Ban, who was the team
medic as well as their sniper. He hurried in the direction
Tak had indicated.

"What's this about the Chinese army?" Tak demanded.

Corporal Dae reported, "Sir, the UAV has movement on
the highway." Dae offered the colonel a video tablet.

Feigning more nonchalance than he felt, Rhee took the
tablet and invited Tak to look as well. Curious, the captain
slung his assault rifle and walked over, standing next to Rhee.

"This is National Route 1," Dae explained, which ran
down from the north and led to their bridge. The infrared
image showed a straight section of highway. It was filled with
a long column of armored fighting vehicles, smaller ones
in the vanguard and a phalanx of main battle tanks in the
center. They were heading south.

Rhee looked at the readouts from the drone. "You've
got the UAV moving south."

"Pacing the front of the column," Dae explained. "About
thirty kilometers an hour."

"And the drone is less than thirty kilometers from
here," Rhee observed, checking its location. *No time to waste.*
"Lieutenant Guk, monitor the UAV and use the binoculars
to watch the far side of the river. Call out if you see any

movement. Master Sergeant, Corporal Dae, get the transmitter set up. Ban, as soon as you've treated the wounded, set up to cover the bridge." If the main column was within thirty kilometers, there could be more scouts closer than that—much closer.

"What do you think you're doing?" Tak demanded angrily, and Rhee explained about the transmitter and how it would help guide the missiles.

The explanation only made the North Korean angrier. "Your aircraft are spying on our country. You are sending missiles to destroy our bridges. When will you leave us alone?"

Rhee tried to stay calm. He also had leftover adrenaline from the battle. "Should we have let the Chinese kill you?"

Ban walked up and reported, "Sir, I've treated them, both bullet wounds. They need to be evacuated, but they should be all right once they're in hospital." Turning to the captain, he added, "There are five others, already dead. I'm sorry. I couldn't do anything for them."

Tak acknowledged the report with a nod. "We just wanted to be left alone," he said sadly, but his anger flashed again. "You've destroyed my country, and now the Chinese are jumping in to help finish us off. We won't go down quietly!"

The remnants of Tak's force, just four more men, had gathered behind their commander. As opposed to the well-equipped Southerners, the group carried basic AKM assault rifles. Rhee saw one handheld night vision scope. They looked underfed and battered by weeks of combat. Rhee wanted them to lose, but they were still Koreans. There was no joy in winning a civil war.

Rhee checked Oh and Dae's progress. They had unfolded the transmitter, and were taking readings with a laser rangefinder. They weren't done yet, but would be soon. There was no time for an extended political discussion, but he had to try.

Rhee spoke to the entire group. "We don't have to fight anymore. The two factions fighting each other in Pyongyang have stopped and joined with the ROK Army. They're turning to face the Chinese as a single force. Come back with us. Your wounded will get excellent medical care, and—"

"Desertion!" Tak shouted. "Betrayal!" one of Tak's men added. Another said, "Surrender? I don't want to be a prisoner."

"You will not be prisoners. Wouldn't you rather fight our common enemy, the Chinese?" Rhee proposed hopefully.

"It's all lies anyway," Tak concluded.

"Are the Chinese a lie?" Rhee countered, pointing to the corpses.

"Colonel, the transmitter checks out and is calibrated," Oh reported. Rhee could see him gesturing with a thumbs-up.

"Dae, send the message," Rhee ordered, frustrated. At least the original part of his mission was proceeding. A moment later, the corporal said, "Message received. Six and a half minutes."

But the radio gave him an idea. Rhee said, "Now contact Third Army, and see if we can get in comms with General Tae. He should be at General Sohn's headquarters."

Rhee turned back to Tak and his men. "I'm going to get you proof that the North and South have joined forces—there is only one Korea!"

Tak and the others shook their heads, but one of his men asked, "What happened in Pyongyang? We've had no word since the city was surrounded."

By the time Rhee had explained about the ROK's truce with Tae's forces in the city, Dae announced, "The headquarters staff is waking General Tae now."

Rhee checked his watch. The missiles were just under four minutes out. The receiver came alive with static, and then, "This is General Tae Seok-won."

"Sir, this is Colonel Rhee. We met on the southern bank of the Taedong River a few days ago."

"The Special Forces brigade commander. I remember you." The flat statement held a question.

Rhee explained where he was, and who he was with. The general listened quietly, then said, "Let me speak with the captain."

Rhee passed the handset to the captain. Dae turned up the volume, and Tak held the receiver so everyone could hear. "This is Tae Seok-won of the General Staff."

Tak's men recognized the name. Some came to attention. Tak did not, but discipline held enough for him to respond. "Captain Tak Ho-rim, Fifth Reconnaissance Battalion. There is no more General Staff, and my leaders say you are responsible for the fifteenth of August and the war."

"The General Staff is gone, but there still is a Korea, and it needs to be protected. I have many divisions under my command, and we're going to stop the Chinese army. What are you fighting for? Your cause is lost. Join us, and fight for your home."

"You are not the rightful leaders of our country!"

"Kim's rule is ended. It cannot be restored."

Tak just shook his head, and gave the handset back to Rhee. After Rhee signed off, Guk announced, "Two minutes."

Everyone looked toward the bridge, and began taking cover. If a missile missed the bridge at all, it might miss by more than a little bit.

"Dae, signal the helicopter. Give them our location for immediate extraction." It didn't matter if the missiles hit or missed. Their job was done, and there was nothing more they could do. And while the sound of small-arms fire might not reach to the troops in the city, the imminent explosions would attract unwelcome visitors to the hill.

Master Sergeant Oh waited near the transmitter, and when he saw Rhee watching, gave another thumbs-up. Everything was working properly.

The laser rangefinders said they were four hundred meters away from the bridge, but he was taking no chances. Rhee was prone, behind cover. Watching through binoculars, he half-expected to see Chinese vehicles approaching the far end.

The first sign of the missiles' arrival was a roar and fireball at the base of the bridge's center pier. A second blossomed at almost the same spot half a second later, and quickly looking left down the valley, Rhee spotted four small sparks in a line, moving too fast to follow, each hammering the same spot on the bridge pier.

Each Hyunmyoo missile had a half-ton warhead, and the impact point was on the west side of the bridge, at the base of the center pier. To Rhee it looked not like one explosion, but the same explosion lasting six times as long, blasting and tearing at the concrete, until the span on each side began to sag, and finally collapsed into the river.

Rhee was glad they were so far away. He'd felt the pressure wave from each blast pass over him, and his ears rang with echoes of the explosions.

Oh was already breaking down the transmitter. They'd take it back out with them. Dae reported, "The helicopter's ETA is fifteen minutes."

They had to move back down the hill, to flatter ground. Still hopeful, Rhee turned to Tak's men. There were seven, counting the wounded. "It will be tight, but there's room for all of you. I promise you will not be imprisoned or punished." Looking directly at Tak, he asked, "At least let me take your injured men with us. They'll be in a first-class hospital within an hour."

After a pause, one of Tak's men spoke up. "My family is south of the capital, if they're still alive. I'll go. I can help carry the wounded." A second man said, "I'll go, too." The remaining two looked at Tak, who said, "I'm staying, but go if you wish," and they hurried to help the others.

The group organized themselves for the trip, each pair of Northerners carrying a wounded comrade. They stacked their weapons and other gear they wouldn't need.

Rhee should have been satisfied, but in the face of Tak's stubbornness, he felt like a failure. He urged, "It's a new chance for you."

Everyone looked at Tak expectantly, but he shook his head, and Rhee gave the order to move out. They had a ride to catch. As he turned to leave, Rhee hesitated, and asked, "Why stay?"

Tak answered, "Because I can't imagine anything else." The captain turned and slung his rifle, and walked south toward town.

Rhee watched the captain disappear, then headed west, down his side of the hill.

5 September 2015, 9:00 a.m. EDT
CNN Special Report

"The European Union and the Association of Southeast Asian Nations have both agreed to impose economic sanctions on China, restricting both Chinese-manufactured goods and sales to China, especially of 'dual-use' items, items that have both civil and military applications. Among other things, this has affected a multibillion-euro joint helicopter program with France, and numerous instrument and computer sales to the People's Republic of China.

"This follows the passage of a sanctions bill by both houses of Congress and awaiting the president's signature. Secretary of State Marie Baldwin spoke after the bill's passage, saying, 'China's attempt to somehow preserve or sustain its client state is both misguided and harmful to the entire Asian region. Sanctions always hurt both trading partners, but the short-term cost to us must be weighed against the potential damage the DPRK could still inflict.'

"In related news, units of the US Seventh fleet have entered the shallow waters of the Yellow Sea with the publicly stated purpose of blocking any action by the nearby Chinese navy against either the Republic of Korea or the former DPRK. Many Chinese naval bases line the eastern and northern sides of this body of water, half the size of the Gulf of Mexico.

"A US Navy spokesman says that while he cannot discuss the precise location of naval vessels, he reported that Chinese and American warships are already 'well within weapons range of each other.'

"The only public reaction from China to these latest developments was a statement released by the Chinese ambassador to the United Nations that 'China would not be intimidated or deterred from acting in its own legitimate security interests.'"

CHAPTER EIGHTEEN
CONFRONTATION

5 September 2015, 1300 local time
Third Army Field Headquarters
Outside Taedong, North Korea

With Operation Gangrim winding down, Rhee Han-gil had expected the summons to General Sohn's headquarters. He would report not only on his own recent mission, but the Ghost Brigade's operations as a whole. As his helicopter approached from the air, he could see the whole complex, sprawled more than half a kilometer on each side, with untidy clusters of tents, vans, and vehicle parks. He also noted antiaircraft emplacements that were thankfully idle. Lanes for vehicles wound through the base, raising dust that hung in the hot air until it found someone to cling to. Its size was appropriate, since it was the forward headquarters for the entire ROK Third Army.

Rhee was met by an anxious aide as soon as his helicopter landed, who led him through the camp to the commander's area. They were meeting in the open, in a tent with three sides rolled up, the fourth shading them from the afternoon sun. A cluster of officers worked at laptops to one side. It was a familiar scene, until he noticed that at least a third of the soldiers in the tent were wearing DPRK uniforms. The sight bumped up hard against a lifetime of upbringing, as well as his entire army career. Intellectually, he wasn't opposed to the idea, but it did take some getting used to.

A senior officer in a North Korean uniform stepped outside. Rhee immediately recognized General Tae. The aide saluted the general, and then left. Rhee also saluted the former DPRK general, who returned it and offered his hand.

"Thank you for not killing those men outside Anju."

"You were the one who convinced them to join us, General," Rhee replied.

Tae nodded, then said, "I'm really speaking of Captain Tak. You didn't shoot him, even though he refused to come with you. We might have to fight him some day soon."

Rhee disagreed, as politely as he could with a general. "You can't change a dead man's mind, sir. I can't really think of 'North' and 'South' Korea any more." Rhee paused, meaning to say more, but realized that Tae probably thought about the issue differently. He started to apologize, but Tae stopped him.

"I could not imagine that I would be here, in this place," Tae explained, "but in truth, I could not imagine any kind of future living under the Kims. To stay sane in the DPRK, one had to live day to day."

The aide reappeared. "General Tae, Colonel Rhee, General Sohn has arrived."

Officially, Rhee was reporting to his immediate superior, General Kwon, but General Sohn, commanding the ROK Third Army, and Tae, representing the former Northern forces, sat in, listening and asking questions.

After describing his own mission, Rhee briefed them about the Ghost Brigade's operations in the last phase of Operation Gangrim. He used a map that showed the

Korean Peninsula north of Pyongyang, marked with lines showing both the Chinese advance, the suspected positions of the Kim faction holdouts, and the "United Han" forces. He stumbled a little over the phrase, and apologized.

"It's not official yet," Sohn cautioned the group. "The National Assembly is still arguing over whether it should be 'United Han' or 'Great Han' Republic. At least they're leaving the flag alone."

"'Han' is a good name," Tae added. "There's history behind it. I believe most Northerners will be able to identify with it, in time."

For Rhee's Ghosts, Gangrim had been a tremendous tactical success, but also a strategic failure. Although they'd struck dozens of targets, and captured or destroyed the vast majority of the North's chemical weapons, none of the missions had yielded a single nuclear warhead. Nobody was naïve enough to believe that the Kims' claims of possessing nuclear weapons had been all bluster. The DPRK had actually detonated several devices. They were there, somewhere.

"They may have been in the area the Chinese have occupied," suggested Kwon hopefully.

Tae shook his head. "Unlikely. Most of the General Staff was unaware of their true location, including myself, but the Kims were always worried about the threat of a Chinese invasion." Gesturing toward the map, he explained, "This is exactly what Kim Jung-un was afraid of. I always believed they were kept somewhere close to the capital. And it doesn't really matter where they were. They certainly could be moved, and almost certainly have been, into the holdouts' strongest, most secure location."

"They're in there. They have to be," Sohn declared, pointing to the marked area on the map.

It was a sweeping assumption, but probably correct, Rhee believed. The Chinese army had advanced as far south as the Chongchon River, which ran roughly east-west across the peninsula. The Han forces, and a few US Eighth Army units, were still some forty kilometers to the south, organizing near Sukchon and Sunchon.

Having delivered his brief, Rhee expected to be dismissed, and began to gather his notes and tablet, but General Kwon said, "Please remain, Colonel. This discussion will affect you and your men, and we would welcome your ideas."

Sohn's intelligence officer, a colonel as well, briefed them all on what was known about "the Stronghold." Scouts were well north of the Han army, watching and searching for the Chinese as well as the Northern holdouts. The scouts' progress, or sometimes lack of it, had allowed them to draw a border around the Kim faction's probable refuge.

From the city of Anju east to Lake Yonpung, south to Sunchon, then west to Sukchon and back north to Anju, an irregular rectangle enclosed a sparsely settled region filled with rugged, heavily wooded mountains, and threaded with river valleys. Numerous intel reports had all came to the same conclusion. The Kim faction had retreated into the highly defendable area, which not only held several army bases, but also a missile base and an airfield. It was also very likely that there were other installations built secretly into the rocky landscape.

"The Kim faction pulled a lot of their best antiaircraft units into the area, so we have very little information from aerial reconnaissance, either by manned aircraft or UAVs. So many UAVs have been shot down that we can't afford to lose the rest. We are using what's left to track the Chinese forces, although it's your prerogative, General, if you want to change their tasking."

Sohn shook his head. "No. We need to know about Chinese movements as well. I don't like fighting two different enemies at the same time."

"But our enemies can also fight each other," the intelligence officer responded happily. "The northern edge of the Stronghold is on the south side of the Chongchon River. It's likely that the Chinese will be able to attack soon. They're bringing up bridging equipment, as well as more artillery, so they can force a crossing."

Tae had to say it. "They may very well be ready to attack before we will."

"The area is all mountains, filled with troops that have had weeks to dig in," Sohn replied. "I won't send in a force that can't win."

"Then let the Chinese attack, and inflict some casualties," Kwon suggested.

Sohn shook his head. "I think we must move quickly. If the holdouts have nuclear weapons, then the risk increases the longer we wait. The Chinese attack across the river may pressure the holdouts to launch." He gestured toward Rhee. "You remember what the colonel reported about the holdouts' sentiments—'they won't go down quietly.'"

Tae was also against waiting. "And if the Chinese do get across the river into the mountains, it could be very hard to push them back out, if it came to that."

Sohn agreed. "Once they've paid in blood for that land, they'll want to keep it, or charge us a high price to give it back."

"When the Chinese invaded Vietnam in 1979, then retreated to their own border, all they left behind was scorched earth," Tae said darkly. "If they couldn't steal it, they blew it up or burned it. My country has suffered enough without them adding more ruin and destruction."

"It's now *our* country, General Tae, whatever the politicians decide to call it," injected Rhee firmly. "We will defend it together."

General Sohn, after nodding to General Kwon, said, "And that's why you're here, Colonel. Our orders to General Kwon are twofold: slow down the Chinese advance, and at the same time find a way to break through the holdouts' defenses. We have to destroy their nuclear weapons and any delivery systems before it's too late."

Kwon pointed to Rhee. "Of the two, you can guess which one has the highest priority. I want you to work with me here, designing missions for all the brigades, not just your Ghosts. You've done well in this fight, Colonel, and we need you to come through for us again."

Rhee carefully aimed his response at all the generals. Smiling, he answered, "I'll do my best."

No pressure.

5 September 2015, 1600 local time
USS *Gabrielle Giffords* (LCS 10)
The Yellow Sea

"Captain, *Yantai*'s getting set for another pass." The OOD's report sounded almost routine.

"Understood." Commander Ralph Mitchell fought the urge to walk out on the bridge wing and look aft. The *Independence* class had been built with sloped, smooth sides to reduce their radar signature. They'd done away with the bridge wings, along with a lot of other things.

The old-style helmsman at the wheel and the sailor standing by the engine order telegraph had been eliminated.

The bridge watch even got to sit down, which would have been heresy in his father's navy. The officer of the deck and junior officer of the deck had their own display screens, and sat on either side of a bank of controls for the ship's operation. To look aft, Mitchell could use the flat-screen display next to the chair, complete with joysticks and zoom controls.

The bridge on the *Independence* class was larger than those on most ships, and it seemed even more spacious with only two people at the control console, instead of the five or six or more on earlier ships. The normal watch section of two men—a commissioned officer of the deck, and a senior enlisted junior officer of the deck—could run the ship under most conditions. In a pinch, one man could do it. The "CO's chair" was to the right of the control console, and came equipped with its own workstation. However, Mitchell often preferred the extra chair immediately behind the two watchstanders. Any similarity to science-fiction starships probably came from similar design goals. Probably.

Mitchell's orders were clear. He was to trail the Chinese formation and monitor their operations. The Chinese clearly didn't want him around, but just as clearly weren't ready to fire on him, at least not yet.

"*Yantai*'s speed is still increasing." When you only had two people on the bridge driving the ship, division of labor was important. Mitchell had set up his teams so that the JOOD would concentrate on conning the ship, while the OOD kept his attention on the tactical situation. Monitoring the ship's internal systems and sensors fell to the four watchstanders in Integrated Command Center 1, or ICC1, just behind the conning station.

Although an enlisted man, the JOOD was a first-class petty officer and technical specialist in one of the ship's main systems—the gas turbines and waterjets, the weapons and sensors, and so on. He'd then received cross-training in the others. Besides, Mitchell could rely on Petty Officer Booth's judgment. One of the good things about serving on *Gabby* was her small crew. You got to know everyone. He trusted Booth to mind the store, which allowed the OOD, Lieutenant Sontez, and Captain Mitchell to focus on the Chinese.

The formation they were trailing had left the navy base at Qingdao three days earlier. Chinese fleet activity had steadily increased since the crisis started on the fifteenth of August, but the sailing of this group had both Seoul and Washington deeply concerned.

It was centered on three amphibious ships, which between them could carry a regiment of troops, with armor and helicopter support. Three first-line guided missile destroyers and five frigates escorted them, while Chinese fighters from nearby bases along the coast flew top cover.

At first, some in Washington had thought the group might be heading for the Spratlys, raising the possibility of a naval confrontation in the South China Sea, but there were two fleets based well to the south that were more than capable of performing that mission, and still might. All doubts were removed when the Chinese task force hadn't turned south, but loitered along the border of the Yellow Sea and Korea Bay.

They were likely a contingency force. If the ground troops hit a roadblock, the amphibious force would land their troops to break it up.

As the Chinese incursion into Korea had developed, this task force had steamed about almost at random, keeping clear of the surface traffic that filled the Yellow Sea, but making no attempt to conceal its presence. Every radar on the Chinese ships was energized, broadcasting electromagnetic radiation as it searched for contacts. Helicopters buzzed around the formation, inspecting nearby surface ships and searching for submarines.

Mitchell and *Gabby* had received orders to proceed westward within hours of a US Navy P-8 getting near enough to identify not only the warships, but the amphibs in the center of the formation. It was a twelve-hour run from the port of Busan, on the southeast coast of Korea, around the peninsula and north into the Yellow Sea, pushing her to nearly forty knots. She could go still faster, but would not have had any fuel when she arrived.

As fast as forty knots was, the Chinese formation could have crossed the water between the two coasts and landed its troops long before *Gabby* got there. Evidently, they didn't want to, because they were still steaming in racetracks when *Gabby* showed up that morning.

Mitchell's orders were simply to watch and report the movements of the Chinese formation. Loitering anywhere between forty to sixty miles off the coast, the Chinese could turn east, go to flank speed, and begin landing their troops in a few hours, anywhere from Nampo all the way up to the Chinese border. Although the eastern half of Korea was mountainous, the western coastal plain made it possible to put their troops ashore anywhere, especially in this age of helicopters and air-cushion landing craft. Mitchell was specifically charged to report immediately if the formation turned toward the Korean coast and increased speed to more than fifteen knots.

Gabby had been hurriedly fitted with an electronic intelligence collection van before she left port, and specialists were monitoring Chinese radar signals and their communications traffic down in ICC2. All comms were encoded, of course, but even the number of radio messages sent and the circuits used could be useful. In truth, they were studying how well the Chinese navy did its job. Mitchell and his crew recorded every aspect of the PLAN's operations they could see, from launching and recovering helos to how well the Chinese ships kept position in their formation.

In the old days of the Cold War, the Soviets used to shadow American naval formations the same way. The "tattletales" were either trawlers converted to carry electronic eavesdropping equipment, or small, expendable warships. Russian doctrine was to follow the all-important NATO carrier groups, constantly reporting on their position and activities. If the transmissions ever stopped, it might be the first warning the Soviets had of a Western attack. Similarly, the first sign of a Soviet strike might be a shadowing destroyer suddenly opening fire with every weapon it had, hoping to cripple the carrier in a surprise attack.

Mitchell's only orders were to follow and report, but one of the five Type 054A frigates was doing its best to chase him off. The frigate kept trying to "shoulder" *Gabby* aside. By rights, this should have been easy. Although only a little longer than *Gabby*, the Chinese ship had twice the mass.

Naval ships tried very hard to stay clear of each other. Even a minor ding in the hull could mean weeks or months of repairs in port, not to mention the paperwork. To shoulder another vessel, one ship would pull alongside, matching course and speed, and then slowly inch closer and closer to the other. Eventually, the ship being shouldered would have to change course or collide. It was "chicken of the sea," although nobody ever called it that.

And there was a trick: by keeping your bow ahead of the vessel you were trying to drive off, if the two ships actually collided, the fact that the other guy's bow struck your ship meant it was his fault—much more paperwork for him, and a propaganda victory for you. Ships attempting to shoulder another vessel always had a camera recording the action.

Mitchell didn't cooperate, though. The formation, with nowhere particular to go, was loafing along at fifteen knots, with the US ship matching course and speed. The Chinese frigate could do twenty-seven, according to the intelligence pubs. But each time *Yantai* had come alongside, Mitchell had let the frigate get even with his bow and then steadily bent on more speed.

The first time, *Yantai* had given up after they'd reached twenty-five knots, falling back to her trailing position twenty-one hundred yards astern. After a short interval, *Yantai* had tried again, this time matching speed with *Gabby* until they reached twenty-eight and a half knots.

This was when Mitchell had really missed the bridge wing, because he would have walked out, the wind rushing over him, and studied the foreign warship, only a few dozen yards away.

The Type 054A was the newest class of frigate in the PLA Navy. The Chinese admirals must have liked them, because there were over twenty in the fleet and they were building more. Like most modern warships, she had clean lines and sloped sides, although not quite as radically as *Gabby*. The Type 054A was well armed for her size, with an automatic 76mm gun forward, two rotary 30mm guns aft, and two flavors of missiles—medium-range SAMs and YJ-83 antiship missiles that could reach out almost a hundred miles. Painted a pale gray, she was emblematic of the "new" Chinese navy that had appeared with the new century.

But Mitchell knew *Gabby* made her look like an antique. Instead of a single conventional monohull, she was a trimaran, with a center hull and two outriggers, with four waterjet propulsion units in the main hull. Ton for ton, trimarans had less of their hull in the water, which meant less drag. Her wave-piecing bow jutted out well in front of the deckhouse, which gave not only the illusion, but the reality of speed.

In fact, everything had been sacrificed to that one goal. *Gabby*'s bow gun was only a 57mm, and her only other weapons were a point defense SAM, short-range Hellfire missiles, and four .50-caliber machine guns. She didn't even carry ASW torpedoes, common on most warships. Too much weight. Besides, she didn't have a sonar, so she wouldn't know when to shoot one.

Racing side by side at twenty-eight–plus knots, the two ships were moving almost twice as fast as the formation, but Mitchell wouldn't let the Chinese skipper get his bow ahead of the US ship. When he was sure that *Yantai* couldn't increase her speed any more, he ordered the OOD to increase their speed to thirty-two knots, and they'd smoothly glided away from the Chinese warship.

Gabby circled back, taking station again, this time off the Chinese formation's port beam. Mitchell had watched the frigate take up its trailing position behind them again, and imagined the conversation between her captain and the Chinese formation commander. He tried to put himself in the Chinese captain's and the Chinese admiral's shoes. This might look like a confrontation between ships and weapons, but it was really a contest of minds.

It must have been a short discussion, because Sontez's report came only minutes later. "She's launching her helicopter."

Mitchell could see it rising from behind the frigate's superstructure. Most warships had helicopter pads and hangars built into their stern, and used them for scouting or sub-hunting missions. Some could even carry light anti-ship missiles. The Type 054s carried Russian-built Kamov machines, quite handy but reminding Mitchell of an over-sized light gray bug.

A helicopter might be slow compared to a jet fighter, or even most commercial aircraft, but this one was fast enough to zoom ahead of *Gabby* and then circle her several times.

"Probably taking pictures," Sontez commented.

Meanwhile, *Yantai* had pulled alongside, matching the formation speed of fifteen knots, but didn't seem interested in racing. Her skipper actually kept his bow back a little. He knew that bringing it even with *Gabby* would trigger another contest that he could not win.

"Watch him, OOD," Mitchell cautioned.

The headset beeped. "Captain, the formation just turned east, new heading two seven five degrees true."

"*Yantai* is closing!" Sontez was almost screaming.

Mitchell was ready. "All ahead flank! Hard left rudder! All hands brace for collision!" Booth hit the collision alarm and the warning sound filled his ears. The Chinese ship was probably close enough to hear it as well.

Where another ship might have heeled over in the turn, *Gabby* just pivoted in the water and leapt forward, away from the frigate's knife-sharp bow. Her trimaran hull gave her stability, but also worked against her. Because of *Gabby*'s radically sloping sides, her hull projected farther out underwater than it did at the waterline. In other words, the frigate was a lot closer than it might look.

They all felt the shock through the ship's structure; people not strapped into their seats were thrown to the deck. Rattled around in his chair, Mitchell watched on the starboard quarter camera as the flat of *Yantai*'s bow slammed into the LCS's stern, the frigate heeling over against *Gabby*'s sloping hull.

The Chinese vessel righted herself immediately, but although the two ships were clear at the waterline, a grinding, scraping vibration lasted for several moments before the frigate fell astern. Mitchell could see a long gash in his ship's thin aluminum hull along the water's edge.

The intercom relayed, "Bridge, Engineering. We've got flooding in at least two of the after ballast tanks on the starboard side hull. One of the fuel tanks may have been ruptured as well. The flooding seems to be contained, but I've sent a damage control team to verify our condition. The propulsion plant is still capable of answering all bells."

"Very well. Have the XO inspect the damage." Mitchell acknowledged the report with relief. The damage seemed to be contained. It could have been much worse. Fortunately, the starboard outrigger took the brunt of the blow. There wasn't a lot of equipment in there to get hurt. The diesels and gas turbines were buried deep in the center hull, and there were no screws or rudders to foul, so as long as that damaged section of hull held together, they were in good shape. He checked the pit log. Their speed was still building, now close to forty knots.

"Any problems, JOOD?"

Petty Officer Booth replied, "She's having a little trouble staying on course, Captain. And she's a bit sluggish in answering the helm."

Understandable, Mitchell thought, considering the starboard outrigger had just been pierced and partially flooded. The extra weight would also slow them down.

He ordered, "Bring us to two seven five degrees," then pressed the intercom. "ICC1, Bridge. Make sure all this is getting sent to Seventh Fleet. What's the Chinese ETA to Korean territorial waters?"

"At twenty-two knots they'll reach the twelve-mile line in two and a half hours. If they stay on this course they'll be off the mouth of the Taeryong River delta. Looks like the Chinese marines are going to try landing on the southern bank. It's on your display, Skipper."

Mitchell checked the screen to his right. From the south bank of the Taeryong River delta it was only twenty-five kilometers to the spot where Chinese bridging had been seen on satellite imagery—on the other side of the Chongchon River.

He carefully marked a spot on the chart just outside the mouth of the delta and asked, "What's our best course and ETA to this location?"

After a moment's pause, a line connected the symbol showing their current position to the new destination. "Course zero four eight, two and a half hours at flank, sir."

"Petty Officer Booth, new course zero four eight, all ahead flank."

Mitchell used the time to personally inspect the damage to the starboard outrigger. He met his executive officer at the access hatch. The XO quickly ran down the list. The two aft ballast tanks were breached and completely flooded. Number three fuel tank was leaking, and he had already ordered the engineering officer of the watch to transfer what fuel was left to another tank. Mitchell then followed his XO to the impact site. There he saw the thin aluminum plating high above the waterline had been deformed inward, but had held. The more severe damage was below.

Sure that his ship was seaworthy, Mitchell then took the time to make a report by voice to Seventh Fleet. After that, he made the rounds—a casual inspection, but an inspection nonetheless. The only place he didn't visit was the signals intercept van and ICC2. His security clearance wasn't high enough. The cryptological tech in charge did report they had been rattled, but not harmed by the jolt, and he'd be very grateful if that didn't happen anymore.

Smiling, Mitchell replied he'd do what he could, and returned to the bridge by way of the flight deck. At forty-one knots, the wind buffeted and tore at his clothes, but he stayed for a while, taking in the horizon, before going back inside. There was nothing to see, though. The Chinese were still too far astern.

Although they weren't in sight, Mitchell knew the Chinese could see *Gabby*, both by radar from their scout helicopters and by her own radar emissions. There was no need to conceal her location. In fact, he was doing everything possible to broadcast his presence and precise location. Often warfare was about stealth and surprise. Today, Mitchell was doing his best to make sure there were no surprises.

The Fire Scout drone helicopter they'd launched earlier had taken over the trailing role. Its radar, data linked to *Gabby*, showed the Chinese formation still on course, at twenty-two knots. The escorting frigates and destroyers could do over thirty, but the big amphibious ships weren't built for speed. Twenty-two was the best they could do, so that had to be the formation's maximum speed.

The drone kept well clear. Its radar had the range to see the formation from thirty miles out, and the radar image was sharp enough to allow Mitchell to identify individual ships by class. He'd placed the drone so far out to make sure the Chinese wouldn't think it was a threat. It was still close enough for the Chinese to shoot it out of the sky if they'd wanted to. That fact that they hadn't was hopeful.

There was no "fog of war" in this meeting. Thanks to the Fire Scout drone, Mitchell could figure the exact moment when the Chinese formation would appear on the western horizon, just over twenty miles away.

He'd placed *Gabby* two miles inside Korean territorial waters, which meant the Chinese had nineteen miles to decide if they were ready to start a fight with the United States. Aircraft from the two sides had sparred over the Korean Peninsula, but that had been more chance meetings than deliberate engagements. This time, if they wanted to land their troops, they'd have to deliberately sink an American warship.

Gabby was at battle stations, which meant a total of eight people on the bridge and in ICC1. Mitchell spent most of the time while they waited in his chair. Pacing the bridge would just make everyone else nervous.

The entire crew understood their purpose, but Mitchell explained over the ship's announcing system, "If we have to shoot, I'm going to wait until the Chinese formation's a mile inside Korean waters. I'll angle the ship to present a narrow aspect while keeping one of the Hellfire modules clear, and I'll take her to maximum speed. Be prepared for sharp maneuvers. If there's time, I'll designate the target, but if they fire first, just concentrate everything on the nearest ship for as long as we can." He paused for a moment, and added. "Good luck to us all, and God bless the US Navy."

Lieutenant Sontez, the OOD for general quarters, asked, "Do you think they'll let us get close enough to shoot?"

Mitchell laughed. "They won't waste any missiles on us. Those destroyers each have an automatic 130mm gun forward. Effective range is thirteen miles. Since our 57's and the Hellfires' ranges are about half that, they have a six-mile margin. But they'll be shooting at a fast, sharply maneuvering target."

Petty Officer Booth added, "Skipper, I understand that we're a speed bump, but I would like to get some hits in before we're gone."

Mitchell said, "Right now, the admiral running that formation is rereading his rules of engagement. We know the Chinese are willing to engage Korean units. Without us here, they'd sail right in and land their troops and raise all kinds of hell. But if we say 'halt,' then the admiral's got to decide if sinking us is covered in his orders. It's even money he's been on the phone to his fleet commander. I just wish I could have listened in."

Sontez reported, "Sir, the lead ship is ten miles from the line."

"And twelve miles from us," Mitchell responded. "Evidently they're not ready to shoot us outright. Well, it's time to see what they have in mind." He picked up the microphone for the bridge-to-bridge radio. "Chinese formation, this is USS *Gabrielle Giffords*. State your intentions."

There was no immediate reply. Mitchell was expecting that. He pressed the intercom. "ICC1, tell me when they are *exactly* five miles from the CTML."

He could do the math. The three-minute rule meant that at twenty-two knots, they'd cover twenty-two hundred yards, just over a nautical mile. Subtracting that from ten nautical miles . . .

It kept his mind occupied, and he was only a minute off when ICC1 announced over the intercom. "Five miles, Skipper."

He keyed the radio mike again. "Chinese formation, this is USS *Gabrielle Giffords*. If you enter Korean territorial waters, I will fire on you." Mitchell repeated it, then changed frequencies, and repeated it again. Not that it wasn't obvious.

He checked the bow gun's display. It had an EO tracker, and it was centered on the bow of the lead destroyer. Even at several miles, it seemed to dwarf the smaller US ship.

Sontez announced, "Three miles." After the captain acknowledged his report, the lieutenant stated flatly, "If they shoot, we're dead. If we shoot, we're dead."

"A strong argument in favor of nobody shooting," Mitchell confirmed. "But we aren't going to let them push us around."

"They're at the twelve-mile limit, Captain." Sontez's report had a hint of resignation.

"Understood, OOD," Mitchell replied. The resignation was echoed in Mitchell's acknowledgment, but his orders were crystal clear. "All hands, stand by to engage the lead Chinese destroyer, bearing two three zero degrees, two eight hundred yards. Helm, come left to 225 degrees, all ahead . . ."

"Sir, they're turning." Even as Sontez announced the turn, Mitchell could see it on the monitor. The lead destroyer was no longer showing only its bow, but its starboard side. He used his glasses to check the other ships. They were all turning.

"Belay that order, Lieutenant! Come right to two five zero at fifteen knots. We'll stay on our side of the line and match their speed and course."

"Aye, aye, sir." Sontez couldn't keep the relief out of his voice, and there were a few muted cheers from the watch-standers in ICC1 behind them. Captain Mitchell just kept the glasses raised, silently watching the Chinese do exactly what he'd bet on. They could still sink *Gabby* anytime they wanted, but it looked like they didn't want to.

6 September 2015, 0400 local time
Seventh Air Force Headquarters
Osan Air Base, South Korea

"This time it was five missiles, Tony. Five!" General Randall Carter and his deputy were watching the stateside reaction to the latest North Korean missile launch. As focused as the newspeople were on the loss of life, they really hadn't absorbed all the implications.

"It was probably every Musudan they had," Tony commented. "It's a big step forward, considering eight days ago, they fired one missile and missed completely."

"It seems they finished reading the owner's manual," Carter replied darkly.

The flat-screen on the wall of Tony's office showed the CNN feed. The banner across the bottom read "Breaking News: Lethal chemicals in warhead strike Guam"; the shaky image showed figures in bright yellow protective suits working with chemical detection kits. At MTV-like speed, the picture shifted to a roped-off wooded hillside, then plastic tents set up outside a hospital.

The on-screen anchor reported, "The chemical agent is still being identified, but it is some form of persistent nerve gas, which is making it very hard to decontaminate the victims. There have only been a few cases requiring treatment, though. Most victims die within minutes from asphyxiation."

"I haven't heard them say how big the affected area is," Carter observed.

"Acres right now," Tony answered. "But it's spreading downwind. The only break we got was that one missile hit Apra Harbor dead center and landed in the water, and the other one a mile away in a park."

"And the battery on Guam shot two down," Carter added. "That gives the bad guys a forty percent success rate, counting the one that broke up in flight."

"But why the sub base at Guam?" Tony asked, secretly glad they weren't trying to decontaminate Osan or Kunsan. "As a military target, US Navy subs aren't their greatest threat."

"They're demonstrating range and striking power," the general answered quickly. "They would have hit Pearl if they could, but two thousand miles is probably the best the Musudan could do." It was supposedly a modified copy of a Russian SS-N-6 sub-launched ballistic missile, but nobody had hard data on its performance, it had never flown before, until now. It could carry explosive, chemical, or even nuclear warheads.

General Carter explained, "Before I came to watch the TV with you, I spoke to my counterpart in Seoul. The Korean government is going nuts, which means Washington will go nuts. Tokyo and Beijing will climb onto the bandwagon, too. And I think they're justified. What's left of the North Korean regime just demonstrated the ability to launch five long-range missiles simultaneously, armed with WMDs. It's likely they have more missiles, possibly with even longer ranges, assuming the KN-08 is real, and we know the South Koreans haven't been able to find a single nuke."

"Do you think the Kim faction will try to bargain now?" Tony asked. "Use the threat of more attacks to make a deal?"

Carter shook his head. "Unlikely. They would have already claimed this attack as a 'demonstration.' There's been nothing. Besides, the South—excuse me, the 'United Han Republic'—would never accept it."

"Then what's the Kim faction's goal?"

Carter laughed, but he wore a grim smile. "Who do you think is driving that nut wagon?"

CHAPTER NINETEEN
REALITY CHECK

6 September 2015, 11:00 a.m. local time
August 1st Building, Ministry of National Defense Compound
Beijing, People's Republic of China

The translator had added a scrolling banner to the CNN image. The Mandarin characters carried either the dialogue or translated other relevant English text displayed on the screen.

They watched the Western broadcast in silence. "They were very fortunate it landed in a park," the air force commander commented. His remark wasn't directed to anyone in particular, but several of the CMC members nodded their agreement. Although only a few of the ministers could speak English, they were all still absorbing the news and understanding the implications for China.

President Wen abruptly entered the conference room and they all stood. Several latecomers followed him. Wen's summons had been simply to meet "as soon as possible."

Wen hurriedly gestured, and as they sat, he asked the defense minister, "Have they said anything new? How many dead?"

"It's up to twenty-seven so far, all from exposure to a chemical agent. Some were first responders who came looking for casualties, and became victims instead."

The Second Bureau minister reported, "My specialists say it was probably VX, a persistent nerve gas. The DPRK manufactured large quantities of it. It is colorless, odorless, and can't be detected without specialized equipment. Inhalation causes almost immediate respiratory failure, as well as convulsions. We know they used both Sarin and VX in the fighting around Pyongyang."

"Horrible. Pointless." Wen shook his head sadly, stopped, and then straightened up in his chair. Addressing the entire group, he said, "With hindsight, Defense Minister Yu's concerns now look more like predictions. Judging from your expressions, I think everyone is as horrified as I am. What's left of the DPRK, concealed in their mountain fortress, is still very much a danger to anyone within their reach. Our army's failure to force a river crossing earlier today only heightens the danger we face. Is the army commander still in transit?"

General Yu answered, "Yes, Comrade Chairman. In his absence, I've arranged a video conference with General Shi, who commanded the assault this morning."

Wen nodded, and within moments, the CNN broadcast was replaced by a man in his early fifties with a weathered, square face in digital camouflage fatigues. He didn't stand, but sitting straight up, said, "General Shi Yushang, commanding the Southeast Security Force." He was inside a command vehicle, and while the video image was sharp, they had problems hearing the general over the background noise. An aide turned off several fans, and the sound quality dramatically improved.

General Shi sounded positive, although the news wasn't good. "My units have regrouped and I can resume the attack tomorrow morning."

"You'd been warned about the risk of chemical weapons, General. Why weren't you properly prepared?" The chief of the Second Bureau sounded angry, but General Shi didn't seem to notice.

"There were not enough protective suits for my entire force, and we prioritized the frontline units that were taking part in the assault, along with the combat engineers laying the bridges."

"And instead, they concentrated on your artillery," the defense minister concluded.

"DPRK counter-battery fire was accurate, and its effects were increased by the mix of chemical and explosive shells." The general paused to rub his face. He looked tired, but that was to be expected. Wen knew he would have been organizing a dawn attack since the small hours. "The holdouts didn't ignore my assault troops. They dropped just enough chemical shells there to force them to keep wearing the protective suits. And in spite of all our training and preparations, I've still got just as many casualties from heatstroke as I do from enemy fire."

"And more from chemical weapons than bullets," President Wen added. "What are your casualties?"

Shi scowled. "Approaching ten percent in the assault units, and over eighty percent in some of the artillery batteries. And I can't just bring in new personnel. The artillery pieces themselves have to be decontaminated. New artillery units have been ordered in, but they won't arrive until after dark at the earliest, and they'll have to set up . . ."

Defense Minister Yu, a general himself, asked, "What kind of attack will you make this time?"

"Early tomorrow morning we will focus on a very narrow front, if the air force can help us out. I will bring up more artillery, but I'll be firing at extreme range, which means it will be less accurate. And they've wrecked the pontoon bridges we did manage to lay, so I'll have to use the reserve equipment, hence the narrow front."

President Wen said, "Thank you, General Shi. Your service to China is an example to us all." They cut the connection, and the president turned to the PLAAF chief of staff. "I assume you're fulfilling his request."

The general scowled. "We are sending him everything he's asked for, but my specialists have their doubts. Aircraft aren't always a good substitute for artillery, and not only do the DPRK forces have excellent antiaircraft defenses, but evidently the targets we are supposed to hit are virtually encased in concrete and rock. We will have to use penetrating precision-guided ordnance, and our stocks are not unlimited." The general smiled. "It's ironic that for many of these targets, the best option would be a chemical warhead."

"But you will be able to do it," Wen persisted.

"We will have to use war reserve stocks, but we will do it. The cost will be high, though."

"Compared to the cost of losing even a single city to a nuclear weapon?" the defense minister asked sharply. Turning to Wen, he added, "General Shu is organizing the delivery of more equipment to General Shi, but the earliest any of it can get to him is very late today, or very early tomorrow. If everything goes smoothly."

Wen nodded his understanding. "And in war, things rarely go smoothly. Minister Yu, I'm going to ask a question, not because I think it's the best solution, but because we can't afford to overlook any possibility."

Yu answered guardedly, "Yes, Comrade Chairman."

"Could the DPRK holdouts and their nuclear weapons be quickly eliminated by several small nuclear weapons?" The senior officers present all looked aghast at the suggestion. Wen had expected their reaction, and quickly continued, "The area is sparsely settled, held by a group now almost universally despised, and possesses weapons of mass destruction that they have already used freely. We could make a strong case that the Northern holdouts pose a nuclear threat, not just to China but all of Asia and a good part of the Pacific."

The president's reasoning intrigued them. General Yu ordered the technicians, "Bring up the map of the holdouts' area, with the known targets." He and the air force minister left their chairs to study the screen, zooming the image until the features became blurs.

After several minutes of quiet conversation, the generals nodded in agreement, and Yu turned to face the group. "Small warheads won't do the job. It would take at least nine large devices, with at least five hundred kiloton yields. Given the accuracy of even our newest missiles, and the hardening of the targets in that area, that gives us a virtual certainty of destroying or crippling all known targets."

"Nine!" Wen exclaimed. "Is that because of the terrain?"

"Yes," Yu confirmed. "The area is somewhat mountainous, and any storage bunkers are undoubtedly deeply buried in solid rock. The irregular landscape means even two nearby targets have to be attacked individually. And since we don't have complete information on all the holdouts' installations, any that are not specifically targeted will likely survive with little or no damage."

The Second Bureau minister, in charge of intelligence, added, "My missile specialists are convinced that we still haven't located their entire launch network."

President Wen summarized, "And unless we target that installation directly, even with a nuclear weapon, we can't be sure it will be destroyed."

The minister nodded agreement. "My people have collected a lot of information, both from the sites we overran, and from South Korean and American news reports. The Kims went to astounding lengths to harden and hide their military installations. This is a case where conventional precision-guided ordnance will likely be as effective as a nuclear device," he finished.

Wen sighed. "Then I won't pursue this option any further—for now." He paused for a moment, as if steeling himself, then continued. "In that case, given the increased level of the threat," nodding toward the defense minister, "and the lack of progress by our ground forces, I believe we must consider a new strategy. Even as I summoned you all to this meeting, I received a message from the president of the United States. I will read the Mandarin version provided by the Americans, which our translators say is a faithful interpretation of their president's text.

"To President Wen, of the People's Republic of China: Our countries' armed forces face each other only inches apart, in grave danger of starting a war that will benefit neither, and distracting us from the far greater hazard posed by a cruel regime's dying struggles. I suggest that instead of fighting each other, we work together to put a swift end to the threat that endangers us all.

"I urge you also to cease your operations against South Korean forces, who are already fighting our common opponent. We will do everything in our power to encourage our ally to work with Chinese forces, as well as American military forces, for the express purpose of erasing every remaining trace of the Kims from the Korean Peninsula.

"Finally, I must remind you, President Wen, that America's guarantee of Korea's territorial integrity is absolute, and if China has any goal other than the removal of the threat posed by the holdouts of a disgraced dynasty, we will not hesitate to defend Korea as vigorously as we would our own homeland."

Wen passed the message to others at the table. Some read it completely, while others barely glanced at it. Several minutes passed in silence before the Second Bureau minister said reluctantly, "It pains me to agree with any American, but he's right. If the intervention expands beyond our stated goal, we face almost certain war with America, which could make our losses so far trivial in comparison."

They all knew he was referring to Scarborough Shoal, now firmly under the Philippines' control, its security guaranteed by the Americans. China could win on the Korean Peninsula and still suffer.

Several heads nodded, and the president asked, "Then how shall we proceed?"

6 September 2015, 1100 local time
Gyeonggi Military Camp
Outside Paju, South Korea

"He's got to be the oldest private I've ever seen," Cho asserted.

"I don't disbelieve you," Kary insisted. "I just don't know enough to agree or disagree."

They were standing outside the headquarters tent, located near the front gate of the Gyeonggi Military Camp.

Kary Fowler was now responsible for five refugee and two military camps, all holding former North Korean citizens. The Korean army ran all the camps, but was more than willing to let her minister to the needs of their residents. Even the military camps filled with ex-KPA soldiers came under her purview, since there was no longer an army for them to be soldiers of, and they had many of the same needs as the civilians. Beyond basic necessities like food and shelter, they usually needed at least some medical attention. There was an amazing demand for dentists. She'd arranged for many of the same classes to be taught as well, since the DPRK army's worldview was even more skewed than the civilians.

Using a helicopter provided by the ROK Army, and with Cho as her escort, she toured one or two camps every few days, being seen and dealing with problems that could only be solved in person.

Kary always walked through the camp first, accompanied by Cho, who wore army fatigues with a sergeant's rank insignia. Then, while Kary met with the camp's officials, Cho wandered about, listening and watching without the distraction of civilian higher-ups.

The military camps held a mixture of DPRK soldiers that had surrendered to South Korean troops or had been wounded and captured in a fight, army deserters that had reached the South or been found and collected in Northern territory, and in a few cases, entire units that had surrendered without a fight, after negotiations with the advancing Southerners.

Any soldier who wished was given a chance to serve, under General Tae, in the new United Han Army. While a fair number had done so, many did not.

Because national service was mandatory under the Kim regime, for many this was the first choice they had ever been allowed to make. With better food than they ever had before, and no longer being shot at, the camp seemed like a great place to be. They still lived under military discipline, including calisthenics, and that's where Cho first noticed him.

The man was in the rear rank of four, falling behind during jumping jacks, and failing completely at push-ups. While Cho had seen few DPRK soldiers that he could call impressive physical specimens, the rest of the group was performing satisfactorily.

The soldier's physical incompetence was almost comical, and Cho had moved closer, intending to see if he was sick or somehow injured. The first detail he noticed was the man's age, easily in his early forties. The second was his rank— a private? That didn't make much sense. Then he noticed the insignia on the shoulder of his fatigues. It marked the wearer as a member of a Light Infantry unit, one of the many former DPRK's special operations forces. Whoever he was, that man was not a special operations soldier.

After the exercises ended and the formation was dismissed, the corporal leading the calisthenics had taken care to inform Private Chun Ho-park that he was "a disgrace to not only both Koreas, but your Han heritage, and how did he . . ."

Cho had other questions. Why was this person attempting, and rather poorly, to disguise himself as a soldier? It was easy to imagine someone using the chaos of a civil war to lose himself—to change identity and make a fresh start somewhere else. There were many in the North who wanted to leave behind an inconvenient, or perhaps criminal past.

Who had this person been before he chose to be a very bad soldier? A party official? Cho was certain he was probably running from something more serious than an unhappy marriage.

Cho had told Kary about him, along with his other observations, after Kary finished her meetings. After some discussion, she decided to trust Cho's judgment. The camp's security officer promised to review the file for "Private Chun" right away.

They hadn't even made it back to Camp Munsan before Kary and Cho received a radio call to return to Gyeonggi as quickly as they could. With her concurrence, the pilots reversed course and increased speed. Half an hour later, the machine landed, not at Camp Gyeonggi, but the 31st Homeland Defense Infantry Division's base next to it.

They were met by Lieutenant Hak, the division security officer, at the landing pad. Hak had noted Cho's observations and promised to investigate the matter. He greeted Kary respectfully as they got out of the helicopter, but then almost embraced Cho in his enthusiasm. He didn't even wait for Cho, still in a noncom's uniform, to salute.

He pumped Cho's hand, and led them toward a waiting jeep. "Sergeant Cho, you've done your country a great service! We can't talk here, but we need to interview you further, and we'll need some information about your parent unit. I'm sure you'll be getting a commendation, and if they don't promote you, I'll want to know why!"

Hak refused to explain further until they reached the division's intelligence section, a cluster of low structures, and were ushered inside the headquarters building. Once through the doors, the lieutenant almost ran down the hall to the commander's office. "Colonel Gyo, they are here!"

Cho was ready this time, and after letting Kary go in first, he stepped into the colonel's office and saluted crisply. "Sergeant Cho Ho-jin, reporting."

The colonel not only returned Cho's salute just as smartly, but stood as he did so, before bowing to Kary and introducing himself. "Colonel Gyo Hwi-soon. I am head of the division's intelligence section. Is Sergeant Cho attached to your office?"

Puzzled, Kary answered, "Yes, Colonel, as my orderly." It was the standard story that avoided lengthy explanations. Cho was more intrigued than confused by Gyo's behavior, although he still felt a little edgy around ROK intelligence types.

"Then we'd like to ask him a few more questions about 'Private Chun.' You may remain, if you like."

Kary did, and for several minutes the two intelligence officers quizzed Cho about how he'd first noticed the impersonator, and exactly what had led him to suspect the man wasn't really a private.

Cho did his best to keep his answers short and specific. The sooner the interview was over and they were done, the better. That also matched his persona as a noncom being questioned by two intelligence officers. But he could tell Kary was curious. Finally, she couldn't stand it.

"Please tell me what you've found out. Whoever Chun really is, he's a resident of the camp, so he's also my responsibility," she argued.

Lieutenant Hak could only look to the colonel, who shrugged. "That's true enough. You'll find out through channels eventually. His real name is Ga Seung-ho. He's a civilian, and an expert in ballistic missiles. He was being escorted by three Light Infantry special forces soldiers from a safe house near Pyongyang to somewhere in the north, probably in the area the regime holdouts are occupying."

Cho was surprised, but managed to remain silent. Kary looked over at her "orderly" and said, "Well done, Sergeant!"

"We'd barely started to question Ga when he broke down completely. He told us who he really was, where he'd been hiding, about the special operators that were escorting him north, everything. The vehicle they were riding in was attacked from the air, and his escorts were killed or wounded. He was on the road for about two days after that before our scouts collected him."

Ban added, "The uniform was his escorts' idea, to make him less conspicuous. He wants nothing to do with the Kim faction or any other part of the DPRK. He tried to pass himself off as a regular soldier because he was afraid of being imprisoned and tortured by our intelligence people. Once he understood we weren't going to put him on the rack, he was willing to tell us everything he knew."

"Except where he was headed," the colonel interrupted. "The only person who knew their final destination was the officer in charge of the escort detail, and he was killed in the air attack. Not that Ga wanted to go there. He immediately headed south, and surrendered to the first ROK soldiers he could find."

The colonel was almost jovial. "We've already sent word to Second Operations Command headquarters and they are on their way here now, to question him further. Even if he doesn't know exactly where he was going, they'll try to gather what clues they can—offhand remarks by his escorts, any maps he may have seen, even how much gas was in the vehicle. Getting answers from him has the highest priority possible."

Kary asked, "A missile expert can probably tell you a lot, but how will it help? The Kim holdouts are already launching missiles. I was watching the news about that attack on Guam earlier today."

"His specialty is guidance systems," Colonel Gyo explained. "He'd been trained in both Russia and China. Their missiles haven't been very accurate so far, and he was told that it would be his task to make them more accurate. It sounds like he knew how to do it, too."

"And then they'd launch a lot more missiles," Kary concluded.

Gyo nodded. "Yes, exactly. Your orderly may have saved many lives. Now if we can just find out where they were taking Ga, we'll know where to look for the missiles themselves. Then we can end this once and for all."

Suddenly the target of everyone's gaze, Cho tried to find somewhere to look. Kary was smiling proudly. Gyo and Ban were grinning at him as well. Cho suspected it was not only at the thought of frustrating the holdouts' plans, but at the praise they'd receive for discovering the missile expert.

But they were all missing something. The other three hadn't done the math properly. Once the holdouts realized that their expert was a no-show, they might just start lobbing their missiles anyway, and to hell with accuracy. Chemical warheads didn't need to be very accurate. Neither did nuclear weapons.

He could have simply nodded and accepted the credit, but he couldn't remain silent. Not any more. "Colonel, I might be able to help with that problem."

6 September 2015, 1900 local time
Thirty-First Homeland Defense Infantry
Division Headquarters
Outside Paju, South Korea

Cho had a small audience now. After his revelation, Colonel Gyo had organized a meal while they waited for the representatives from Second Operations Command. They included the deputy commander, a two-star general, as well as military intelligence people and two civilians who simply gave their names as "Park." Given that Park was the one of the most common surnames in Korea, they might as well have given no name at all, but not giving a name would have been considered very rude.

Kary had insisted on staying with Cho, first asking politely, then pulling rank and insisting that she be party to any interrogations. Naturally distrustful of the military, she was doubly suspicious of anyone involved with espionage or counterintelligence. What she had learned from Cho only reinforced her impression.

After the Second Operations Command officers arrived, it had taken some time, and a few phone calls, to explain Cho's exact status and his wearing of a Republic of Korea Army sergeant's uniform. The general was quite unhappy, and was almost ready to arrest Cho for the offense, but the intelligence people were more philosophical.

In the end, Cho Ho-jin found himself facing a division commander, the command's deputy commander, their intelligence staffs, and other unnamed intelligence types. Kary, wearing civilian clothes, was a splash of bright color on one end of a wall of camouflage battledress. For someone who'd spent his life avoiding attention, it was near torture.

Cho drew strength from Kary's presence. By nature and profession, he was a private person, his life a closed book that was never meant to be read. But they needed to know what he knew, and that they could trust that what he said was true.

"I was eight when my father was killed. I still remember clearly the house we lived in. It was on Taesong Lake, a little outside Pyongyang. It sat on a hill facing the lake, and I didn't understand until later how luxurious it was. We had plenty to eat, and I even had toys.

"My father was often gone, and I had no brothers or sisters, but my mother had servants, and a military orderly that I played with. I was spoiled and told that because of our family, I could look forward to a life of privilege and accomplishment, in return for our absolute loyalty to the Kims.

"When the last war began, I remember my mother worrying about my father, as all women worry about their men when they go off to war. Although he'd be away from the fighting, any headquarters was a valuable target, so it was not unjustified. As far as I know, she never imagined that his own leaders would kill him.

"We didn't get a lot of news about the fighting while it was going on. Even I was old enough to recognize that we weren't being told the truth about what was happening, but my mother justified it, because of security, she said. Spies were everywhere." Cho smiled at the irony, but there was no humor in his expression.

"The first time we knew the war was over, or that the war was lost, was when they came for us. It was late morning, and an officer pounded on our door. When my mother opened it, the man loudly read a proclamation that my father had committed treason, betrayed the state, and paid for his crimes with his life.

"They almost dragged the two of us into a waiting car. My mother was in tears, but neither the officer nor the driver would answer her questions. We were driven to a small village northwest of the capital, and almost dumped in front of an empty house. The officer informed us that if either of us were ever discovered outside the village, we would be shot. He took the time to read the proclamation aloud again, so that the citizens of the village would be 'properly warned,' and then drove off.

"We had nothing, or even less than nothing. The house was a ruin, a derelict nobody wanted. With only a few things she had managed to snatch before we'd been taken away, she had to barter the clothes on her back for our first meal. I did what I could to help, finding work a child could do, but the villagers knew they could prey on us at will. I quickly learned how to fight, and how to read people. Who was trying to trick you, who would help, who would wait for the best moment and attack you unaware.

"My mother only lasted a few months. Early in the fall, she became sick, and died on a pallet of rags, the only bed we had. I left the village, almost daring the authorities to come after me and just try to kill me, but they didn't care."

Cho sighed. "After that, I lived by working and stealing until I was twelve. I was in Najin, a port city far in the north, looking for work, when the Russians recruited me. They first offered me food, then an education, and eventually the chance to strike back at the regime that had murdered my family and made my life hardship.

"I returned to the DPRK from Russia when I was twenty-two. I spied on the North's military, its political structure, and its economy, whatever my handlers wanted to know. I usually used money, because loyalty was cheap under the

Kims. Even when money didn't work directly, it could usually buy what my target wanted: drugs, sex, sometimes a favor from an official that they couldn't normally approach.

"I mapped military bases for the Russians, including many that were underground. I learned to ask the locals, because local labor was often pressed into service. Injuries and deaths were common, so I listened to widows and those maimed in accidents. Often, all I needed was bottle of good alcohol. A basket of food, or some Chinese medicine, was more than enough, and I would follow up with some good detective work. I had to be careful, of course, but even the organs of state security have their price." He smiled grimly.

"And where do you believe Ga was going?"

"There are several bases that have been dug into the mountains in that area. They were all extensive enough to accommodate surface-to-surface missiles. I can show you the ones I found, and how I found them."

Once the Second Operations Command officer left to give the necessary orders, Kary managed to arrange for a few quiet moments with Cho, "to go over some organizational matters." The 31st Division's officers seemed reluctant to let him out of their sight, and Kary felt the same way. Privacy was impossible, and they settled for the near-empty officer's mess, with Lieutenant Hak on the far side of the room.

They sat on opposite sides of a small table, pretending to drink their coffee. Kary couldn't hide her uneasiness. "If you are unsure about doing this, we can wait. We could ask Colonel Little for his help."

"To do what?" Cho asked. "Guarantee my safety? It looks bad when you're more worried about your own side than the enemy."

"And you don't need to come back to Munsan for anything?" she asked.

"My home is in a tent with twenty-three other men. Everything I own fills about half of a footlocker under my cot . . ."

"I'll hang onto it for you until you get back."

". . . and the most precious thing I have in the world is right in front of me."

She smiled at the compliment, but still fussed. "I wish they'd let you have a phone. Not *that* phone," she hastily added, "but a regular phone, so we could talk, at least a little."

"I will very much miss talking to and being near you, Kary Fowler, but this should not take long, and then I will do my best to remain by your side for as long as you can stand me. And did you hear the general?" Cho laughed softly. "At first he was mad at me wearing the uniform, but then he said, 'If you're going to wear the uniform, you should just sign the papers.'"

She laughed. "And then you tried to bargain him up to lieutenant!"

He shrugged and smiled. "It was a long shot. Still, I might do it anyway. Starting as a sergeant is an intriguing offer. Besides, I need the pay."

Kary's brow furrowed. "For what?" she asked, curious.

"I don't like living in a tent. When this is over, I want to buy a house. On a lake." He reached over and squeezed her hand gently.

"That sounds wonderful," she replied.

Chapter Twenty
Strange Bedfellows

6 September 2015, 1800 local time
United Han Army Field Headquarters
Outside Taedong, United Han Republic

At first, Rhee didn't like it. It jarred. He understood why Cho Ho-jin needed to keep a low profile. The army agreed. They had even made up a fake ID card for him. Or maybe not so fake. How was he different than the other Northerners who had answered the call to join the United Han Army? But then they really were soldiers, not just someone playing the role. Maybe it was because Cho wore a sergeant's stripes. He hadn't earned them, the way Master Sergeant Oh had.

Cho was earning his pay now, though, assuming they were paying him. Rhee had been allowed to sit in on Cho's debriefing by army intelligence. He'd be betting his life on what Cho told them, after all.

The intelligence people were using one of the purpose-built trailers that had been brought to the base. It was electronically shielded, and had map displays and other equipment that let the analysts fit Cho's information into the bigger picture. And he was filling in a lot of blank spots.

In addition to Rhee, representing the operators, there were regular army intelligence officers and a counterintelligence specialist from the National Intelligence Service. Everything Cho said was recorded, both on video and paper. That was good, because Rhee thought it would make a great book.

The Russians had trained Cho well, from his early teens, according to what Lieutenant Hak had heard. Cho could speak Russian fluently, and decent Chinese, but very little English. He'd demonstrated an excellent memory, and when pressured by the intelligence types, had responded calmly. They couldn't rattle him.

Using many false identities, and with currency supplied by his Russian patrons, he'd operated successfully in one of the most repressive police states in the world. He'd been a peddler, a farmer searching for a runaway child, a soldier many times, and of course different government functionaries. Cho had bribed, deduced, and tracked down information the Russians wanted from the time he was twenty-two until now, twelve-plus years later.

He'd remained alive by never staying in one place too long, never forming any attachments, and by total dedication to one goal: revenge against the Kim regime. Rhee was proud of what he'd done as a special operations soldier, but as he listened to the former spy, he had to admit that he could not do what Cho had done.

Cho used a digital map, zooming in to show fine detail, to trace his movements, where he'd gathered information, and where the clues had led. In his travels, often by foot, he'd found roads and rail lines that weren't on any map, and signs of construction in narrow mountain valleys. Tracing power lines, in that energy-starved country, was a good technique. Crisscrossing the entire DPRK, he'd noticed long-term changes that hinted at deeper meanings. Once, he'd discovered the remains of a thriving village that had been forcibly moved, for no apparent reason.

The spy—former spy, Rhee corrected himself—had been all over the DPRK in the course of his work, but of course intelligence only needed to know what he had seen in the area occupied by the Kim holdouts. Cho knew about several installations in the area, including three bases that intelligence already knew about.

Although they could not possibly serve as the hiding place for the missiles, the intelligence people questioned him at length about those locations as well. Comparing their information with his was a good way to establish his credibility, and his capabilities.

He'd also located two installations that intelligence hadn't known about. One was a facility for producing boot-leg drugs, the other an extensive complex with several over-sized armored doors, surrounded by pillboxes and other ground defenses. He'd interviewed locals in nearby villages, who, for a little food, were glad to share their stories of being blindfolded before being taken to work underground excavating huge chambers. It had to be the place, and Cho was confident of its location. He'd been close enough to see the pillboxes and the carefully camouflaged doors. Rhee listened carefully to every detail.

The debrief had lasted for hours, and they'd taken occasional breaks outside the van. The air outside was warm and thick, but the windowless van felt confining. Seeing the sun and taking more than three steps in a straight line refreshed them all.

Of course, there was no shoptalk outside the van, but during one such break, Rhee found himself standing next to Cho, the ex-Russian spy he was slowly coming to respect.

Although they'd been introduced when the debrief began, Rhee had listened and said very little. Now, standing next to Cho, he felt he had to say something.

Feeling a little uncomfortable, Rhee asked, "Have you actually joined the army?"

Cho quickly shook his head. "No, Colonel. The uniform just helps me blend in," he replied formally. "I'm sorry if it . . ."

"No, it's fine," Rhee responded. "For what it's worth, you'd make a good sergeant."

Cho smiled, recognizing praise when he heard it. "Thank you, sir."

After only a moment's pause, Rhee added, "Your father was a good general. The last war was a hard fight. He deserved better."

Cho's smile disappeared but he said "Thank you" again, then added, "May I ask you a question, Colonel?"

Rhee nodded, and Cho asked, "You're going to plan the operation to capture the missile complex, aren't you?"

"Plan it, and lead it, if I have any say in the matter," Rhee responded firmly. "I may not have the same personal grievance that you do, but I won't rest until the Kim regime is wiped from the earth."

"Then take me with you," Cho answered suddenly. "I've been through Russian infantry school and parachute training. The Russians even sent me to some of their special operations courses. I'm not as physically fit as your troops, but I've been on the ground where you're going." Rhee had heard dozens of new recruits with the same desperate tone, but he knew Cho's determination came from a different place. "I have to be there," Cho finished, almost begging.

Rhee paused for a long moment, but answered, "I'll consider it." After another pause, he added, "If I think you'd increase the chance of the operation's success." And after another pause, the colonel warned, "And as long as you're not bent on personal revenge."

Cho shook his head, "No, Colonel, although once, I might have been. Now, I have things to fight for, not fight against."

The headquarters tent was larger than the intelligence section's trailer, but it was becoming just as crowded. Many had heard rumors about a "special asset" arriving at the base, but the counterintelligence people had spread so many false rumors that nobody knew what to believe. In spite of tight security, many of the headquarters staff had found reasons to be at the briefing.

It was clear something was up. In the assembly area, there was more "hurry up and wait." Fuel and ammunition stocks were being topped off. Stragglers were being quickly recalled. A few units had "relocated" that morning, supposedly to some other part of the area, but nobody seemed quite sure where.

Security was going to extremes. No new personnel were being allowed on base. Anyone away from their unit had to have a reason, and the orders to back up their story.

For the briefing, the headquarters tent, located near the center of the base, was surrounded with jammers that would scramble cell phone and other UHF frequencies. Several nearby tents were cleared and then occupied by security personnel, and anyone who had business near the tent had to have it cleared with the chief of staff.

Most drastic of all, the headquarters tent's side flaps, normally rolled up to take advantage of any cooling breeze, had been lowered. Fans and portable air conditioners had been set up in their stead, but it was not completely effective. The temperature in the closed atmosphere was not helped by the high number of attendees.

Rhee would give his brief after the intelligence section. Although his Special Forces were only one part of Operation Kut, his team would have the final and most important role. A *kut* was a Korean cleansing ceremony. Performed by a shaman, usually a woman, it exorcised evil. The name hadn't been Rhee's suggestion, but he completely agreed with the choice. Anyone who had grown up in the South would feel the same way.

Cho's arrival and information had triggered a series of events that was still cascading outward. Within minutes of concluding Cho's debrief, Rhee and Kwon had retired to the SOF planning cell to rough out an attack plan. The intelligence staff began their own work, analyzing and then preparing the many reports that were needed by the air staff, the ground forces, even the navy.

Less than an hour later, General Kwon had assured General Sohn that the complex could be taken, and Sohn had issued warning orders to ground and air units all over Korea, then summoned his commanders.

While he waited for the higher ranks to arrive, Rhee continued to work on what was an uncomfortably rough briefing. Special operators tended to be detail men and perfectionists, because the details could be just as important as the big picture. He liked to have answers to any questions his audience might have. Rhee wasn't alone, though. Two chairs over, he could see the deputy G2, a colonel like himself, typing furiously.

But they couldn't afford to wait. They didn't know what the holdouts' timetable was. All they could do was move as quickly as possible. While Rhee gave his brief, General Kwon was taking their general concept and turning it into a proper operational plan. The colonel couldn't think of anyone he'd rather have putting the plan together.

According to the chief of staff, General Sohn was ready to come in, but wanted everyone else there first. All Rhee could do was work quickly, and hope that they wouldn't mind a few "to be determined" on the slides.

Kevin Little, representing the US forces, had arrived some time ago, but except for a hurried nod in greeting, Rhee had ignored his old comrade. He had work to do.

General Long had also arrived, with his interpreter. He was deputy commander of the Chinese Southeast Security Force, and had arrived late last night as the Chinese liaison. Rhee took the presence of a high-ranking Chinese officer as a good sign. Long was senior enough to make decisions, and not just relay everything back to headquarters and wait for a reply.

Long had also brought a gift: a list of all the installations known to Chinese intelligence related to any of the DPRK weapons of mass destruction.

It was foolish, but Rhee took some pride in knowing that while the new information filled in some gaps, they hadn't known about Cho's site, either. The Chinese also confirmed that they had not found any nuclear devices at the locations they had occupied.

The two Chinese representatives had spent the morning at the operations center, coordinating communications and making sure that the two armies, now cooperating, wouldn't shoot at the wrong people. Luckily, the geography of the Kim redoubt area made it simple. The Chinese would attack from the north, across the Chongchon River, while the

American and Han armies would attack from the east, west, and south. The three sides also shared intelligence about the redoubt and its defenses, and coordinated reconnaissance.

The two Chinese had come over from the nearby ops tent within minutes of General Sohn's summons. Now Long sat quietly, studying the map on the large flat-screen display and making notes. Evidently, Long spoke excellent Russian, and passable French, but no Korean or English, so everything would have to be relayed through the young captain who sat at the general's elbow.

General Tae, who had been out in the assembly area, finally arrived and bowed politely to the Chinese general before taking his seat. Neither man smiled.

Moments later, General Sohn entered and, even as everyone came to attention, waved them back into their seats. Evidently warned about the Chinese interpreter, Sohn spoke in short sentences, with frequent pauses. He managed to get his point across.

"We know, with high confidence, where the Kim faction holdouts have their nuclear weapons hidden. What we don't know is their timetable. Therefore, we will move tonight." That got a reaction. A major operation like this would normally take days to organize. "We cannot wait any longer. If the enemy learns of our preparations, they may launch another missile attack before we can stop them. Tonight, it ends!"

Taking a lead from Sohn's urgent tone, Colonel Won, the deputy intelligence chief from Sohn's staff, quickly walked over to the flat-screen display. It showed the area held by the holdouts, now described with the Chinese term "the Redoubt." He said simply, "The missile site is here, about fifteen kilometers northeast of Sukchon. The area is mountainous and heavily wooded."

He pointed to a place on the map almost in the center of the area controlled by the holdouts. A long valley formed by two high ridges ran north and south. A narrow road, little more than a track, ran the length of the valley. There were no signs of habitation in the valley, but a military base occupied the north end, and the Sunchon air base sat at the southeast corner. Won pointed to a symbol in red a third of the way up the valley from the air base. "It's here."

The intelligence officer pressed a key and the map was replaced with a rough schematic showing a tunnel network that extended well within the mountain and ran three stories deep. The colonel began pointing out different parts of the installation: the missile magazines, the liquid fuel tanks, a storage area for the multi-wheeled launch vehicles. There were strong defenses both outside and inside, including pillboxes guarding the entrances and even a series of decoy tunnels . . .

General Tae was amazed and interrupted the colonel. "This is very detailed information. No one on the General Staff was aware of this place. Are you sure your source is reliable? Can any of this be confirmed from other sources?"

In the meantime, Won had looked to General Sohn, who gave a small shake of his head. The colonel answered Tae, "Collecting more information has been discussed, sir. We've avoided sending UAVs or other aircraft into the area, to prevent tipping our hand. The air base at the southern end has been attacked several times, as have some of the other nearby installations, but this missile complex itself has remained untouched and unnoticed. A special operations team would take too long to get in, collect the data, and get out. And then there is the risk of them being discovered, which is assessed as being high."

Rhee agreed emphatically with Won's explanation. He'd been asked earlier in the day by Sohn's staff about the feasibility of a Special Forces scouting mission, but it simply couldn't be done quickly enough. They'd have to wait until dark to even begin, cover many kilometers of rough, wooded country to get into position, and then wait till first light to actually get a good look at the complex. It would mean postponing the attack for at least two more days, and a recon team couldn't do much more than confirm the site's location and any outer defenses. It just wasn't worth the delay.

Through the interpreter, Long asked, "Then could we interview the source ourselves? Ask him some questions to determine the accuracy of his statements?"

To see if you believe him, Rhee thought. It was not unreasonable, but General Sohn was more direct this time. "His information has been confirmed to the best of our ability, in the time available. We will move using what we have."

Won started again. "We can't tell how many missiles, or even of what type, they have inside, but the complex is large enough to hold about a dozen BM-25 Musudan intermediate-range ballistic missiles. Since they've launched five missiles already, we're looking at possibly seven to eight missiles in the storage bunkers. Alternatively, there could be about half a dozen Hwaseong-13, or KN-08, intercontinental ballistic missiles. We have reason to believe that some KN-08 missiles are there, because during Ga Seung-ho's debrief, he said that the people who summoned him were concerned with 'progressive guidance errors over long ranges.'"

Kevin Little's Korean was good enough to keep up with Won, but he was still grateful for the pauses that gave the Chinese interpreter a chance to work. General Long reacted strongly to the phrase "over long ranges," but Little could see him work to control it. The BM-25 and KN-08 were both crude by modern standards, but the former could cover almost all of China, as well as Japan. The latter could hit targets as far away as European Russian and India. Neither had been tested before the civil war, but four Musudan missiles had managed to find their way to Guam—operational test completed satisfactorily.

As for payloads, he'd heard a lot of speculation since the crisis began about how many nuclear weapons the DPRK possessed, or how big they were, or what they could fit into the nose cone of a missile. To Kevin's thinking, it didn't really matter. A nuclear explosion anywhere, of any size, would be a disaster. He found it hard to imagine the calamity more than one would create.

Won had moved on to the defenses in the area. There was the Sunchon air base nearby with a squadron of MiG-29 Fulcrums. Like so many military installations in the North, most of it was underground, with only the runway and a couple of hangars vulnerable to attack. Based on other such installations, the entire squadron could be sheltered underground. Both the runway and taxiway had been pummeled during earlier strikes.

The air defenses also included an unknown number of surface-to-air missile launchers that emerged from behind concrete doors just long enough to fire, and then were retracted to reload. Batteries of radar-guided guns were emplaced in hidden revetments on the hillsides, with mobile AAA guns that could be set up for aerial ambushes, and then moved before they could be targeted.

The Chinese, Koreans, and Americans had all lost both UAVs and manned aircraft to the air defenses. Cruise missiles had a difficult time threading their way through the terrain to reach their targets, and even if they could, they didn't have the ability to penetrate the hardened bunkers. It was just as hard for manned aircraft as well. Flying at a safe height would expose them to the full force of the defenses. Missions were still being flown, but bringing the pilots back safely meant choosing their targets carefully, and giving them a lot of support they wouldn't usually need. And even with Cho's information, the striking aircraft lacked the exact coordinates to put GPS-directed weapons onto the bunkers—a near miss just wasn't good enough.

The colonel was winding up his part of the brief, and the captain-interpreter relayed, "General Long would like to know if the source you mentioned earlier had any information on the holdouts' timetable."

"No, General," Won replied apologetically. He explained, "The working theory has always been that they were having problems with the ballistic missiles' guidance systems. Our capture of the ballistic missile expert Ga confirmed this, but it is much harder to gauge the holdouts' patience, especially about something as irrational as revenge."

General Sohn spoke up. "I believe that the remnants of the Kim faction have no expectation of survival. History has often shown the military forces of a dictatorship collapsing when they sense that the end is near. That is not the case here.

"I believe these troops are defending the last bits of their territory so fiercely because they are buying time for their leaders to prepare a retaliatory strike. I realize that this is an assumption based on another assumption, but what evidence we have fits this theory."

Rhee barely waited for Colonel Won to sit down before beginning, and he spoke so quickly that Kevin wondered if there was a getaway car behind the tent with its motor running.

"Operation Kut will begin just after dark with an assault by the Chinese all along the Chongchon River front, concentrating on Anju in the northwest. This will occupy the holdouts' attention while US forces to the south and Korean forces to the west and east move into final attack positions. Two hours later, regardless of Chinese progress, the American and Han forces will attack, concentrating on taking the towns of Sukchon in the southwest and Sunchon in the southeast. Both are road junctions and the largest towns in the area. They are important military targets in their own right, but the attack on Sukchon will hopefully mask our operations near the real target."

As he explained the first part of the operation, Rhee tapped the keyboard. A long blue line appeared along the Chongchon River, and then a second line appeared marking the western edge of the redoubt, and two more bordering the south and east. "All forces will have heavy artillery and air support."

General Tae spoke up, asking, "What kind of losses do you expect to your air support?" Little was impressed with Tae's diplomacy. The subtext to the question was "Remember the air defenses? You could lose a lot of planes."

"Much of the first wave will be air-launched decoys. Both the Americans and Chinese have them in numbers, and some are being transferred for use by Korean aircraft as well. They can mimic the flight path and profile of a fighter. We expect the holdouts to waste missiles on them, and hopefully reveal any camouflaged gun emplacements.

"We will expend almost all our stocks of decoys, and will also have many of our remaining UAVs in the area to observe. The UAVs are smaller and won't be flying attack profiles, so they should live long enough to do their job."

Rhee nodded toward General Sohn. "Once the commander is satisfied we have identified as many of their air defense installations as possible, he will signal a massive artillery barrage. This will use every long-range tube we have, and the multiple-barrage rocket launchers as well. We will not use aircraft to attack the air defense positions, although we'll use any surviving UAVs to check the results." He smiled. "It's best not to hunt duck hunters with ducks."

He nodded toward the Chinese general. "I apologize for not sharing this plan with you before the meeting, but to be honest, we're still working on the details. It means a lot of your heavy artillery will be out of position to support your own troops, but it should reduce your aircraft losses significantly."

Through his interpreter, Long answered, "It is satisfactory, although I would suggest that any artillery positions that are discovered also be targeted." Sohn nodded his concurrence.

Rhee continued, "My team will follow the artillery strike in, and land here." He marked a spot on the map just two kilometers from the missile bunker. "We'll be using a full company from my Ninth Special Forces Brigade for this attack. We'll approach the landing zone from two different routes through the mountains. This will increase our chance of success, just in case one group runs into functional air defenses." He traced paths that wound through the landscape from the west. Both ended in a meadow that was shielded from the bunker's view by a sharp ridge.

"In addition to our flights, attack helicopters will supplement the troops' advance with close air support strikes along the outer defenses, and the air base here"—he tapped the location at the south end of the valley—"will also be attacked by Korean special forces and aircraft. All this is in addition to the general attack by Korean, Chinese, and American troops into the Redoubt itself."

General Long spoke again, this time asking, "This is a sound plan, but what if the simple fact of an attack makes them decide to launch the missiles? How much warning will we have if they intend to launch?"

Rhee frowned. "It depends on the missile type and number of missiles . . . maybe forty-five minutes, possibly an hour." He called up the schematic of the missile complex again. "The missiles are likely assembled and mated to their transport-erector-launcher, but they won't be fueled, since this would make them too heavy to raise to launch position. The TELs will have to emerge from one of these three doors, which are all armored, drive a few hundred meters away, and bring the missiles vertical before they can be fueled. If they're clever, they've already prepositioned fuel and oxidizer tanks, and pre-surveyed the launch coordinates down to the centimeter."

He paused for a moment, and Colonel Won added, "At the very best we're looking at an hour, tops."

Rhee then picked back up. "However, once my team arrives, we can bring any launchers that emerge under fire, and before we get there, the UAVs will be watching. If there is any sign that the launchers are setting up before we get there, General Sohn will order a continuous hold-down barrage of the area. That will obviously affect the ground troops' support . . ."

Long interrupted. "The ground attacks are simply holding exercises—not feints, but secondary to the real objective. I concur. But what if the barrage is not successful?"

Rhee responded, "Colonel Little has confirmed that several US radar planes will be watching the area closely. They'll be supporting the attacks, of course, but they can also track any ballistic missile launches. They will quickly calculate the impact area and provide a warning."

Then the colonel shrugged philosophically. "After that, the nation that is targeted will have to respond to the threat separately."

Kevin smiled grimly. Not only did China have dozens of potential targets, but their best antiballistic missiles were purchased from Russia, and were barely enough to cover Beijing, and perhaps a few other cities. Even the vaunted Russian S-400 couldn't guarantee a sure kill, and nobody had forgotten about the unsettling appearance of decoys in the earlier missile attacks. He fervently hoped North Korea hadn't developed any other surprises.

"Then I wish to propose an alternative plan," Long began. He stood, and the interpreter relayed his words. "You have developed a fine plan, with as good a chance for success as any military operation can have, but nothing is certain. All we can know for sure is that it will be a desperate fight, with many losses.

"However, in this situation, there is a need for both urgency, and certainty. With the permission of the Korean government, and on their behalf, I believe that the surest and simplest course is to use a ballistic missile, which cannot be intercepted or shot down by the Kim holdouts. Our DF-5 can place a five-megaton thermonuclear device within half a kilometer of that missile complex, and no amount of rock will be enough to shield them."

Rhee, appalled at the suggestion, stood openmouthed for half a moment. He wanted to reply, but in that pause

Tae, sitting next to the Chinese general, stood and backed away, recoiling from the very idea. "Absolutely not! You can't protect yourself by destroying half our country!"

Long didn't need the interpreter to understand that while Tae's was the most extreme reaction, nobody was nodding agreement. Evidently, he'd expected this, because he calmly replied, and then waited for his interpreter to relay his response.

"Seoul, even Anchorage are at as much at risk as Beijing if the missiles are the longer-ranged Hwaseong-13, what the Americans call the KN-08. The mountain valleys will contain the blast, and the region is thinly settled."

Long continued quickly, before anyone else could reply. "If I relay these coordinates to our rocket forces, they can have a missile targeted and ready to fly in less than half an hour. Flight time will be something less than fifteen minutes."

He'd been speaking to the entire group, but now he turned and addressed General Sohn directly. "Consider my suggestion carefully, General. It doesn't have to 'end tonight.' It can end in an hour, and how many lives will be saved?" Long sat, still holding Sohn in his gaze, and waited for an answer.

Nobody spoke. Finally General Sohn stood. He spoke carefully, as if still forming a response. "I will speak for the Korean government and unilaterally reject your proposal. You oversimplify the decision. While such an attack would solve the military objective, I'm fighting for the future of a newly united Korea. This weapon would create a wasteland not just from the impact, but the fallout the bomb would create.

"Even this 'thinly settled' region holds tens of thousands of civilians. Should they all perish because of the holdouts'

desire for revenge? This operation is not designed to anni-
hilate our opponents. With some luck," he nodded toward
Rhee, "the colonel's plan will destroy the missiles and frus-
trate the diehards' plan for revenge. I am sure that Colonel
Rhee's men, even in the center of the holdouts' resistance,
will accept the surrender of anyone who offers it."

Sohn's voice rose a little. "Our war has always been one
of liberation, not conquest. I know that some of my men will
become casualties, but they know they are fighting to save
the rest of our countrymen. He gestured to General Long.
"Some of your men will become casualties as well, but that is
the price China pays for her security. Buying your safety with
thousands of Korean lives is simply unacceptable!"

Long nodded his understanding. "We respect the decision of the general and completely understand his rationale.
But I must inform you, with all respect, that of necessity I
will pass the information on the target's location back to my
commander. While we will spare no effort to make tonight's
operation a success, I already know that my government will
spend a sleepless night monitoring our progress."

Long took care to look in Kevin Little's direction as well
as Sohn's. "Please inform your governments that if we detect
a missile launched from within the Redoubt, whether it is
aimed at Beijing or not, our rocket forces will unilaterally
respond with an attack as I've already described. If your
operation fails, if the Kim holdouts begin launching, then
China will act, for the protection of our country and all of
Asia."

Rhee rose defiantly, insulted as much by the Chinese
general's recommendation as his innuendo that Rhee's
plan wasn't good enough. Staring straight at Long, he said
tersely, "We won't fail."

6 September 2015
Seventh Air Force Headquarters, Operations Center
Osan Air Base, United Han Republic

"This is no way to run a railroad," muttered a frustrated Tony Christopher. He shifted about the overloaded desk, lifting one folder after another until he found the spreadsheet he was after. Supply issues were whittling away at his F-22 contingent as one ship after another dropped offline due to maintenance gripes. And even though the requisition for the repair parts had been submitted, there weren't enough of them on hand to keep the aircraft up—more parts had to be shipped from the contractor in the US. *Just in time maintenance my ass*, thought Tony.

His bad mood wasn't caused solely by the USAF's annoying maintenance system; no, the main source of irritation was that he was a fighter pilot flying a desk during a war. It wasn't that Tony didn't appreciate the importance and necessity of what he was doing; "experts study logistics," or so he was told. But it didn't change the simple fact that he would much rather be strapped into a jet, hip deep in a furball in contested skies. It's what he did . . . emphasis on did.

"Saint!" shouted General Carter as he strode into the ops center.

"Yes, sir."

"I need you to get your butt to Kusan, ASAP. We just received a mother of a strike package and I want you down there to help organize it. This is a maximum force effort with a tricky time-on-target schedule; we can't afford any screwups. You leave immediately."

"Understood, General," replied Tony as he quickly turned to leave. Since the beginning of the conflict, he kept an overnight bag packed in his office, and it would take him only a minute to grab his gear. He was just reaching for the doorknob when Carter called back to him.

"And Saint, no shenanigans. You're to keep both feet firmly on Mother Earth, clear?"

"Of course, sir. No shenanigans."

"Good. Now off with you."

Chapter Twenty One

Stronghold

6 September 2015, 1915 local time
Kunsan Air Base
Gunsan, United Han Republic

The emergency response vehicles wailed as they charged down the taxiway toward the subsiding orange fireball. At the far end of the runway, a returning F-16C had just plowed into the field, tumbled, and burst into flames. Tony held his breath as he watched the ejection seat shoot skyward moments before the jet blew up and prayed the pilot had escaped unharmed. That was the third aircraft the 35th Fighter Squadron had lost that evening, and the massive attack on the Kim redoubt was still to come.

The preliminary strike was a large-scale suppression of enemy air defenses, or SEAD, raid by seven squadrons—three US, two Korean, and two Chinese. The objective was to make the holdouts believe a massive air attack was underway, and trick them into engaging with their SAMs and AAA. The ruse worked well.

Apparently, it never occurred to the defenders that almost all of the "targets" that their radars detected were decoys. They held nothing back, and an eruption of missiles and shells poured out from the mountains against the phantom raiders. Once the weapons' locations were exposed, the aircraft began launching anti-radiation missiles and GPS-directed bombs against the radars, missile launchers, and guns. The result was a bloodbath. The initial battle damage assessment intelligence cell concluded that over eighty percent of the air defense assets were either destroyed or damaged. But even though the SEAD raid had "severely degraded" the Kim air defenses, it wasn't without cost—eight aircraft were either missing or known to have been shot down.

Tony looked on as the F-16C fighters taxied to their hardened aircraft shelters and came to a stop. As soon as the engines had shut down, an organized horde of aircraft maintenance specialists and ordnance mechanics swarmed over the aircraft, furiously prepping them for their next mission. The pilots jumped down from their aircraft and headed straight to a waiting van. The vehicle whisked them over to the squadron's ready room for a quick debriefing; the squadron intelligence shop was working frantically to update the raid's damage assessment.

Seeing the flurry of activity, Tony was dragged back to the last war. He vividly remembered being the one hurrying over to the ready room with his wingman, Hooter, both of them bubbling over with an adrenaline overdose. Now, he was a general officer, one of the senior leaders, who sent young men and women downrange in their Falcons to fight. At that moment, he would gladly trade his star for an aircraft.

"General Christopher!" came a shout from behind him. Tony turned to see the wing commander, Colonel Graves, jogging in his direction.

"What's the status of that pilot?" Tony called out while pointing toward the crashed fighter.

Graves' expression was one of relief, but the roar of a passing F-16 made it impossible to hear his response. It wasn't until he got closer that he could finally answer. "He got out clean, sir, but landed as hard as you'd expect. He's over at the infirmary now, being treated for some minor cuts and bruises. He'll be sore in the morning, but otherwise he should be fine."

Tony unconsciously rubbed his right arm, recalling a similar injury he sustained when he ejected from a crippled aircraft so many years ago. He shook himself from his musings and asked, "So, what's the damage, Colonel?"

Graves and Tony walked into one of the shelters, mostly to get away from all the noise. "Confirmed three birds lost, including the Thirty-Fifth's squadron commander, Lieutenant Colonel Ortiz. His wingman said his aircraft was hit on the way out. No one reported seeing him eject, and he has yet to report in. Right now he's listed as missing."

"Damn it!" Tony cursed in frustration. The next strike had to be airborne in an hour, and the loss of the squadron commander was a severe setback. The Eightieth Fighter Squadron had taken off thirty minutes earlier and would soon be over the target area to plaster anything they found in the open. No one expected this attack to get the ballistic missiles, but it would force the Kim faction to keep them buttoned up in their hardened caves. The artillery bombardment was carefully timed to occur just as the second wave of strike aircraft cleared the area. Thirty minutes later the ground troops would begin their assault. By then the 35th was supposed to be back on station, loitering to the south, waiting for the SOF guys to provide the precise location of the bunkers' armored doors. The schedule was very tight, and unforgiving. In the back of Tony's mind was the Chinese threat to level the whole area with one honkin' big nuke.

"How good is the deputy squadron commander, Andy?" he demanded.

Graves hesitated for just a moment, but the delay spoke volumes, "Major Jackson is a good man, General, but he's barely been with the squadron for a month and . . ."

That was enough for Tony. Pivoting quickly, he spotted the crew chief working on the F-16 in the shelter. "First Sergeant!" he shouted loudly.

The man turned about, annoyed by the interruption. However, once he saw Tony waving to him, he broke out at a run. "Yes, General. What can I do for you?"

"Get me a ship."

X Corps Headquarters
Northeast of Sunchon, United Han Republic

Tae watched with satisfaction as the second wave of aircraft bombarded the redoubt's outer defenses. The explosions were so numerous that they continuously lit up the night sky. The sheer amount of ordnance being dropped on that parcel of land was difficult to comprehend. He momentarily felt sorry for the Kim faction, pinned down in their holes, thinking they might yet somehow endure to cause untold death and destruction on all their enemies.

That their ultimate defeat was inevitable wasn't in question; it was whether it would come by way of the American/Han plan, or the Chinese plan. The general still shivered when he thought about the Chinese suggestion to drop a five-megaton nuclear warhead on the redoubt and be done with it—an option they refused to take off the table.

Major Ryeon walked up quietly beside his general and stared in amazement. He was also having trouble grasping the weight of firepower pouring down on his former countrymen. "How could anyone survive such a pounding?" he asked.

"Impressive, isn't it?" remarked Tae as he kept his eyes on the flashes blooming on the horizon. The delayed rumble that followed could easily deceive someone into believing a storm was approaching—a bad one.

"And yet, you'd be equally shocked by how much of the Kim faction's strength will remain intact. Don't get me wrong, they will suffer many casualties, lose many fortified positions, but they will still be a force to reckon with. Our approach won't be a leisurely stroll in the countryside, Major." He briefly looked down at his watch and noted the time. The air strike would be ending soon.

"Are the unit commanders gathered?"

"Yes, sir, they're assembled in the command tent," replied Ryeon.

"Excellent! Then let's not keep them waiting." The two men turned and walked quickly for the makeshift tent city a hundred meters behind them. As they approached, a guard lifted the flap. Inside a South Korean officer ordered loudly, "Attention!"

"Be seated!" Tae barked, gesturing for everyone to sit. As the men took their seats, the general noted the blend of uniforms—soldiers from the North and South fighting together. He was still struggling with the concept, even though he'd worked hard to make it happen, and silently conceded that it would likely take him the rest of his life to reconcile his mixed feelings. Although hastily built from various former DPRK and ROK units, his command was nearly a full-strength corps, with a brigade of the North's best tanks, four infantry divisions, and several batteries of excellent South Korean artillery. Many of these men had served with him from the beginning of the civil war and he knew how worn out they were, even though their faces beamed with excitement. They had just one more battle left to fight.

"Comrades, in less than ten minutes the artillery barrage will begin. Our units are already in position for the final assault on the Kim stronghold. As soon as the artillery commences firing, Major Ro will lead two Reconnaissance Bureau comp . . . Correction, two Han special forces companies against the Sunchon airfield. Once the airfield has been taken, we will step off and attack along the southeast corner. The Chinese have already begun their assault to the north, and surveillance reports indicate the Kim holdouts have committed some of their reserves. We will attack from the opposite direction and force them to use what little they have left to try and fend us off.

"We must make them believe that our three corps attacking from the east and south are a crushing threat to their survival, so we must strike fast, and we must strike hard. The goal is to force the Kim faction to pull assets away from their western flank and thin their lines for the special forces assault group. We cannot hold back tonight. We must hit the enemy with every drop of our strength."

Tae paused and stepped away from the map board, approaching the first row of chairs. Looking intently at his audience, he spoke with a tempered voice. "For many of you, the adversary we face includes individuals we once knew as comrades, colleagues, and perhaps even friends. I understand your mixed feelings—the confusion, even the awkwardness of working with our Southern kinsmen. I understand, because I share them as well. But you must put that all aside tonight; for tonight we fight for our land.

"For the people in those mountains do not share our dreams for the future," stressed Tae as he pointed toward the redoubt. "In fact, they are doing everything in their power to prevent that dream from coming true. They either cannot, or will not, see the possibility of a new way of life—one without constant fear, one without 'the state,' one with hope. After tonight, if you wish to stop being a soldier, and do something of your own choosing, you will be free to do so. But tonight, I need you to fight one last time to free our people from the deadly plague that is the Kim regime. Are you with me?"

The cheering was deafening.

Han Special Forces Assault Group—Ghost Brigade
45 KM Southwest of the Landing Zone, United Han Republic

Cho looked out the window of the Surion helicopter and saw the greenish-hued terrain pass by in a distorted blur. He didn't even want to think how low they were, or how fast they were going. Both were undoubtedly in the "very unsafe" category as far as normal civilian operations was concerned. *What was I thinking?* he thought to himself. Cho raised his night vision goggles and closed his eyes. He struggled to concentrate on happy thoughts as the helicopter bounced about unevenly in the night air. *Stay calm. Don't think about your stomach.* It would look very unprofessional if he threw up on the Ghost Brigade command staff.

The twenty-four helicopters flew in two long columns a mere fifty meters off the ground. Each of the formations was led by three US Army AH-64D Apache Longbow gunships as escorts for the nine troop-carrying Korean Surions. The Americans would also provide close air support should the Korean assault group run into resistance, and act as a backup just in case something went wrong with the strike aircraft. Each of the Surion helicopters carried two pilots, two gunners, and nine commandos. Between the eighteen transports there was a handpicked company of the Ninth Special Forces Brigade—about to be unceremoniously dumped into the heart of the Kim redoubt.

A hand grabbed Cho's shoulder and gently shook him. Opening his eyes he saw Master Sergeant Oh in the dim light; he was holding something in his hand. "Here, chew on this. It'll help keep your gut from rebelling."

"What is it?" asked Cho.

"Ginger gum." The commando smiled broadly. "It's our best defense against lunatic pilots. They're always trying to get us to vomit. They think it's a cute game. Sick bastards!"

"Thank you," Cho replied gratefully. He popped the stick of gum into his mouth and immediately felt a tingling sensation from the strong spice. It didn't take long for the soothing effect to quell his upset stomach.

"Sergeant Cho, what unit do you belong to? I don't recall ever seeing you before with any of the ROK Special Forces brigades, and your accent sounds northern," inquired Oh.

Cho looked at the senior enlisted man with wariness, uncertain if Oh was just trying to make small talk to pass the time, or if his question was of a more probing nature. "I'm not at liberty to discuss my affiliation, Master Sergeant. Let's just say I've been to where we are going."

"Ah, I see. Well, it's always a good thing to have a guide in a strange land," Oh replied politely. Then leaning closer, and with a more serious tone, he said, "Since you're probably not a special warfare operator, stay close to me and do as you're told. Before you do anything, and I mean anything, make sure Colonel Rhee or I give you permission. And for

God's sake, don't do anything heroic. If you follow these instructions to the letter, there is a reasonable chance you'll survive this mission. Am I clear?"

"Perfectly," Cho answered with a note of irritation. As far as Oh was concerned, the new sergeant was an amateur who needed a last-minute introduction to Special Warfare 101. Unfortunately, there wasn't time, so the next best thing was a harsh warning. Cho understood Oh's motivation; the man was a consummate professional and expected the same from his colleagues. Clearly Oh didn't like having an "untrained" individual on this mission. But even if he meant well, the gruff delivery left Cho's ego bruised. He didn't like being treated like a child.

Rhee waved his hand, grabbing everyone's attention. Pointing to a tablet, he marked their location and said, "We've reached the break-off point. The other formation will peel off and take their own route in. The ride is liable to get a bit rough once we start flying down these valleys, so make sure all your gear is secure. We land in sixteen minutes."

Cho braced himself. *Now* it's going to get rough?

Hellcat Strike
Over Incheon, United Han Republic
It had been awhile since Tony felt so good. He was in heaven, literally. The sixteen F-16Cs of the Hellcat strike were organized into four flights, flying high above Incheon as they headed north to their loiter station. Each flight had one bird with two GBU-31 2,000-pound armor-penetrating bombs for the hardened missile storage bunkers, and three aircraft with four GBU-38B 500-pound high-explosive bombs for everything else. Once the SOF guys pinpointed the location

of the armored bunkers, fifty-six bombs would descend on them like a pack of wild dogs, or cats, in this case.

General Carter was fuming, and he let Tony know it as the strike passed by Seoul. But Carter wasn't so angry that he ordered Tony to abort. No, Carter knew this raid had to work, or else. And as much as he would hate to admit it, both men knew Tony was the right guy, in the right place, at the right time. Oh, there might be a disciplinary hearing afterward; perhaps a letter of reprimand would find its way into Tony's record, maybe. But in the end, he was at peace with his decision. This would be his last chance to fly a combat mission, and any punishment the air force could come up with would be well worth it.

Still, Tony knew there would be hell to pay when Ann found out about his little junket. And Randy Carter would make sure Ann knew about it. "*C'est la guerre*," Tony mumbled to himself.

"Puma lead, this is Lighthouse. Hold you on course three four five, speed five hundred, angels thirty. Nightstalker one and two have delivered the package and are holding to the west. There are no friendlies above angels five. There are no bogies to report," concluded the air battle manager on the E-3C Sentry.

"Roger, Lighthouse. Hellcat strike proceeding to station," replied Tony.

"Puma lead, DPI coordinates will be relayed by Dog Pound via JTIDS."

Tony acknowledged the report that the E-8C JSTARS command and control aircraft, code named Dog Pound, would be relaying the aim points from the special ops team to his strikers by digital data link. All the pilots had to do was release the weapons within parameters and the GPS guidance would do the rest. With the team on the ground providing a differential GPS correction, the bombs should land within a handful of inches of the target—more than close enough.

As Tony was signing off, the air battle manager chimed back in once more with a cheery, "It's good to see you back in the saddle again, Saint. Good luck. Lighthouse out."

Smiling, Tony radioed his instructions to the other three flights. They'd be on station in fifteen minutes.

X Corps Headquarters

Tae was pleasantly surprised that the commandos took so little time to secure the airfield. On the one hand, the general was pleased with their rapid progress; on the other he knew the air base had been practically unprotected. Only a minimal troop complement had defended it, and rather badly at that. Most were untrained conscripts; they were zealous, but had no chance against Ro's professionals. Very few surrendered.

"Comrade General, Major Ro reports the bridging units will be in place shortly and his commandos are ready to forge ahead," reported Ryeon.

"Very good! Tell Ro to have his commandos scout out these two main roads to the southwest." Tae pointed on a map to the roads that climbed into the foothills. "I need to have a better idea of what defenses are up there. We've met almost nothing! They must be concentrating their forces up there in those heights. And get some of those miniature UAVs up there as well!"

"Yes, sir!" shouted Ryeon on the run.

Tae shook his head. *Where were the Kim forces?* he silently wondered. Both the Chinese to the north and the American and Han armies to the east and south had met very light resistance and were advancing quickly into the hilly terrain. Either they had grossly misjudged the Kim faction's strength, or they were holed up in a reinforced central core. Tae was betting on the latter. Frowning, the general started trotting over toward his aide. "Major Ryeon! Get me a vehicle! We're heading in!"

Ghost Brigade

Rhee's half of the company worked their way quietly up the ridgeline a little over a kilometer from the landing zone. Major Maeng's half landed about four kilometers to the east and would be making their way to the northwest. With any luck both groups would get a fix on the target and set up their real-time differential GPS transmitters. The US fighter-bombers tasked with making the main attack would have the most precise target fix possible.

They met no opposition as they landed, and a quick survey of the area showed it had been hit repeatedly by aircraft ordnance. Many of the destroyed positions they inspected were decoys—the gun emplacements made of steel barrels and piping. Rhee had expected some of this, but the lack of any bodies made him wonder where the Kim faction had put its strength. Did the earlier Chinese attempt to cross the Chongchon River draw most of their assets to the north? Rumblings of artillery from all around him told him the battle along the perimeter still raged.

Cho hung close to Master Sergeant Oh and an American colonel named Little. After jumping out of the helicopter, Cho briefly considered hugging the ground. The ride in through the valleys was unspeakably bumpy. Rhee's warning that things would get "a bit rough" was a gross understatement. Cho reminded himself to thank Oh for the ginger gum again. Without it, Cho would have certainly embarrassed himself.

Cresting the rise slowly, Rhee pulled up his night vision binoculars, made a quick sweep, and then focused on where they needed to go. What he saw answered his earlier question. Some two hundred meters ahead was a heavily reinforced defensive line with real machine gun emplacements and what looked like mortars. The defensive positions were hidden in a grove of trees and had multispectral camouflage netting over the top. Rhee couldn't see the bunkers behind the tree line—their intended overlook position.

Dropping back down, he motioned for Little and sergeants Cho and Oh to get close. Whispering he said, "We have a little problem. We can't use our preplanned survey site. There is a strong defensive position in the trees ahead. We'll have to maneuver to the secondary site to our right."

"Rhee, that grove of trees is almost a semicircle," observed Kevin. "We have to assume the Kim defenses will follow along the tree line. There isn't a lot of cover to our right; you'll have to set up the DGPS transmitter in the open. You'll need a little distraction to shift their attention from that part of the line."

"True. Any suggestions?"

"Colonel," volunteered Cho. "There is a slight ravine that curves along this rocky outcropping, here. It's not on your map, but it will offer some cover while allowing a clear line of sight to the target area."

Little nodded. "Yes, that should work. Particularly if we combine it with a diversion to the left."

"Care to take that on, Colonel Little?" Rhee asked.

"Absolutely. I can take the four FLASH teams and set up over here." Kevin pointed to a rock ledge that would give them a slight elevation advantage. "If the incendiary rockets don't scare the shit out of them, they'll have to stay hunkered down. The blast should wreck their night vision, and the Apaches can use the heat signature for suppression fire if we need it."

"Excellent! Master Sergeant Oh, you go with Colonel Little . . ."

"Sir, if I may," interrupted the Korean senior NCO. "I think it best I stay with you and the DGPS transmitter. I can get it set up and calibrated faster than anyone else here. Staff Sergeant Jeo is more than capable to assist Colonel Little."

"Very well, Master Sergeant. Colonel Little, you take two-thirds of the men and make a lot of noise. The rest of us will set up the DGPS station."

Hellcat Strike

They had been milling about smartly for almost half an hour. Fortunately, the trip from Kunsan to the loitering station only required the fuel in the two drop tanks, leaving a full internal load for the attack run and return trip. Still, just hanging around wasn't Tony's idea of fun. So far, there was no word from Dog Pound. He knew the SOF team had to hike their way to their survey sites, set up their gear, and calibrate it before they could transmit the data. He just hoped they weren't taking the long way around.

X Corps Headquarters

The explosion was far off to Tae's left, but pieces of dirt and rock rained down on him and Ryeon. The X Corps had plunged almost ten kilometers into the hills before they ran into any real resistance. The defenses weren't along the mountainside as he expected, but were placed at ground level by key intersections of the limited road network. This suggested a lack of experience, or time, or both. Regardless, Tae's forces were now fully engaged and, at the moment, pinned down.

A South Korean officer wiped off the dust from his micro-UAV display and pointed to several mortar batteries just behind the ridge off to their right. The video feed showed the mortar crews loading and firing furiously. There seemed to be no attempt at adjusting their fire, just an emphasis on volume. Tae was dismissive. "Very sloppy. Probably some incompetent political commissar! Major Ryeon, have the Second Field Artillery Group put counter-battery fire on that location immediately. And where are my tanks?"

"General, the Fourth Armored Battalion is coming up now with twenty Chonma-ho tanks. They've been alerted to the positions of the machine gun emplacements."

"Very good. Tell the battalion commander to engage those emplacements at his earliest opportunity and have him set up his 122mm howitzers here." Tae pointed to a flat piece of land behind him and to the right. "I want fire laid down on that ravine, right here, where the road runs straight between these two hills. That's a perfect place for an ambush."

"Yes, sir, at once," responded Ryeon as he grabbed the battlefield radio handset.

Tae didn't bother to wait for his aide; he'd catch up when he was done. The general slapped the South Korean sergeant on the back and roared, "Come, Sergeant, let's see what more mischief we can cause with that toy of yours!"

Ghost Brigade

Kevin kept low as he and Lieutenant Guk and Staff Sergeant Jeo hugged the rocks, positioning themselves to direct fire as necessary. The fifty commandos were spread out in a rough line some seventy meters long. The FLASH teams were placed at regular intervals. Although an old weapon, the four-barreled bazooka-like flame assault shoulder weapon was perfect for close-in fighting. It could fire incendiary rockets out to a range of seven hundred fifty meters, but it was aimed with a standard reflex sight, which meant it wasn't all that accurate. However, in this situation, Kevin was counting more on the shock value of the weapon. Besides, they were firing from much less than half the maximum range; hitting wouldn't be an issue.

"Ghost One Alpha, this is Ghost One Bravo. We are in position and ready to initiate," he said over the secure radio.

"Ghost One Bravo, initiate," ordered Rhee.

Kevin flashed a small light toward Guk and Jeo. They flashed back; the troops were ready to commence firing. Kevin then held down on the light and the four commandos with the FLASH launchers perched them on their shoulders, took aim, and fired. Chaos descended on the Kim positions.

Rhee saw one explosion after another erupt along the left side. The FLASH launchers kept up their volley of rockets, while disciplined rifle fire came from Little's troops. The Kim defenses fell into total panic and began spraying machine gun fire and rocket-propelled grenades inaccurately back in the general direction of their assailants. The colonel motioned, and his men took off at a run across a short opening and down the hillside. They scurried down loose rock and gravel and finally down into the ravine that Cho had mentioned. The location was perfect.

While Master Sergeant Oh and two corporals began setting up the DGPS transmitter, Rhee positioned his men to defend against any potential attack. He then took his binoculars and looked down into the small trough behind the elevated grove of trees. There he saw the doors of the armored bunkers were open, and four missile TELs positioned at their launch pads some hundred meters away from the cave entrances. Three of the missiles had been raised into a vertical position and were being fueled. He watched as the fourth was raised to the vertical. They were bigger than any mobile missile he'd seen before.

"Ghost One Alpha, this is Ghost Two. We are in position and ready to take ranges, over," squawked his headset. Major Maeng's team was set up and ready to use their laser rangefinder to take the measurements.

"Ghost Two, stand by," Rhee instructed.

"Standing by. Ghost Two, out."

It took Oh just a few more minutes to finish setting up and check the calibration; after one last inspection, he signaled Rhee he was ready. The colonel waved for him to take the ranges.

"Stay here," Oh told Cho. The master sergeant then crawled on his belly to a small cluster of rocks several meters away. Peeking over the top, he raised the laser rangefinder and started measuring the distance to the bunker doors and launch pads. Within moments of Oh triggering the rangefinder, machine gun fire began peppering their location. The master sergeant was hit in the shoulder and thrown to the ground—out in the open. Without thinking, Cho dove across and pushed Oh out of the line of fire. The man had been hit twice and was badly wounded.

"Didn't I tell you not to do anything heroic!" Oh gasped in pain.

Cho didn't reply but grabbed his first aid kit and tore open the master sergeant's uniform near the wound sites. Oh pushed back and grunted angrily, "Take the damn ranges, you moron!"

Feeling frantically around the ground, Cho found the cable and pulled the laser gun toward him. Rhee signaled him to hurry as the commandos began returning fire. Crawling to the rock, he raised the laser and, exposing as little of himself as possible, began shooting the ranges. A bullet ricocheted off a boulder to his right, stinging his face with small shards of rock. It took all of twenty seconds to get the ranges. Once Rhee gave Cho thumbs-up, the former spy threw down the laser gun and crawled back to Oh.

"There, are you happy now, Master Sergeant?" exclaimed Cho. Oh didn't respond. Fear seized Cho as he hunted for a pulse on Oh's neck—there wasn't one. Oh was dead.

Rhee had little time to see what was going on with his master sergeant. Once the shooting had started, he ordered Ghost Two to take ranges and transmit. He also alerted Maeng to expect return fire; the Kim faction apparently had laser-warning sensors.

One of the corporals flashed Rhee an OK sign. They had the data and were ready to transmit. Rhee pushed his finger skyward and yelled, "Transmit!"

Hellcat Strike

"Puma lead, this is Dog Pound. DPIs received, data being transferred by Dolly. Commence attack by flight, over."

"Roger, Dog Pound," said Tony as he quickly looked at the center flat-panel display. The data link, brevity code Dolly, had uploaded the sixteen-digit UTM coordinates for his four GBU-38B bombs into his computer. He took a brief moment to scan each designated point of impact to make sure they were close to each other. He had no desire to drop a bomb on the friendlies hiding nearby. "Dog Pound, DPI coordinates confirmed. Commencing attack run."

Tony then took a deep breath and called out to the other flight leaders. "Commence attack by flight. Puma will go in first, then Lynx, Leopard, with Jaguar bringing up the rear. Let's not keep the snake-eaters waiting."

As he listened to their acknowledgments, Tony pointed his F-16 to the northeast and punched it to full military power. He looked to his left and right and saw the shadowy outlines of the other three jets in his flight. Keying his mike he radioed his wingman, "You go first, Wookie. You've got the two big boys."

The flights of Hellcat strike quickly formed a line and, guided by their heads-up displays, flew to the release point. One by one, the onboard computer automatically released their bombs. Tony pulled his ship up and to the left as soon as he felt the bombs fall off the racks. Again looking over his shoulder, he tried to watch the other flights during their runs, but it was too dark. All he could do was listen in as each flight lead announced ordnance release, and when they were clear. Once Jaguar flight was done, Tony radioed the E-8C JSTARS.

"Dog Pound, bombs away."

Before the JSTARS aircraft could respond, the E-3C air battle manager broke on line. "All flights, this is Lighthouse. I have six bogeys, bearing zero three zero, range fifteen miles, speed four hundred, angels seven. Negative IFF."

Ghost Brigade

Kevin flinched as an RPG hit the rock face to his left, the shock wave travelling through the solid wall. The defenders had apparently calmed down a little, as their fire was becoming more accurate. So far, they hadn't ventured from their protective cover, but that would only be a matter of time— and there were a lot more of them than his band of commandos. They needed help.

"Nightstalker One, this is Ghost One Bravo, request immediate close air support. Target is illuminated with incendiaries," shouted Kevin. What he heard in reply was disheartening.

"Negative on CAS request, Ghost One Bravo," said the helo pilot. His voice betrayed his disappointment. "Airspace is closed due to inbound strike. I suggest you duck and cover."

Oh great, thought Kevin.

Two more commandos were hit as the Kim forces pushed toward their position. The holdouts were attempting a rush, but it was poorly coordinated, and Rhee's men beat them back. He'd heard the decline for close air support over the radio; the air strike was on its way. All they had to do was hold their ground for just a little longer.

Cho hugged the small boulder closely as the bullets whizzed by. He managed a few shots with his assault rifle, but had no idea if he hit anything worthwhile. But when an RPG round fell short, he knew he had to get back behind better cover.

Just as he was about to make a run for it, the attackers made another charge. The accurate fire from the commandos dropped many of those rushing their position, but there were simply too many, and a number of attackers managed to get over the rocks. The fighting devolved into a hand-to-hand skirmish. Again the commandos had the qualitative advantage, but the Kim faction had numbers.

Cho watched as Rhee took down three with his pistol and then crush the windpipe of a fourth with a forceful knife-hand strike. But it was the fifth soldier that caught the colonel on his blind side, delivering a sharp blow with the rifle butt. Stunned, Rhee was thrown to the ground. The soldier paused to take careful aim, but before he could shoot, Cho ran across and slammed into him, driving the man headfirst into the rock. Dazed, the soldier shook his head, pulled his combat knife, and rushed toward Cho.

He lunged to his right, the quick move causing the soldier's main thrust to miss, but he swept the blade downward and caught Cho's left leg squarely in the calf. The pain was incredible and he let out a scream of agony. Cho hit the ground hard. He struggled to get back up, but with his right leg under his body, and his left useless, he couldn't move quickly. The soldier approached with a wicked smile; Cho looked frantically for a weapon of any kind. None were within reach. All he could think of was how cruel this war had been to Kary. Just as the soldier raised the knife, a sharp crack from Rhee's pistol put an end to his lethal intentions.

Rhee then looked around and saw many of his men were wounded, but the latest charge had been beaten back. He glanced at his watch, and then yelled at the top of his lungs, "EVERYONE DOWN!"

Then the ground started shaking.

The bombs fell in such a rapid interval that it seemed like one big, long explosion. The 2,000-pound penetrators tore into the mountainside and ripped the walls apart, causing a landslide. Bodies, living and dead, bounced off the ground as the shock traveled for kilometers. Then the high-explosive bombs hit the launch pads. The fuel and oxidizer tanks of the KN-08 missiles were shredded. Freed from their containment, the hypergolic chemicals poured onto the ground and mixed, enhancing the explosive effects many times over. Rhee felt the intense concussive blast and heat from the exploding missiles, even though they were over five hundred meters away, and shielded by over a meter of hard rock. No one on the other side of that wall could have survived. After what seemed like an eternity, the ground stopped shaking.

Hellcat Strike

Tony snapped his head hard right and saw six sets of blue flames below him. The fighters were coming up fast, at full afterburner. "All flights, tally on bogeys, four o'clock low."

Reaching over to the control panel, Tony dumped his empty drop tanks and pulled his ship into a hard right bank. He was the farthest away from the approaching enemy aircraft and had to quickly get back into position. He watched in horror as two of the bogeys flew right into the trailing element of Jaguar flight. The other four kept on coming, right toward him. They had no intention of running, or returning alive.

"Stick with me, Wookie," exclaimed Tony as he continued his right bank and pushed his nose down. His maneuver threw off the approaching pilot, who tried to pull a steep turn while at afterburner.

"Saint! You have a bogey slipping into your six o'clock!"

Oh shit! Tony thought to himself. *I'm being double-teamed!* "I could use a little help here, Wookie!" he said.

"Rog. I'm engaging!" Soon after, Tony heard "Fox Two!" indicating a heat-seeking missile had just been launched. The sudden bright flash told him Wookie had got a kill. "Splash one!"

Tony finished his barrel roll and found himself just off the bogey's port quarter; the pilot had overshot his target. Lining up the target in his HUD, Tony selected an infrared-guided missile and waited for the loud growl that told him his AIM-9X had locked on to the target. As soon as the welcome noise filled his headphones, Tony pulled the trigger and announced, "Fox Two!"

The missile leapt off the rail and flew a straight path to the hostile aircraft, aided by the concentrated heat from the afterburners. Tony watched as the bright plume of the missile's exhaust merged with the target, disappeared, and then exploded, shredding the enemy fighter. "Splash two!" he called out.

Lynx and Leopard flights soon reported the downing of the remaining two aircraft. His body loaded with adrenaline, Tony did a full search of the night skies, looking for any more hostile aircraft.

"Puma lead, this is Lighthouse. All bogeys have been splashed. Repeat, all bogeys have been splashed."

"Roger, Lighthouse. Thanks for the update. Where did those jokers come from?"

"Dog Pound picked them up before we did. Looks like they used a highway as a runway. They didn't come from any of the nearby air bases."

"Sneaky little bastards," grumbled Tony as his blood pressure finally began to drop.

"That they were, Puma lead. Oh, and congratulations on number eighteen, Saint!"

Tony shook his head; it hadn't even sunk in yet that he'd scored another kill. "Oh, yeah, right," he mumbled. "I must be getting old." Then keying his mike, Tony ordered, "All flights, this is Puma lead, return to base."

X Corps Headquarters

A huge mushroom cloud erupted from the mountain ahead of him—a monstrous pillar of bright orange and red flames. A thundering roar soon followed, the sound echoing off the surrounding hills. At first, Tae could only look on in utter despair. He feared the Chinese had carried out their threat and used a nuclear weapon to destroy the missile site. Disheartened, he waited for the shock wave and wall of fire to put an end to his life. And he kept on waiting.

But as he watched the cloud dissipate, he realized that blast wasn't a nuclear device, but the exploding remains of the Kim nightmare. In a most unprofessional manner, Tae let out a shout of joy and gave Ryeon a bear hug.

There would still be some more fighting, but it was all a mop-up campaign now. The new United Han Republic would survive. His land would survive. With a light heart, he started walking back up the road.

EPILOGUE

9 September 2015, 4:40 p.m. local time
Munsan Refugee Camp
Outside Dongducheon, United Han Republic

She hadn't been waiting for him, not exactly. There was more than enough to keep her mind occupied. With the final defeat of the Kim holdouts, the army had started talking about repatriating the Northern citizens, which was good news, but this had added "travel agent" to her job description. The army wanted her input on who should go home first, and where they wanted to go, and didn't understand why it was such a difficult question to answer.

She'd shifted her chair a little so she had a clearer view of the door. And she checked her phone more often than before, although she knew he didn't even have one. He could borrow someone's cell phone, after all.

Late in the afternoon, absorbed in a file that was supposed to list the home provinces of everyone in each camp, and didn't, she noticed a shadow across her keyboard and looked back over her shoulder. It was Cho.

Startled, she shrieked "Eep! How long have you been standing there?" Then happiness replaced surprise, and she quickly stood and welcomed him back with a hug. He pecked her on the cheek, which felt completely normal, and only made her happier.

Taking a step back, she looked him up and down while he stood, smiling broadly. "You're all right?"

He shrugged. "I'm here, still breathing. I would like to get off my feet, though."

"Oh, of course," she said and let go.

He gratefully plopped into a chair next to her desk. "I'm exhausted. My cot in tent six actually looked homey."

"Well, don't get too settled. The army will start moving people out of here in the next few days." She gestured toward her laptop. "There's a lot to do."

"And I'll be glad to help." He smiled warmly.

When he didn't say anything else, she prompted, "So? What happened? You've been gone for three days."

He sighed. "They debriefed me in this stuffy, windowless van. I got very little sleep. They said my information was very useful. And as soon as they were done with me, I came back here, as quickly as I could."

She reached over and squeezed his hand. "I'm proud of you for speaking up. I know you didn't want to."

Cho nodded, agreeing. "Absolutely. We former spies still like to keep a low profile."

She laughed, but said, "Later, I want to hear all about what you told the army. I'm sure it helped, because the day after you left they destroyed the holdouts' nuclear weapons in a missile complex, and now they're hunting down the last of the stragglers. But you must know all about that. It's been all over the news, of course."

"I haven't seen a television in days," he answered.

"Then you should," she said enthusiastically. "They're showing pictures of the ruined complex. And there was an air battle, too. They've got video of a MiG-29 fighter being shot down."

She looked at the clock. It was almost time for them to go for dinner. She obviously wasn't going to get any more work done. "Come on. I'll buy you a cup of coffee and you can catch up on what's been happening." She headed for the coffeepot.

After a pause, Cho got up and followed her. She poured two cups of coffee and handed one to Cho, who turned and walked slowly toward the tent next to theirs. "You really are tired. I guess I'll have to take care of you," she remarked brightly, taking him by the arm.

The rec tent was as large as the headquarters tent; it held a ping-pong table at one end and a large-screen television at the other. The chairs in between the two were all turned to face the TV. Two-thirds were filled with people, all in a festive mood, laughing and sometimes clapping at the news.

Several members of her staff saw them come in and recognized Cho, welcoming him back. "Congratulations! Good work!" Others teased Kary, asking her what it was like having a hero for a boyfriend. And they were glad to see Cho hadn't been badly wounded.

Their words made no sense to her. "I don't understand," Kary said. "We just came in to watch the news about the battle."

"Exactly!" someone answered. They made room for her and Cho in the front row. Another person said, "They have been running the footage almost continuously."

Completely confused now, Kary could only ask, "What footage?" She looked to Cho, who managed to look both confused and apprehensive.

"You'll see. Just sit and watch for a few minutes."

That had been her intention anyway, so she and Cho sat together watching one of the Korean news channels. She held his hand tightly, giving it an occasional squeeze.

There was nonstop coverage of the war. The first piece they saw had aerial views of the missile complex, now a blackened and smoking ruin. Her blood ran cold at the thought of how close the missiles had come to actually being used.

The next segment featured a hidden cache of currency and gold that had been found during the search of a North Korean diplomat's house in Switzerland. It was worth tens of millions, and was one of many such hoards being discovered around the world. *So much greed,* she thought. The diplomat was in custody until he could be repatriated to Korea, where he would probably face money-laundering charges, among other things.

"It's the top of the hour," someone announced. "They'll run it now." The staffer was smiling broadly, which only added to Kary's confusion.

The image shifted to show a clearing, with a wooded mountainside in the background. "This is video that just reached us of the special forces soldiers that attacked the Kim holdouts' fortress and destroyed the missiles inside."

The camera centered on an older officer in battle-stained fatigues. His helmet was off, and he was wearing a black beret, a sure sign the battle was over, and he was taking a long drink from his canteen.

Helicopters were taking off and landing behind him. "Colonel Rhee Han-gil, shown here, the commander of the Ghosts Special Forces Brigade, personally led over a hundred and fifty of his elite troops through heavy fire, at times engaging in hand-to-hand combat, to destroy the missile complex."

The camera panned right to show groups of soldiers, obviously very tired, sprawled on the ground. Medics were working on some who were wounded. "The army won't release any casualty figures until all the next of kin are notified, but described their losses as 'lower than expected.'"

Rhee walked into the frame from one side, and the camera zoomed in to follow him as he stopped to speak to different soldiers, then knelt next to a wounded trooper sprawled on the grass. His helmet and assault rifle lay next to him. The camera zoomed in a little more, centering first on a bloody but bandaged leg, then on their faces as they spoke.

Kary realized the wounded soldier was Cho. Then she immediately dismissed the idea. It must be someone who just looks a lot like him. She looked at the man sitting next to her, then back to the screen, searching for some difference. Her confusion grew when she couldn't find one. Was this really Cho in the video?

Astonished, she watched the two figures on the screen. It was clear from their manner that the colonel was praising the soldier, and Rhee patted him on the shoulder, then grinned and saluted the man—Cho—before straightening and moving on.

"As a matter of policy, the authorities do not release the names of soldiers in special forces units. Colonel Rhee, as the leader of the attack, is an exception. Questioned about the wounded soldier Colonel Rhee was speaking with, an army spokesman identified him as someone who was critical to the success of the attack."

The report ended, and thunderous applause filled the tent, punctuated with cheers. Cho was bright red with embarrassment. If he wanted to keep a low profile, this was an epic failure. Confusion and surprise whirled inside Kary; then the pieces began to fall into place.

She looked Cho straight in the eye, a deep scowl on her face. "Pull up your pants leg," she ordered in a no-nonsense tone.

Cho nodded and pulled up the cuff of his fatigue pants. She saw nothing but leg.

"Nice try," she said. "The other one, please." There was a sharper edge to her order.

This time, he got the trouser up no more than a few inches before she saw the white of a bandage. Her medical training kicked in. The wound had obviously been treated already. "How bad is it? Was there any infection? And why are you walking on it?"

Cho winced as he rolled the pant leg down. "It's not too bad. It only went through the soft part of my calf, and they've pumped me full of antibiotics. And they gave me a crutch, but I don't—"

"Where is it?"

He pointed to a spot on his calf.

"Not the wound, the crutch!"

"Oh, that. I left it outside your tent. I wanted to see how well I could get by—"

"You didn't want me to see you were hurt! Later on, you can tell me which of the several bad reasons you used to justify that decision."

She turned to one of her staffers sitting next to her. She asked sweetly, "Helen, would you please get the crutch for us?" Helen, like everyone else nearby, was following the conversation closely, the news channel ignored. She nodded and dashed from the tent.

Kary found it was possible to care deeply for someone, to believe that someone was a wonderful person, and still want to throttle him.

She was aware of the many people around her, but didn't feel embarrassed or self-conscious. If Cho was uncomfortable with his less-than-low profile, that was too bad.

She watched him closely. "Tell me the truth. Were you in the battle?"

Cho sighed. "Yes, I was in the battle."

"You lied to me about the van!" she accused.

"No, no!" he insisted. "I was in the van. The battle was later."

Her understanding grew. "So you just skipped the part about the battle. Did they make you go, or did you volunteer?"

After a short pause, he answered, "I volunteered. It turned out—"

"And when were you going to tell me about this?"

"I was looking for the right time! I didn't want to upset you."

She laughed. "What? Were you afraid I would go to pieces? After everything we've been through? When was that time going to be? 'Right away' would have been good."

"I was working on it!" he protested. "I promise, it wasn't going to be long." Cho noticed Helen standing to one side, offering his abandoned crutch, and desperate for any distraction, took it gratefully. "Thank you so much."

Kary nodded, and said briskly, "Good. Now that you're mobile, let's go somewhere and have a long talk, unless your leg's too sore. We could just stay here."

Levering himself up with his crutch, Cho said, "No, we can go."

The two left at a measured pace, with Kary slowing her steps to match Cho's progress with the crutch. She ignored the rising buzz of conversation behind her.

Even while one part of her mind automatically and calmly planned his convalescence, the rest boiled with a dozen questions she wanted to ask and another dozen things she was going to tell him.

If I don't kill him first.

10 September 2015, 8:00 p.m. local time
CNN Special Report
"This evening, Seoul and Beijing announced an agreement in principle for the rapid withdrawal of Chinese forces still in former DPRK territory. Citing vague 'security concerns,' the PRC had previously avoided discussing when their troops would leave, even though all former DPRK weapons of mass destruction had been located and turned over to the US Eighth Army for destruction.

"Acknowledging China's concerns without addressing their exact nature, the Korean foreign minister, meeting with his counterpart from Beijing in Tokyo, said that, 'building a relationship of trust with Korea's northern neighbor will be an important part of the United Han Republic's new foreign policy.'

"The former DPRK maintained the fifth-largest standing army in the world. Its sudden removal from the region means that the large and expensive US presence in Korea is no longer necessary. The first point of agreement is that while America will continue its alliance and serve as a guarantor of Korean sovereignty, the bulk of its combat forces will return to the United States. Medical and logistical units will remain for some time to assist in the massive humanitarian effort.

"With the removal of the US combat forces, and the expected partial demobilization of the Korean army, Chinese forces in the region will also be reduced.

"The economic benefits of this are far-reaching. In addition to the reduced military budgets, all three nations stand to gain, especially since China was providing the equivalent of over two billion dollars in direct aid annually to Pyongyang for decades. This represented half of China's entire foreign aid budget each year. While it will lose an equal amount of trade income from goods it sold to the DPRK, China stands to gain many times that amount in trade with a united Korea.

"The one very large, very dark cloud on Korea's economic horizon is the massive cost of repairing the damage in the north caused by the war, and of upgrading—indeed, almost rebuilding—the infrastructure of the entire former DPRK.

"Economists familiar with the integration of East and West Germany estimate that reconstruction will require seven to ten percent of Korea's gross domestic product for the next ten to twenty years. This is a staggering amount, a lump sum of about half a trillion US dollars. These same experts note, however, that Germany faced a similar hurdle and overcame it. The determination of the Korean people is at least as great.

"In that economic context, as a second point of agreement, the United Han Republic has pledged the equivalent of ten billion US dollars in trade to China for at least the next ten years. This will include construction contracts, immediate purchases of foodstuffs and fuel for the relief effort, and even some ammunition and repair parts for the former DPRK's military hardware. The details of the agreement will be worked out in Tokyo over the next few weeks, but social media reports some Chinese units are already moving north.

"An additional incentive for the PLA's withdrawal is that it relieves their army of responsibility for the Korean civilians in the areas they occupied. Han army units, now engaged in a humanitarian effort instead of a combat mission, are following closely behind the Chinese troops. It is possible that all former DPRK territory will be clear of Chinese forces by the end of the month."

Kunsan Air Base
Gunsan, United Han Republic
Tony Christopher turned off the television and tossed the remains of his lunch into the trash. He wanted to know why, if the fighting was over, he was so busy? But he knew why. They'd flown the wings off their aircraft, and now all that deferred maintenance had to be dealt with. And the war really wasn't over for the transports. They were still bringing in relief supplies, as well as replenishing stocks of parts and ammunition that had been seriously depleted in the few short weeks they'd been fighting.

But a lot of that matériel would have to be removed in the very near future. It was hard to imagine the Eighth Fighter Wing, the Wolf Pack, anywhere but Kunsan, but his boss, General Carter, was in Seoul right now with the rest of the Pacific Command, planning the biggest redeployment of the US armed forces since Desert Storm. Yet Carter had promised Tony that he would do a full tour in country. The Seventh Air Force wasn't going away that quickly. In fact, he hinted that for his next tour, Tony might end up with Carter's job, provided he didn't fly any more unauthorized combat missions.

On top of everything else, the crisis had deferred his house-hunting. Ann was still waiting for him to find a place for them to live, and wasn't being all that patient. If there was a drawdown, he might be able to pick up a nice place for less than they had planned.

And wait until she heard there was a chance for back-to-back tours.

11 September 2015, 1000 local time
Third Army Field Headquarters
Outside Taedong, United Han Republic

It was the first visit to the territory of the former DPRK by the president of the newly united Korea. Lingering security concerns and the rapid-fire press of events had prevented President An Kye-nam from making even a short trip above the former DMZ. Besides, the occasion was historic, and needed to be properly choreographed.

An's helicopter, Korea One, approached Taedong after a forty-five minute flight from the Blue House in Seoul. A wedge of Apache gunships escorted the aircraft, while fighters provided high cover for the flight.

The presidential helicopter flew a little past the landing pad, then turned into the wind to make its final approach. The commentators covering the landing used the time to discuss the political problems facing the Seoul government as it organized elections in the shattered north, and tried to cope with new political parties well to the left of traditional Korean politics.

As the helicopter's wheels touched the pad, whistles blew and with all the pomp and circumstance it could muster, the victorious army welcomed its civilian leader. A band flown in from the capital played the "Aegukga" while the honor guard came to attention and presented arms.

In concession to the ongoing military operations, the soldiers welcoming President An wore battledress. This was not only more appropriate for a field headquarters; it allowed General Tae and other former KPA soldiers to avoid wearing their Kim-era dress uniforms. The idea was to blend in with their Southern colleagues, and camouflage served that purpose well.

President An Kye-nam emerged first, followed by a huddle of officials trying to stay close to the president while avoiding the rotor wash. They waited nearby, half-crouched, for a moment while the helicopter's engines spooled up again and it flew off.

While most of his entourage waited to one side, the president reviewed the honor guard, made up of special forces troops that had taken part in the assault on the missile complex, then greeted the generals, arranged in order of rank: Sohn, Tae, and Kwon.

An greeted Sohn warmly, and had a lengthy conversation with Tae, and beamed as he acknowledged Kwon's salute. Rhee might be the hero of the hour, but everybody knew who Rhee worked for.

After speaking with Kwon for a few minutes, An nodded in agreement. He walked back to stand next to General Sohn. The band struck up the "Arirang Nation" march, and the different staffs quickly rearranged themselves while the general strode to a nearby podium. He barked out a short command. In time with the martial music, a new group of individuals marched onto the landing pad, forming a neat line facing the dignitaries. The commentator announced the name of each one.

Once they were in position, the president stepped in front of the podium and Sohn called out, "Colonel Rhee Han-gil, front and center."

While Rhee crossed the distance in front of the podium, General Sohn read, "For considerable skill in executing the attack on the Sukchon missile complex, and displaying exceptional leadership and conspicuous bravery during the action, Colonel Rhee Han-gil is awarded the Taeguk Cordon, First Class." A staffer produced the decoration and handed it to the president, who pinned it on the colonel.

Standing at one end of the line, Kevin tried not to smile too broadly as Rhee received Korea's highest military honor. One was supposed to maintain proper decorum at these events. Rhee's deputy was next. Then several enlisted soldiers who had done some extraordinary things during the fight. As the sole American, he was okay with being last.

There was a reception after the awards ceremony in the mess tent, which had been decorated with oversize Korean flags and the insignia of the Ninth Special Forces Brigade. Curiously, a DPRK flag, somewhat tattered, occupied a place of honor. It was a trophy that been taken from the missile complex before it was destroyed, and was headed straight to a museum after today's festivities.

There were two crowds in the tent—one surrounding Rhee and the other at the refreshment table. It had been hot under the sun, and Kevin decided rehydration had priority. His rank as well as his recent award gave him an edge, and he managed to redeploy with a cool drink to a quieter part of the tent.

General Tae had chosen the same tactic, and when he saw Kevin approaching, he smiled broadly and offered his hand. "Congratulations on your award, Colonel."

"And to you on your success at the airfield, General. It's much better to have you as an ally than as an opponent."

Tae acknowledged the remark with a raised glass, then quietly asked, "But will America be an ally to all of Korea? The North was your enemy for over seventy years."

"Americans were always able to distinguish the Kim government from the Korean people." Little shrugged. "If you want to take the long view, when the peninsula was divided in 1945, the Soviets promised to hold elections in the north. That never happened, and the first Kim came to power. Now, three or four generations later, the North Korean people will finally get a chance to have that vote."

The general nodded agreement. "It will be an interesting experience for everyone." He paused thoughtfully, and asked, "I'm hearing a lot about the South Korean democratic system, but I'd like to know more. Would visiting America help me learn more about politics?"

Kevin was taking a drink, and a little of it went down the wrong way. He coughed, but recovered quickly. "Are you thinking of going into politics?" In the process of translating that question from English into Korean, Kevin tried to mask some of his surprise at the idea.

"Not right away. I believe the military government will have to run things for several years. Actually, President An just asked me if I'd delay my retirement and take part in the negotiations with China, representing the interests of the Northerners."

"Politics is all about give and take, General," Kevin answered brightly. "And the talks are in Tokyo. Japanese-style democracy is very different from both Korean and American."

"Good point," Tae agreed. The general looked at something past Kevin's shoulder, and he turned to see Rhee standing there.

The colonel took care to greet General Tae before his old comrade, but then he slapped Kevin's shoulder. "Congratulations on your award, Kevin! Third Class,

Chungmu Cordon! That's like the American Silver Star. You should be proud."

"I am," Kevin answered, "but I'm especially glad for you. That medal makes you untouchable." He turned to Tae. "There were some high-ranking officers in the ROK Army who were upset with a mere colonel treating with a three-star general."

Tae laughed. "Generals, jealous? Who ever heard of such a preposterous thing?"

"Actually, it's no longer a problem," Rhee said, and showed them a small white box. He opened it and they saw two silver stars, one for each shoulder.

"Brigadier General!" Kevin remarked happily.

Rhee grinned. "General Sohn just handed them to me. He says if I'm going to act like a general, they might as well make me one."

Kevin saluted his friend, and Tae shook his hand warmly. "This is not too far from where we shook hands for the first time," Tae remarked.

"We've covered a lot of ground since then," Little commented.

"We're here because of you, General Tae," Rhee said. He touched his medal. "This belongs to you as much as me."

Tae accepted the compliment with a smile. "We had a different awards system in the KPA. Not getting shot was popular."

25 September 2015, 11:00 a.m. local time
Lake Taesong, United Han Republic
They'd borrowed an army jeep, driving from the port city of Nampo northeast, back toward Pyongyang. Restrictions on civilian traffic had been lifted now that all the areas affected

by chemicals had been marked, and the main roads cleared of unexploded ordnance.

Kary tried to imagine the pain Cho had felt The roads were busy, but a good deal of it was still foot traffic. Kary saw vehicles with Southern license plates mixed with the military transports. Only a few Northern vehicles were on the road. She knew gasoline was still very precious.

Civilians plodded along on either side. She studied them, trying to guess their story. A local farmer? A mother and child looking for the rest of their family? She saw several demobilized soldiers, probably headed for home and hoping it was still there.

Cho turned off the main road and headed northwest, keeping the city on their right. The two-lane road was less traveled, but there were scattered clusters of farm buildings. They drove for no more than a few kilometers and she saw they were headed for a line of low hills.

Curiosity building, she finally said, "I still don't know where we're going or why."

"We're almost there," he answered, and the road curved around a low hill, paralleling a small river. The river and road both reached a lake and they drove along the shore for few minutes, before stopping near a ruined house. Built on the hillside, it had suffered a fire or other damage, and looked long abandoned. Several small trees were growing inside the outlines of its foundation.

He parked the jeep and got out carefully, favoring his left leg and using the crutch as Kary had taught him. He reached out with his free hand and beckoned, "Please, come."

She nodded and followed, trusting that he would eventually explain.

Traces of a path led up to the house. The closer she got to the structure, the worse it looked. The masonry walls were shattered, as well as blackened by fire. The tallest part of the ruin was no more than a meter high.

They stopped near what was once an entranceway, and Cho announced simply, "This was my house. This was where I lived as a child."

Kary, surprised but also shocked at the extent of the ruin, asked, "Did this happen when you . . ."

"No," Cho answered. "We were simply taken away. But years later, on one of my first missions for the Russians, I was near Pyongyang, and I came back here. We'd been forced to abandon almost everything when we were arrested. I suppose I wanted to find some relic, maybe something my mother had owned. I found the house like this. The army had used explosives to level the place, then set everything on fire. I spent a few hours picking through the rubble, but couldn't find anything. They probably looted it first."

Kary tried to imagine the pain Cho had felt back then, the hurt he must still feel. She hugged his arm, searching for words, but could only say, "I'm sorry."

"Don't be," Cho answered. "This is what my life felt like until I found something better, something to live for."

Kary could only hug him even more tightly. She fought to control what would be tears of happiness, but she knew once she started, it would be very hard to stop.

"I want to build our house right here," he announced. "This was the last place I could call home. We'll tear out all the wreckage, then build a place for us." After a moment, he added, "Once we clear the site, I'd like to have a shaman perform a *kut*. Would that bother you?"

Swallowing hard, she answered, "Of course not. This sounds wonderful, but what about the mission? You know I want to rebuild that."

"What mission? You mean the new full-sized hospital, school, and church? Your CFK organization did so much in spite of the Kims, I'm curious to see how much they'll be able to accomplish now." He paused for a moment, and became more serious.

"You know you can't rebuild at Sinan. The village is empty, and it's contaminated. But there's plenty of room to build right here. Actually," he said, pointing back down the road, "back there a few hundred meters. Room for everything, and to grow after that. I've already surveyed the site."

"What?" she exclaimed. "Is that what you have been doing the past few days? And what do you mean 'surveyed'?"

"I've talked to a few people, and I'm starting a construction company." He grinned. "It's a growth industry, don't you know?"

Korean Language Terms

Ajumma	A respectful term for a middle-aged woman.
Dongji	"Comrade", referring to someone of higher social standing.
Dongmu	"Comrade", referring to someone of equal or lower social standing.
Halmeonim	Grandmother
Oppa	"Older Brother," literally and figuratively. Used by women only.
-seonsaengnim	A respectful term used for a doctor or teacher
-ssi	Honorific used between people of the same social status
-yang	Similar to –ssi, but for unmarried women/ female minors only.

GLOSSARY

AA: Antiaircraft

AAA: Antiaircraft artillery

AEW: Airborne early warning

AH-1F Cobra: US attack helicopter.

AH-64D Apache: US attack helicopter.

AIM-9X Sidewinder: US infrared-guided air-to-air missile.

AKM: Russian Kalashnikov modernized automatic rifle.

APC: Armored personnel carrier

ASAP: As soon as possible

AT-3 Sagger: Soviet first generation anti-tank guide missile.

AT-4 Spigot: Soviet second generation anti-tank guided missile.

ATGM: Anti-tank guided missile

BM-11: North Korean rocket launcher based on the BM-21.

BM-21: Soviet 122mm rocket launcher.

BM-24: Soviet 240mm rocket launcher.

BM-25: aka Musudan, a North Korean intermediate range ballistic missile.

BTR-60: Soviet 1960s era eight-wheeled armored personnel carrier.

BVS-1: US Navy submarine optronic mast, replaces an optical periscope.

C-130: US transport aircraft.

CCP: Chinese Communist Party
CEP: Circular error probable, basic measure of a weapon's accuracy.
CFC: Combined Forces Command
CFK: Christian Friends of Korea
Chonma-ho: North Korean main battle tank based on the Soviet T-62.
CIA: Central Intelligence Agency
CIC: Combat information center
CMC: Central Military Commission
CNN: Cable News Network
CNO: Chief of Naval Operations
CO: Commanding officer
CP: Command post
CT: Cryptologic technician
CTML: Conventional twelve-mile limit
DF-5: Chinese Dong-Feng (East Wind) 5 intercontinental ballistic missile.
DGPS: Differential global positioning system
DMZ: Demilitarized Zone
DPI: Designated point of impact
DPRK: Democratic People's Republic of Korea
E-3C Sentry: US Air Force airborne early warning and control aircraft.
E-8C JSTARS: US Air Force ground surveillance, command and control aircraft. JSTARS stands for joint surveillance target attack radar.
EO: Electro-optical
EMCON: Emission control
ESM: Electronic support measures
ETA: Estimated time of arrival
F-16 Falcon: US fighter-bomber.

F-22 Raptor: US stealth fighter.

FBI: Federal Bureau of Investigation

FLASH: Flame assault shoulder weapon

FLIR: Forward looking infrared

FUBAR: Fouled up beyond all recognition (polite definition)

G2: Army command senior intelligence officer.

GAZ: Gorkovsky Avtomobilny Zavod or Gorky Automobile Plant a major Russian automotive manufacturer based in the city of Nizhny Novgorod.

GBU-31: Guided Bomb Unit-31, a 2,000 lb GPS guided bomb.

GBU-38B: Guided Bomb Unit-38B, a 500 lb GPS guided bomb.

GPS: Global positioning system

HEAT: High-explosive anti-tank

HHB: Headquarters and Headquarters Battalion

Humvee: Slang for the High Mobility Multipurpose Wheeled Vehicle (HMMVV), a four-wheel drive military automobile.

HQ: Headquarters

HUD: Heads up display

Hwaseong-5: aka Scud B, North Korean copy of the Soviet R-17 short-range ballistic missile.

Hwaseong-13: aka KN-08, North Korean intercontinental ballistic missile.

ICC: Integrated command center

IFV: Infantry fighting vehicle

J2: Joint command senior intelligence officer.

J-11: Chinese version of the Russian Su-27SK Flanker fighter.

JAG: Judge Advocate General

JOOD: Junior officer of the deck

JSA: Joint Security Area

JTIDS: Joint tactical information distribution system

K1A1: South Korean main battle tank based on the US M1A1 Abrams.

K2 Black Panther: Advanced South Korean main battle tank.

K21: South Korean infantry fighting vehicle.

Kh-35/SS-N-25 Switchblade: A small Russian anti-ship missile, similar to the US Harpoon.

Klicks: Slang for kilometer.

KN-01: North Korean version of the Soviet export P-20 (SS-N-2A Styx) anti-ship missile.

KN-08: aka Hwaseong-13, North Korean intercontinental ballistic missile.

KPA: Korean People's Army

KS-30: Soviet heavy 130mm antiaircraft gun.

KWP: Korean Workers' Party

LCS: Littoral combatant ship

M4A1: A shorter and lighter variant of the US M16A2 assault rifle.

M-46: Soviet 130mm field gun.

Mi-8: 1960s era Soviet transport utility helicopter.

MAC: Military Armistice Commission

MiG-19 Farmer: 1950s era Soviet jet fighter.

MiG-21 Fishbed: 1960s era Soviet jet fighter.

MiG-29 Fulcrum: 1980s era Soviet jet fighter.

MP: Military police

MOPP: Mission oriented protective posture, levels of protective gear used to safeguard personnel in a toxic environment.

MQ-9 Reaper: US armed, unmanned aerial vehicle.

Musudan: aka BM-25, a North Korean intermediate range ballistic missile.

NBC: Nuclear, biological, chemical

NCO: Non-commissioned officer

NK: North Koreans
NIS: Republic of Korea, National Intelligence Service
OOB: Order of battle
OOD: Officer of the deck
OP: Observation post
OPLAN: Operations plan
OPREP-3: US Navy message format used to inform a senior authority of an incident that is of national-level interest.
Osa I: Soviet Project 205 guided missile patrol craft.
P-8: US Navy maritime patrol aircraft.
PAC-2: Patriot Advanced Capability – 2, US Army surface-to-air missile.
PAC-3: Patriot Advanced Capability – 3, US Army surface-to-air missile.
PACOM: US Pacific Command
PLA: People's Liberation Army
PLAAF: People's Liberation Army Air Force
PLAN: People's Liberation Army Navy
Pokpung-ho: North Korean main battle tank based on the Russian T-72 and Chinese Type 88.
PRC: People's Republic of China
RAM: Rolling airframe missile, US Navy short-range point defense missile.
Rodong-1: aka Nodong, a North Korean medium-range ballistic missile.
ROK: Republic of Korea
RPG: Slang for rocket-propelled grenade. In Russian, it stands for "handheld antitank grenade launcher."
S-400: Russian long-range air defense missile system.
SAG: Surface action group
SAM: Surface-to-air missile
Sarin: A nonpersistent nerve agent.

SATCOM: Satellite communications

Scud: Family of short-range ballistic missiles of Soviet origin.

Sea Sparrow: US Navy short-range point defense missile.

Second Artillery Corps: A separate service within the People's Liberation Army responsible for ballistic missile forces, both nuclear and conventional.

SOF: Special Operations Forces

SM-2: Standard Missile 2, US Navy long-range air defense missile.

SS-N-6: Soviet R-27 submarine launched ballistic missile.

Surion: South Korean transport utility helicopter.

T-54/55: Soviet main battle tanks introduced at the end of World War II.

T-62: Soviet 1960s era main battle tank.

Taepodong: A North Korean intercontinental ballistic missile.

TAO: Tactical action officer

TEL: Transporter erector launcher

TOW: Tube-launched, optically tracked, wire-guided anti-tank missile.

Type 033: Chinese copy of the Soviet Project 633 (Romeo) diesel-electric submarine.

Type 054/054A: Chinese guided missile frigate

Type 69: Chinese main battle tank based on the Soviet T-54 and T-62.

Type 88: Chinese main battle tank.

UAV: Unmanned aerial vehicle

UAZ-469: Warsaw Pact bloc produced light utility truck.

UH-1N Huey: US utility helicopter

UN: United Nations

USFK: US Forces Korea

UTM: Universal Transverse Mercator coordinate system.

VIP: Very important person

VX: A persistent nerve agent.

WMD: Weapons of mass destruction

XO: Executive officer, second in command of a warship.

Y-8: Chinese medium range transport aircraft used from numerous missions.

ZiL: Zavod imeni Likhachova, or the Likhachov Plant, a major Russian automotive manufacturer based in the city Moscow.

Made in the USA
Coppell, TX
29 August 2022

82256066R00298